A REALM UNDONE

JL LIENHARDT

This book is a work of fiction. Any references to historical events, real people, or real places are used fictitiously. Other names, characters, places, and events are products of the author's imagination, and any resemblance to actual events, places, names, or persons, is entirely coincidental.

Distributed by Simon & Schuster

Print: 978-1-998672-10-3
Ebook: 978-1-998672-11-0

FIC009020 - Fantasy/Epic
FIC009100 - Fantasy/Action & Adventure
FIC009070 - Fantasy/Dark Fantasy

#ARealmUndone #TheSeveredEra

Follow Rising Action on our socials!
Twitter: @RAPubCollective
Instagram: @risingactionpublishingco
Tiktok: @risingactionpublishingco

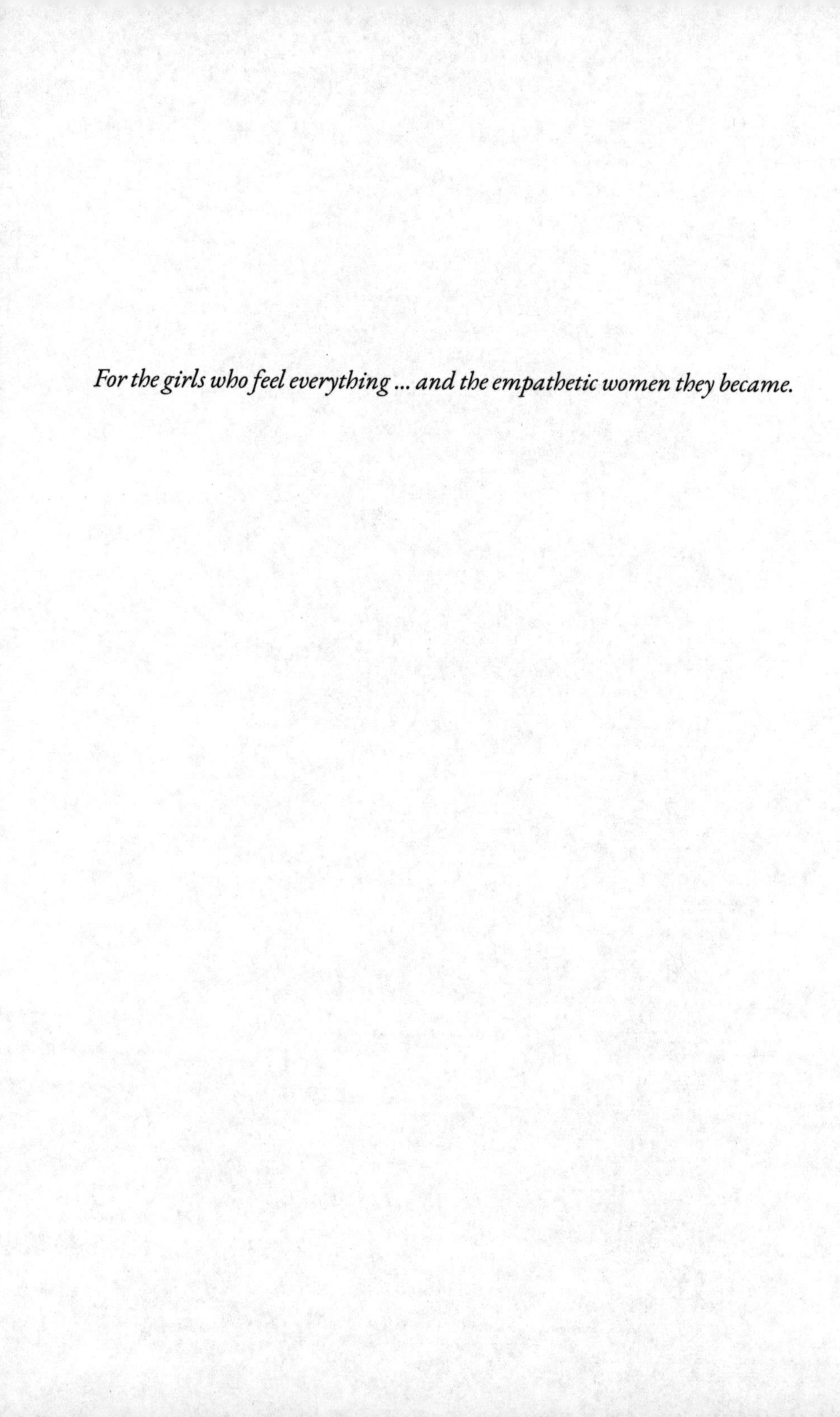

For the girls who feel everything ... and the empathetic women they became.

A REALM UNDONE

BOOK ONE
THE SEVERED ERA
TRILOGY

I

The city still stood.

Alia swore her home had crumbled years ago. The streets had collapsed into snaking chasms up to the palace square. The sun-stained brick buildings crowding each curve had fallen too, claimed by the churning sea. And the stark limestone palace had been smashed into a heap of powder atop the cliffs, swept up by a gale until it blanketed the once-glittering remnants, each spark of magic stifled.

But here it was.

"You said Sheath was a ruin," Lena grumbled beside her.

Her daughter was old enough to know better. Lena must have heard tales of the most renowned city in the realm in every hinterland village they passed through. Enough to know that Alia's recollections could not be relied upon. And still, Lena felt the need to prod Alia over another lie, as if that would make her change their course.

It didn't.

"We should keep going." Alia glanced at the sky; there was no telling when night would return.

"It's crowded." Lena switched tactics, the tremor in her voice rising above the clamor of the busy road. "Let's go north instead."

She couldn't fault Lena's attempt, not this time. They *should* go north. Anywhere other than Sheath. "No. Hurry."

Alia dragged her daughter back into the procession of travelers, their shoulders pressed together on the crowded road. Lena matched Alia's height, sharing her curling dark hair, olive complexion, and stubborn jaw. The only marked difference was the hue of Lena's eyes, golden brown flecked with garnet, as her father's had been.

How Alia wished that Lena's eyes were the only thing about her appearance that set her apart from the others seeking refuge in Sheath.

A long-sleeved cloak, unsuitable for the press of summer, covered her daughter's skin up to her throat. Despite this attempt at concealment, a perceptive eye could catch a glimpse of coal-colored tendrils inching up Lena's neck.

A rumble of hooves sparked a collective shudder through the dense pack of commoners. They all must have heard whispers of the hooved creature storming through the kingdom of Mandal, moving ever closer to the palace. Alia looked back at the wood bordering the city to the east, searching between the trees.

What a fitting homecoming it would be: slaughtered by a monster in the shadow of the city's gates.

But it was only a team of horses, pulling an ornate carriage boasting Mandal blue, a hue stolen from the waiting sea. Sighs of relief were short-lived, as the carriage picked up speed as it merged onto the main road. Those too old or too laden to move quickly were struck and forced out of the way as the carriage hurtled along worn ruts.

Most nobles had fled their hinterland estates for the safety of the palace as soon as the unforgiving winter had receded. The chill which had spread across Mandal and Royce had been more akin to the frozen mountaintops of Parth than the once mild countryside. The nights had stretched on, the longest Alia could remember. But shivering in the dark was nothing compared to what many villagers suffered in the jaws of the

Oucura.

Their night would never end.

Alia and Lena were forced back by the carriage, tripping over the uneven ruts. While Lena maintained her balance, Alia pitched forward. The hard-packed dirt scratched her palms. But before she could regain her feet, a man struggling onward stomped on her left hand. Alia's bones cracked under his heavy boot, and pain lanced up her arm. She spat her curses into the dust, trying to suppress the hurt.

Even without seeing the shattered bones, Alia could sense the disruption and see a shadowed outline of her crushed fingers. It took all of her will to rouse her magic, and even still, she only managed a sluggish response.

Once, she would have been able to repair this injury in mere moments. To meld the bones back together, to knit vein and tendon with a rush rather than a sputter.

"Bastards." Lena helped Alia to her feet before glaring ahead at the carriage.

Before Alia could distract her, the carriage's harness burst into splinters. Freed horses galloped down the hill, the carriage crashing into the dirt.

"Lena," Alia scolded through clenched teeth, still waiting for the pain to subside.

"Someone had to do it." Lena shrugged.

Alia yanked Lena away from the road. "It didn't have to be you."

"They hurt you. More people would have been hurt, too, if I hadn't."

"More could be because you did," Alia repeated the same lesson that never seemed to permeate. "Is it coming?"

"I'm fine."

But her daughter's eyes glowed garnet, her palms bore crimson marks of heat, and the menacing black ink tracing Lena's veins expanded yet again, reaching her chin. If this small exertion caused another magical outburst, there was little Alia could do to contain her.

Alia placed her right hand on Lena's cheek, forcing herself to calm. She counted out the rhythm of Lena's heart, waiting for the racing pulse that always preceded an outburst. The moments ticked by. The only change was her daughter's growing impatience.

"I said, I'm fine." Lena tried to spin out of her grasp.

"You are this time." Alia adjusted Lena's cloak to hide the marks. "We need a place to rest." Even if using magic didn't end in an incident, Lena was easily drained.

Lena's ferocity dulled as they continued on. Her flush faded to pallor; the burst required to sever the horses from the carriage taking its toll. Alia slid her unharmed arm around Lena, keeping her slowly healing hand tucked against her chest.

The crowd moved downhill towards the relative safety of Sheath. The waves encroached on the city walls, the stone straining against the sea. Even as Alia savored the bite of salt in the air, she couldn't ignore the angry swell of the tide. It looked poised to drown Sheath's low-lying neighborhoods.

Alia raised the hood of Lena's cloak as they passed through the gates. She didn't need a Mandal guard taking an interest in Lena's markings. They moved in step with other commoners, thrust into the swarming city.

"That should have been harder." Lena yanked her hood down and gulped a breath like she'd been suffocating.

"At least we're here," Alia said, trying not to let Lena's observation claw at her. The guards had barely looked at them, and she hadn't sensed any magical barriers in place. Anyone could walk into the center of

Mandal.

Anything.

"How's your hand?" Lena's forehead creased.

"It'll heal." Alia focused on plotting their way toward the palace. "Probably long before those noble fools make it down the hill."

Lena yielded a feeble grin, the tension between them easing.

The pattern of Sheath's streets came back to Alia, unfurling with each step. Alia had spent more time in the depths of the city as a girl than her parents would have liked, precisely for that reason. She had yearned for the illusion of anonymity provided by disappearing among the winding streets and narrow alleys. Her years in the hinterland had only sharpened that skill.

They skirted the hastily made shelters, the tents erected for the refugees streaming into the city. The scurrying menders and cries of the injured reminded Alia of the waves of wounded from the war with Veillant that had filled the streets when she was a child.

A war back then, rather than the work of one creature.

An unbidden memory awaited Alia as they strode up the main thoroughfare. On this street, Cormac had first taken her hand. He hadn't known the way and clung to her to avoid falling behind. Alia remembered the feeling of his calloused palm engulfing hers.

She had never wanted to let him go.

The sun remained high as they searched for a room. With so many fleeing to the city for refuge, the lodgings were already bursting. At last, Alia selected an inn a few blocks from the palace. It appeared reputable enough to provide some notion of safety, but not luxurious enough to garner attention from the blue-cloaked guards patrolling the streets.

Inside, Alia kept Lena behind her, hiding her appearance from the portly man at the helm. She tucked her injured hand inside the fold of her cloak.

"My lord." Alia forced a smile.

"No lords here," he said, eyeing her shabby attire. "Three silver pieces a day by the palace count, night or not. Doesn't include food or washing. No exceptions."

"By the palace count. Tell me, how long did the last night last?"

The innkeeper only scowled.

Alia maintained her grin, attempting to be disarming. "We have something far more valuable than coin to offer. How long has that knee been bothering you?" Alia could feel his bones grinding against each other as he moved and ignored the way Lena shifted uncomfortably behind her.

"No, no, no. I want silver; take your gimmicks somewhere else."

"I assure you, no gimmicks." Alia held out her hand, palm up.

He muttered a curse but gave Alia his hand, nonetheless. Within a moment of touching her, the innkeeper's eyes widened. It was a cruel trick, a simple manipulation of nerves, providing numbness rather than healing. He flexed his right leg, now painless.

"When we are ready to depart, this will be your payment. Until then ..." Alia squeezed his fingers and drew out a grimace. Magic flowed from her hand, effortless and punishing. Healing was difficult. But causing harm was instinctual for someone like her.

The innkeeper narrowed his eyes as he handed over a key.

"We'll take bathwater and dinner when you're able. May the sun stay high."

They ducked around the lively pub, making for the stairs to the guest rooms. Lena sulked after her, even more miserable than she had been on the road. "You could have just tried to heal him. He might have been grateful."

"But now we have a room for as long as we need."

“I’m not allowed to use my magic because I might hurt someone. But you use yours to hurt people whenever you want.”

“Our magic is not the same,” Alia snapped, unlocking the door to the room, just large enough to fit the bed inside it.

Thank Orlast for that.

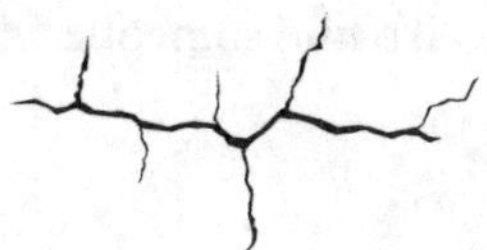

Once they washed and ate a meager meal, Alia unpacked a nightgown for Lena and selected a plain dress for herself. Most of their clothes were made by her own hand, though Alia had little talent. This dress had been payment, part of the fee Alia took for placing wards around a caravan market. Other than healing and hurting, barriers had been the only other type of magic Alia had ever taken to.

Her hand had improved with time; Alia could extend her mending fingers. As she forced Lena’s damp hair into plaits, the ache receded even further.

“Where are you going?” Lena eyed Alia’s only good dress.

“To gather information.” Alia tugged slightly on Lena’s hair to straighten her neck.

“I thought you had what you needed.”

“I have a start.” According to the whispers on the road, King Isaac’s sickness had progressed.

Lena sat up in the bed, twisting again. “Take me with you.”

Alia kept a firm hold on her daughter’s braid. “No.”

“I feel better. I can help.” Lena’s insistence didn’t erase the risk.

Alia paused, assessing the dark veins at the nape of Lena's neck. "Do you want to have an outburst on the steps of the palace?" Her words echoed in her head, sounding too shrill, too harsh. But she didn't retract them.

"Why are you going to the palace?" Lena winced as Alia pulled the strands tight.

Alia took a deep breath. "To find someone who can make you better."

"But you said—"

"Enough."

Lena scoffed and jerked her shoulders away.

Once Alia was satisfied with Lena's hair, Lena climbed into bed, pulled the blanket up to her chin, and turned away.

"I'm going to place a barrier—"

"I know, I know. I'm locked in this room. My dungeon until you return."

"I'll be back soon."

Lena feigned sleep; Alia steeled herself and grasped the doorknob.

"Mother."

Alia paused, caught by the softness of Lena's voice.

"Promise to come back?" The flicker of candlelight exposed Lena's tears.

"Of course, I'll come back," Alia said. "I will never leave you."

Lena nodded, hardening her mouth. "Even though you should. I could have killed you if I'd—"

"It was not your fault." Alia wilted. She was outmatched when it came to comfort. No words rang true. The first outburst hadn't been Lena's fault. Nor the second. Nor the rest. But that gave no guarantee it wouldn't happen again—that Lena's power wouldn't rip through everyone near her without discernment.

"You're sick, Lena. And I'm going to find someone to help you," Alia managed a hollow assurance.

Lena's head bobbed again, but her gaze dropped to the creaking floorboards.

"I'll be back before you wake." Alia shut the door behind her and traced a barrier around the room, sealing it with a ghostly web. Only an experienced mage would be able to penetrate it ... or one of Lena's uncontrolled bursts. She had to trust Lena wouldn't attempt it, for her sake and for those of the other poor souls sharing the inn.

Alia stepped back out into the city streets, shelving her concern to reclaim her bearings. Even though it was a few blocks away, the palace already towered above her. The place she had once fought so hard to be free from was now where she desperately needed to be.

The sun sank as Alia stalked towards the palace entryway. She paused in the square, taking in the statue of King Orlast, the first king of Mandal. The likeness stood between the palace and the rest of the city, a beacon of the First Monarchs. The King, forever memorialized, held in one hand his spear, outstretched to deal the killing blow to the Tiarcon of the Moon, and pressed the other over his heart. Stone rivulets of blood ran down his chest, the sign of his broken oath to the immortal tyrants.

The Spear of Orlast had given the city its name, the place Orlast had chosen, and finally set aside his weapon to build anew. An entire kingdom to rival the Otherworld.

But what was once held in reverence, fortified with purpose, had weathered, the marble statue along with it, as the polish had been eaten away by salt spray. There was still a divot notched into the old king's arm from when Alia had scaled the statue in her youth to hang Harlan Gust's breeches from the tip of the Spear. Cormac Barton had put her up to it, of course, and she had been neither able to refuse amusing him nor proving herself.

A bell rang out over the square, emanating from a large circular dial mounted on the palace gate. Alia squinted to make out the various hands of the dial, marking the day, month, and year. The bell signified nightfall, arriving just after midday this time. The crowd cried out at the tolling, protesting the brevity of daylight. The shifting patterns of light and dark struck fear across the mortal realm.

Fear that the Otherworld hadn't forgotten the lurchers of Entien and the magic that had been taken from them.

Commoners roiled, the atmosphere of the square bordering on unrest. Alia hoped the commotion would help distract the guards from her movements. There were cries for sun, demands for bread, and desperate appeals made to a king who had long ago stopped listening.

Alia set her mind to her task. The surest way to draw the Captain of the Guard out of the palace was to show him an acute threat. She made sure her hood was raised and her gait even as she slipped behind the guard lines.

She extended her hands out in front of her, fingers flexed. With a flourish of her right hand and a slight glow, she summoned a deep purple mist, careful to only disturb a wisp of the brimming dark that resided within her. If she released too much, she'd be attracting more than the captain. It would bring the entire Tower down on her.

Her fingers slid along the nearest guard's cerulean cloak, his armor doing little to protect him. The mist transferred from her hand to his back, coursing down his body until it found the complex bones in his ankle, the ghost of the old injury beckoning to her.

She crushed his ankle with a flick of her finger.

The guard clattered to the ground, armor and steel striking the stone of the square as he fell. Alia pretended to draw back in surprise with the rest of the crowd, as the guard's comrades rushed in. Commoners scattered, as they knew to expect blind and harsh retribution. Alia ran with them, curving her way to the guards on the other side of the square who had not left their post to aid their fallen fellow.

Alia repeated the process three more times, exploiting old injuries without guilt. The fallen would have ample access to healers, and the pain would just be another memory. They would likely even get the remainder of their shift to rest, a rare luxury.

She slid towards the east entry of the palace—the servants' entrance. It had been her favorite way to sneak in and out, as the guards took less notice of the churn of stewards and maids than they did the commoners at the main entrance. A fresh brigade of guards would be deployed from this entry to respond to the attack in the square. Alia positioned herself near the opening, shrouded behind an empty merchant stall.

Looking out over the guards and servants filing out of the palace, Alia searched for the familiar Captain of the Guard. Captain Stephan would be ancient by now, but Alia hoped he had been too stubborn to die. Not because she cared to see him, but because she knew he was crooked. King Isaac hadn't burdened himself by calling scrupulous men into his company.

Patience served her as she waited, taking in every weary face that passed by. Finally, she caught the crest she hunted.

Alia knew in a moment that the man bearing the captain's crest was not Stephan and nearly laughed at her fortune. Unlike his men, the captain strode forward without armor. He was a giant man, his uniform stretched tight across his muscular chest and equally impressive biceps. The final beams of dusk illuminated his thick black beard, umber skin, and bright eyes. His head was shorn bald, adding to the intimidating mantel he was trying to project. Mandal's Captain of the Guard was none other than Harlan Gust, a man she counted among her closest friends at one time—when their pack of noble wretches had roamed the palace.

"Clear the square," he ordered, sword in hand. His guards obeyed in a flurry.

Alia stayed put as Harlan stomped forward, moving clear of the servants' entry, and scanning the square for a sign of the perpetrator. She had to draw him away from the square, away from his men. She dipped her hand into the purse secured at her waist, finding only a single copper and the ring she had never been able to part with.

Harlan quelled the brewing riot, and Alia waited. As darkness claimed the streets, Alia offered her last copper to a child, instructing her to go to the captain with her message.

The captain bent down from his considerable height to hear the child when she approached. He followed the child's pointed finger to where Alia stood. Alia took down her hood and lifted her face to the torchlight before walking down the street. She had to hope that seeing her would be enticing enough for Harlan to obey the second part of her message—to meet her at a pub.

Harlan had made Alia shift her strategy. Instead of finding a way into the palace, she could convince Harlan to bring a healer to Lena.

Anxiety seized Alia as she stepped into the boisterous pub, the dark doing little to discourage its inhabitants. Alia was aching to return to Lena's side, to make sure she was resting. That her condition hadn't worsened.

The Harlan she had known was amiable as long as he wasn't on the training grounds. He would help her; he could be convinced by the dregs of their friendship.

But at the same time, Alia could not expect him to be the man she once knew. Anything could have happened in nearly two decades. There was no telling what lies had been told about her.

Or which truths.

When the captain entered the pub, Alia let a confident mask fall over her features. The other patrons of the pub shied away from him, making her assume he'd earned a reputation for demanding order in the rowdy streets.

"Ali?" He approached with caution.

"How many of your men are waiting outside?"

A flash in his sharp blue eyes confirmed her suspicion. He recovered quickly. "How do I know you are who you claim to be?"

"How about you go outside, dismiss your entourage, and bring me an ale on your way back?" Alia folded her arms across her chest.

Harlan slowly sucked in a breath. "I trust it was you who dispatched my men in the square."

"I had to get your attention somehow."

"A relief really. I thought it was ..." They both knew what he thought it was. The Oucura. But the Captain should have known the beast didn't attack with subtlety. "How do I know it is you, Ali?"

"You took the lashes for ruining Lord Milan's prized ruby saddle, even though it was Flora who stripped the gems and left the leather in the lake." Harlan had always been completely devoted to his friends, even to his detriment.

The corner of Harlan's mouth twitched.

"Baldric walked in on you bedding one of the Paxton girls when you were fifteen; I think he described you as—"

"Ali," Harlan interrupted her, casting an anxious look over his shoulder. He fixed her with a grim nod before ducking out of the pub. He returned a few minutes later and dutifully went to the bar to retrieve two tankards.

Harlan set the mugs down on the table and then reached for Alia, yanking her from her chair and crushing her into a hug. Her shock kept her immobile for a moment before she softened and returned the embrace, relieved he had retained some affection for her.

"We thought you were dead." Harlan set her back down and sat across from her, brimming with excitement. "How are you not dead?"

"What was happening in the square? What was everyone yelling about?" Alia dodged his question.

"Oh, that? A common occurrence these days. They were watching the palace count. Sunlight only lasted seven hours this time." Harlan took a drink. "And Cormac announced a new Master Mage. A Veillanti."

Alia almost forgot her purpose at the news, and wrinkled her nose in disgust. The post had been vacant for over a decade, but surely the situation wasn't so desperate as to need to choose a leech to oversee the education of Mandal's mages. "How did Cormac convince King Isaac to allow that to happen?"

"King Isaac hasn't been ... active ... for some time now. Cormac has taken on all his duties. He is going to have a fit when he hears that you are back."

Alia put a hand up, pleased that her information about King Isaac's illness had been correct. "I am not back, and I will not be seeing Cormac."

Harlan's face fell. "Ali—"

Alia lurched forward, taking Harlan's hand in hers, appealing to the softness that somehow still resided in him. "No one can know I'm here. Not even Cormac. They'll kill me, Harlan."

"Cormac isn't going to let anyone hurt you," Harlan protested, then seemed to think better of it. "Or, at least—"

"You do know, don't you? What I did, what I can do?" Alia whispered, locking eyes with her old friend.

Harlan withdrew his hand. He knew.

"I need help, and then I'll be gone again."

Harlan's struggle played out in his posture as he tensed, shook his head, and sighed. "What do you need?"

"A healer."

The smile was back. "Why would you need a healer?"

"It isn't for me." Alia didn't want to explain to him that her magic was not as he remembered.

"Oh?" Harlan lifted his eyebrows. "Who is the healer for then?"

"You don't need to know."

"I do need to know. I took oaths, Ali."

Oaths that required him to tell his sovereign about the presence of a fugitive in the city. Alia had long lost faith in notions of fealty, but Harlan would have sworn his life to the Crown in order to become captain. Which meant he needed a compelling answer to bend his vows. "It's for my daughter," Alia said, looking into her lap. She hadn't wanted any of them to know about Lena.

"Your daughter? How old?"

"Will you bring me a healer or not?"

Harlan took a drink and carefully considered. "Ali, no matter what they said ..." He shook his head, casting off a memory. "I never believed it."

Alia opened her mouth to speak, but thought better of it. If she told Harlan all he had heard was likely true, he would report her.

"I'll bring a healer for your daughter."

"Thank you." Alia held onto his hand as she told him the name of their inn. She couldn't help but add, "How is my sister?"

"I've looked after her, just as you asked me to." A smile spread across Harlan's lips as his eyes drifted downward. He was holding back, not wanting to bring up Cormac again. As if Alia hadn't already known. The marriage of the crown prince was news that even permeated the hinterland.

"Good." Alia tried to picture Elowen as a grown woman. She had been a child the last time she saw her. "And ... the others?" As much as she had suppressed memories of her old friends, being back in the city made her yearn for them.

"Baldric is down at the southern coast—King's orders. Flora married Geoff Frulin and moved all the way to Waterston. And George ..." Harlan paused. "We lost George in a skirmish with the Veillanti nearly five years ago."

A twinge of sadness ran through Alia, and she let a grimace show. George had been a reluctant and clumsy warrior in his youth; she couldn't imagine what had possessed him to become a soldier. "I hope you avenged him," Alia murmured.

"Baldric did." Harlan nodded. "Deserted his unit for a time and hunted every Veillanti soldier on the continent."

Violence had always been Baldric's preferred form of expression. "Good."

"And you? Where have you been all these years? Why risk coming back now?"

Bristling, Alia took a drink. "I told you."

"These are dangerous times, Ali."

Alia dropped her voice low. "Is it the veil?"

"No one knows how the Oucura crossed the veil. It has been impassable for hundreds of years. It's as if—" He stopped himself from saying more.

"They are saying on the road that it tore its way through." Alia leaned forward, trying to prompt Harlan for more information. "Is that possible?"

Her movement betrayed her, as Harlan's gaze caught on her boot as she crossed her leg over the other. He fixated on the worn leather, the sole barely still attached to the rest, the holes in her stocking visible through the tears. A reminder that she wasn't the noblewoman he'd known

"That is a question for the Tower." Harlan tipped back the last of his ale.

The captain may have been glad to see her, but he was still wary.

He was right to be.

2

Captain Harlan Gust kept his word.

Dark still held Entien; Alia had to ground herself in the pattern of bells ringing out each hour from the palace. She counted the tolls, increasing in number until midday, until Harlan made his appearance, towing a palace healer.

The captain pushed inside the quaint room, removing the hooded cloak that had covered his face. Alia found herself crushed into another embrace, peering over Harlan's shoulder at the woman he'd brought.

The healer had hidden beneath a cloak as well and was hurriedly smoothing her light plaits. The woman's frown deepened as she looked around the room, apparently aggravated at having been forced into the city. The palace healers Alia had known would never deign to leave the palace grounds, a symptom of their noble blood. Alia could feel the healer's magic, its strength denoting that she descended from an established bloodline of elemental magic.

Harlan held his arms out to Lena, but her scathing glare put him off. Alia was encouraged to see a bit of fight in Lena, but lethargy quickly settled in again.

Alia had spent the resting hours perched against their bedframe, watching to ensure that Lena's chest was rising and falling with each breath. It had become her preoccupation, one that Alia reclaimed from the first few weeks of Lena's life. Back then, Alia had barely been able to keep herself alive, let alone an infant. So, she had hovered over her child, not able to take her eyes off Lena, certain some horror would befall her.

And now it had.

"Lady Quinn, please meet my friends." Harlan avoided using Alia's name.

Quinn's chin jutted out, assessing Alia, eyes roving up and down as she was trying to place her. Harlan must have been sure to select a noblewoman who wouldn't recognize Alia. "Who are you?"

"Remember what we—" Harlan cut in.

"I know a quotidien like yourself can't feel it, but these two are teeming with magic," Quinn snapped. "I have a right to know who I'm healing."

"Of course you do," Harlan said. "Just as I have the right to imprison you for what you took from the infirmary."

Harlan's threat cowed Quinn. She sidled past Harlan and Alia, kneeling beside the bed where Lena sat. Quinn closed her hand around Lena's wrist, trying to discern her affliction. Just as Alia had done time and time again.

"What are your symptoms?" Quinn asked Lena.

"I'm fine." Lena jerked out of Quinn's hold.

"It started about a year ago, the marks," Alia stepped in. "They keep growing and she keeps getting weaker."

Lena grudgingly pulled at the high neckline of her tunic, exposing the angry black veins writhing beneath her skin. They had begun with only a few pinpricks over her heart. Now the markings were a tapestry covering Lena's skin, a poison was seeping outward.

Quinn made a disapproving sound in her throat. "A year without seeking a healer?"

"My mother is a healer, a slow one, but still," Lena said.

Quinn peered back at Alia, seemingly pleased she had pegged Alia's magic accurately. If she had a full understanding of Alia's capabilities, she would have fled the inn by now.

"It doesn't feel like something to be mended or removed," Alia explained.

"Need I say that she should be in the palace infirmary?"

"Just tell me what's wrong with her."

"I don't yet know." Quinn pursed her lips. "Has she ever had any other ailments?"

Alia shook her head. "I've looked after her. But since she's had the marks, she's also had ... episodes."

"Episodes?"

"When she uses her magic, she can become agitated. Fever, shaking, outbursts. I can contain her, but they are getting worse."

Harlan raised an eyebrow. He was right to be concerned; the latest episode had nearly leveled an entire village.

Quinn muttered a curse. "If it is a magical issue, she should be evaluated by the Tower."

Alia tried to suppress a shudder. There was no way she was letting the Tower or its mages near her daughter. Alia had only barely escaped that place. "Can you help her or not?"

"I'll try," Quinn conceded, bending her head down to focus on Lena.

Quinn's exam was painfully thorough. Lena tolerated it well, much to Alia's surprise. Harlan stood silent beside Alia the whole time, at one point trying to place his hand on her shoulder before Alia flinched away. She didn't need comfort; she needed an answer.

When Quinn finally got to her feet, Alia stepped forward expectantly. "I've never seen anything like it," the healer admitted. "I need to return to the infirmary to see if I can find anything in our records. I'll be back tomorrow."

"Tomorrow?" She had piled her hopes on the palace healers having the remedy for Lena's problem so they could quickly escape Sheath.

Quinn's glower appeared well-practiced. "Or you could bring her into the palace infirmary. Now."

"Tomorrow will be fine." Harlan ushered Quinn out of the room.

He returned moments later. "I'm guessing you won't reconsider?" he asked Alia, who merely shook her head.

"They aren't going to be able to do anything." Lena stood and pulled a blanket around her shoulders to cover the blemishes. "Healers are fools. If it isn't bleeding right in front of them, they're useless."

"Your mother is the finest healer I've ever met." The corner of Harlan's mouth twitched. "And she is not a fool."

"She doesn't know either." Lena sighed. "The healer will consult her precious books, brew me an ineffectual tonic, and then claim that I'm telling tales about my symptoms."

"Your aunt—" Harlan began before Alia's sharp gesture stopped him. "Lena, has your mother ever told you about her childhood?"

Lena snorted. "She never tells me anything."

Harlan's questioning gaze tried to catch Alia, but she turned away. She'd never been able to share her past with her daughter. The darkest parts, those that had driven her from Mandal, she kept locked away so tightly that they had nearly taken the whole of her childhood with them.

"Ah, then allow me. The palace was complete mayhem because of Alia."

"As if I did it alone," Alia whispered, shocked that Harlan hadn't run back to his post at the first chance.

Harlan began to regale Lena with the tales of young Alia.

How she'd convinced their friends to drink mead until one of them vomited. How she split her head open scaling the south wall of the palace so no one would catch her out in the middle of the night. How she led a squad of palace guards on a chase from the palace to the Fen and still managed to get away.

"Who are you?" Lena turned from Harlan to question Alia.

Alia hoped Lena would never find out. "I'm sure Captain Harlan has other demands on his time."

"Of course." Harlan's grin faltered, only for a blink, before he joined Alia at the door to the room. "I brought this for you." He handed over a satchel. "I know grain is becoming hard to come by."

Alia peeked inside to see bread and silver, more than they'd had in months. Shame burned her cheeks, but hunger didn't permit her to refuse it. "Thank you."

"If Lady Quinn can't find a solution, you know there's another option." He kept his voice low. "Your sister may be able to do something the healers cannot."

"I'll consider it," Alia promised, although she already was set against the suggestion.

"May the sun rise." Harlan clasped his hand around hers.

"And the moon forever fallen."

Once he was gone, Lena flopped on the bed, crumbling in the absence of opposition. "Does he really think he can tell a few stories and act like he knows you?"

"Harlan means well."

"Then where has he been the past ten years? If he is truly your friend, where was he when we needed somewhere to sleep? And some captain; he hasn't sent a single soldier to protect the villages before they were ripped apart by the Oucura." Lena's anger was rising, and Alia feared it would tax her ailing body.

"Protecting his palace," Alia said, agreeing with the sentiment but not wanting to add to Lena's distress.

"Father would hate that you brought me here, crawling back to them for help."

Her words bit into Alia, the truth echoing through her mind. "Just until you're well again."

"He'd want us to go back to Dihlmere."

Alia felt the same nostalgic pull to Lena's first home. Her heart swelled remembering the quiet cottage, the embrace of the forest around them, and the ease Lena's father brought to every room he was in. Then her heart plummeted, remembering it all aflame, all lost.

"There's nothing there anymore, Lena." *He isn't there anymore.*

"There's nothing here either."

Alia nearly drowned in the pain surging across Lena's face, her shortcomings as a mother reflected in each line. Perhaps she wouldn't have failed so spectacularly at protecting Lena if she had help, if she had Finn.

"I'll go fetch us a meal from downstairs." Alia plotted her escape from Lena's ire, setting the bread on the table and tying the clinking satchel to her belt. Her daughter didn't move as Alia slipped out of the door.

She took each step slow, her footfalls heavy. The burgeoning surge of anger towards Finn was unproductive. Blaming him wasn't going to change the fact that she was all Lena had left.

When Alia reached the bottom of the stairs, she froze.

"There she is! The extortionist!" the innkeeper shouted across the meager dining area, his audience a pair of guards in blue cloaks.

No. Not yet.

The guards swiveled in her direction, plying the innkeeper with a few silvers for his information. "We do not suffer thieves in Sheath," one of the guards said with menace, moving towards her.

The palace harbors much worse than thieves.

After years of schemes, she had managed to choose an establishment with a manager surly enough to turn to the enforcers rather than hide from them. As she turned to run, wisps of mist escaped her hands, seeking out the guards and slowing their advance.

She swiftly climbed the stairs and grasped the doorknob to their room. Alia slammed the door shut behind her, casting a barrier in the same breath.

"Get up." Alia tried to maintain a shred of clarity as her mind whirled. The only thing she needed to do now was get Lena away from them. "We'll go through the window. If the guards catch me, you need to keep going. Find Harlan. I think they will be satisfied with me, so you should be able to get away."

"We've bested marshals before; we can fight them back," Lena said, her garnet eyes flashing.

"Hinterland marshals and palace guards are not the same. You can't risk using any more magic. Lena, listen to me." Alia placed her hand on Lena's back, urging her towards the window. "Even if they take me, I will find you."

There was no time for an embrace, even if it may be their last.

With her pack slung over her back, Alia opened the window shutters. Just as she evaluated the three-story drop to the street, a banging came at the door. Alia's skin prickled, sensing a mage on the other side of the door.

The Tower had come for her.

She could feel the mage chipping away at the barrier she had made. There was no way it was going to outlast a Tower-trained mage.

Lena scrambled out of the window, well-practiced at scaling down the building façade. Alia followed behind, the gaps between the stones leaving plenty of room for the toes of her shoes and fingers. As she descended, she sensed her barrier crumbling. She maneuvered herself lower, closer to the ground, but she wasn't fast enough. A rough hand snatched for her, tangling in her plaits, and yanked her upwards. Alia anchored her feet and grasped the wall with her left hand while she sent a jolt of mist through her right, breaking the guard's fingers.

"Mother!" Lena screamed from the street.

"Run!" Alia ordered, but her daughter did not listen. Even though the path to Lena's freedom was open, as the street was not yet filled with guards, she planted her feet. Alia could see Lena's chest heaving, her garnet eyes molten with an all too familiar look of fury.

Not here. Not now.

Wind tore at Alia, nearly peeling her off the side of the building. She blinked against the onslaught, seeing Lena in the center, skin turning crimson. "Breathe, Lena!" Alia shouted, finally touching her feet to the ground. Alia constructed another barrier around her daughter as people in the street began to flee. The heat reached her, swirls of balmy air meeting the biting cold. Through the torrent, Alia fought to get to Lena.

Alia grasped Lena's burning skin, meeting her furious eyes, and trying to push calm over to her. "Lena, please." She held her daughter tight, healing herself as rain pelted her face and the heat burned her skin. The buildings around them shuddered, doors and shutters pulling free under the strain.

A woman in mage robes was standing before them now, trying to contain Lena's outburst of power. A mage Alia hated. Lady Rosalynn Paxton.

She was whispering a spell, but Alia's new barrier held, wrapping a cocoon around the two of them. "Lena, don't."

Except that she did.

Lena doubled over in pain, screaming as her entire body shook. Alia tried to ply her with healing magic, but there was no relief. She held her daughter, as difficult as that proved to be, trying to soothe her convulsions.

The wind intensified.

Another group of guards arrived, Captain Harlan leading them. He likely had only made it a few blocks before being called back.

"Undoing Mage!" Rosalynn shouted. "Surrender yourself."

Even as she was surrounded by enemies, Lena's scream was the only thing Alia focused on. "Lena, please," Alia repeated, willing each bit of healing magic into her daughter, but it was too weak, ineffectual. The waves of magic flowed from Lena, each one smashing into the barriers Alia had tried to build around her daughter's wracking body. She was in so much pain.

The swirling wind only howled, knocking Rosalynn to the ground and disrupting the guards' advance. As the last bits of Alia's strength left her, her failings crystallized. She couldn't protect Lena; she couldn't save her.

The palace would claim her. The palace would claim them both.

3

Alia woke to her own groaning. She slammed her eyes shut as soon as they opened, the torchlight making the pressure at her temples flare. One glance had been enough to tell where she was anyway. The white stone walls, the equally snowy curtains, and the overwhelming herbal smell—the palace infirmary. Where she had spent endless hours learning how to heal.

Now it was a prison.

The laden air disrupted her memory, the heat from the torches on the wall mixing with the oily billows. They banished the persistent dark looming through the window, where sunlight used to stream.

Her entire body felt like it had been stuffed with iron, her limbs too heavy to lift.

Alia's magic was gone. Worse, Lena was gone.

She'd been drained, and there wasn't even a hint left to ease her own headache. Alia groaned again, throat rasping. The last thing forced down her throat must have been the draining tonic; she could still taste the bitter poison.

Some Undoing Mage she was.

"Welcome back." An ancient healer sat beside her, silver hair carefully coiled and a healthy glow on her sienna wrinkles. Alia recognized her—Harriet, the crest on her robes marking her as Chief Healer.

"Lena?" Alia managed to cough.

"The young woman? In the next room. Drained, as you are. For our safety."

Alia's inventory of curses had no effect on Harriet's serenity.

"I wonder if..." Harriet said, hands hovering above Alia's torso, teasing out a sphere of light, her magical aura. The ball was a spectrum of purple hues, ranging from the deepest plum to a calming lavender. As Alia watched, the darkest specs multiplied and overtook their lighter companions. Harriet closed her fists, and the sphere returned to Alia at the base of her ribcage, her fine display of elemental magic at an end. "You used to be more light than dark."

Alia glared. Of course, there had been more light in her aura once. Back when she was a talented young mage, an unparalleled healer. Back when her power had matched her to Crown Prince Cormac Barton, deeming her strong enough to join with the royal bloodline and produce the realm's next ruler. But that, and so many other things, had been taken from her.

Back before the Undoing.

"Your healing magic is far less powerful than it was," the Chief Healer observed.

"Devoured." It was a loss that Alia scarcely let herself feel. The effortless ability to preserve life, to heal, had been snatched from her by the emergence of the Undoing. Thinking of it threatened Alia's semblance of dominance over her magic, the tight lid that she kept over the Undoing to keep it from spilling out. There was no starving the Undoing, no denying it, and despite her best efforts, no pretending that it wasn't there.

As soon as the notion of it invaded Alia's mind, she felt the Undoing pulse within her. That aspect of her power was not the slightest bit diminished by whatever they had given her, a magic so insidious it could not be extinguished. Alia shivered; she could prove their ignorance in an instant. She could unleash the Undoing, break herself free, and show them the beast they already assumed her to be. It was always there, coiled and hungry.

Alia's own fear smothered the plot. If Lena was indeed just in the next room, she couldn't risk it. There was no telling if she could stop once it began, if she could control whose life was taken.

"What's wrong with Lena?" Alia asked. If anyone could diagnose her, it would be Harriet.

"We are examining her. But she is not a threat in her current state." Harriet pressed her lips into a thin line. "Is she ... is she like you?"

"No," Alia said harshly, and Harriet's forehead smoothed.

Undoing Mages aren't born, they are made.

Harriet looked like she was going to ask another question, but thought better of it. "I will let the guards know you're awake."

Alia stared at the ceiling. After almost twenty years of escaping Mandal justice and she had been caught just two days after returning to the city. Utter foolishness had led her here.

Desperation, more like.

Execution was the only logical sentence for her past crimes. Time wouldn't have lessened the punishment; her abscondence only made it worse. An admission of guilt. Banishment would be a gift, but none of the Mandal nobility could sleep soundly knowing that she was out there somewhere. They would have to kill her.

Lena would be killed alongside her or left alone with them.

Elevated voices sounded outside the door. She tried to lift her head, only making it an inch before falling back down into the pillow. Alia struggled to recognize the voices, the blistering headache interfering. At last, two people entered the room, slamming the door shut behind them.

They crowded above her, hovering on either side.

Harlan and Elowen.

Her sister looked every bit the princess, from her intricately braided chestnut hair to her fine gown. Alia's breath caught in her throat as she waited for Elowen's reaction. Elowen's chest heaved as she looked down on Alia. She placed her hands on her sister's cheeks as if to verify she really was there.

Elowen let out a long breath and whispered, "Oh, Ali."

Leaving her younger sister to the snakes of the palace had made her departure all the more difficult, but Alia had been confident that things would be different for Elowen. And Elowen had done well. She was married to the prince.

Elowen drew Alia into her arms, tears escaping the princess's eyes despite the attempt to keep her royal composure. When Elowen finally straightened, she dabbed her face with a handkerchief, somehow managing not to smear the paints which evened out her olive skin.

"Ali, I'm sorry," Harlan sputtered, his eyes bloodshot. "You were reported to the guard, and they were doing their job."

"Harlan." Elowen's soothing voice silenced the captain. "Can I talk to my sister alone?"

Harlan's mouth opened and shut without sound, as his head shook from side to side. "Princess, it is not—" Even her old friend thought she was a threat.

"My big sister is not going to hurt me," Elowen said with a reckless amount of certainty.

"I will be just outside the door," Harlan promised, receiving a nod from Elowen.

"I always knew you were alive. I felt it." Elowen's tears resumed as she grasped onto Alia's shoulders. "But Ali, you shouldn't have come back."

The tears were telling: the Mandals would execute her, and Elowen couldn't save her.

"Lena, the Oucura, I had to," Alia choked out, trying to sound as pathetic as she felt.

"I just looked in on Lena. She is beautiful. She looks just like you." Elowen's smile was sweet, a practiced habit of distraction from unpleasant things snapping into place. "You found a man out on your travels?" Her question was a not-so-subtle plea. Elowen was asking—hoping—her husband wasn't Lena's father. Hoping Alia hadn't fled the palace all those years ago pregnant with Prince Cormac's child.

"Yes," Alia reassured her. "I met Lena's father in Royce not too long after I left Mandal."

Elowen's relief was palpable. "Is he here?"

"He died. Almost ten years ago now." Alia did her best to control her emotions as she spoke, not wanting to dissolve completely.

"Orlast keep him." Elowen seemed to mean the words. Perhaps, despite the years apart, Elowen's heart was still malleable enough to help a criminal.

"Lena doesn't have anyone else, Elowen." Alia didn't try to keep the whine from her voice. "I know I have no right to ask anything of you, but when I'm gone—"

"Stop," Elowen pleaded. "We'll have to find a way, Ali. I won't let them take you from me. We'll show them you're good, that you couldn't possibly have meant to hurt anyone."

Alia's hopes sank. Her sister's belief in her redemption was nearly as crushing as the knowledge she was wrong.

There wasn't any good left in her. It had been stamped out.

"Lena is sick. I've taken her to healers in Parth and Royce. No one seems to know what is amiss with her. Can you help her, Wen?" Her sister's eyes widened at the old nickname. "Please?" While Alia had been a natural healer, able to tackle any malady, Elowen's magic was channeled through the natural properties of plants.

Elowen grasped Alia's hand tightly, prepared to fervently give her oath. "I will. And I will be making your tonics from now on. Whoever mixed this batch has sapped all your strength, not only your magic."

"It could be dangerous for you to be seen aiding me. Help Lena; I can take it." Even her own sister could not sense the Undoing's undaunted strength.

Elowen's pity was far more useful than her fear.

The princess chewed on her lip, a nervous tic that royalty hadn't drummed out of her. For a moment, she looked just like she had as a girl. "About Cormac ... " Elowen began.

Alia shook her head with great difficulty. "You don't owe me an explanation." When Alia had fled the palace, she knew Cormac would find someone else to marry. The crown prince was required to supply an heir after all. And while she hadn't anticipated that someone to be her sister, Alia could hardly fault Elowen for it. Alia knew if there was blame to place, it should be reserved for their mother. Either way, she couldn't afford to lose her sister as an ally in protecting Lena from squabbling over her former lover.

"Ali, I don't know how to make any of this right. Tell me how." Elowen lay her head on Alia's chest and wrapped her arms around her once more. Alia's casual graciousness seemed to have triggered a rush of guilt from Elowen, all but ensuring that her sister would do as Alia asked.

"You can keep my daughter safe," Alia charged. "She isn't like me; she is innocent. You have to protect her from the Bartons, from the Meadors. Please, Elowen."

Elowen lifted her head, understanding that Alia had just asked her to protect Lena from the royal family and their own parents. Elowen was part of both families, but nowhere near as brutal as the rest of them, or at least Alia hoped. "If it comes to it, Ali, I will care for Lena like my own. I swear it."

"Thank you," Alia said, her eyelids heavy. Her objective had been achieved.

"I think they mean to put you before the King's Council," Elowen said. "Father sits on the Council still; he'll ask for leniency. They're good men, really. It's just—these are dangerous times. Tensions are high."

Harlan's identical statement echoed in Alia's ears. "Have there been attacks here as well?"

"Nearby and getting closer. Imagine it here, all these defenseless people." Elowen's anxiety was plain.

"As defenseless as the people in the hinterland?" Alia couldn't stop herself.

"I didn't mean—" Elowen's shoulders slumped. "Have you seen it?"

"Only the aftermath." Alia tried to push the images away, bodies strewn with no one left alive to bury them.

"Did you ever think—" A shiver went through Elowen. "I remember learning about them. Immortals. Tiarcons. We're supposed to defend ourselves from stories."

From what Alia had seen, there was no defense. Only escape. "Do you know how it came through?"

Elowen paled, leaning in as if afraid the walls would hear. "Cormac thinks the Veillanti have finally found a way through the veil. That they've betrayed us to the Otherworld and are seeking to destroy Mandal as retribution. The attacks, the short spurts of sunlight, even the Council is asking questions."

Elowen's point in mentioning this was clear. With so much fear, Alia was just another magical beast too similar to the treacherous Otherworld. She was another threat to the mortal kingdoms and had to be dealt with before she grew beyond their control.

Damn the Undoing. Damn the Meador bloodline.

A knock at the door signaled Elowen. "I'll do what I can." Elowen squeezed Alia's hand.

Thanks to Elowen's gentler tonic, Alia could support her own weight by the time Harlan returned. Still, she was feeble and unkempt from days of draining draughts. The prince would have to judge her this way.

Before Harlan could speak, Alia pressed, "Can I at least see Lena once more?"

Harlan's gaze fled to the floor. "My orders were clear."

"What could I possibly do?" Alia held up her trembling hands for effect.

"I can't defy him again." There was no humor left in Harlan, only bowed shoulders. Cormac must have been furious when he found out Harlan hid her presence in Sheath.

"Is he going to have me executed?" Alia tried to provoke some sympathy, a last effort to see Lena. A quick execution might be the only kind of mercy Cormac allowed. His father, King Isaac, wouldn't even give her an audience before ordering her death. And he would be sure to make her end as brutal as possible, a spectacle. It would amuse him to see just exactly what would kill an Undoing Mage.

"You attacked his uncle." Harlan scratched the back of his neck.

He wasn't going to give in to her. Besides, he was right.

Alia had often thought about how it would be to see Cormac again. In her imagining, she was wholly unaffected by the man she once loved, impervious to his title and authority. But instead, she would go before him as a prisoner.

She knew where Harlan was taking her before they arrived. She had joined Cormac in spying on the council chambers on more than one occasion. As children, they had always been thrown out, but now Cormac presided over it.

When they arrived at the chamber's golden doors, Harlan stopped her with a light touch on the shoulder. "Ali, I'm sorry."

Harlan's apology twisted like a blade. Guards ushered them in, and Harlan's grip tightened. Beyond the gold doors, the high-ceilinged chamber glittered with lanternlight, casting shadows on the stone table at the center.

The table had persevered in her memory, a map of the realm first carved in Orlast's time. The borders of the four kingdoms of Entien might have shifted since she'd last seen it. Parth swallowed up the northern mountains, Royce to the eastern plains, and across a strip of sea to the south, the Isle of Veillant. The landscapes had been a curiosity to her then, but now she saw lands she'd haunted. The Spear of Orlast remained etched across the kingdom of Mandal, the one weapon powerful enough to kill a Tiarcon, lost for centuries.

Eight high-backed seats were placed at the table, all set three steps lower than the outskirts of the chambers where the attendants were made to wait. The chamber was from Orlast's time, the fledgling mortal kingdom rejecting the lofty thrones of the Tiarcons. Deliberating allies and subordinates would have filled the higher levels back then, rather than prisoners.

Several feet from the end of the table, up on the first steps, sat two chairs. The one on the left was hers, and magical bonds snapped around her wrists as Harlan pressed her down into it. Alia looked to the other chair; her daughter's garnet eyes overflowed with hatred for the men seated before them.

They had dragged Lena from her sickbed to suffer judgment.

"Lena," Alia whispered, struggling against the magical ropes.

Lena swung around to face her, and Alia fought the urge to gasp. The dark marks had reached her mouth. The skin around her eyes was sunken.

What have I done?

"I'm sorry," Lena panted. "I didn't mean—"

"Whatever you hear, Lena, whatever they say." Alia tried to hold Lena's attention. "I've only ever wanted—" Even now, when the proper words were required to buffer what Lena was sure to learn, Alia couldn't find them.

I've only ever wanted to control what you saw in me, what you knew of me.

Lies had been far easier than explanations.

Alia forced her attention to the men around the table, the ones who would stand in judgment. Most hadn't bothered to inspect the prisoners bound before them, keener to posture amongst themselves. Those who did look over regarded Alia with suspicion and Lena with abject terror. Alia lifted her chin; she hadn't survived for this long to cower before the Crown's closest allies and grasping rivals.

She found a pair of emerald eyes like her own, sharp with attention. Lord Edgar Meador, the head of the most brutal family in the kingdom, his council seat bought in blood. He did not greet his daughter and granddaughter. There was no smile, no assurance offered. Just his unwavering attention. Alia wasn't sure what she'd expected. Her father wouldn't dare to spare a bit of his influence to save her; she was a criminal. He would prefer to keep his hands clean of her misdeeds.

Cormac arrived last, as not a moment of his time could be wasted waiting for others. His dark blonde hair was longer now, emphasizing a slight wave as it was brushed back. His shoulders had broadened, sculpted by decades as a warrior. A shadow of a beard graced his angular jaw, up to his well-defined cheekbones. His skin was paler than she recalled, porcelain, cold without the brush of the sun. The years had taken the mischievousness out of his bright eyes, but one look at him still had her reeling.

Alia opened her mouth.

His brow furrowed, and those ice blue eyes narrowed. Cormac's gaze seared through her, his mood shifting and darkening from across the room. Anger, disgust, and frustration; no hint of the love that had once flourished between them.

"Master Dorian, barrier. Now." Cormac looked to the middle-aged man seated on his left, clad in black mage robes with a Mandal blue sash belted around his narrow hips.

The mage stood with an affirmative nod, magic bristling around him as he moved.

"Hello," he greeted Alia and Lena as he stood before them, smoothing dark locks that sprang back up the second his hand passed through them. "I'm Master—"

"Get away from us, leech." Alia glowered, not wanting to give the mage the chance to assess their strength.

Despite her hostility, there was warmth in his deep brown eyes; they were so dark the irises were almost indistinguishable from his pupils.

Alia picked up his accent in the few words she'd allowed. Mandal's new Master Mage, a Veillanti by birth.

He wasn't entirely sullied by worshipping the Otherworld. In fact, his features were more pleasing than cultish, his short beard making him look several years older than his smooth skin would belie. But as he moved closer, Alia could see the odd markings along his temples, dark scars standing out on his light brown skin, connecting along his hairline. Veillanti markings.

Lena spat at his feet, enforcing Alia's insult.

"Charming." His lips lifted into a smirk, letting Alia and Lena's combined aggression fester. "I'm going to place a barrier around you. Just a precaution." It was an unnecessary precaution; the Undoing was as useless as ever. There was no way that Alia could attempt to employ it without risking Lena.

The barrier shimmered around Alia and Lena, summoned in a blink. Even though his task was complete, the mage lingered. He watched Alia through the barrier, head tipped to the side.

"Shall I test it?" Alia threatened, trying to disrupt him. Mages of his caliber often possessed affinities, and she didn't want to experience what his were.

The mage bit back a chuckle. "That won't be necessary," he said before retreating to Cormac's side.

The prince began the proceedings, speaking from the chair at the head of the table, facing Alia and Lena. "Lady Alia Meador stands charged for crimes against the Crown, including a vicious attack on Master Mage Ruben Barton with the intent to take his life, and evading the King's justice. For some of you, these events are burned into your memory; for others, they predate your time on the King's Council. Therefore, we will review these charges."

Cormac had never sounded so callous.

"I thought—" Lena raised her head with discernable effort. She turned her gaze on her mother. "This is about you?"

It was about the Undoing. As significant as her crime was, the Council would be preoccupied with the nature of her magic, afraid of what else she might do.

"Bring in the Queen," Cormac ordered before Alia could answer Lena.

Alia braced herself, regret searing through her. She should have killed Rheta.

Stewards brought a ninth chair to the table for the Queen. The years had marked Rheta's skin, but her sharp blue eyes, Cormac's eyes, still brightened her face, gleaming like her golden crown.

"Alia." The Queen studied her, seeming to delight in every uneven seam, each wayward curl, and all the marks the road had left behind on Alia's skin. "If you had any decency, you would have rid the realm of your presence."

"If I had any decency." It was foolish, beneath her, but Alia embraced the youthful brashness that Rheta inspired.

Cormac's glare sliced through her; Edgar rubbed his temples. Harlan leaned back in his chair to position himself in Rheta's path to Alia. It was unclear which woman he sought to protect.

"How far you've fallen." Queen Rheta clasped her hands together, barely suppressing applause. "One of the swine."

"Those swine are giving their lives in the fields that feed you." Lena strained against the bonds, garnet light smacking against Master Dorian's barrier.

"Muzzle your whelp." Rheta's eyes flashed.

"Enough." Cormac seized control of the session, pausing long enough for complete silence to reign. "Mother, please recount the crime for the good of the Council."

Queen Rheta feigned distress, the perfect victim. "Most of you remember my dear brother, Ruben. As Master Mage of Mandal, he dedicated himself to the education of the next generation of mages, to making sure Mandal could defend itself should the Otherworld attempt to rival us. At that time, I worked closely with him as the Intercessor. He gave his considerable magical talents in the pursuit of identifying the most powerful combinations of magical bloodlines."

Master Ruben, the defender of Mandal, the only hope for the mortal realm of Entien. Alia knew better. The man wielded the worst of the Otherworld, preying on those he was supposed to instruct.

"If his work had not been interrupted, Mandal would have warrior mages to protect itself during these troubled times." The queen heaped the blame for Mandal's struggle against the Otherworld on Alia's storied ledger.

"My brother devoted himself to teaching Lady Alia. He was thrilled by what her healing magic could do for our soldiers and mages. But my dear brother, for all his mastery, was blind to her treachery."

The bonds bit into Alia's skin as she jerked against them, aching to scratch her nails across Rheta's throat. Anything to stop her from speaking. *Lies. Lies. Lies.*

"The night of the attack, my brother was upset. Lady Alia had become volatile, unpredictable, and he had finally begun to see what she was. I had never met an Undoing Mage, but when I came upon my brother writhing in pain, encased in a lethal mist, I knew." Rheta paused for dramatic effect. "You have all heard the stories of Lord Silas Meador. You know an Undoing Mage brings death as easily as the rest of us draw breath."

Alia remembered the uncontrollable darkness, the complete shock when the mist surrounded her. At first, she thought Master Ruben had done something to her. By the time she realized that the Undoing was coming from within her, it was too late.

"Ruben fought back, saving me before she could kill me, but he couldn't save himself. By the time he overpowered her, he had been under her influence too long, too damaged. He lived, but my brother was never the same man again after that evil marked him."

How Alia wished she had been strong enough to finish the task. If there was one purpose for the Undoing, it should have been to kill Master Ruben. And his complicit sister.

Alia shrank away from Lena's scathing stare; the past she had hidden from Lena was now laid bare. Lena had never been told of the Undoing or Master Ruben, lest the knowledge of their darkness spur the like within her.

"Wise councilmembers, a rogue Undoing Mage is a threat to the entire kingdom. She cannot be contained, and she cannot be left alive."

Queen Rheta might as well have taken a bow.

The councilmembers could hardly look at Alia now, fidgeting in their seats. Fear came off them in waves.

"Are there questions for the witness?" Cormac asked.

"What could there be to ask?" the man to Cormac's right said. "The Undoing Mage must be executed."

Alia scrutinized the man's mousy face. He looked like a Wexworth, a house that was once respectable, but in recent generations hadn't produced a single magical heir. A Wexworth making any statement about a mage should be a crime.

"Mother," Lena murmured. "What are they talking about? What's an Undoing Mage?"

Alia maintained focus on the Council, as they could influence Cormac.

The Veillanti mage strummed his fingers on the table, frenetic as he leaned forward. "Your Highness, if I may ask, what precipitated the attack on Master Ruben?"

Queen Rheta looked down at the mage, her distrust evident from across the table. "Not that it should matter to you, Veillanti, but I wasn't there to witness it. I do know my brother hoped to help Alia turn away from her troubling behavior."

"I will remind you, Mother, Master Dorian has defected," Cormac chided with thinly veiled irritation.

The mage didn't blink as the queen huffed a correction. "Had you ever seen Lady Alia exhibit such magic before that day?"

"No one knew what she was until that night." Queen Rheta looked at her son, pity crossing her face. Alia imagined the shame the Undoing had brought the prince.

"We are through with questions." Cormac's patience had clearly waned. The rest of the council remained silent, wise on their part. "Thank you, Mother. You may go."

"My son, Lords of Mandal, I trust you will see justice done." Queen Rheta weighed on the decision with a supplication.

Cormac remained silent, hands clasped before him, until the door shut behind the queen.

Look at me.

Cormac started, as if shaken from a trance. "And now we can hear from the accused."

He trudged towards Alia, abandoning his place at the head of the table. He stopped at the edge, only a few feet from where she sat bound. This close, his presence was overwhelming. Memories tugged at Alia as she sat in thrall of him, the man who had loved her.

"Lady Alia—"

Ali, your Ali.

"—do you have anything to say for yourself?"

I never wanted to let you go.

Her insides churned, but her face remained impassive. "You know what I am." She met Cormac's gaze, declaring herself his equal, still. That is what he had loved about her most, the challenge. Now it only served to infuriate him further. His hand tightened on the back of Harlan's chair, fighting for control of his infamous Barton temper.

"Your Highness." Edgar, ever the polite courtier, drew Cormac's attention to him. "There is no excuse for my daughter's actions. I will not quarrel with the punishment you determine fitting for her."

Alia's lip curled at his speech; the man who had raised her would never submit so thoroughly without having his own solution in mind. Her father's manipulative nature was unmatched, and Alia had been his finest pupil.

"I will, however, ask for your mercy before the ruling is made. This disastrous incident aside, the Bartons and Meadors have been staunch allies for generations. The strength of the Meador bloodline is unquestioned, and with our power comes the potential of an Undoing Mage. I will remind you that it was the last Undoing Mage, Silas Meador, who aligned with your great-grandfather to begin the Barton reign."

Alia grimaced. Silas Meador used the Undoing to overthrow the previous ruling family, the Truaths, killing nearly every single member at the behest of the Bartons. He promptly gave in to the darkness afterward, taking his own life.

The Undoing had a cost.

"You like to forget that Silas was due for his own trial, disowned by the first Barton king for slaughtering children." Lord Tristan Palmer glared at Edgar from across the table.

Edgar's honeyed words turned sour. "A bitter day for the Palmers, even now. How you must still grieve the Truaths, the death of your influence."

Lord Daniel Solreen, white-haired and frail, coughed. "Lord Palmer raises a valid point. The Meadors had long produced powerful mages, but volatile, violent ones."

"For volatile, violent times," a lord Alia didn't recognize countered.

Edgar weathered the insult, pushing back from the table just far enough for the hilt of his sword to catch the torchlight. "My daughter could have further value to Mandal. My granddaughter shows considerable magical potential, and without the taint of the Undoing. Alia could still produce additional warrior mages for Mandal."

Alia thrashed against her restraints again, ignoring the burn. After all these years, she was still just chattel to her father. To be kept alive until he could see what else he might extract from her.

Her control fluctuated as she felt the all too familiar pull of the Undoing seeking to be released. Alia slammed her eyes shut, trying to hold back the force that gathered within her. It yearned to pour out, to end this entire council, taking her and her daughter along with it. Despite her attempts to retract it, the pressure only built.

Until it abruptly subsided. A pleasant warmth pushed in, helping satisfy the Undoing and contain it. It had been years since the Undoing had settled, not since their home burned. When Alia opened her eyes, Master Dorian's were boring into her. *He* had stifled the Undoing, but she was too stunned to distinguish how.

Regaining power over the Undoing was a temporary victory. Now, the Master Mage knew the attempts to drain her magic didn't apply to the Undoing. The queen had been right; the Council could not let her live.

"Considerable magical potential." The Wexworth lord scoffed at Lena. Alia followed his gaze over to Lena, her quivering limbs, dark veins, and bowed head. "What is wrong with her?"

"She's sick." Harlan seemed to find his voice for the first time.

"She's not sick." Master Dorian continued to strum his fingers on the table. "She's untrained."

Cormac's head snapped in his direction and away from Alia's distress. "What do you mean?" He echoed the question at the forefront of Alia's mind.

"I've been through Master Ruben's records. Lady Alia is one of the few wielders of high magic in Mandal, which her daughter also possesses. That kind of capability is essential if we should hope to stand against the power of Alasar. Or as you say here, the Otherworld." Dorian's gesticulations matched the pace of his speech.

Her high magic was a burden born of the land Mandals long refused to acknowledge by name. Veillanti had no such aversion.

"Ali can stop the Oucura?" Harlan questioned the mage, slipping into familiarity.

Dorian nodded. "According to my studies."

"You can't fight one evil with another," Wexworth protested.

Dorian's hands continued to tap. "Isn't that what mortalkind has always done? Used Tiarcon magic against them?"

"It won't work," Alia cut in. "It-it-it—" she stammered to explain the destructive force within her. How it refused to obey her, how it had dampened any other affinities she once had.

"We will reconvene after midday," Cormac said, yielding. "Captain Harlan, secure the prisoners until then, separately."

Harlan laboriously got to his feet, giving Master Dorian time to drop the barrier.

"Lena." Alia found the courage to turn to her. Even as her life was being ruled on, a bit of hope flared. From Master Dorian's description, Lena could be set right; there was an end to her condition.

"Who are you?" Lena asked once more, her lips trembling.

"I'll explain," Alia promised as she was pulled away.

The magical bonds on Alia's wrists remained as Harlan led her to the adjacent room. It was a small space without windows, without any chance of escape.

"I tried to talk with him." Harlan's voice was barely audible.

"He never could be reasoned with."

"It's his father. The Council is already questioning his rule. He thinks the best response is to provoke them. Show them he isn't afraid."

Cormac's instincts hadn't changed, his destruction spelled out by his own brutality. "Killing a Meador would be bold."

The two sat in silence as the minutes stretched on. Alia relished the opportunity to stand after being chained in a chair, stretching her muscles as much as her shackles would allow.

The queen wanted her dead, still.

Her father wanted to breed her.

Master Dorian would have her be a weapon.

Cormac showed no sign of leniency.

And Lena didn't recognize her.

Harlan jumped, shielding her, when a door appeared on the wall before them. A white hot light traced its outline and cut through the stone. Prince Cormac stepped through, chest heaving and eyes ablaze.

"Leave, Harlan."

"Stay." Alia put every shred of fear into her appeal to Harlan. To stand between her and a royal desperate to prove himself.

Cormac advanced as Harlan hesitated, sweat gathering on his forehead.

"Leave us."

Harlan ducked out, mumbling about oaths by way of apology to Alia.

"Come to say farewell before my execution?" Alia tried not to outwardly react to being alone with him. "How does one kill an Undoing Mage?"

Cormac bristled, moving to rest his back against the opposite wall. He must have been told in a gentler way than she had about the end that had befallen all the previous Undoing Mages in her bloodline.

Ruben had delighted in speculating about her fate, his words still etched in her memory '*Succumbed is a word my predecessors favored in their records. But myself, I preferred consumed, devoured.*'

In the written records of Mandal's master mages, one had never recorded an exact manner of death for an Undoing Mage. Rather, only that they imploded in a manner that could only be of their own doing.

"Your daughter."

"The one you pulled from the infirmary. A sick child put before the Council in restraints."

"Hardly a child. How old is she?"

Alia's eyes dropped to the floor, not wanting to admit Lena was nearly grown. "Nearly seventeen."

Cormac bent to meet her eyes. "Is she mine?"

This had been his reason for cornering her, for Lena's presence at Council. Alia considered lying to the prince, letting him believe Lena was his daughter, to buy her protection. But Lena would never comply; she knew who her father was.

Alia shook her head.

"You married?" Cormac fired the question without emotion, but Alia could feel his anger still.

Had he wanted Lena to be his?

"A Roycan, yes."

"Which house?"

"None."

"You left me and married a commoner?" His voice rose to a dangerous pitch.

"Lena is legitimate. If she were to claim a name, it would be Meador. But we have no use for titles." Whatever Finn had been mattered little now.

"You just want my healers," Cormac grumbled. "You returned after all of this time, and you went to Harlan for help?"

"You're the prince."

"You thought that I would refuse you."

"No, I thought you would do exactly what you're doing now—prosecute me," Alia bolstered her voice to match his.

Cormac raised his fists. "What choice do I have?" he raged. "You leave without a word of explanation—not even a farewell—you ran. After attacking my family, you ran." His temper was no longer contained by royal expectations.

"What use is there in talking about this? It is finished."

We are finished.

He drew closer as Alia held her head high and her feet rooted. She did not meet his gaze even when he stood right in front of her, fearing what she would see in his eyes, fearing what hers would divulge in turn. He raised a hand to trace her jawline.

"Stop." Alia clenched her jaw. "You belong to Elowen."

"I belong to no one," Cormac said, his hand cupping her cheek. "It is just as well you left."

"I heard. A perfect family."

"Yes, Elowen gave me two strong sons to carry on my legacy." Cormac smiled in a show of self-satisfaction. "And the throne is within my grasp."

"How lovely for you."

Cormac's smile widened before his expression hardened again. "What happened that night, Ali?"

Alia was unable and unwilling to shrink away from his touch. Everything about him was still too familiar.

"Why didn't you come to me?"

"They were never going to let us be together once they knew what I was." Alia's voice broke into a whisper. No one would have an Undoing Mage as a royal.

"I could have convinced them." Cormac caressed her cheek with his thumb. "You never gave me the chance."

Alia stayed silent; a familiar panic was seeping into her bones. She still didn't have the strength to explain it all to Cormac. Cormac looked down at the bonds on her wrists, banishing them with a spell. He didn't fear what her hands could do.

"An attack on the royal family cannot go unpunished."

Alia placed her hand on his chest, feeling the pounding of his heart. The prince was conflicted, wavering. It was dangerous for her to encourage him, to let him feel the power he'd always craved. But this was a way to survive, as long as she knew when to step back.

She met his gaze, not to provoke him but to soothe. "It is within your power to decide."

Now that her bound hands were no longer between them, he took her into his arms. Alia buried her face in his chest, her strength fleeing. They were drawn together, circumstances forgotten. Alia leaned into him, the feeling of him drowning sense. If she could just stay here, like this, with him, then everything else would melt away. She could be who she had been, the woman he had loved.

But Cormac broke the embrace. He stepped back and held her from him, searching. His touch was almost painful as he whispered, "You shouldn't have come back."

An inconvenient complication. The kingdom of Mandal had continued on without her, indifferent. It would have been better if she had stayed away, stayed dead. "Help Lena. Then I'll go. We'll both go."

"You know I can't."

He couldn't let her go. The magic that had taken root inside of her couldn't be left alone. Neither could Lena's power.

Cormac left through the door he had cut. He glanced back, but only to summon bonds to hold her wrists together. Alia crumpled against the wall, sliding down to sit on the ground as the Council met in the next room to decide their fate.

4

Seeing Lena was the only solace as the guards dragged Alia back into the confines of the council chamber. But the reprieve abated; Edgar stood beside her daughter. Both guards strained to tame Alia's flailing as they deposited her in the chair, Cormac's spelled ropes snaking around the arms.

"Alia."

Just his acknowledgment provoked her. "Get away from her."

"I am her grandfather." Edgar puffed out his chest, brandishing a ringed hand.

"You have no right—"

"Council," Cormac began, making Edgar slither back to his seat.

"Lena, please." Alia tried to learn towards her.

Lena made no sign that she had heard.

"The Council has provided deliberation and advice, but the burden of ruling falls on me alone." Cormac's words were a warning to the rest of the Council; dissention would not be tolerated. "In the name of King Isaac, I sentence Lady Alia Meador to indefinite confinement within the palace." Cormac spoke to his Council, rather than to Alia.

Her breath caught in her throat; relief cut short by dread. *Not execution, but a cage.*

"Lady Alia will honor the order of the Crown and exhibit civil behavior befitting a lady of her noble stature. Furthermore, Lady Alia and her daughter will be trained at the Tower and tasked to contribute to Mandal's defense whenever summoned. Finally, both women will report as eligible to the Intercessor to see if an appropriate magical pairing can be made."

The chains are never coming off.

Mandal had laid claim to them, their magic, their bodies. Something threatened to tear loose within her, but Alia capped her fury for Lena's benefit.

"A just ruling, your Grace. I will see your order enforced." Edgar bowed deeply.

"Captain Harlan will see to Lady Alia's confinement," Cormac said, regarding both men. Perhaps this was Harlan's punishment for hiding her presence from his prince. "And Master Dorian will see to their instruction."

Caged and weaponized.

"A merciful ruling," Wexworth jeered.

"My prince, what if there is another incident?" Tristan Palmer's fists were on the table.

"If Lady Alia commits another transgression against the Crown, her life will be forfeit."

A short leash.

Their freedom was gone, stripped away in one statement. But the Mandals were confident enough in their means of control to keep both of them alive. Which meant there would be a way out, eventually. Alia had escaped the palace once; she was sure she could do it again. Lena was spared the worst of the sentence, the worst of their fear. Even still, Lena's magic became unhinged at the prince's ruling, waves of heat and light pouring off her.

"Lena, no." Alia braced herself for an outburst. Her daughter glowed and sparked, magic strengthening and control waning.

Master Dorian approached, seemingly unbothered by Lena's combustion. With a twitch of his fingers, he constricted his barrier around Lena, absorbing the heat and searing light pouring out of her. Alia stilled, eyes wide; no mage had ever been able to stymie Lena's magic. Alia had only ever been able to contain the worst of it before Lena tired.

While one hand orchestrated the barrier, Master Dorian summoned Lena's aura with the other, warm light pouring from his palm. Lena's body jerked, her magic distilling into garnet ribbons, fighting the mage's summons. But her strength ebbed, and a garnet sphere burst from the base of Lena's ribcage.

While Alia's aura was stagnant, save for the infection of the Undoing, Lena's fractured magic spun in rings. Dorian teased out a single strand of light, pulling it out of the frenzy. Isolated, the speck of magic obeyed Dorian's direction. He pulled at another strand, creating a procession, smooth and orderly. He continued to pull as the rest of her aura followed, winding it back in on itself like a spool of thread.

Instantly, Lena dimmed and her shoulders hunched over in exhaustion.

"What are you doing?!" Alia shrieked, even as she could see the sickness beneath Lena's skin start to retreat.

Master Dorian ignored her, admiring his work as he returned Lena's orderly aura with a wave of his hand.

The mage then reached over, relieving Alia of the glowing bonds around her wrists. "We can pretend these were more than ornamental," he said in a voice low enough not to be overheard.

An irritating awe stunted Alia's ability to respond. She flexed her hands and turned away from him, setting herself between Lena and the

Veillanti. He'd known how uncontained her magic was. He could have exposed her and had chosen not to. And he knew how to help Lena.

"I'll see you shortly," he called after her as Harlan approached.

Harlan helped Alia lift Lena out of the chair, her daughter recovering from the subsided outburst.

Princess Elowen, flanked by noble attendants, beamed at them as they exited the stale council chamber. Elowen wouldn't be smiling if she knew Alia had just been in her husband's arms. If she knew how wretched her sister was.

Cormac should have had her killed.

"It is a harsh sentence, but we'll make it manageable," Elowen whispered in her ear. "I had chambers made up for you both. Let's get you cleaned up." Elowen's soft hands burned Alia as the princess dismissed her attendants, two young noblewomen who were regarding Alia with a sadistic fascination.

Elowen pulled her through the palace's brightly lit passageways while Harlan followed with Lena hanging on his arm. They went in the opposite direction of the royal apartments, towards the oldest section of the palace. It had been known as the Olden Wing even when Alia had lived there. It was far from the luxurious royal apartments and too shabby to be considered proper lodging for anyone of note.

The ideal prison for a pair of disgraced noblewomen.

The corridors dimmed, narrowing as they skirted the section built against the cliff. The air was instantly cooler, more damp. Every step away from the council chamber made it easier for Alia to breathe.

The suite was simple, furnished with necessities, but it was more than Alia and Lena had enjoyed in years. The door opened up into a sitting room, adorned with a few faded chairs and a torn couch clustered around a single worn table, the wood stripped and scratched from years of use.

The walls were free of decoration, rows of stacked, yellowed stone that the builder hadn't bothered to even.

Down a narrow, barren hall were three separate chambers. Two had been made suitable, recently dusted, and thin linens put onto mattresses. Lena quickly claimed the chamber with the window, leaving Alia with the larger one with room for the bed, a small armoire and mirror, and a single closet.

"I can have them bring pieces from your former chamber," Elowen offered, trailing Alia as she surveyed the space.

"No need." Alia smoothed the sheet with her hand, imagining how it would feel to lie down on a proper bed, how the fabric would feel against her skin. There was no reason to muddy the hurriedly tidied chamber with relics of her past.

The most remarkable part of her new prison was the expansive balcony looking down on the rest of the city, resting upon the side of the cliff. The glow of the city and spray of the sea reached her as the dark stretched on. Most of the Olden Wing was pressed against the rocks themselves, but Elowen had selected apartments that looked over the sea. She had remembered.

"Look here, the water is warm." Elowen pointed to the bath set up in the third chamber as maids in royal uniforms prepared towels and fresh clothes.

"Lena?" Alia found her voice.

Lena huffed, then disappeared into her selected room and slammed the door. Alia heard the soft sigh of the mattress as Lena flopped down on it.

"Then for you." Elowen's smile didn't fail. "I'm sure rest will do her some good. Don't you want her to see you well, despite it all?"

It was a notion their mother had imparted to them. As long as one looked well, it didn't matter what the reality was. If her dress was pressed, plaits orderly, and face carefully painted, no one needed to know what festered within.

Your beauty is your armor.

Alia supposed that having been born quotidien—without magic—in a noble bloodline, had driven Mariana Meador's obsession with the wares she did possess. Not that she hadn't lusted for more; after all, she had produced two magical daughters.

"The guards will be right outside the door. You can summon me at any time," Harlan said more to Elowen than Alia.

Alia watched his retreat into the antechamber, wanting to follow him. Elowen's polite urging stopped her. If she were ever going to free herself from this place, she would have to discern what means Cormac would use to keep her locked away. And Harlan, as her jailer, was sure to know. But that investigation would be for another time, when Princess Elowen wasn't present.

Alia had forgotten what it was like to be waited on. The maids took her old, worn clothes, hopefully to be burned, and brought her soaps and oils as she lay in the pleasantly warm bathwater. Her confinement was to be a comfortable one, with luxuries she had only dreamt of on the road. She might as well take advantage of it while it lasted.

She fought the impulse to hide the rough callouses on her hands and feet, the blistered scars from walking too far in worn boots, and the grime that seemed part of her skin now. They scrubbed her until it hurt, and still she was marked by a life outside of the palace. She wouldn't let it give rise to shame.

Once the maids concluded their efforts, Alia was wrapped in a robe. She found her sister at a wooden table in the larger chamber. The princess had ordered a feast from the palace kitchens, and it covered every inch of the tabletop.

"I am glad the quarters are to your liking." Elowen sat perfectly straight in the chair, watching Alia eat. "Drink this." She pushed a cup towards her. Elowen's tonic smelled bitter but spread warmth through Alia's body like a flame.

Her beautiful little sister with her kind, gentle magic. Alia remembered this tonic, how it would always appear during one of her dark days, when she returned from the Tower and shut herself away from everyone, even her family. There would be a small scratching at her door, and she would open it a crack to find a warm cup there, one that could trick someone as defiled as her into having hope.

Elowen brewed life, and Alia overflowed with the power to take it.

Alia couldn't say if they were two sides of the same coin or complete opposites. They were similar enough to have fallen in love with the same man, to have both dreamt of becoming royal. Alia knew that they shared even more than that, the daunting expectation of relentless parents, a fearsome legacy as Meadors. But somewhere their paths diverged.

When Alia fell out of favor, it must have all changed for Elowen. She must have been thrust onto the pedestal, the hopes that their parents had for Alia placed on her shoulders. And her one companion, who knew what it was like to grow up a Meador—her older sister—had been branded a monster, then vanished in the night.

"Tell me more about Lena's father," Elowen said, bridging the silence and sipping her own cup of tea.

"His name was Finn." Alia gulped down Elowen's reviver, forgetting propriety.

"Finn," Elowen repeated. "What was he like?"

Alia had to look down at her plate, nearly empty now. Her view of her husband, once so delightfully sincere, had become increasingly murky in the years that he had been gone, the night of his death looming over all the pleasant memories. "He was steady. Immovable," Alia responded, lacking a more fitting description.

There was a glimmer of despair in Elowen's eyes before her smile reached them. "Steady indeed to hold you still. I wished I could have met him. He was a commoner?"

"A farmer," Alia said, at least it was what he purported to be. She couldn't quiet the incessant nagging in her mind that he had been playing a part, just as she had.

The Undoing had quieted during her years with Finn, subsiding to a dull groan. Alia had foolishly believed that she had gained control, but when Finn died, so did whatever had repressed her darkest tendencies, leaving her with a child, without a home, and firmly in the grasp of the deadliest magic in Entien. Elowen didn't need to hear all of that.

"Your charm won him over, I'm sure." Elowen chuckled.

"How could it not?" There had been no charm left in her when Finn found her, just raw agony.

"Mother would whip me if I allowed you about without your hair fixed." Elowen's ever-present smile did not falter. She gestured at the maid to begin brushing and plaiting Alia's dark curls.

"Is Mariana here?"

Elowen winced. "She's always here. I don't think she'll ever return to the Meador lands; she is accustomed to the ways of the palace. She became the Intercessor shortly after you ... departed."

"The Intercessor? Of course," Alia mocked humorlessly. "She always could twist any situation to her advantage." There was no doubt in Alia's mind that her mother had found a way to make Alia's downfall her path to another honorific. Being the Intercessor no doubt suited her, as she had been obsessed with magical matches for her daughters, and now she could lend that obsession to the entire kingdom, finding the most powerful bloodlines to combine.

"She's anxious to see you. I asked her to give you some time to settle in." Elowen braced her palms on the table.

"I will never be settled enough to see her," Alia snapped, trying to breathe through the anger. "She must be all too pleased with the ruling. She has fresh blood for her pairings."

"She's been so distracted with Master Dorian; I think you'll escape her attention for the time being."

"Master Dorian is letting her match him?"

Elowen nodded with wide eyes. "It was one of the conditions of his defection."

Alia let out a low whistle. "I can only imagine courtiers crawling over each other to grab hold of a fresh magical bloodline."

"It has caused quite a stir."

"And nearly a riot among the commonfolk." Alia remembered the crowds when she had arrived in the city. The wars with Veillant had left empty beds all across Mandal, not to mention the hardship wartime rations had imposed. While tensions hadn't turned to open war in thirty years, the losses were still remembered, hatred stoked for another few generations.

"They'll need to become accustomed to Cormac's leadership. He has many ideas to move Mandal forward." Elowen beamed.

The only ideas Alia remembered Cormac having were those that benefited him. But it was somewhat endearing to see Elowen's pride in her husband. He was going to need her support if these were the kind of choices he was going to start with.

A Veillanti for a Master Mage.

Neglecting to execute an Undoing Mage.

Allowing the Oucura to rampage the hinterland unchecked.

"Now, get a dress from your closet and let's wake Lena." Elowen stood, tucking a stray hair behind Alia's ear and taking her arm in hers again.

"She's only just found out what I am, she may not be ready to—"

"Ali, the last thing she needs is to be left in the dark any longer."

"She's my daughter." Alia chaffed at Elowen's interference.

"Exactly."

Alia tensed but did as her sister bid. She had only planned on divulging the Undoing to Lena if she showed signs of it. But she should have known that in coming to Mandal, Lena would discover her secrets. Some of them.

"Lena?" Alia hovered over the door. She turned the knob to find Lena sprawled out on the bed, staring at the ceiling.

"Did you do it?" Lena didn't look at Alia or Elowen.

"Do what?"

"Try to kill that man?"

Alia sighed as Elowen pushed her along. "I did."

"Did he deserve it?"

"He did." Alia sat beside Lena on the bed, silently begging her not to ask why.

Lena pressed her lips together. "The Undoing, that's how you hurt people, isn't it?"

"Yes."

"And that's why they're scared of you?" Lena propped herself on her elbows.

"Yes." Alia traced her hand over Lena's cheek, where the black veins no longer stretched. "But you don't need to be."

"I don't understand. Your magic has always been pathetic." Lena's eyebrows drew together.

"Your mother is one of the most powerful mages in Mandal," Elowen spoke up, attracting Lena's suspicious gaze.

"Lena, this is your Aunt Elowen. Princess Elowen Barton." Alia stifled a chuckle at Elowen's expense.

"Married to that ass of a prince?" Lena snapped.

To her credit, Elowen only gaped for a few seconds. "I'm glad you're feeling better, Lena."

Lena turned back to Alia. "What was the leech saying about me, about high magic?"

"Master Dorian has officially defected from Veillant." Elowen sounded exactly like Cormac. "He is Mandal now."

"My father said—"

"I have high magic, the Undoing," Alia cut in. "It is our bloodline; at the time of the Severing, our ancestors had been gifted magic from the Tiarcons. Which has been strategically concentrated for generations."

It was a gentle way to describe how the Meadors married and murdered.

"And you?" Lena gave Elowen a sideways glance.

"Only elemental." The corner of Elowen's lips twitched downwards. "Neither of my parents had it. Just Alia."

There was more to Elowen's explanation, the crux of the division between the sisters, between Alia and the rest of their family. Even with the pains taken to produce the strongest mages, some were only able to practice simple expressions of magic. Somewhere along the line, mortals had abandoned the delineation of the eight Tiarcons for four divisions more suited to their new realm and dampened magic. Alia envied Elowen's elemental magic, earth magic that was common enough in Entien not to draw suspicion.

"Do I have the Undoing?"

"No." Alia shook her head. "Never. Your magic is not like that."

"But—"

A scuffle in the drawing room interrupted them. After hearing Harlan's raised voice, Alia and Elowen crowded the hall. They came upon the Captain of the Guard and the Master Mage bickering.

"I told him that you were not to be disturbed." Harlan's apology was to Elowen; he was behaving less like a jailer and more like a steward.

"Princess Elowen." Dorian bowed his head. "Lady Alia. There is simply no time. You and Lady Lena need to come to the Tower now and begin instruction. We must prepare for the Alasaran."

"Alasaran?" Lena emerged from her room.

"Creature of the Otherworld, servant of the Tiarcons, whatever it is that Mandals have chosen to call them these days." Master Dorian smoothed his dark curls behind his ears, another futile effort as they hung in his face a moment later. "We need to be prepared to face it."

Lena stepped forward. "You'll teach me how to kill it?"

"Ideally." Master Dorian let out an apprehensive sigh.

"Lead the way."

"Lena, no." Alia grasped her shoulder, holding her in place. She turned to Dorian. "You may think you know what's coming from your perch in the Tower, but we've seen firsthand what that thing does to people. Lena is a child; she can't be expected to fight that kind of madness."

Dorian's fingers twitched, and he tapped the tip of each finger to his thumb in turn. "Which is why it behooves us to have an Undoing Mage."

"Her magic doesn't work." Lena pulled away from her mother.

At that, Dorian chuckled, giving Alia a probing look.

"Ali, please. Think of our people," Elowen added. Now she was the one pulling at Alia's strings with sisterly affection. A Meador, after all.

"Not the Tower." Alia held firm. "Send your instructor here, and they can train Lena under my watch."

"Instructor?" Dorian advanced, looming just before her. "No one knows more of high magic and Alasar than a Veillanti. I am the only one who can teach both of you."

"Not you," Alia said, refusing to back away from him. She could let Lena learn magic if it would make her well again. But she would not let Lena be subjected to a Master Mage, not after what Ruben had done. And never to a Veillanti, a people who worshipped the Otherworld, desperate to serve the Tiarcons again.

"We do not have time for whatever prejudice you carry." Dorian's jaw clenched. "I am Mandal's Master Mage, Veillanti or not, and I can—"

"You can flaunt your title until the Otherworld shatters the veil for all I care. You know what happened to the last Master Mage." Alia squared her shoulders to his, the Undoing roiling, begging for an outlet.

Dorian's saturnine eyes held hers, accepting her challenge. Alia ceased breathing, all focus held on keeping the intensity of her glare without belying the struggle to stifle the Undoing.

His gaze wobbled first, likely unable to ignore the mist curling around Alia's wrists. He snatched her hand where violet light had begun to eat away at her fingertips. "I think your magic works just fine."

Elowen wrung her hands. Harlan released his hilt. Lena brushed against Alia's shoulder, staying close.

"Ali. If you do not comply with Cormac's order, the conditions of your confinement will worsen," Harlan warned.

"It'll be for the best for Lena—" Elowen began.

"I'm her mother!" Alia's shout echoed through the suite, the impasse ringing out. Her sentence had scarcely begun, and already she felt like the Mandals were clawing her daughter away from her, trying to manipulate the distance between them.

"You are." Dorian's demeanor shifted, his agitation giving way to calm. "I can teach Lena here, under your watch. I can help her, keep her magic from making her ill. And if you deem that she is able to use it to defend Mandal, then I can teach her to do that as well."

Alia didn't trust the sudden serenity from the mage; it reeked of condescension.

"Mother," Lena pleaded. "This is why we came here. No one else we've come across has ever been able to help me. You aren't strong enough to contain me. It needs to stop."

Alia froze at Lena's words. She didn't trust the Master Mage, certain he would find a way to twist this opportunity. But at the same time, Lena was right. Alia looked from Lena to Elowen, from Harlan to Dorian.

"Under my watch," Alia conceded, already dreaming of leaving Mandal behind.

But she would comply, for now, until Lena was strong enough to leave this place to its fate.

5

Dorian insisted on holding the first lesson out on the balcony. He summoned flame to light the wall-mounted torches, illuminating the lines on Lena's chest and neck. Harlan and Elowen had left as soon as the tension eased, likely desperate to avoid the next conflict.

Alia shadowed the doorway, silently swearing that if Lena's condition worsened, if the dark lines spread an inch farther, she was going to stop Dorian's meddling.

As Master Ruben had, Master Dorian began with meditation. The similarities were scorching as Lena grudgingly sat beside the mage, closed her eyes, and tried to pattern her breathing.

'*Without me, you can't contain that darkness inside of you.*'

Alia pushed Ruben's words away. She shifted her attention to the sound of the sea, the steady waves. Master Ruben's window had overlooked a similar vantage point, all the way to the rocky shore. Alia had focused on the rough sea, getting lost in it rather than having to be in her own body. She had imagined that she was floating free on the winds, untethered.

'*It will devour you.*'

Alia strode forward, needing a distraction. "If Lena's sickness is due to high magic, why didn't the same thing happen to me?"

Lena opened her eyes and peered at her mother, either eager for Dorian's answer or a break from her task.

"There's something unique about Lena." Dorian rubbed his tidy beard. "Her symptoms are a sign that she is coming of age, her magic strengthening. Her aura has been battling with itself, causing the deterioration of her corporal form."

"Lucky me." Lena folded her arms across her chest.

"The more we sort out your magic, the more we'll sort out the reasons behind it all." Dorian's nerves had apparently evaporated, making him almost sound reassuring. "What is the nature of your father's magic?"

"My father was quotidien." Lena's posture stiffened at the mention of Finn, emphasizing the past tense.

So he said. Alia didn't have the truth to contradict the lie.

"Quotidien?" Dorian asked, skepticism apparent even as he tried to take Lena at her word. "How about you show me what you know."

Lena's eyes widened; it'd been a long time since she'd been given permission to use magic. Alia drew nearer to Dorian, anxiety peaking. "Is that wise?"

"I realigned her aura, but the order won't take unless she practices."

Lena opened her palms as Alia wrapped her arms around herself, holding herself together. A ball of garnet-colored light danced in Lena's hands, brightening the balcony and making Alia's pulse race. Lena let out a triumphant shout when her magic didn't spiral into an outburst.

"Good, what else?"

Lena's face fell, and the light went out. "I can't do everything on command."

"Tell him," Alia said.

"When I'm angry, sometimes there's wind, and heat, and rain..." Lena scraped the toe of her boot against the ground.

"Is that a Meador affinity?" Dorian asked, and Alia shook her head.

"What else?"

"I'm good with making things grow." Lena's skill had been invaluable on the road until it became too dangerous for her to use it.

"That is Meador," Alia offered in anticipation of Master Dorian's question. "I used to be able to—" the memory stalled her, savoring how it had felt to breathe life into a shriveled flower. "I saved half of the royal garden during the first drought."

"And why do you believe that you no longer could?"

He told me.

Alia was lost in her mind, plunging into what had been taken from her. Her ability to grow, to heal, was stunted beneath the crushing weight of the Undoing. The only thing that had been close to the magic she had once felt was giving birth to Lena. That moment of life from the void, light from dark. How desperately she needed to feel it once more.

"She gets like this," Lena explained to Dorian as she grasped Alia's hand, pulling her back to the balcony. "Mother?"

"Mmhmm?" Alia's eyes focused again.

"Let's take a break," Master Dorian suggested, walking past them and back into the sitting room.

"What happened to your urgency?" Lena was still holding onto Alia's hand.

He gestured for them to sit opposite him. "Forgive my impatience earlier, sometimes I... forget myself."

Alia knew the feeling.

"The prince is looking to me to stop the Oucura. Demanded it, even though no mortal alive has faced one and lived." Dorian's twitching persisted. "And then you two arrive, and I finally feel like we may have a chance."

"We aren't weapons." Alia placed her hand on Lena's shoulder.

“I know, I know.” Dorian opened his palms. “You’re not even here of your own volition.”

“Thanks to you and your fellow councilmembers.”

“I argued against your confinement, Lady Alia.”

“So you could use us to battle the Otherworld for you.”

Lena jerked away from Alia, looking between her and the Master Mage.

“Because I do not think you are to blame for the incident with Master Ruben.” Dorian’s words reverberated in Alia’s ears.

Alia pursed her lips, rejecting the hope his words inspired. “You don’t know me; you weren’t here when it happened.”

“I don’t know you, Lady Alia,” Dorian agreed. “And you are the first Undoing Mage I’ve ever come across. But I do know that Undoing Mages are created in the harshest conditions. And at the time of the attack, you must have been just coming into your power and quite ignorant of how to use it.”

“Conditions?” Lena said. “What conditions?”

When Alia wouldn’t answer, Dorian spoke again, “Regardless, I doubt your actions were unwarranted.”

Alia regarded the man before her, then wrapped her arms around herself once more. From this vantage point, she could see clearly that the odd markings on his face weren’t inked. The series of inverted arrows at Dorian’s hairline was more like scars than tattoos, half obscured by the shiny black hair that hung to his shoulders in loose curls. The warmth of his dark eyes was unmistakable as he stilled under her estimation.

The mage had quickly come to a conclusion that people who had known her intimately still failed to grasp. “It doesn’t change the outcome,” Alia said.

“It isn’t right, keeping you both here,” Dorian added. “And if you ever decide you want to leave, I can help you get away."

"Escape?" Lena perked up. "What about the Oucura?"

"You would disobey your new sovereign?" Alia pressed.

"I swore an oath to teach and protect Mandal's mages. That includes both of you."

"How would you help?" Lena asked.

Dorian smirked. One moment, he was seated before them, and the next, he was just... gone. Alia held her breath for a few seconds, staring at the place where Dorian had been. And then, without a sound, he was suddenly back. He dumped out a handful of rocky sand onto the floor. "From the shore," he said with a grin.

Lena had gotten to her feet, mouth parted. "How did you do that?"

"It is called *flickering.* It is high magic. It takes study to master, but now I can do it as easy as blinking," Dorian said, his tone just shy of boastful. "I think I can teach you, Lena."

"And you can take us with you?" Alia's mind was churning with the possibilities.

"Let me show you." Dorian moved quickly to her side, wrapping his long arms around her too quickly for her to break away. In a blink, she was standing atop the palace's highest tower, looking out on the stormy sea. She would have fallen forward if Dorian hadn't kept her upright, his wiry arms surprisingly strong.

When she tried to catch her breath, her chest constricted, pain feathering outward to her fingertips. Her head throbbed, vision blurring. She tried to harness healing, to defend herself, but nothing responded to her call.

Dorian cursed and pulled her close.

And then they were back in her chambers. And the pain was gone.

Alia cradled her head, reeling from the burning sensation. "What did you do to me?"

Dorian was slow to let her go, hands trembling. "I'm sorry, I forgot. The conditions of your confinement pose a complication."

Cormac had put more than guards on her. A magical binding unleashed agony if she tried to leave. But if it could be bested, she could get out. Dorian could transport them anywhere instantly, and there was nothing Cormac's entire army could do to stop them.

"And if I—we," Alia amended her question when Lena glared daggers at her, "make the decision to leave Mandal, you will help us?"

"I swear it." Dorian placed his fingers to his lips and then his heart.

"Teach me," Lena insisted, looking back at Alia. "We'll never have to run again."

Alia's heart pounded, the sensation of travelling in an instant keeping her off balance as Lena peppered Dorian with questions. Lena had so quickly relaxed in his presence, sparing him the scrutiny that she subjected all others to. But there was no telling which brutal affinities the Master Mage harbored, no matter how enlightened he purported to be. And her ability to escape Mandal couldn't rest on him alone.

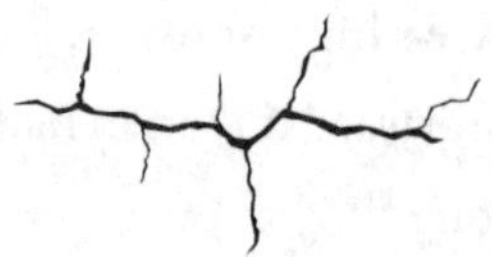

Despite the obligations Master Dorian was sure to have at the Tower, he came to the Olden Wing prison as the palace bells chimed mid-morning each day. While Alia refused invitations to join the lessons out on the balcony, she kept a close watch. Dorian's promise to help them escape confinement made him tolerable, not trusted.

The mage was the only one other than palace servants to enter the apartment. Neglect, whether born out of fear or indifference, stifled Alia's hopes of finding a way out. Her frustration, paired with Lena's restlessness, made for silent meals and long afternoons spent in darkness.

But when the sun finally rose a week later, Elowen offered a reprieve. The princess arrived, beaming, with Harlan at her hip to take them to the royal gardens for Lena's next lesson. The princess wielded particular influence, stretching the terms of Alia's confinement to the other end of the palace.

Elowen led the way, curving around the halls of the Olden Wing and climbing the main stair. Her sister and daughter walked arm-in-arm, the former chattering about each tapestry they passed. Alia stayed close to Harlan. He must know about the spell that kept her bound, enough to expand her movement at Elowen's whim. But she'd already tapped the extent of the captain's pity; he wouldn't disobey Cormac without cause.

The royal quarters lorded over the palace from its peak, where the sprawling limestone turrets condensed into five points. The tallest tower sat atop a hexagonal floor. The king's chambers. It lightened Alia's step to think of King Isaac abed, purportedly wasting away. Healers could only keep a failing body alive for so long.

The three women and a complement of guards didn't ascend to those heights. Instead, they veered off on the last floor before the royal apartments, a buffer between the monarch and the rest of the nobility. It was there that the builders had seen fit to create a plot of land suitable for gardens, a conscious task for the cliffside palace.

The royal garden had been one of the first places Alia had tried out her magic, willing life into flowers yet to bloom. Lush, viridescent hedges encircled the garden, punctuated by pearly limestone pillars. Soft petals weaved their way through the paths, willfully overgrown.

Alia looked over the peach quince and crisp white dogwood, the delicate blooms of the coral bell, and wanted to tear off every petal. Her dress suddenly felt too tight, the sun too harsh. "What happened here?"

"We've had to replant." Elowen had the audacity to be proud. "These are much more tolerant of drought and sparse sunlight."

The plants Alia had nurtured were dead, wilted under the shrouded moon. They'd been ripped out and replaced, discounted as the realm changed around them. Replaced by others with the tools to survive. It was too much to hope for proof she'd been someone else before the Undoing. That her power had healed, sustained beauty. That too had been lost.

It was foolish to mourn flowers, something that bloomed only to die.

"And how much grain was left to shrivel in the fields?" Lena smoothed the front of her breeches. Despite having a closet full of gowns, Lena refused to deviate from the fashion of the road.

Elowen only sighed and kept walking, already learning that nothing good came from arguing with Lena. "There are those." Elowen shielded her eyes and pointed upward. "They keep spreading. It hasn't seemed right to take them down."

It was the south-facing palace wall, the limestone smoothed into a nearly seamless façade. But flowered vines bloomed in every crevice, lavender petals of starcrest looking out over the garden. The vine had once been guided along the arched walkways but must have found its own way up the wall.

"If only your people could eat them," Lena said, disrupting Alia's admiration.

"I don't remember the gardens ever being this crowded." Alia eyed the clusters of parading noblewomen. It made Elowen's diversion more puzzling; the Crown was flaunting its presence among members of the

Court.

"Cormac expanded permissions, especially when there's sunlight." From Elowen's smile, the change had been her idea. King Isaac used to only allow his most trusted advisors and their families up into the gardens, not risking having anyone out of favor this close to the royal section of the palace.

"How kind of him." Lena stretched her hand out, gently unfurling a nearby leaf.

"Wait for Master Dorian." Alia closed her hand around Lena's outstretched fingers. Beneath Lena's fastened tunic, dark veins stretched up to her neck.

"He's late."

The palace bells tolled, and a group of ladies passed them on the path. Lady Quinn was among them, trying hard to stare into the sun rather than at Alia.

"Princess Elowen," the leader preened. The young noblewoman's jeweled gown clung to her statuesque figure and matched the pins in her tightly corded, flaxen hair. Her voluminous grey eyes sat above a delicate nose, reminding Alia of a self-satisfied feline. When her lips curled at Elowen's greeting, the resemblance was even more striking.

"Lady Lillian." Elowen took a step forward, remarking on the beauty of the morning before introducing her to Alia and Lena.

"It is a pleasure to meet you after all of the tales I've heard." Lady Lillian Palmer inclined her head. Alia did not return the respectful gesture, still studying the woman and deciding she would have been only a child when Alia left. She had to be the daughter of Tristan Palmer, her father's hated rival on the council, which made her both interesting and dangerous.

"Captivity suits you, Ali," one of the women noted, distracting Alia from recalling where the Palmers fell in Mandal's magical rankings.

Alia stood and squared her shoulders, placing herself between Lena and the gaggle. That woman, she did know. "Ah, Wylann, I see your hair grew back. Mostly." She regretted the words as soon as she said them, watching the noblewoman's face dim and hand fly to the back of her head. Alia hadn't had a good reason to terrorize Wylann and of half Court back then, and even less of a reason to be cruel now. But the impulse persisted.

"Lady Wylann Stanton now." The noblewoman poked her weak chin forward.

Lord Stanton had sat in judgment of Alia the week before, the one member of the Barton Council she hadn't recognized. One of the men who had been too cowardly to look her in the eye. Elowen had provided his identity but left out that he was married to Wylann.

"You look well, Lady Wylann," Elowen said, likely attempting to diffuse the brewing tension.

"Thank you, Princess." Wylann curtsied.

"Lady Quinn, how is the king today?" Elowen asked.

"Strong, very strong," Quinn bowed her head, her quivering words obviously a lie.

It made Alia smile.

Whether trying to escape Elowen's questions or unnerved by Alia's glee, the women excused themselves. "May the sun stay high."

"And the moon forever fallen," Elowen responded.

Their skirts swirled as they walked away, designed to capture the eye.

If worn properly.

Alia allowed her shrewd upbringing to filter in, immediately seeking out faults. A pointless exercise.

Lena stared after them. "Friends of yours?"

"Never any of mine." Alia shook her head. She'd scared away every noblewoman except Flora.

"How much does a dress like that cost?" Lena eyed the intricately sewn, gem-encrusted bodice of Lillian's gown.

"Enough for you to eat for a year, at least," Alia said, breathing in the fresh scent of the garden.

"At least? How could you grow up in a place like this?"

Elowen stiffened beside Lena. "The highest-ranking families look after entire sections of the kingdom. They provide more than they consume. If you'd join us at Court, perhaps you'd feel differently."

"I'd rather—"

Alia sensed Rosalynn Paxton's magic before she saw the imposing woman. Her dull blonde hair, as ever, was severely bound at the nape of her neck. Her features blended into her pale face, plain and clever.

The mage was headed towards them, so Alia moved to intercept her.

"Alia," the mage said, leaving off Alia's title and any form of greeting.

"You can have no purpose here." Alia didn't care that she was the prisoner and Rosalynn the high-ranking mage.

Enjoyment bloomed across Rosalynn's face. "Master Dorian was detained. He sent me to train Lena."

"And how do you train young mages? Exactly as Master Ruben did?" Alia advanced on her, hands at her sides, the Undoing threatening.

"No one will ever be a more brilliant instructor than Master Ruben, Orlast keep him."

Alia nearly spit. "But he failed to teach you the difference between brilliance and lunacy."

Elowen's broke through Alia's rage. "Lena, how would you like to go riding with me?"

Alia turned, seeing an elated gleam brightening Lena's golden eyes.

“Horses?” Lena looked to Alia for permission.

“Go along, Master Dorian isn’t coming,” Alia granted, not moving from Rosalynn’s path. “*You* can crawl back to the Tower.”

“The Master Mage will hear of this. And the Queen.” Rosalynn bowed her head to Elowen before turning around.

Sweat dripped down the back of Alia’s neck as she waited for her knees to unlock. She was beginning to think the Olden Wing prison had been a sanctuary, protecting her from people like Rosalynn. The palace was sure to be littered with them, and Alia’s hatred had only become more concentrated over the years.

“I’ll explain to Master Dorian that Lady Rosalynn is not a proper substitute,” Elowen promised, grabbing Lena’s hand. “Let’s go to the stables.”

The garden provided a direct route to the stairs, one that stretched from the base of the palace all the way up to the meadow. Most had to climb the entire way on the exposed stairs, while those with favor enjoyed a much shorter route through the palace.

As soon as the three women began to make their way, Harlan abandoned his distant perch. “Your Highness, the gardens were far enough.”

“Captain.” Elowen placed her hand on his arm. “You can protect us just as well from the meadow.”

Once again, the captain bowed to the Princess’s will, trailing them up to the pastures atop Sheath.

The view was as inspiring as Alia remembered, the entire city spread out before her before miles of crashing sea. She stayed on the outside of the fence as Elowen and Lena went into the stables to select their horses. Harlan and his guards kept their feet on the ground as well; they were there to watch Alia, after all.

She rested her back against the fence, shielding her eyes from the sun with one hand to take in the view. Idleness embraced her; she was almost enjoying herself until a voice plunged her into ice.

"You still haven't gotten over being thrown from horseback?"

Alia's chest tightened; Elowen had betrayed her. "You taught me to learn from my mistakes."

Edgar Meador's smile was wry. "And instead of learning, you ran from them."

"I prefer to think of it as a strategic retreat."

Her father kept his distance, facing the meadow. "The terms of your confinement seem... lax."

"Would you rather me be locked away until I produce a magical heir for some pathetic lord? Which family are you most eager to dismantle at the moment?" Alia chuckled. "That is the Meador way, isn't it? Marry, breed, destroy. Do the Bartons know what is coming their way?"

"The sooner you demonstrate your worth, the better. We don't want any impropriety of yours causing trouble for your sister."

"If I'm causing Elowen trouble, then she will say so."

"Your sister has a weakness when it comes to you."

"Thank Orlast you aren't similarly afflicted." Alia had never understood her parents when she was young, and she understood them even less now that she had a child. She had once craved their affection, pleaded for protection, only for them to withhold both.

Edgar shifted his attention over to where Elowen was instructing Lena, each riding a fine black mare. "You would do well to distance yourself from the girl, for her sake."

"I'm all she has."

"I heard her father was of common stock?"

Alia only scoffed.

"Still, her affiliation with Meador is strong enough. I think once this sickness of hers is resolved, she could make a fine match for a second son."

Alia turned to steady her hands on the fence, her control cracking. Darkness gathered between her fingertips. "My daughter is not a horse for you to sell for her breeding attributes."

"And what kind of life will you secure for her? A farmer's whore, perhaps? Your debasement needn't hobble your daughter with the same future." Edgar's daggers were launched without malice. It was as if he were speaking of the disappointing crop yield and not his granddaughter.

'No one else would want you if they knew.'

"You returned under your own power," Edgar said. "Did you not think of what that might require? Have you forgotten?"

Alia clenched her fists so tightly, the Undoing began to eat away at her fingertips.

"Mother!" Lena must have sensed Alia's magic stirring and steered her horse into a gallop towards her. When Alia's focus returned, Edgar was heading back to the palace. Harlan edged closer to her.

Elowen rode over. "I didn't know he would be here."

"Yes, yes. Go back to your riding." Alia eased her mood and opened her fists, dispersing the escaping mist.

Alia retreated towards the tree line surrounding the pastures. Harlan trailed her, leaving the rest of the guards behind with Elowen and Lena.

Alia waited to be among the trees before she let her tears fall. All these years later, and still her father held the ability to scold her whenever he saw fit. How she hated him, this palace, this city. They were right not to trust her; she could not control her impulses.

"Your father is a fool," Harlan commented.

"I'd rather be a farmer's whore than that lord's daughter."

Finn had coaxed her out of the sullen place, helped her reassemble herself piece by piece. He loved her, cared for her, believed her—and then they'd had Lena. For years, they'd lived in Dihlmere simply, happily. Those years were a golden contrast to what had come before and what came after.

But it was pointless to dwell on what could never be again.

Alia fought through the hurt. She was alone with Harlan now, and there were pressing questions. "You can't let me out of your sight, can you?"

Harlan's shoulders dipped as he retrieved a golden pouch from his belt. "If you stray too far from this, I'm told it'll be painful."

Explosively, from her brief experience. "Let me see it." Alia drew nearer, feeling the magic humming in Harlan's hands.

"It's just a—"

"Harlan."

He muttered under his breath as he gingerly shook out the pouch, wrapping a small object in the fabric so that it didn't touch his skin.

"That bastard." It was small, the size of a brooch and dwarfed by Harlan's palm. The metal contained some sort of gold, mixed and robbed of its luster. But the way it was formed was unmistakably Cormac's workmanship. The warped gold had been formed into the likeness of a woman, from waist to crown. He had molded each curl of the woman's unbound hair, even etched a wry smirk on her face.

It was intimate, an invention spurred by memory. It was her.

Alia placed her hand over her chest, remembering her inability to breathe when Dorian had transported her to the tower. She was tied to the emblem by Cormac's magic, the connection molded by his flames.

Her cheeks flushed. "That is a foul thing to be carrying around."

"I had no choice."

"Give it to me." Alia thrust her hand forward.

"You know I can't." Harlan's loyalty to Cormac snapped between them.

Before she could argue, the ground trembled beneath her.

"Please, Ali." Harlan sighed.

But it wasn't her. No matter how destructive the Undoing was, it couldn't make the earth move.

A force rumbled towards them from deep in the forest. Disruption followed in the wake of the sound, the same feeling Alia sought to remedy while healing. There was something broken approaching, crashing through the forest and getting closer every second.

"Harlan ..." Alia grasped the sleeve of his uniform.

The crackling sounded again, and Harlan spun, becoming the commanding Captain of the Guard and bellowing for his men. Harlan gathered a handful of guards, rushing towards the noise as the ground continued to shake.

"Get back to the stables," Harlan ordered, rushing towards whatever was coming at them through the trees. "You three, go to the Princess," Harlan directed his men. She barely noticed as Harlan passed the emblem, once again obscured in the pouch, to the eldest of the three.

The pounding of hooves overtook all else.

The Oucura.

Alia picked up her skirts and broke into a run, the three guards quickly overtaking her. The ground's quaking nearly tripped her as the crackling pitch intensified. When she burst out of the trees, the meadow was already filled with scurrying Mandals, all trying to escape what was coming.

"Into the stable!" one of the guards shouted to Elowen and Lena as they sat atop their steeds, gaping in her direction. They needed to be in a defensible position when the Oucura arrived, not out in the open.

Elowen galloped ahead of them, leading Alia and Lena.

Once Elowen and Lena dismounted, the three women huddled into a vacant stall as the guards stood with their backs to the stable, the last line of defense. Through the seams of the wooden planks, they peered out into the forest. Alia put up a barrier for lack of another weapon. Master Dorian had been right to be hasty with Lena's training; the Oucura was closer than they thought.

He had seemed so hopeful at having an Undoing Mage at his call. He'd had no idea she would be useless against it. The crackling got closer and closer as trees exploded on contact, sending showers of splintered wood up into the sun. The Oucura's hooves pounded the ground with such ferocity that the entire structure above them swayed.

"We need to keep it away from these people." Lena's eyes darted around the stall.

"We need to stay alive," Alia said, preferring shelter to charging.

"Master Dorian said you can—"

"I can't." Alia shook her head. "I'd kill you before even wounding the Oucura."

"The guards will protect—" Elowen was silenced by the Oucura emerging from the tree line.

The branches snapped, breaking themselves for the beast, with it having to touch them. The creature was nearly twice Alia's height, with long, curved horns terminating in dagger points. It stood upright like a man, but its furred legs terminated in black bull hooves. The rest of its body was a bizarre mixture of man and beast, fur and leathery skin.

But the worst part was its face. Dried blood covered its cheeks and chin, marking the beast with red streaks. Its mouth protruded, with curved fangs among flat teeth, designed for piercing and crushing. And at a distance, Alia could see the wildness of its clouded yellow eyes as its gaze roved over the meadow.

The Oucura—harbinger of death in every hinterland village—had arrived in Sheath.

And it didn't look the least bit daunted by Harlan and the guards that had remained under the trees.

Alia took a deep breath as it stepped into the meadow, pawing at the ground. The beast could see them, its animal eyes showing cognition. The sense of disruption was even stronger now, coursing across the meadow, like the ground wanted to split in half. It emanated from the Oucura.

Rather than being contained, its magic radiated outward, influencing and affecting the very air, shaking the ground. The Oucura was a transforming force, making the entire meadow volatile.

Elowen wrapped her arms around Lena. "Your mother will protect us." The princess leapt from one savior to another.

Lena lacked her aunt's confidence. "Even I can break through her barriers."

"What is it doing?" Alia abandoned their crouched position to rise and get a better look. "It's just standing there."

"Stay back," the guard warned.

As if it had heard her, the Oucura's brief pause was over. It raised its face to the darkening sky and bellowed, then galloped straight at them. There were screams from the others who had sought shelter with them.

"The Undoing, Ali," Elowen urged.

"I can't." There was no time to explain to Elowen that the Undoing wasn't some switch to be turned on and off, some all-powerful ability Alia could tap into whenever she wanted. It demanded sacrifice and required control that she did not have.

"You have to!" Elowen screamed, face white with terror.

"You'll be crushed." Lena shook Elowen off and stood shoulder to shoulder with Alia.

"Stay back, Lena." Alia's attention was split as the wind picked up.

The huffs of the Oucura intensified, its horned crown lowering as it continued its charge. Alia held her barrier, but the impact sent her sprawling into the hay. It pushed the breath out of her lungs, making her shake alongside the stable as it reeled from the Oucura's charge.

The stable held, but her barrier had shattered. Nothing but wooden beams stood in the Oucura's way now.

Alia looked from the ground to see Lena's arms spread wide. "Don't."

Lena summoned a torrent of wind, creating a whirlwind around the Oucura as it backed up for the next run. Her magic only succeeded in angering the beast, its stomping intensifying as it moved towards them. A yell escaped Lena's lips as a ball of garnet light gathered in her hands. Lena's eyes blazed crimson, dark veins pulsed. Her magic was overtaking her.

The Oucura cut a path through Lena's whirlwind, its mass too great to be detained. Lena slumped, and her body bucked, the all too familiar signs of her internal struggle. Elowen was too close, and there were too many other people in the stables. They were all going to be torn apart.

Except the ground had stopped shaking.

The Oucura tipped its head back to the sky, something held to its mouth. The sunlight glinted off the red sheen that now covered the beast's chest, dripping down to its fur-covered torso. It was then that Alia caught sight of what it had in its hands—a body, clothed in Mandal armor, now without a head. A curdling snap accompanied each movement of the Oucura's jaw.

Elowen shrieked. "Ali, please!"

The Oucura let out a roar that made the entire stable tremble. It silenced the screams of those trapped and the swirling of Lena's storm until the roar was the only thing that existed.

Alia felt a tugging within her, like a gate had been unlatched and swung wide open. Her throat went dry as the roar shook all her thoughts loose. It was all she could hear, the Oucura, the only figure in sight. The roar clawed inside her, seeping into her mind. She was part of the Oucura now, a creature of bloodlust and rage. Its agony grabbed hold, a singular torment that could only be lessened with violence.

And then it was gone, the Undoing surging over the places the Oucura had tried to hollow out. Darkness filled her, but this was familiar. Rage she'd nurtured for years, unable to leech it from her bones.

But the others did not have the same defense. In front of her, the two remaining guards turned away from the Oucura, swords pointed at the other. They hadn't been able to expel the Oucura's roar, hadn't been able to free themselves.

Screams filled the stable again, as Mandals turned on each other, consumed by the Oucura's bloodlust and drawn into madness. Elowen produced a knife from under her skirts, crawling towards them with clouded eyes. She raised the knife over her head, the dainty Princess Elowen of Mandal transformed into a killer before Alia's eyes.

Alia grasped Lena, pulling her out of range of Elowen and gripping her to her chest, cupping her chin to get a good look at her eyes. The sparks of red had faded, replaced by a milky shimmer. Lena put her hands on either side of Alia's head, her nails digging in. Alia bit her lip to stop from screaming, blood rushing over her tongue.

She managed to cast Lena off, slamming her back against the remnants of the stall. There wasn't anywhere to run, and even if there was, she couldn't leave Lena behind. "Lena, Elowen, please."

"They can't hear you." Master Dorian materialized beside her. His eyes were dark pits, but sharp and free of the creature's hold.

Dorian dodged as Elowen lunged for him, the knife cutting strips into his robes as she fell forward. Alia struggled to keep Lena from her throat as the wind continued to swirl around them.

Dorian pressed his fingers over Lena's temples, rendering her unconscious and still. Alia looked over to see Elowen in the same state. The wind stopped; the heat faded.

The two guards had fallen, impaled on each other's swords. The Oucura was taking its pick of the Mandals; they were too focused on fighting amongst themselves to realize its approach.

"You weren't affected," Dorian said as he caught his breath.

There was a simple explanation. She could resist the Oucura's call because there was already a force inside her mind with a firm hold. She was already claimed by madness.

"Where have you been?"

"No one else is coming," Dorian said, surveying the carnage across the meadow. "The prince won't risk losing others to this frenzy. You have to end this."

"I can't." Alia glanced down at Lena and Elowen. "I'll hurt them."

"You won't." His words were definite. Warmth grew inside her, like the sun was reaching her skin through the stable slats. It was the same feeling from the council chambers, coming from Dorian. "I'll help you."

Alia's attention hastened to the Oucura, which was discarding its latest victim in a heap.

Summoning the Undoing wasn't the difficult part; it was calling it back once it unfurled. If healing was a process of mending, this power was about breaking, destroying.

While she had managed quick expressions of Undoing, a broken bone here and there, she had never really let it free since the night it attacked

Ruben, for fear of what she would do to someone else, for fear of what else it would do to her.

But her daughter and her sister lay at her feet, the rest of the meadow already darkened with blood. No one else was coming, and the Oucura was advancing, killing as it went. Alia couldn't shake the memory of the broken villages they'd seen, what Sheath would become if the Oucura weren't stopped.

The palace was visible from where she stood, gleaming despite their struggle. Alia could take Lena and run, let the Oucura turn Sheath into a tomb.

The city wasn't hers to save. She owed it nothing.

But the Oucura was robbing mortals of their will, their ability to control themselves. The immortal magic reeked of inculcation.

And that, she couldn't allow.

Alia extended her fingers, bringing her hands out in front of her, and pointed them towards the Oucura. She rolled her neck and exhaled, uncapping the tight lid she kept over her magic.

Her hands glowed violet, the mist gathering at her fingertips. The mist traveled the distance to the Oucura of its own volition, creeping forward for a life to take. The darkness was limitless, as all the strife she had suffered was on hand to sustain it. The Undoing whispered its way to the Otherworld beast, teasing around the Oucura's horns and massive hooves and finding a home in its chest. The mist wormed its way in, covering its heart.

The Oucura drew to its full height, dropping a stablehand to turn towards Alia. It bellowed with claws outstretched as it shredded through the stable doors. Alia gasped, drawing back to shield Lena and Elowen as she lost her focus. Dorian's hand sparked, fire coursing from his fingertips and striking the Oucura, slowing its progress.

"The fire won't kill it. It has to be you." Dorian grunted, maintaining his attack.

The cord connecting her to the Undoing was still intact. Alia got back to her feet. She could feel the Oucura's heart, the rhythm of each beat, even the strain of its struggle against Dorian.

Every inch of the Oucura was mapped out by the Undoing. She could sense the seams, knitted skin where the Oucura had been wounded before, places it had healed. She thought of the mortals it had murdered, the minds it had pillaged, and felt the Undoing peeling away at its scars. Alia's heartbeat started to match that of the beast, pounding a stuttered rhythm in her ears.

A gaping wound opened across the Oucura's forehead, its blood mixing with that of its victims, which dripped down from its chin. Next, the Oucura's right leg buckled, incapacitated by an old injury. Cuts and scrapes scattered across its skin, and the roar shifted to one of agony.

The Undoing found every hurt the Oucura had ever had and tore it open.

And then the darkness she had sent forth turned back to her for confirmation, for permission to dismantle the creature completely. Alia granted it, her uncaged power soaring at finally being allowed to fulfill its purpose.

Her magic dug deeper, whittling down the Oucura. The creature began to collapse on itself, muscles withering, joints failing, bones unable to withstand its form as blood stained the grass. The Undoing flooded over the besieged beast, eating away as it flailed towards her.

There was a soft groan as the Undoing tore apart the Oucura's heart. And then silence.

The Undoing gathered, collecting from the husk of the Oucura. It continued to flow from her hands, curving its way through the meadow, sucking the life from the grass and sneaking inside mortal and beast alike. It consumed her hands and forearms, the skin flaking away and reforming in the same breath.

"Pull it back," Dorian's breath was warm on her cheek. "Command it."

Alia slammed her eyes shut, sensing every bit of her magic across the field. Inhaling, she called it back, fixing it back within her. But it was too much, as her darkness returned, so did *he*. The price of the Undoing burned through her, ravaging her mind. This was it, the end that had befallen Silas Meador. A magical failsafe to ensure this magic could only do so much harm. All that evil, turning inward.

Ruben took hold of her.

'No one else would have you if they knew.'

Ruben was standing before her, as she last remembered him. She could feel the pressure as he gripped her chin, squeezing painfully to make her believe his words.

Terror seized her, numbing her just like inculcation. She had just felled a beast, but she couldn't break free from his hold.

"Again," Ruben ordered.

Alia couldn't respond, couldn't argue as she extended her hand over the flame. Heat seared through her outstretched palm; she pressed her lips together to suppress the scream that was sure to infuriate him. She knew what would happen if she pulled her hand away before he allowed it, if she didn't readily offer it again every time he asked.

It would be worse than this.

So, she kept her hand over the flame, even as the stench of charred flesh made it impossible to breathe. Even as her skin blackened, the pain subsiding as the feeling was burned away. Alia looked up at Ruben, her teacher, silently pleading for relief as fire ate a hole in her hand.

But he was scribbling in one of his journals, barely even paying attention to her suffering. Indifferent when the hand supporting her buckled, slamming her cheek into the floor of his office, while she fought to keep the hand in the flame still.

Ruben yanked her head from the ground by her hair.

"Alia!" Dorian broke through the Undoing's onslaught. He lifted her from the bloodied ground, the warmth of his containment spell returned.

"I can't." Alia wrapped her arms around herself, wrenching away from Dorian's hold and curling her knees into her chest. She couldn't bring any more of it back.

Dorian let her crumble, standing over her to rope in the dregs of Undoing with whips of golden light. He gathered the last of it, pulling her magic from innocents before bottling it up inside of her. It ached as it writhed in her chest, sorting itself back into place, until only the echo of Ruben's words haunted her.

When Alia regained awareness, her hands shimmered with mist, light permeating her skin. The power, which had been keen to destroy her moments ago, purred.

Dorian stalked to where the Oucura lay, making sure it was indeed dead. "It's over. For now."

Alia drank in the sight of the beast who had terrorized the hinterland for weeks, dead at her hand. Curled in on itself, the Oucura looked smaller. Horns shorn, hooves gone. It almost looked like a man.

When Dorian looked back at her, concern spread across his brow. "Your hands."

The last dregs of the Undoing pulled at her fingers, snaking a path of destruction across her skin. Alia wrapped her arms around herself, turning away from the mage. The remnants were a meek reminder of what the full force of the Undoing could do to her.

From far across the meadow, a bedraggled group of Mandal guards, led by Harlan, emerged from the trees. She sighed with relief that her friend hadn't fallen to the Oucura.

"Princess Elowen," Harlan panted, taking in the dead Oucura before hurrying to his princess's side.

"She'll come to shortly," Dorian assured him.

Harlan stood and looked over the scene, the bodies of his guards close at hand. Alia could see tears glistening in his eyes.

"Harlan," the condolences died on her tongue.

The captain sniffed and sheathed his sword. "They died defending our princess. A worthy end." There was a stubborn strength in his words, a belief in Mandal that could not be whittled away by the attack.

A belief that Alia could not share.

When Alia tried to back away from the slaughter, Harlan caught her arm. "You did well, but stay close." He edged toward the fallen guards, stooping over the bloodied grass to reclaim the emblem and tying it at his belt once more.

Killing the Oucura hadn't made her any less of a prisoner.

Alia turned back to Elowen and Lena, bending to touch her daughter's cheek. She was terrified about what another outburst would mean for Lena.

"Allow me." Dorian waved a hand, and Lena's eyelashes fluttered. Alia couldn't look at the mage, not even to mutter thanks. Doing so would be to acknowledge what they both now knew: she needed him. Owed him.

Dorian lifted his hand to revive Elowen.

"I've got her." Harlan stepped in, taking Elowen into his arms.

Lena sat up, yanking Alia down. Lena's fingers dug into her back, a clinging embrace. “What happened?”

“It is dead.” Alia looked over Lena’s shoulder at the fallen form of the Oucura, blood still dripping into the grass. “I killed it.”

“You?” Lena pulled back, her gaze searching for signs of deceit. “Did I—”

“Master Dorian stopped you.”

And me.

“I wanted to protect them.” Bodies lay strewn across the meadow, tinged in blood and mud. Alia fought the impulse to shield Lena’s eyes.

“Others failed them, not you.” Mandal didn’t deserve their protection, nor Lena’s guilt.

They made an ambling return to the palace, as guards and healers rushed by to aid the survivors.

6

The sunlight lasted over ten hours that day, heralded in Sheath's streets as the reward for victory over the Otherworld. Mandals took it as a sign: killing the Oucura had weakened the malignant influence responsible for the scarce daylight. Alia could see the outline of the crowd from her balcony, hear the music, each toll of a sun-filled hour breeding euphoria.

But she shared in none of it.

For now, Dorian had said. He believed there was more to come. There would be cause to use the Undoing again. And that would mean living through Ruben once more. It hung over her, the memories she had buried coming to her in the sunlight, echoes of a dead man in her mind.

This was it, the cost that had been too high for all the Undoing Mages before her. The voices that drove the Undoing inward. Ruben would kill her after all. His memory, his words.

When the night did come, Alia welcomed it.

Even though Lena's magical outburst had sapped her strength, Dorian demanded they press on with daily lessons for the next week. The mage appeared unchanged by the devastation in the meadow, content to move on just as the rest of the palace had. Except the day after the Oucura, he moved too slowly to contain a beam of light from Lena's hands, only managing to deflect it upward into the night sky. And while he managed a twinge of a smile every time he caught Alia watching him, she more often found his lips tightly drawn. As if it all weighed on him just as much as on her.

It would be a basic courtesy to engage him, to return his attempts at conversation, as if talk about the waning summer heat could smooth over what he'd done. But even when Alia had the slightest inclination to humor Dorian, the memory of him pressing darkness into her chest made her go sharp.

It didn't stop him from trying.

"Care to demonstrate a proper barrier?" Dorian called from the balcony.

Alia snorted and turned back to the book in her lap, one of the many Dorian had brought for Lena. Alia had snatched it from the growing stack in Lena's bedroom in case there might be mention of a way to sever her connection with Cormac's emblem. Thus far, it was only rambling nonsense about the birth of Entien.

Out on the balcony, Lena's attempted barrier spewed garnet sparks, nearly setting fire to Dorian's dark robes.

Dorian maintained his upbeat demeanor as he patted away embers. "A bit closer that time, Lena. Again."

"It was exactly the same," Lena snapped, but lifted her hands again anyway.

Alia tucked the book under her arm and hovered beneath the arch leading onto the balcony. The shrouded moon loomed overhead, outshone by the mounted torches.

"The Battle of the Moonlands?" Dorian drew near, reading the spine of the book crushed to her side.

"As useless as the rest of them."

The diary from one of Mandal's former master mages covering Silas Meador's demise, the compendium of immortal creatures, and the exhaustive historical accounts of the Severing. None explained the effect the Undoing had on the Oucura or how long she had before the Undoing turned on her.

"You could join us then."

Another kind invitation. As if he wasn't planning on manipulating her weakness, waiting until it best served him. "You're teaching her barriers. What good is a barrier against one of them?" Alia brandished the book. "Did you not see how the Oucura shredded through mine?"

"We are building—"

"You didn't see, did you? You weren't even there until after."

Dorian stiffened, his entire form bristling with guilt. "I was detained."

"Detained?" Alia curled her lip. "They are going to throw me in front of those beasts until it kills me. And then what? They'll send Lena?"

The mage balked, his soft eyes shifting to Lena's sputtering magic. "I—"

But his response was stifled by Harlan's entrance. The captain crossed the antechamber with heavy steps. His uniform was rumpled, smelling of smoke and bitter ale.

"May the sun rise." His greeting was equally subdued.

"Too much celebrating?" Alia examined him, tilting her head to the side.

Harlan's lips twitched downward. "It took a few days to make enough boats."

Alia bit into her cheek. The captain had been putting the dead to sea, ferrying them to the next realm. She might have noticed the flaming vessels if she hadn't been so steeped in her own misery.

She bowed her head. "I hope the next realm is kinder to them."

"And they'll be remembered in this one." Harlan sought her hand, fingers dusted with stone powder. He'd been carving names onto the

Wall, leaving a mark of each person behind. It was a startling thing to see such tenderness in Mandal's Captain of the Guard. But Alia was grateful he had been allowed to endure, be kept whole, despite his station.

"Have there been reports of any other attacks?" Alia asked.

"No." The crease in his brow remained.

"Out of gratitude for saving his ass, Cormac is going to let us leave?"

A flinch rippled through Harlan. "To thank you for your service to the Crown, the queen and the princess have invited you to dine with them."

Alia's hands shook. "A social outing? We were nearly eaten."

Sweat broke out on Harlan's brow. "They intend to honor you."

"No. Tell them no." A meal with Rheta was just another torture.

Harlan grimaced. "I am under orders from Cormac. Lena has been invited up to the royal apartments as well, to spend time with her cousins. This is progress."

Cormac was forcing her into the fold, back into palace life. Harlan spoke of progress, but it was just another form of control. Like Elowen pulling them to the gardens, a meal with the queen would be noted.

"The queen has advocated for Lady Alia's execution on multiple occasions," Dorian said from where he hovered behind Alia.

"Which is why Prince Cormac selected you to serve as escort, Master Dorian." Harlan's face smoothed. "To ensure that no harm is done."

Alia sputtered, early syllables escaping her lips without conclusion. It was bad enough that she had to tolerate the Veillanti every day during Lena's lessons.

"Forgive me." Dorian scratched his temple. "But is that not your charge?"

Alia couldn't tell if Dorian didn't want to be in her company any more than she his, or if he was following her lead.

"The prince requires me elsewhere." Harlan unfastened the golden pouch at his belt. "These are his orders."

The casual nature in which Harlan placed her leash in the Veillanti's hands made her head throb.

"You are expected." Harlan gave a small bow before leaving the apartment.

Dorian had the decency not to open the pouch as he tucked it in his robes with a sigh.

They retraced their steps between the Olden Wing and the royal apartments, this time climbing all the way to the top floors. Each step heightened Alia's dread—another confrontation with Rheta on the heels of having to see, to feel, Ruben again was not something she could prepare for.

Dorian fussed with his robes; he had to be assured several times that his attire was appropriate for a royal engagement. "Mandals waste so much time. Every meal has to be a production."

"I presume in Veillant you're too busy prostrating yourselves in front of your beloved Otherworld to eat." Alia tucked Lena's arm in hers, pulling her close and glaring at every guard that passed by.

Dorian hacked a short laugh. "You really hate the idea of anything more powerful than yourself."

It was true, she hated the idea of anyone having power over her. Which now included the mage. "I hate the idea of mortals being forced to serve tyrants."

Amusement lit Dorian's eyes. "The Tiarcons are just like any other beings; there are nuances."

"Veillant would have us serving them in chains."

"Aren't you serving your kingdom in chains?" Dorian asked, eyebrows ticking upward.

The wound he prodded was too deep, too fresh.

"Do you still believe as the Veillanti do?" Lena asked, her tone without accusation. "That we'd be better off living under Tiarcon rule?"

Dorian looked ahead, hiding his expression. They took a few turns before Dorian answered, "I don't know."

"You also don't know the way to the queen's entertaining rooms." Alia sighed and climbed the stairs ahead of him.

They were the last to enter the royal parlor. Queen Rheta sat on the couch, her crown towering over a mass of well-crafted silver locks. Her gown was adorned with an impressive cape with a fine brocade of pearl and jade. The dour look on her face confirmed this engagement was not her idea.

Elowen sat beside her, demurely dressed in comparison, with her sons on either side. Thomas, scarcely younger than Lena, was every bit a Barton, fair-haired and sullen, while Owen had Elowen's soft features.

The other guest made Alia reflexively tighten her hands into fists, keeping them hidden in the folds of her skirts. Her mother, Mariana Meador, was perched on the queen's couch. Being in the same room with her sharpened Alia's hatred, allowing each ounce of betrayal she tried to keep jarred to resurface.

"Alia," Mariana acknowledged, searching every inch of her appearance, and ignoring Dorian altogether. "Just as I feared, you never grew into that nose."

That nose. Straight and strong, a matching profile to her father.

And in Mariana's opinion, far too prominent compared to the delicate roundness of the one Elowen had inherited from herself. Alia had tried cutting it once, hoping to shape the flesh as she healed it. But not even her untainted magic could heal conditions of birth.

Alia kept her expression blank, masked. Mariana had always craved reactions, delighting in her ability at provocation.

"Lena." Mariana grasped for her granddaughter's hand. "It is truly a pleasure."

Where Edgar riled the Undoing, Mariana stifled it. Numbness spread through Alia, staying the rage that usually propelled her. She watched, silent and still, while Mariana pulled Lena away from her. There was a stunning audacity to the way her mother latched onto Lena, one that robbed Alia of her base instincts.

Dorian's arm brushed against hers.

"Please see the children to their table," Queen Rheta said with a wave of her hand, shattering the hold Mariana had on Alia.

A steward sprang forward, taking the princes and Lena to the next room. Lena squeezed Alia's hand as they separated. As the distance widened between Mariana and Lena, Alia began to breathe again. This could be endured; Alia was capable of sitting down with the queen who wanted her dead, the mother who abandoned her, and the sister who had replaced her.

She managed through two courses before Rheta cornered her.

"Alia." Queen Rheta twirled her knife. "I have assured your mother she needn't apologize for you. Some children are simply born rotten, no matter how upstanding their parents are."

Alia swallowed. "What a relief that must be to her."

"Take your sister here. A fine lady in every way. She is a testament to your mother's nurturing," Rheta continued.

"You are too kind, Your Highness," Mariana slathered on the praise while Elowen bowed her head at the compliment. Alia held back the impulse to laugh at the thought of Mariana Meador as nurturing in any sense.

"But you, I knew you were born wretched the moment I saw you. And your poor mother, how it must grieve her for you to be this way."

If Mariana grieved for her, it was only because Alia had slipped from under her thumb.

"Wretched as you are, I never imagined you were also daft. Was I not clear in our last conversation about what would happen to you if I saw you again?"

Alia noticed Elowen flinch ever so slightly and turn her chin to Mariana, who went about eating as if nothing had been said. Dorian's eyes bored into Alia, but Rheta appeared to take no notice of him.

"You were clear, Your Highness."

"And yet here you are."

"Yes, I am." There was no use arguing against this adversary.

"And, apparently, you have made yourself of use somehow. So, I am to tolerate you in my house."

"You are so very kind to do so, Your Highness." Mariana bowed her head.

"I will allow your presence. But you will conduct yourself respectfully," Rheta hissed.

Here we go.

"You will bring your daughter to Court and have her educated as a lady, as your mother wishes."

"That will not be possible, Your Highness. Lena's studies with Master Dorian require all her time and energy," Alia interjected.

"Is that so?" Mariana narrowed her eyes.

"I hear she is very talented," Elowen offered to lighten the mood.

Rheta was equally put off. "Master Mage, is there truth to this?"

Dorian nodded, his eyes catching Alia's. "Lady Lena is very dedicated to her studies."

"Oh, I remember how dedicated to your studies *you* were." Rheta sneered at Alia. "Why my poor brother, Orlast keep him, thought he could teach you anything, I'll never know."

"Orlast keep him," Mariana and Elowen parroted.

"Which reminds me—do not think I have forgotten what you did. While you dwell in my palace, you will not utter a word of your filthy lies about my dear Ruben. He did everything he could to help you, and all you did was twist his kindness." Rheta was nearly spitting.

Alia let the words roll over her. No one had believed her before. Not even her mother had entertained the possibility she was telling the truth. She had dared to speak out against the queen's beloved brother and paid for it.

But the horrified look on Elowen's face startled Alia. Though her sister didn't speak, her eyes were wide with alarm.

"What a lovely meal, Your Highness. Don't you think so, Elowen?" Mariana called Elowen to task.

"Master Dorian, is it true your instruction leaves no time for the girl to join Court?" Rheta asked.

"Oh." Dorian's eyes slid again to Alia, who inclined her head slightly. "No, Your Highness, because Lady Lena is beginning her training so late, her time and focus must be on developing her skills."

"Because her ignorant mother kept her in the woods for so long." Rheta could always find the insult. "Your daughter has deprived you once again, Mariana."

"I have grown accustomed to disappointment where she is concerned,

Your Highness," Mariana said.

Dorian eyed the exchange timidly, then dropped his fork to fold his hands in his lap when his fingers twitched.

"But I suppose there is always you, Alia." Rheta gave her a cruel smile. "The least you could do for your family is to produce another mage."

"I'm afraid my childbearing years are past," Alia said.

"Nonsense." Rheta eyed her gleefully. "You still bleed."

Alia's arguments stalled; Rheta did not possess the power to sense such things, but the maids may have reported her request for linens.

"Surely there is someone who would take a disgraced widow as a wife. You will join us at Court and do as your mother bids."

Alia opened her mouth to protest, but the queen silenced her with a look.

"I will never understand why my son let you live. Know that if my dear Isaac's strength returns, the first thing he'll do is take your head for what you did."

Alia sprang to her feet, the Undoing overflowing at the threat of the king's brand of justice. Before the mist could spill out, a hand on her elbow pulled her back. Dorian restrained and contained her.

"You will present yourself at Court gatherings henceforth. And your daughter shall attend as well as her lessons permit. I'm sure Master Dorian will see to it that she is able." Queen Rheta stood, fury twinged with fear. "Lunch is over."

The dismissal was unnecessary; Alia was already storming in the direction Lena had gone with the princes. Her mother hissed sharply behind her, demanding that she turn around. She refused.

The adjoining chamber was empty, save for the remnants of a meal and the stewards clearing the table. They were quick to inform Alia that the children had gone out to the royal courtyard. Alia forced her way through a staging room; no one had to show her the way to the courtyard.

"Wait, please." Dorian ran to catch up as she raced down the steps. "You have to stay close."

The emblem.

The pain that was sure to come if she strayed too far from it.

"Keep up then."

The mage panted after her until the royal apartments opened up into ornate, pearl-arches, crisp pools of rainwater, and curving vines. Lanterns swayed in the breeze, like stars dotting the square. Alia had played in this courtyard—her friends endlessly climbing up to the highest ledge and knocking each other off.

But instead of a game, Alia came upon the aftermath of an altercation. And a royal guard had his hand clamped on Lena's upper arm.

Thomas and another boy his age were strewn across the stones, tunics torn and forearms bloodied. Owen cowered between Lena and a young woman in mage robes.

"I need my father," the other boy whined, a tear running down his cheek. Alia didn't recognize him, but his pathetic tone struck a chord.

"If you don't let go of my daughter immediately..." Alia gave the guard little chance as she threatened him with her open palms. The rumors of the Undoing were enough to make the guard jump to release Lena.

"She's hurt, Mother," Lena called, directing her towards the young mage. Dorian had already freed his student from the other guard, delivering her to Alia's hands. The young woman looked at Alia with increasing terror. Alia released her, trying to ease her panic.

"You have a cut, I can help," Alia coaxed. When the young mage agreed to tolerate Alia's touch, her healing magic responded more fervently than it had in years. The cuts vanished, leaving skin unblemished within moments.

Before Alia could marvel at her magic's resurgence, she was faced with a trio of outraged fathers.

"What happened here?"

Prince Cormac rushed out ahead of the rest to Thomas' side. Lord Jaremiah Wexworth flew forward to the other boy, who must be his son, Gawain Wexworth.

Alia wrapped Lena and the young mage in a barrier as Edgar Meador came into the courtyard. Dorian remained at Alia's side.

"Father, she attacked us," Gawain thrust the accusation at Lena.

"They were hurting her," Lena said from behind Alia.

"We were sparring," Thomas said.

"Two against one isn't sparring. And it isn't sparring when someone is screaming for you to stop. Owen saw it all!" Lena yelled.

The youngest prince shrank away at Lena's claim.

"Just a spat among children." Edgar donned his genial smile. "I apologize if my granddaughter was a bit harsh, but there is no harm done. I can see the boys to the infirmary this minute."

"Except harm was done," Lena said, putting her arm around the young mage. "To her."

"I'm certain the Truath provoked this," Lord Wexworth said.

Truath?

Alia looked at the young mage in alarm, taking in her black hair and night sky eyes, stark against her beige cheeks. She must be one of the few living descendants of the Truath bloodline, the rest of which had fallen at the hands of the last Undoing Mage in Mandal. It was no wonder Alia's presence terrified her.

"It was unprovoked!" Lena shouted.

"Are you going to let an attack on your son go unpunished?" Wexworth asked Cormac.

Cormac looked at Alia, the first glance since the sentencing. His gaze quickly passed over her to narrow on Dorian. "The Meadors will be charged a fine, due to the royal treasury for this behavior."

"A fitting punishment." Edgar bowed his head.

"But they're the ones—" Lena began to protest.

"I believe you," Alia whispered, taking Lena's hand. Lena had not grown up in the palace; she couldn't understand. Even though Lena was telling the truth, using magic against the crown prince's heir was not to be tolerated. Alia needed to make sure a fine was the only punishment there would be.

"A fine?" Jaremiah sputtered. "This menace attacked our boys." He left his son's side to come towards Lena. He ran straight into Alia's barrier, which knocked him back.

Cormac glowered at Alia, telling her she was only making things worse.

"Lashes—I demand lashes." Lord Jaremiah scrambled to his feet and back into Cormac's ear.

"No one is touching my daughter."

Cormac oscillated between Alia's wrath and the brutality the Barton family was known for. She knew before he opened his mouth which side would win out.

"Five lashes on the palms in addition to a fine for the Meadors," Cormac decreed, choosing to satisfy Wexworth. "Lord Edgar, I trust you will see this punishment carried out. I need to take my son to see the healers."

Cormac ran from the outcome of his order, placing it in her father's hands.

"I will witness." Wexworth folded his arms and licked his lips.

One of the royal guards went to fetch a switch as Lena trembled beside Alia. "I won't let them hurt you," Alia promised.

When the switch was delivered into Edgar's hands, he frowned at it before shaking all emotion from his expression.

Alia stepped forward. "Since this punishment was assigned to a Meador, any bearing the name can claim it. I will take the lashes."

Lord Jaremiah looked delighted at this turn, and Edgar only nodded.

"You can't do this." Lena hazarded an appeal to Edgar.

"It will be fine," Alia assured.

"Full swings, Meador," Jaremiah warned Edgar as Alia stood before him. "And no healing until the end."

Edgar managed indifference, though he grunted as he brought the switch down on her hands as hard as he could. Lena gasped. The pain seared through Alia, and a bloody line slowly blossomed across both hands. Alia hardly had time to take another breath before her father struck her again. The following blow came just as swiftly.

Edgar Meador was well-practiced in this kind of punishment. He was the reason Alia had never taken to horseback riding, and the reason Elowen excelled. Every time he found them slouching in the saddle or too stiff, they met the end of Edgar's hunting whip. Tiny, swift stings that cut into flesh, even through clothes. Alia had healed Elowen, taking her pain away as quickly as their father delivered it. Her own wounds had healed too, but she had not forgotten who had administered them.

Alia's arms shook all the way to her shoulders as the fourth and fifth blows came. Her palms had become bloody messes, a crisscross of flesh. She absorbed every blow without a sound, for Lena's benefit.

"Is it done?" she asked. Edgar nodded even as Jaremiah's expression soured, disappointed by her composure.

A flutter of magic responded to Alia's call, tingling across her ruined skin with urgency. She turned her back on Edgar, hiding her still-bleeding hands in her skirts. She bid Lena and the young mage to follow her, knowing that Dorian would trail after them.

Once they were safely away from the courtyard, Alia stepped aside and bent to look at each of them. "Do either of you need to see the healers?"

When they both shook their heads, Alia straightened.

"You should get back to the Tower," Dorian said to the Truath girl.

She soundlessly nodded, eyes welling up as she risked a glance towards Lena.

"What is your name?" Lena asked.

She squirmed. "Madeline."

"Lena." Her daughter's smile was soft, one Alia hadn't seen grace her face in too long.

Alia turned away and let the two girls speak. They were similar enough in age, and it would be good for Lena to have a friend, even if she was a Truath.

"You weren't much help back there," Alia said to Dorian.

"You didn't seem to need it."

Alia kept her aching hands hidden in her skirts while following a sulking Lena to their apartment. When Lena immediately fled to her room, Alia followed. Dorian wisely stayed in the sitting room, close enough to spare her pain but not intrude.

Lena paced the small room. "Why didn't you fight for me? I didn't do anything wrong. I defended—"

"They were never going to let an incident involving Thomas go unpunished. The hierarchy in the palace is just as brutal as it is on the road. There is no fairness or justice, just those with power and those with none," Alia tried to explain.

"We could have fought them—we have power."

"I used to think that way. These people, Lena, they always win. Even with magic, they will find a way."

"Because you let them."

Her words stung. "You need to learn how things work here."

"So, the next time I see the prince kicking a girl on the ground, I should walk away because he's the prince? Is that what you would do?"

Alia had never been blighted by righteousness, not even at Lena's age. "When I was young, I would have been right there with Thomas."

Lena sank onto the edge of her bed but didn't prod further. "I don't like the prince." She didn't specify which prince, not that it would matter.

"I'm going to find a way out of here."

"Leave? We can't leave."

"We don't belong here." Alia would have thought Lena would be begging to leave the palace.

"We don't belong anywhere. You never let me."

Because belonging meant having something that could be taken. That it could burn, that it would have to be left behind.

Lena brought her knees to her chest. "Get out."

It was a pattern they'd settled into, arguments demanding space to smolder.

Alia returned to the sitting room, defeated. And furious.

Dorian lingered in one of the shabby armchairs, elbows resting on his knees. An object in his palm caught the firelight, the emblem of her.

"The prince fashioned this himself." Dorian lifted his head at the sound of her footsteps, forehead creased with concentration. "With your blood."

Her stolen likeness in the hands of a stranger was a violation, the power it gave the mage over her even worse. "Give it to me."

"You can't carry it." Dorian held the emblem up to the light before slipping it back into the pouch. His tone was almost apologetic. "It has to be near you but never in your possession. Let me see your hands."

Alia kept her hands folded in her skirts. "They'll heal."

"I can help you along." Dorian reached out faster than she could recoil, taking her bloodied hands in his.

The sensation of sunlight bolstered her, that of Dorian's power numbing the sting. He summoned a cloth and water, dabbing away the blood as the striped wounds closed.

The mage's touch was gentle, trembling. When Alia realized that she wasn't just tolerating Dorian's assistance but finding comfort in it, she promptly pulled away.

Alia flexed her hands, marveling over the resurgence of her healing magic, but not wanting Dorian to notice. "My tutors whipped my palms and knuckles so often, it's a wonder I can feel anything. And if you don't cry, it just makes them angrier."

"Ah, but if you sob, it could make them think you've had enough."

"Is that how one survives Veillant?"

Dorian went still, his habitual tics quieting. "It would depend on your definition of survival."

The sentiment took the air out of her next attack. She was moments away from comforting him if she stared any longer at his morose expression. "Why did you defect? Why would you leave your people?"

A spark of frustration usurped his sadness. "Why did you?"

"I didn't defect."

"Absconded then?" He tried to catch her eye. "Banished?"

Rheta's screaming filled her ears, the final orders issued over Master Ruben's prone form.

"Fine," he said, retreating back to the chair. "I had a disagreement with another mage and was caged in a tiny, windowless cell. I didn't like enclosed spaces to begin with, and now I ..."

Alia pursed her lips, trying to imagine the lively mage locked away and trying even harder not to care why. "What was the disagreement?"

Dorian shook his curls forward, hiding his carved markings. "Just what you would expect from a leech. I betrayed him."

A twinge of guilt joined the roar of suspicion. "Why?"

"Isn't it your turn to answer my question?"

"I never agreed to that."

"Alia." Dorian groaned, scratching the back of his neck. "We need each other."

He needed a killer.

And she needed someone strong enough to stop her when she lost control.

"You carry my prison. We don't need to exchange wounds."

"Magic like ours is best learned through trust."

Alia hacked out a laugh. If the mage sought her trust, he would never be satisfied.

Her callousness set his brow in a firm line. "Your control has not improved. We need to begin your training."

"Lena is taking to her classes."

"Lena is talented, but she is woefully behind in her studies for someone her age. I hoped you might show some interest in gaining dominance over the Undoing. The ability to take life as easily as you can should not be treated lightly," Dorian lectured.

"Do you really think I don't know that?"

"You act like you don't."

"You know, the next time something comes through from the Otherworld, I'm going to step aside and let it cut you down."

"Your threats only convince me of your stability."

Alia felt her anger boiling over. Without touching her, Dorian's magic met hers, dousing the heat. Even if she wanted to lash out with the Undoing, she was contained inside whatever bubble Dorian had put her in.

She didn't have the will to fight her way out. "I can't help you."

"You could if you harnessed your full ability."

"It can't be harnessed!" Alia yelled, her fingers digging into her palms. "I am not a tool to be used. And I don't owe you, Cormac, or Mandal, anything else."

"You don't," Dorian said, tapping each of his fingers to his thumb in turn. "But you also cannot deny what you are."

An Undoing Mage. A monster.

"Get out." Lena's words came from Alia's lips, leaving no room for Dorian to speak further.

But even as Dorian wisely backed away into the hall, her deep breaths did little to quiet the pounding in her head. She pressed her back against a stone wall, ignoring the bite of the uneven edges. Alia curved her arms around herself, gripping her ribcage. It was hers. Her arms, her chest, her throbbing head, her bloodied hands.

She may not have been the one to wake the Undoing, but it was hers to deny.

7

"So, this is Court." Lena tugged at the tight bodice of her gown, trying in vain to stretch the fabric and ribbing as she stood between Alia and Elowen.

"You wanted to come." As much as Alia tried to dissuade her, Lena's insistence won out.

Especially tonight, when Mandal's nobility gathered for one of their most sacred ceremonies. The shrouded moon had vanished and plunged Entien into true darkness, the empty sky serving as a sign of triumph over the Tiarcon of the Moon. The ideal for a pairing ceremony, a practice as integral to Mandal's survival as magic itself.

"I wanted to get out of that room." Lena rocked back and forth on the soft-soled slippers before glaring at Elowen. "You tricked me."

"The dress is the least of it." Elowen took Lena's arm. "Now, the pleasantries."

Alia chuckled as Elowen led Lena away, satisfied to watch Lena's instruction in the ways of nobility from afar. At Rheta's command, Alia had begun attending Court, keeping to the corners, and participating as sparingly as possible.

Six weeks in Sheath, and she had slipped back into the guise of a noblewoman. Alia straightened her gown, high-necked and modest, seeking to cover as much of herself as possible. Her tightly woven plaits were flawless, each strand of hair smoothed down with wax. And, as always, she had enough simmering anger to overpower any other emotion that threatened to show itself.

Across the hall, Jaremiah Wexworth refilled Cormac's cup and laughed uproariously at something the prince said, his pandering sickening even from a distance. And to think, at one time, she wanted to rule all of it. Court gatherings had been her arena of choice, the social core of the palace, her battlefield.

Your beauty is your armor. As well as her wit, arrogance, and utter selfishness.

Even before Cormac had made his intention to marry her clear, she had the other girls in her thrall. She had only needed to make an example of a few of them before the rest fell in line. Alia found Lady Wylann in the crowd. Her carefully styled hair hid the patch of scarred scalp. Alia had latched onto using flame against others, just as Ruben had done to her.

Lady Wylann caught Alia looking and flinched.

Harlan approached and settled beside her, one of the few people she actually enjoyed speaking with. "Your sister is enjoying making Lena a lady." Harlan sipped from his tankard.

"A waste of time." Alia smirked.

"I think she'd do well here. If that's what you wanted for her."

There hadn't been time for Alia to consider what Lena's life would be like when she grew up. In truth, Alia hadn't wanted to think of a time when her daughter would no longer need her.

Mariana and Edgar entered the hall, cutting a clear path to stand beside the thrones. Alia frowned. "I know what I *don't* want for her."

She would never seek to place a crown on her daughter's head or a sword in her hand.

Alia's own dance with royalty was lesson enough. Even now, she was tormented by it. Alia could still feel Cormac's arms around her, no matter how fleeting it had been. No matter how distant he had been since. The prince had neither sought her out after the ordeal with the Oucura nor after the incident in the courtyard.

It was vile to begrudge the lack of attention from her sister's husband.

"Well, well, well—Ali!" A woman with shining crimson hair burst through the sea of courtiers to stand before Alia and Harlan.

"At last," Harlan exclaimed, stepping forward to take the woman's hand and bring it to his lips. "Back home where you belong."

"And I'm not the only one who has returned." Her hazel eyes twinkled.

"Flora." Alia grinned as the taller woman wrapped her arms around her shoulders.

"I've just come in from Waterston—the trip was dreadful. I am going to need an entire bottle to set me right." Flora treated the room to her theatrics. "You should have sent for me the moment you arrived."

"I haven't exactly been in the position to send for anyone."

"Harlan told me." Flora rolled her eyes. "It is just a show so Cormac can appease his mother. You'll be free soon; Cormac could never stand to disappoint you for too long. And compared to whatever backwater hovel you've been staying in all these years, this still must be paradise. We used to think so, at least. I can barely stomach Waterston most days."

"Some paradise." Alia took a sip of her drink. "Why would you marry a man from the most miserable keep in Mandal?"

"Well ..." Flora waved her arms dramatically, drawing attention to the jewels that adorned her neck, highlighting her golden complexion. "And someone has to keep the insufferable Roycans within their borders. I have a household of my own, a doting husband, an army of children, and

I've never been so bored."

Flora hadn't changed at all.

"Did you ever stop to think about how frightfully dull my life would be when you ran off? Did you ever consider what would happen to me?"

The second question held a glimmer of earnestness. Alia had erased Flora along with the rest of her memories of Sheath, even though they had been inseparable for years. "An oversight."

"Tell me about your adventures and don't leave out any details—especially not about this pauper husband of yours. And you killed a beast?" Flora waved Harlan off and took custody of Alia.

They toured the hall, Flora questioning as adeptly as Alia evaded. It was their dance, practiced phrases and controlled expressions, each trying to see what the years had left behind. If nothing else, Flora was a welcome distraction, brimming with Court gossip and suspicions.

After a full circuit of the room, Flora leaned into Alia and murmured, "Why is Elowen avoiding us?" Flora didn't pause to hear Alia's answer before marching over to the princess and placing herself firmly in her path.

"Lady Flora, welcome back," Elowen said, her posture too wooden for her smile to be genuine.

"Wonderful to see you, Princess." Flora bowed low. "Where is your husband? Have you lost him?"

Elowen blushed deeply. "He's just there, talking to Lord Stanton."

"How awful for you to be unattended." Sarcasm slipped from her bright lips.

"You manage well with it. How many years has it been since Lord Geoff graced us with his presence? Enjoy the evening, Lady Flora. Ali," Elowen said before excusing herself.

"What was that about?" Alia asked Flora once they walked away.

"My husband loathes Sheath as much as I love it. She just can't stand that I can do as I please. I never forgave her for moving in on Cormac the second you disappeared." Flora snapped her fingers. "And she knows that I know about her dalliances."

"Dalliances?"

"You don't know?" Flora drew Alia into a corner away from the other revelers. "This is why you need me. No one else tells you what you need to know. Elowen and Harlan."

"What about them?"

"Elowen *and* Harlan," Flora repeated suggestively.

"No." Alia's shock came out as a whisper. There was no way her sister would have an affair with Harlan behind Cormac's back.

"Oh yes." Flora nodded. "It's been going on for years. Harlan told me."

"Does Cormac know?"

Flora shrugged. "According to Harlan, he wouldn't care if he did. Apparently, Cormac hasn't touched Elowen since the boys were born, and they hardly ever interact in private."

Alia shifted between shock and pity. "And Harlan?"

"Madly in love. Didn't you wonder why he never married and sought a station at the palace?"

Alia had assumed his devotion to Cormac had kept him here, but this made even more sense.

"I think it's somewhat poetic. Elowen must have known when she married Cormac that he would never love her the way he loved you. But she wanted to be royal so badly." Flora's judgment arched her brow. "I can't believe no one told you. Have you honestly not had a dalliance of your own with Cormac yet?"

"He married my sister," Alia hissed, but she felt a wave of nausea. Flora had the uncanny ability to see through the best liars at Court.

"Just to punish you, Ali. But he's only punished himself, hasn't he?"

"It doesn't matter why he married her."

Flora fixed her with a piercing stare. "Of course it does. You still love him. You've always loved him."

"He married my sister." Alia didn't know if she was reminding Flora or herself. "Anyway, a lot has happened since I left." And she looked pointedly at Lena.

"Yes, yes, I know all about your years of slumming it."

Alia couldn't stop a bark of laughter. Her guilt significantly lessened with the knowledge that Cormac and Elowen's marriage was loveless, but it made her continued preoccupation with Cormac more dangerous.

"I know I've only just arrived, but some advice." Flora scanned the room. "Pick one of them before they choose for you. For you and your daughter. Too many bloodlines have run dry."

"Come now, Flora. We've never had a choice."

Only the illusion of one. Even if she attempted to appease the preening crowd, they'd find a way to bring her down in the end. The only thing she could do was refuse, stay apart.

The composure buoying Flora held, the glittering noblewoman finding a more diverting topic. "Now, here is the man I came to see." Flora spun, tracking her quarry. Alia followed her gaze across the room to where the mages gathered. Lena was among them, talking animatedly with Madeline Truath. Flora's eyes were settled on Master Dorian.

"And I thought you came to see me."

"Young for a master. And much more handsome than old Ruben."

Alia shuddered as an unbidden image of Ruben burst into her head. When she refocused her eyes, Flora was watching closely, so Alia grabbed her by the arm, "I can introduce you, but need I remind you he is to be paired tonight and you are already married."

"Know him, do you? To the Otherworld with Cormac then! You didn't tell me you had your eye on Mandal's most sought-after bloodline."

Alia stiffened. "I don't. He's Veillanti, a traitor."

"That would make him an unthinkable attachment for you then."

As they watched, Lady Lillian Palmer approached the Master Mage, offering her hand to him with a gleaming smile. Dorian took her hand, his eyes darting around as if hoping for an interruption. Alia looked between them with mild interest, wondering if the Palmers were about to be the victor in the competition for Dorian.

"It is a smart match for Cormac to encourage," Flora whispered. "Lord Tristan grumbles of the old order every few years, and Orlast knows the Palmers could use the influx of magic. He must have sworn generations of loyalty to the Bartons for this."

"But a Palmer with Dorian's magic." Alia slipped back into her old role despite herself. "Wouldn't that be an even larger threat?"

"Ah, wouldn't that be?" Before Dorian could properly bow to his lady, Flora confronted the soon-to-be paired couple by thrusting Alia out ahead of her to perform the necessary introduction to the Master Mage. The glazed sheen shook from Dorian's eyes as he turned towards them.

"I'd like to present Lady Flora Frulin." Alia smirked as Flora held out her hand for him.

"Lady Flora." Dorian kissed Flora's hand.

"May your pairing serve Mandal." Flora beamed. "Lady Lillian, you look absolutely beautiful. Let us fetch some wine to put some blush on your cheeks." Lillian sank into Flora's clutches and allowed herself to be taken off towards the banquet table.

"Have I finally met a friend of yours?" Dorian asked, looking after

Flora.

"Hardly," Alia appraised, shifting to stand beside the Master Mage. His curls were more orderly, robes belted above a crisp blue tunic. The markings on his head were faded scars, and from a few paces away, one would hardly recognize him as Veillanti. "You almost look the part."

Dorian brushed off his robes, preening. "Your approval is hard to come by," he said, taking her hand, intending to bring it to his lips.

Alia recoiled from his touch. "You don't take a lady's hand unless she offers it."

"Wasn't it improper that you did not offer yours?"

"It wasn't as if we had just met. We are far too familiar for such a greeting."

"Familiar?" Dorian's smile broadened. "I didn't realize Mandal familiarity involved multiple threats to an acquaintance's life."

Alia suppressed the urge to smile. "Customary for a Meador."

"Noted."

"You didn't mention that you were being paired. I had to hear it from my sister."

"I didn't know that it would be such an ... ordeal."

Alia's lips twitched at Dorian's choice of words. "Do they not have pairings in Veillant?"

Dorian shook his head with a smirk. "Most of us don't bother with marriage at all."

"Your Queen Odessa certainly believes in the institution," Alia said, which drew a grimace from the Master Mage.

"Just not in its longevity."

Odessa traded husbands too often to recall their names or for any one of them to amass influence to rival hers. "What about the rest of you? How do you protect your magical bloodlines if not through marriage?"

Dorian shrugged. "We are encouraged to explore magical unions. Any resulting children are brought up by the Order."

"What does that mean? You give up your children?"

"We don't claim possession of children that same way you do here. They are provided for, nurtured, and educated."

"Do you have children?"

Dorian lifted his open palms, but his eyes held shadows. "I may have fathered children, but they are not mine to have."

Alia couldn't imagine giving Lena away to someone else to raise. "That is madness."

Dorian let her indignation settle before speaking again. "Like I said, the Mandal system is very ... rigid. It takes some getting used to."

"What do you do if you fall in love?"

"You just love each other." Dorian chuckled. "You don't have to be married to love someone."

Alia bristled.

"You certainly do not." Flora made herself known, passing Alia a glass of wine. She quirked her eyebrow and looked between Alia and Dorian.

"But what a blessing it would be to have both," Lillian angled herself towards the mage. "Master Dorian, my father would like a word." Her eyes settled on Alia for the briefest of moments, the calm demeanor fading away to expose hardened edges. It was a look Alia had perfected herself, a warning, a claim.

Flora leaned in, speaking in Alia's ear, "If you are going to challenge Lillian for him, you'll have to warn me. She is nearly as formidable as you were."

"Your willingness to defend me is touching, but unnecessary."

"I need a good fight. Ah, there's Cormac." Flora poked Alia's ribs and dragged her towards the group of self-aggrandizing nobles. When they approached, Cormac's arm went possessively to Elowen's back.

"Lady Flora, I am so pleased you've returned." Prince Cormac gave Flora a glowing smile that would have shattered Alia if it had been directed at her.

"Pairing a Master Mage was far too intriguing for me to stay away." Flora's lips curled. "And, of course, finding out that our dear Ali was alive and well. You must be so pleased."

Elowen's royal composure held out. "We are all so grateful to have my sister back."

"What a shock it must be to return to the palace. Surely much changed from the accommodations you're accustomed to, Lady Alia." Jaremiah Wexworth's comment garnered a laugh from the rest of the hovering sycophants.

"And somehow I'm accustomed to far less filth than I find here," Alia snapped back at the lord.

"Compared to being forced to manage a commoner's household?" Jaremiah remarked with distaste.

"I was not forced." Alia pulled back her shoulders and lifted her head.

"There is still time for you to find someone better suited," Lady Wylann offered.

Alia's emotions flared, but she knew what to expect here. "Not all of us can be as lucky as you and Lord Stanton, so very well-matched, not a bit of sense between you."

"Perhaps Lady Alia can pick her next conquest out of the dungeons then," Lady Wylann said.

Alia lifted her glass and plastered a smile on her face.

"Perhaps behind bars Lord Stanton would finally be faithful to you," Flora added, making Wylann's turn away, face red with shame.

As the conversation moved on, Alia felt a tug on her elbow and turned to find Lord Jaremiah. "A private word, my lady." He wasn't asking permission.

Harlan broke away from the group to join them. "Is that wise?" he challenged the much smaller nobleman.

"I assure you, I'll be fine." Jaremiah tapped the bejeweled hilt at his hip.

Harlan raised an eyebrow while Alia shrugged. She supposed it was better to have the conversation now and end whatever idea Jaremiah might have. Harlan turned and stepped away, but he could still hear every word Jaremiah said.

"I'm glad we were able to put that unpleasant incident with the Truath girl behind us."

She hadn't.

"I cannot help but feel sympathy for your predicament," Jaremiah began, his smirk of privilege nauseating her. "I would like to offer my assistance."

"I do not need your assistance," Alia said as Jaremiah's eyes roved over her.

"The prince is a very close friend of mine." Jaremiah leaned close, breath reaching her cheek. "I could speak to him on your behalf, ask him to reconsider your confinement."

"And why would you do that?" Alia had to fight the impulse to send the Undoing to a particularly sensitive region of Jaremiah's body.

"I could convince him to release you to one of my estates. You and your daughter would have every comfort that you could possibly want. You wouldn't be subjected to the indignity of having your every move watched." Jaremiah looked over at Harlan with a frown. Alia took the opportunity to scan the room, only to meet Cormac's fiery gaze.

Her breath quickened, and Jaremiah continued, "I could give you anything you desire. And you needn't mind my wife. Be assured, I would claim our children as mine, as true Wexworths."

Alia's fury snapped, as her attention returned to the ridiculous man in front of her. "I'd sooner face execution than bed a Wexworth," Alia spat.

"You are the most—" Wexworth shook with rage, but was interrupted when Harlan moved in, towering over the man once more. He swallowed his words and backed away, presumably to make someone else's night miserable.

"Well done." Harlan nudged her with his elbow.

"I may be a captive, but I still have some pride."

"Cormac would never have gone for it anyway. Your father tried to persuade him to exile you to the Meador keep, and he would hear none of it."

"I am to stay here, under his thumb." Alia could still feel the burn of Cormac's eyes. "Especially since someone else is diverting his wife's attention."

Harlan nearly spat out his drink.

"I told you to look after her," Alia said in a low, harsh tone. "Not seduce her."

Harlan was now deep in a coughing fit, and Alia gave him a thump on the back.

"Lady Alia."

This is why she avoided clusters. Lord Tristan Palmer engaged her this time, striking in his burgundy tunic, his fair hair tinged with gray. As he brought her hand to his lips, his touch sparked, the form Palmer magic often took, given generations of breeding fire and water mages.

Lightning.

"I'm glad to see your daughter and Madeline have become such friends." Tristan offered pleasantries, gesturing across the hall to where the two young women gathered. "She was my ward before she was old enough to train at the Tower."

A fact that certainly burned the Bartons. The Crown hadn't intended to let any Truaths survive to retake the throne. But they hadn't had the will to challenge the Palmers on their lands, not while the glimmer of breeding lightning magic into the royal line existed. It was a practice that had become customary under the Barton reign; sequestering magical bloodlines out in the family lands should the Crown ever have use for it. Confined, just as she now was.

The Palmers had deftly avoided mixing blood with the Bartons and Meadors over the years, although all it had yielded them of late was quotidien children. The infusion of Dorian's bloodline was their last chance at maintaining influence without merging with the other lines. Even with their predicament, the Palmers would fare better than the Truaths. Madeline Truath would never be granted royal permission to marry, never be able to hold a title.

"A Meador and a Truath." Alia itched to be free of Tristan, but Harlan was no longer hovering. Or at least, nowhere she could see. While Harlan had been eager to interrupt Jaremiah, he allowed this interaction to fester. He wanted to know what Tristan would say, and she was an all-too tempting pawn left unattended.

"Hatred isn't in our blood, despite what your father might claim. We've instilled it; I am just as guilty as he."

"And still you argued for my execution." The Undoing twisted in her stomach. She had gleaned as much from Harlan; there had been only a few voices urging leniency.

"True. Because I suspected exactly this. That your father would try to distract the rest of the council with you and your daughter. To make them curry favor just long enough."

It didn't sound like something Edgar would do, with Elowen acting as his messenger.

"Then perhaps you should have made a more compelling case for my death." As much as his accusation bothered her, she wasn't keen to entertain it.

"Perhaps there is another way forward. One not so bleak."

There would always be the scramble for blood and influence. Just as it always had been. "Perhaps."

Flora walked up. "Lord Tristan, your daughter is looking for you. The pairing is about to begin."

"Thank you, Lady Flora." The older man grinned, alighting at Flora's presence. "I look forward to speaking with you again, Lady Alia."

"What did he want?" Flora asked once Tristan had moved towards the throne.

Alia shook her head. "To hear himself talk."

"The pairing hasn't even happened, and he's already smug."

"I hope Cormac knows what he's doing."

"What are they going to do?" Lena joined them in the crowd, nobles moving towards the throne to witness the pairing.

Flora leaned in and whispered in Alia's ear, "You really didn't bother educating her, did you?" Then she stepped up to embrace Lena. "I have heard so much about you, young lady. I am Flora, your mother's oldest friend."

"Some friend, if I'm just hearing of you now," Lena responded with a standoffish glare.

"Well, aren't you lovely?" Flora reached forward to cup Lena's cheek. "A pairing ceremony is done before anyone of magical blood gets married. It indicates if the pair will produce powerful children."

"Your grandmother is the Intercessor, appointed by the royal family to oversee that appropriate magical matches are made," Alia explained. "To concentrate the magic we have left."

"Master Dorian is being paired with Lady Lillian Palmer. Orlast knows Lillian doesn't have a lick of magic, but the Palmer bloodline is strong. Personally, I think it is a waste. The Master Mage could do far better."

All eyes focused on Lady Mariana Meador, the Intercessor. Her ceremonial robes were Mandal blue, trimmed with gold. She wore an expansive headpiece which stretched across her forehead and fastened into her plaits. It wasn't quite a golden crown, but certainly close. Mariana was in her element, elated by her station and the glorious attention.

The musicians quieted, and Mariana lifted her hands. "We honor King Orlast, the First Monarch, the slayer of the mad Tiarcon, and protector of all mortalkind. It is our solemn duty to hold the veil between this realm and the next, to defend our freedom."

Alia looked at Master Dorian, hoping to see his amusement at the Mandal beliefs, but found the mage drawn and humorless. Lena was rapt with attention beside her.

"What is she doing now?" Lena whispered.

"See the bowl." Alia pointed at a shimmering silver saucer. "Now the Intercessor pours in the elixir." It was a potent mixture of natural and magical elements designed by the Tower to bond the blood of two people, mimicking the result of a child.

"And now Master Dorian and Lady Lillian will mix their blood into the bowl," Alia explained as Mariana drew a ceremonial dagger across the outside of their forearms. The Master Mage and his lady then stood side by side, arms pressed together and extended over the saucer, deep red drops mixing with the elixir.

Alia had watched the ceremony countless times. It had always held intrigue for her, wondering what would befall her when it was her turn. She had seen a range of outcomes, successful pairings and disappointment, but each time it seemed like destiny was weighing in and bonding two people together.

The last pairing ceremony she attended had been her own. With Cormac.

"What is supposed to happen?" Lena whispered, as the entire room held its collective breath.

Alia was too distracted by Dorian and Lillian to answer immediately. Dorian looked faint, beads of sweat appearing on his brow. Not the picture of an eager partner. Lillian seemed anxious, but her luminous eyes were hungry; Dorian was something to gain. There was desperation in the way that she moved. Alia pitied both of them.

"A reaction," Alia said softly. "Sometimes it takes a beat."

It had been instantaneous with her and Cormac. As soon as their blood had dripped into the elixir, sparks had erupted, nearly setting the entire hall aflame.

She hadn't known then what rotted inside of her.

The moments dragged on, and nothing happened. Still, the room waited in silence for what seemed now inevitable, the declaration of an unsuccessful pairing.

Mariana feigned distress, her voice grave. "This pairing does not serve the Kingdom of Mandal."

There was the obligatory outburst from the Palmers, and Tristan raised an objection. With Dorian being the Master Mage, the issue was obviously with Lillian. If she couldn't produce magical children with the most powerful mage in Mandal, then it was likely she wasn't destined to produce any at all. Her sobs tugged at Alia's heart; the favored daughter had fallen. Dorian appeared contrite, helping the poor woman back to her mother.

Alia turned her back on the scene; it felt indecent to make further spectacle of their pain.

"Just as I thought," Flora murmured as the din in the hall picked up. The music had turned sorrowful, and the servants carrying tankards and glasses multiplied.

"Bizarre," Lena blurted as they turned away.

"It is necessary." Alia shivered. If Cormac's sentence was carried out, both her and Lena would be forced to submit to a magical pairing.

"Now what?"

"Now, we drink." Harlan walked up from behind them. "That part is always the same if the pairing is made or not."

"Poor Master Dorian." Flora's grin didn't match her words.

"I think he'll be just fine," Harlan said with a wink.

"He will." Alia looked back, passing over the shallow mass to look for Cormac. The onlookers had begun to disperse, the ceremony coming to an end.

Madeline rejoined Lena, who had begun a spirited debate with Harlan over how ale in Sheath compared with the hinterland. Flora was whisked away by another painted face Alia didn't recognize.

The gathering moved on, and Alia kept looking for him. No longer entangled with Elowen, the prince wore a solemn mask as he spoke with a circle of noblemen. Commanding, almost a king. Alia wondered if somewhere wrapped up in his heart was a remnant of affection for her. If his chest ached the way hers did every time she laid eyes on him.

"Alia." Mariana approached, taking Alia's arm.

She wrenched away from her mother's grip. "What?"

"Get your daughter under control."

A few paces away, Lena was now showing Harlan how ale was consumed in the hinterland. Alia had often found Lena hiding in taverns, watching revelry as the day ended. She assumed Lena must have been drawn to the vibrancy and brashness of it all, the novelty.

And brash she was. Ale was spilling out of the sides of her mouth and splashing onto her dress. She had captured the attention of nearly the entire room, most looking on in horror.

Alia sighed and approached the spectacle; Harlan was offering his encouragement, goading Lena on. She snatched the tankard from Lena.

"What the fuck?" Lena wiped her mouth on her sleeve.

There was a collective gasp from the ladies present.

Alia fixed Lena with a look that conveyed disappointment. "It is time for us to retire."

"I don't want to go back." Lena stormed off, Madeline Truath at her hem.

There were too many eyes on them; Alia knew better than to show how angry she was. It was best to end the spectacle, to let it subside.

"Damn you, Harlan," Alia said in a harsh whisper, pushing the tankard into his empty hand.

"She was having fun," Harlan whispered back, handing the dripping tankard to a servant. The crowd turned away now that the sport was finished. Harlan caught her arm, "Come on, we did much worse when we were young."

"Not in the presence of the entire palace."

Once she was satisfied that attentions had moved on, Alia left the hall to find Lena.

She stomped through the corridors, scolding Lena silently. Lena would need to be more careful, but they couldn't show a rift without inviting the vultures.

But Alia only found herself alone in the halls, the darkness of the moonless night pressing in on her. The torches on the walls were lit, but there wasn't even the echo of a footstep ahead of her.

When she turned the corner, her breath grew short. Her chest tightened, with strikes of pain tearing through her.

The fucking emblem.

She must be too far from Harlan. Cormac's spell was taking hold. And it was excruciating.

"My son should know better than to let you wander about."

The voice chilled Alia.

"There is no telling what you'll do."

Alia turned to face Queen Rheta in the desolate palace hallway, trying to pretend that she wasn't in agony. "Your son's men will be along any moment to find me."

The old queen's grin crinkled her skin all the way to her eyes. "*My* men, you ghastly whore."

The Undoing surged, fighting Alia to be set free. Alia wasn't in a state to deny it. "It must burn that he didn't heed you."

The blue of her eyes electrified, Rheta's magic showing itself. While the queen hadn't been as powerful as her brother, there was a reason why Isaac Barton had chosen her to bear his children. As twins, Ruben and Rheta's affinities had been related. Ruben's inculcation was high magic, Rheta's compulsion only elemental.

Elemental or not, Rheta's influence struck Alia swiftly, binding her arms to her sides and holding her still. Rheta struggled under the strain of containing Alia, only able to do so because Alia had once let her at Ruben's instruction.

"Did you wish I had killed him before the end? Was it worse to watch him slowly slip away?" Alia said through gritted teeth, overcome with the need to hurt Rheta, to cause her as much pain as possible.

"My only wish has been to be the one to put an end to your depraved influence on honorable men."

Rheta moved in; dagger extended.

"Mother!"

The dagger vanished beneath her skirts, and Rheta released her hold, leaving Alia to crumple to the ground. "Thank Orlast you're here, Cormac!" Rheta wailed. "She was trying to use the Undoing on me."

Alia stayed on the floor, trying to gulp air.

"Did she hurt you?" Cormac touched his mother's shoulder with concern.

"I fought her off." Tears streamed down the Queen's face.

Cormac called out, and a Mandal guard responded. "Take Queen Rheta back to her quarters and fetch her a healer, just to be sure."

Rheta cast a cruel smile over her shoulder as Cormac gripped Alia's upper arm. "What just happened?" Cormac lifted her to her feet and crowded her against the stone wall.

"Nothing." Alia's chest heaved, the distance from the emblem making her blood flame. "I need—"

"What did you do?" Cormac was in no hurry to end her suffering.

"I didn't do anything."

"I warned you..." His hold on her arm was still tight. "I told you there would be consequences if you caused any disruptions."

Tears sprang to Alia's eyes despite her attempt to suppress them. "I didn't do anything," she repeated. "She compelled me."

Cormac searched Alia's face for deception, his gaze full of desperation. His fingers relaxed around her arm, but his body held her still against the wall.

Alia took shuddering breaths through the pain. "Please, it hurts."

Cormac blinked, stepping back. "What—" He stopped himself, as if just now remembering his own spell. He looked down the hall, finding it empty now that his guards had ushered his mother away.

"I have to get you to Harlan." Cormac lifted her into his arms.

Alia circled her arms around his neck, clinging closer as he rushed back towards the hall. Their heartbeats pressed together; Alia was too aware that he was to blame for each sting. But still, she sank into the smell of smoke on his skin, the softness of his fair hair as it brushed against her fingers.

She tried to tell herself that it was just the memory of their pairing. Or that he'd been the first person she allowed to touch her all those years ago.

"Harlan!"

The captain was just down the hall. The pain had already subsided, her blood stilling.

"I'm sorry. I—" Harlan huffed like he'd been running.

Cormac gently placed her on her feet. "Are you alright?" He smoothed her hair with care she thought he no longer possessed, his face soft.

Alia nodded, taking a step back towards Harlan and away from the prince. Her retreat robbed Cormac of his fleeting kindness.

"You are supposed to stay with her," Cormac chastised Harlan.

"I found Lena—"

"Do not fail me again," Cormac threatened before stalking off, leaving them in his wake.

Alia could finally breathe again, but she might have let the pain linger if it meant staying in Cormac's arms.

8

"Look who I crossed paths with."

Alia jolted upright, her back protesting a night spent sprawled on the threadbare couch. Harlan had deposited her back in this prison the night before, promising Lena was safe with Madeline. Still, Alia had waited in the sitting room, hoping to catch Lena's return.

Instead, it was Flora at the door, clutching Dorian's arm.

"Morning, Alia," Dorian said, head bowed.

"Lena?"

Dorian guided Flora inside, revealing Lena behind them.

"Where have you been? Whose are those?" Alia eyed the mage robes Lena now wore.

Lena's shoulders lifted in defiance. "I thought I would spare you the humiliation of my presence." Lena glowered, stepping around Alia and toward the balcony. "I have a lesson."

Dorian shuffled backward towards the balcony, looking at Alia with a furrowed brow. "She was in the mage quarters; those are Madeline's robes."

Seeing Lena draped in the Tower's uniform overwhelmed Alia, dulled her ability to respond as Dorian joined Lena.

"He calls you just Alia then, hm?" Flora asked as she peered after Dorian through the doorway, twisting a lavish gold chain around her fingers.

"I don't think they spend time on etiquette in Veillant."

"You just watch them?" Flora asked, eyebrows raised.

"I keep an eye." Alia sought Lena's attention, but her daughter was set on ignoring her. When Lena was in such a surly mood, it was better to allow her space. Even if the distance between them was a stinging wound.

"Then you won't mind if I join you," Flora's lips curled as she settled into the couch. "I am surprised you're allowing it. You always said magic was a pathetic way for women to seem more desirable."

Alia had told Flora that and had harassed her enough to stop her from going to the Tower altogether to learn how to use her elemental water magic. It was a ploy to keep Ruben away from Flora and to explain Alia's own aversion to the Tower.

"It wasn't my choice." None of this was.

"Where are your maids?" Flora scrunched her nose at the condition of the room. Flora's condescension was tolerable, primarily because Alia knew its origin. The family Flora was born into didn't have the legacy of the Bartons, Meadors, or even the Gusts; her position of favor was still novel to her, precious.

"Need I remind you that this is a prison?"

"That won't do." Flora stuck out her lip before popping up and leaning on the doorframe with a hand on her hip. "Master Dorian, can you be a darling and summon us wine from the kitchens?"

Lena groaned at the mere thought of alcohol, clutching her stomach.

"At this hour?" Annoyance slipped into Dorian's sideways glance.

"If the sun can't be bothered to rise, then I can't be bothered to be sober," Flora said, casting her loose hair over her shoulder.

She earned a grin from Dorian as he folded his arms across his chest. "I don't recall seeing you at any of the Tower training sessions. If you attended, perhaps you would have learned to summon your own wine."

Alia's head snapped towards Flora, eager to see how her old friend took his challenge. Flora's eyes dragged over Dorian, making a show of sizing him up. "What makes you think you could teach me anything?"

Dorian shrugged and nodded towards Alia. "I haven't given up on her yet."

Flora quirked an eyebrow. "I like a persistent man, even when it borders on foolish. But alas, I'm still thirsty. Maybe this can be a lesson for Lena; Ali and I will even pay attention."

"I can do it." A healthy flush had returned to Lena's face.

Dorian sighed, bowing to Flora's will like so many before him. "The first thing you need to be mindful of when you try to summon an item is that we are not creating anything; we are simply moving it from one place to another. A shift."

Twice during Dorian's explanation, Lena looked like she might retch again, but she kept focus. After three failed attempts, Lena broke out in a sweat. But on the fourth try, a flagon of wine and glasses appeared on the table.

"Thank you, Lena." Flora dipped her fingertip into the wine, sampling it before pouring each of them a hefty glass. When Dorian and Lena returned to the balcony, she continued, "He seems to be managing his failed pairing well."

Alia took a glass from Flora's hand. "I doubt he even understands the implications."

"Still, already much better than the last Master Mage. You always said he was awful, right, what with the mind control and all?"

Inculcation could be understood in many ways, all of them equally unsettling. "Right," Alia said, keeping her response simple to avoid bolstering Flora's interest.

"I always found Rheta a bit repellent, too. Not that I should speak ill of her now." Flora barely took a breath between words.

"Why is that?" Alia asked, thinking of how close Rheta's dagger had gotten to its mark.

Flora's gasp was too practiced. "How have you not heard?" Flora asked, with her hand over her heart. Of course, Flora had gossip. And she knew very well that she would be able to be the first person to tell Alia, which is why she had come at all. "The king is dead."

King Isaac Barton had finally fallen. The man who had been all fire and bluster, dead without a sound, without even being seen by his people one last time.

Alia let out a staggering breath of relief, the threat of King Isaac suddenly regaining his faculties disappearing. Rheta would be out of power, her influence lessened to whatever Cormac granted her. And Elowen.

"Everything is going to change now." Flora took a sip of wine. "To Cormac and Elowen, long may they miserably reign."

Alia couldn't stop her next question, even though asking it divulged far too much to Flora. "Did the Meadors demand the title for Elowen when they married?"

It had been the most difficult part of the negotiation before Alia was paired with Cormac. Mandal tradition dictated that the princess be conferred the title of queen at the king's coronation, but it was never left to chance. Cormac had promised Alia the honor after their first night together.

"They did." Flora pursed her lips, rolling her eyes.

"To the new king and queen, then." Cormac had been waiting for this day for years, and Elowen was surely being heralded by the Meadors. "Do you think he'll reconsider my confinement now?"

The glow left Flora's face, her performance cracking. "It is best if you don't think of it that way."

"How else could I think of it?"

"You're home." Flora didn't waver. "You're one of us. Cormac will be the fourth Barton king. You know no family has held the Mandal crown for more than four generations."

"And Mandal transfers of power are never bloodless." Alia slumped back in her chair. Not even Orlast's bloodline had been able to maintain the throne.

"With an Undoing Mage at his side, who would dare defy him?"

Alia scoffed. Lord Tristan hadn't been too far from the truth.

"Enough of this, Ali." Flora snapped her fingers. "You have the power to serve your king. It is our purpose."

"He sent you here." Alia leaned forward, studying the shifting of Flora's hands, the way she pulled her skirts smooth.

Flora's smile gleamed. "Finish your glass; you'll be glad you did. The king needs you."

"You have the emblem."

"I hear you don't like it. I would find it flattering."

Ali looked out to the balcony, where Dorian, seemingly encouraged by Lena's summoning, was teaching her to flicker in short jumps.

"Harlan will be here any minute to escort you," Flora said. She was not just here to gossip and to see how Alia fared. She was here at Cormac's behest, another link in the chain binding Alia here, where she'd be made to serve, her choices made for her. "I'll watch Lena for you."

Alia knew she shouldn't go, shouldn't be driven to the side of the very man keeping her here. The one who could barely spare her a thought.

But when Harlan arrived, Alia went with him.

Harlan abandoned Alia within Cormac's apartments along with the emblem she couldn't touch, swearing it would be best if he left before Cormac returned. His confidence carried notes of unease; Cormac must be in a state after the death of his father.

The air was weighed down by smoke. A chair was overturned in the sitting room, a place where she'd spent countless hours with her friends. The furniture had been switched out, fabric the same hue as the hottest flame. The tapestries were new, too, changed from Barton portraits to maps and depictions of battles. Weapons were mounted beside them, ones Cormac must have wielded in a bout or skirmish. A man of conquest, violence.

He entered from the hall that led to his private chambers, swaying on his feet. His sleeves were rolled to his elbows, and the laces at the neck of his tunic were undone. Drops of sweat dotted his face, mixing with the streaks tears had left behind. How Flora thought Alia was the best person to reach him when he was like this was beyond Alia's understanding.

"You came," he observed, sounding neither pleased nor surprised.

"Not sure I had much of a choice." Alia fidgeted under his attention, knowing the scattered hours of rest on the couch had disrupted her plaits and wrinkled her skirts. "I'm sorry about your father."

"That bastard," he cursed, eyes roaming the room for something to break. "Do you want to know the last thing he said to me?"

Alia didn't want to know, didn't want to care. "It doesn't matter; it was just the ramblings of an old man."

"That he wished he could have given me more time to mature into a king," Cormac sputtered. "As if I haven't held the role for months. A better king already than he ever was. As if I wasn't already a better man than he'd ever be."

Alia murmured agreement, not the least bit astounded that King Isaac had no kind words for his son while on his deathbed.

"He was too far gone to even know we were attacked by the Oucura. He didn't even know where he was that day. And I'm the disappointment. I'm the one who isn't ready?"

"Cormac," Alia steadied him.

"You knew. You knew what he was like." His eyes, wild as a churning sea, fixed on her.

It was then that Alia understood why Flora had brought her here. Cormac was grasping, struggling to dull his grief. And at this moment, he wanted to hate his father. There was no one better to join him in that than Alia. She'd been tasked with bringing comfort to her captor, and they knew she would. She tried to tell herself that she was only complying to try to convince him to let go, but the urge to be close to him was stronger. "He was a tyrant."

"You threatened him when he caught us. You weren't afraid of him. You were never intimidated by anyone," Cormac said with a ghost of a smile on his lips.

She had a vague recollection of the king bursting into the bedchamber when they were young, furious to find them alone, and spewing all kinds of hatred at her. It paired well with Rheta's insult the day before. "I've never taken kindly to being called a whore."

"You're the bravest person I've ever known." Cormac's intensity made her pause.

Alia couldn't bring herself to tell him precisely how much bravery she lacked. "I'm sorry he's dead. I'm sorry he was never what you needed when he was alive." The feeling was all too familiar.

Cormac slouched against the side table, nearly knocking off a bottle of amber whiskey. "Why do I bother mourning him then?"

"You can still love him, even if he was complete shit."

His shoulders quivered, trying to shake off years of pain. "I always thought things would be different with him. And now ... there is no more time left for it to change."

"It wouldn't have. Do you really think I hope for Edgar or Mariana to change?"

"Would you like me to command them to?" The corner of Cormac's lips twitched.

"They're too far gone."

"Am I?" Cormac asked, reaching for her. He rubbed her lower lip with his thumb. "Am I too far gone?"

Her body was having trouble distinguishing between the past as it responded to Cormac's touch, craving more. Time stretched on as her reason abandoned her, knowing that it was she who was too far gone, unable to back away from the man she had loved. Her sister's husband. A man who only seemed interested in controlling her.

"Ali ..." Cormac's lips were in her hair. Alia didn't back away, savoring the feeling instead. Cormac's hungry mouth trailed down her neck as he pressed her against the wall. His body was heavy, and the rhythm of his heart was slow, too slow.

Alia's mind cleared long enough to realize something was wrong with Cormac. Her healing magic sensed it, like dark specs in every corner of his body, overcoming him.

"What did you do?" Alia questioned, but Cormac just nuzzled into her and leaned his weight on her even more.

By the time Alia managed to shift him enough to get him on the couch, Cormac could barely move. Alia flailed around the apartment for some hint of what might be ailing him. On his bedside table, there was a stack of tobacco papers, and beside them, something that certainly wasn't tobacco.

"Cormac," Alia cursed and returned to the barely conscious almost-king. "Wake up."

Cormac didn't move.

Panic set in. "Guard!" she screamed as loud as she could before a hacking sob took her breath away. She had already done this. She had already said goodbye to him once. "Guard!"

No one came.

Alia's hands were shaking as she tried to calm herself enough to channel her healing magic. She pinpointed every single tiny bit of the opiate in his system. She began removing it, pulling each dark spec from his bloodstream and into an empty glass. She started near his heart, working outward to remove the toxins. Her progress was slow; her magic slightly improved, but not strong enough.

"Someone, help me!"

Cormac looked like he had fallen asleep, his handsome features smoothed into a peaceful expression. Her energy was waning, and each bit took more strength to remove and more time. The pulse of Cormac's heart was slow, but constant.

"Guard!"

"I think he sent them away."

Alia picked out Dorian's voice, not taking the time to confirm he had flickered into the room. "Help him, please."

"I'm not a healer, Alia," Dorian said, his warmth reaching her like sunlight on her skin. "You are."

Dorian's influence bolstered her, her magic filtering Cormac's blood at a steady pace. With each extraction, the weight on Alia's chest lightened.

Once Cormac's heart was beating normally and his breathing even, Alia leaned back against the table, still sitting on the floor. She looked at the mage, who was standing at the door. "How did you hear me?"

"I felt you."

"How?"

"Sensing magic is one of my many affinities."

"Your many," Alia grumbled, feeling darkness creep into her vision, exhaustion taking her. "You must want to know why I'm here."

"I've heard the talk."

"Spare me your judgment."

"I'm not—" Dorian cleared his throat. "When will he wake?"

"I don't know."

"Is there something you can do to get him up?"

Alia glared up at Dorian. "I'm spent."

Dorian edged forward, the warmth he exuded growing stronger and spreading throughout her body to replenish her. His eyes were shadowed. "Please."

"Why?" Alia reached for Cormac's hand, sleep taking away the turmoil he'd been drowning in. "He needs this."

"We need him." Dorian sighed heavily. "He is the king of Mandal now. And there has been another incursion."

9

The midday tolls echoed as the council members shuffled into the stale chamber. Stewards flitted to light more of the mounted lanterns, banishing the persistent dark.

"Alia," Edgar summoned her to his side. He rested his hand on the back of her neck, wrapping his fingers around to press into her collarbone. The gesture could have been interpreted as comforting, but from Edgar, it was a tether. Alia tolerated it, entertaining herself with the prospect of breaking each of the fingers of the hand that had so often sought to keep her in line. And while her ability to breathe let her know that she was close enough to her emblem, she didn't know who held it.

Dorian finally trailed in, dazed. After Alia woke Cormac, she was dismissed to the council chamber while Dorian summoned the rest of the Council. He was fidgeting even more than usual, tapping each fingertip to his thumb, and repeating the gesture over and over.

The councilmembers took their places around the king's table. Lord Daniel Solreen spun his jeweled rings around as he waited. Lord Eamon Stanton fished his spectacles out of his pocket, focusing on the map on the table. Lord Tristan Palmer kept his distance as Jaremiah took his seat beside the head of the table. None of them trusted each other enough to even speculate about the reason they had been gathered.

Dorian sat opposite Jaremiah; Edgar guided her to sit in his seat. The arms of the chair reached the edge of the table, and with Edgar behind her, Alia was trapped.

Cormac trudged into the chamber with Harlan clinging to his shadow, hefting a large black bag. He had changed out of his dirtied tunic, donning one of crisp cerulean instead. A crown had been placed atop his head; he carried it as if it were weightless. “Council,” Cormac acknowledged.

“My king.” Jaremiah bowed deeply, leading the rest. Alia stayed confined to the chair but whispered the words.

Cormac appeared satisfied to be recognized as the king without question before a coronation could be performed. With a touch of strain, Harlan heaped the bag onto the table, tugging at the bottom to force its contents out onto the surface.

Alia tried to push away in disgust. Lying at its center, obscuring the map of Entien, was a carcass. It was an eagle, golden feathers dull in death. A spear had been thrust through its entire body, skewering it, with the sharp tip jutting out of its head. Its blood still dripped, the kill fresh.

“A coronation gift.” Cormac claimed the head chair. “From Queen Odessa. Left in my chancery.”

The councilmembers fell silent and still, gazes dragging from their king to the eagle’s crumpled body. Alia craned to look at Dorian, who was now standing back from the table, looking anywhere other than at Odessa’s grim message. Even from afar, Alia caught the wildness in the mage’s eyes.

Cormac rapped his ring on the table, echoing throughout the chamber. “The gift came with the threat of another incursion. And earlier today, Master Dorian detected just that. Veillant has long threatened our tenuous peace, testing every boundary we set. And now, right into the heart of Mandal.”

Veillant found a way through the veil.

Alia studied each of the councilmembers, seeing shock tighten to fury. A murderous fervor whipped across the table, feeding Cormac.

"There can be only one recourse," Cormac's tone was grim, but his eyes were bright and clear.

He wants this. He wants war.

"King Cormac," Lord Edgar said, thrusting his chest forward. "The might of the Meadors is at your command. Our forces and our forges have beaten back this enemy before, and we will do so again."

"The old leech will be made to answer for this." Jaremiah shook with anger. "I will fight until it is her head on this table."

Alia's gaze followed a fly as it found the eagle's unseeing eyes. There was still pain in those eyes, frozen in time at the point of its horrific death. This is what war would achieve; this is where it would lead them. She tuned out the oaths as they spun around, Harlan and his sword, Daniel and his ships, Eamon and his war plans, and Tristan and his whole brood of wind mages. Only Dorian declined an oath, still standing away from the table, looking wretched.

"Was there more to the message?" Dorian asked, voice wavering.

Cormac fished a folded paper from his pocket, spreading it onto the tabletop for all to see. "She demands the Spear of Orlast be delivered to her."

"They know that the Spear of Orlast is lost," Edgar said.

"An impossible task, an excuse to justify her attack," Harlan agreed.

Dorian grabbed the note, holding it close to his face as he read. "In Veillant, they believe the Spear of Orlast could be used to tear down the veil."

"What do you believe, Master Dorian?" Jaremiah glared.

"You could benefit from my knowledge or distrust it." Dorian's voice had more edge than usual. "Your choice."

"It matters not. We cannot allow a mortal kingdom to destroy our realm from within. We will gather our army, prepare our ships, and summon our allies to join our attack on the Isle of Veillant. The last attack." Cormac stood.

"Parth and Royce will have to side with Mandal." Eamon nodded in affirmation. "But we must tend to this incursion first."

"Agreed." Dorian's eyes were closed, his aura volatile. He drew a deep breath as if he were in pain. Alia tried to reach him with her healing magic, but couldn't find physical harm. She received a grateful glance from him, nonetheless. With a wave of Dorian's hand, the eagle carcass disappeared, and he leaned over the map of the realm. "Here."

Dorian identified the edge of the hinterland, not too far from Sheath, in the direction of the border with Royce.

"What is it?" Harlan asked.

"I won't know until I see it," Dorian said.

"Especially not if you're the one summoning it," Jaremiah muttered.

"It is a half-day's ride from where we stand," Cormac formed his plan. "Harlan will assemble a company of soldiers and send for the mages." The only indicator that he was the least bit uneasy was the bulging vein at his neck.

"Immediately, Your Highness," Harlan said.

"Wouldn't it be safer to wait here?" Jaremiah suggested. "Behind the palace walls?"

"We will ride out to meet it. Keep it away from Sheath."

Alia would have admired Cormac's instinct to protect the hinterland if not for his frothing bloodlust.

"What of the coronation?" Edgar asked. "Mandal needs to see its king before to goes to battle."

Cormac's fist tightened. She knew he had dreamt of this day. "Mandal needs its king to protect it. We can tend to crowns and titles when this threat is dealt with."

"I can go ahead and ..." Dorian trailed off, and Alia realized that the eyes of the men had turned to her.

"No." Alia tried to sink into the back of the chair. Venturing into the forest to face the next Otherworld beast was for these bloodthirsty fools. Not for her.

"I never knew Meadors to be cowards," Jaremiah said.

"Alia will accompany Master Dorian," Edgar assured Cormac. "She will fulfill her duty to Mandal."

"And what exactly do you expect me to do?" Alia folded her arms across her chest. She tried to summon some sort of loyalty to her home, to fake a deep connection, but it had been stamped out. They needed her to kill their enemies. But when the threat was over, she would be just another creature too dangerous to go free.

"There are others you could take, Master Dorian." Tristan regarded Dorian with malice. "Everyone should choose their own death."

Lord Tristan's attempt to align with her was feeble, far too late, but noted.

Cormac scowled before nodding to Dorian. "Lady Alia will go with you."

Edgar's hand went to the back of Alia's neck, daring her to protest. Mandal was supposed to provide safety for her and Lena, and it was about to be a kingdom at war with the Isle of Veillant, beset by the Otherworld.

"Lord Edgar, the guard will need orders in my absence," Harlan approached, putting his hand on Edgar's shoulder and leading him away to discuss the safety of the city.

She had to get away. In the shuffle of amassing soldiers and mages, surely there would be an opportunity. Identify who had the emblem, grab Lena, and start running.

The council meeting ended, lords rushing to their tasks.

"Lady Alia," Cormac called her back as the chamber emptied.

Alia paused, sending a bit of her own magic through her pounding head.

Once they were alone, Cormac drifted to position himself beside her. "I need to know. Are you with me?"

"With you?" Alia avoided looking at him.

"Mandal needs you. I need you." Cormac grasped her hand and made her turn towards him.

"I didn't know if you were going to wake up."

Cormac looked down, focusing on their intertwined hands. "You've always fought for me. And you killed the Oucura."

"You weren't there," Alia said. "You didn't see. We barely survived."

"But you did."

He didn't know how the Undoing barely heeded her, the risk he took each time he urged her to deploy it. "It was just one Alasaran; who is to say that my magic will have the same effect on another?"

"Ali." Cormac cupped her cheek with his palm. "We both will do as we must. Our people need us. Our ancestors sacrificed for this."

His touch was distracting, seeping into the fear that stoked her dissent. Her Meador ancestors failed to inspire her; their misdeeds were well known across the kingdom. As for the magic that lurked within her, it didn't even belong to her. But still she paused, considering Cormac's plea.

Am I with him?

"What will you do for me in return?" Alia challenged, even though she knew her position was tenuous.

Cormac's other hand went to her back, pulling her against him. "Your service to Mandal could justify your release in time."

Alia rested her head on his chest, feeling herself fall deeper into the trap she was in. Cormac rubbed her back, his comfort rewarding her compliance.

"And I need you to watch Dorian," Cormac said, lifting her chin.

"Watch Dorian?"

"Did you see his reaction to the eagle?"

Alia recalled how Dorian immediately stood up from the table and the sickly look he bore afterward. "He was horrified. He was as surprised as any of us that Odessa would be so bold."

"Our kingdom is the one threatened, and he had a stronger reaction than any other member of my council." Cormac rubbed his chin and shook his head. "It could have been an act."

Alia had done all that she could to think ill of Dorian, but now that Cormac was suggesting his treachery, she instinctively rejected it. Dorian had been the one to come to her side during the Oucura attack, the only reinforcement brave enough to risk it. If he had still been loyal to Veillant, he would have stood back and allowed them all to be slaughtered. Alia didn't want to believe Lena's only guide out of her predicament was looking to hand the mortal realm over to the Tiarcons. Cormac was seeing shadows in the dark of night. "Nonsense."

"Odessa's gift found its way to my private chancery, which I seal personally," Cormac said. "Who other than a powerful mage would be able to gain access? Who other than someone who has been there before? How did she learn of my father's death so quickly?"

"Any number of Tower mages, informants."

"You seemed determined to defend him." Cormac crowded her, making her take a few steps back, feeling caged in the small room. "You spend a lot of time with him."

"For Lena."

"Just watch him. If he'll divulge other motives, it'll be to you. I've seen the way he looks at you." Cormac's hand found her hip.

His mind was still clouded. "He only wants the Undoing."

"Are you with me?"

"Cormac, I am not—" Alia's protest was hushed when Cormac bent down, his breath on her neck sending shivers down her body.

Reflexively, she threaded her nails through his hair, resting her hand on the back of his neck. It was the encouragement he needed to press his lips along her collarbone, trailing up to her neck until she let out a small gasp. His lips turned bruising and frenzied as she slipped her other hand beneath his tunic, feeling her way across his muscled torso.

His hands roamed beneath her skirts, pulling her ever closer. When his lips reached her mouth, he paused there. "Ali, I need you with me," Cormac repeated, seeking surrender before taking her any further.

The order chased away Alia's desire long enough for her to feel the underlying unease. He thought he could placate her with kisses, capture her affection, and keep her close. She pushed back on his shoulders, startling him into stepping back. She smoothed her dress and took several measured breaths. "I should go fight your battle."

Cormac didn't prevent her from leaving the chamber.

Dorian was standing a few paces down the hallway, pretending not to track Alia's approach. He was still drawn, ailing from the revelation about Veillant. Or perhaps it was as Cormac said, and he just wanted to appear as such.

Alia did her best to slip indifference over her features, a barrier between her and the Veillanti. She fell into step beside him, putting distance between herself and any chance of running back to Cormac. "I trust Lena will be among your mages?" She'd rather drag Lena to a confrontation with the Otherworld than leave her with the beasts at the palace.

Dorian's twiddling fingers slowed. "She can be." He waited for Alia's affirmative nod. "She isn't ready for combat, but she can serve her fellow mages and learn from them."

"And you think I'm ready?"

"You have more experience with Alasar than the rest of my mages." Dorian deflated, his brow furrowing. "We need to stop at the Tower so I can give my orders."

Alia's stomach churned. "How about I go back to the Olden Wing, explain everything to Lena, and you can find me there?"

Dorian turned abruptly. "So you can run?"

He knew already. "You knew that there would be another incursion. You knew that the Veillant had betrayed mortalkind to the Otherworld. We should all be running, shouldn't we?"

"If Veillant has its way, there is nowhere in this realm that will be safe for you and Lena." Dorian pulled the emblem out of his robes. "If you want to go, I'll help you overcome the king's spell, but I'm asking you to come with me. To the Tower courtyard at least."

Alia turned away, curses pouring out. She could stomp and rail that she owed Mandal nothing, that they had no right to put any strain on her shoulders. That the Undoing was not the kind of darkness that saves, that it only brews more of the like. That the monster she had been made into was just as bad as what the Otherworld threatened. "The courtyard is fine."

Dorian hesitated. "You might want to heal yourself before."

"Heal?" Alia followed Dorian's gaze to her neck and clamped her hand over the marks that Cormac had left there. Her magic didn't lessen the burn on her cheeks.

The Tower courtyard materialized before her. Alia stared at the four stone spheres in the center, swinging in the sparse light. Each sphere represented a pillar of elemental magic. For hundreds of years, the spheres kept up a steady dance, swirling around each other, the iron cords weaving and unraveling. But now, all four swung towards the sea rather than connecting with each other. No ticking rhythm, just a haphazard swing, back and forth.

She'd heard whispers that Dorian was blamed for the disruption in the magical rhythm, but Alia was sure the decay of the Tower had started with Ruben. Leaving each form of magic to toil on its own.

Dorian had taken her to the central point and the practice yards surrounded her. There were features for each kind of elemental mage to practice their craft, pools for the water mages, stone walls for the earth mages, chimes for the air mages, and an inexhaustible number of things for the fire mages to combust. And rising above it all was a single basalt tower that was both a part of and separate from the gleaming limestone palace.

Alia kept her eyes on the spheres to stop herself from gazing at the Tower and remembering. She involuntarily grasped Dorian's arm, fastening her fingers to his forearm. Again, a warmth permeated her terror, soothing her and allowing her to bask in it. Alia opened her eyes to the sky, relieved to see a hint of light spanning across it, the harbinger of sunrise.

Dorian called his adepts to him, directing them to mobilize a section of mages while leaving others behind to defend the palace. A third of the Tower's standing warrior mages were to travel with the king, a substantial force.

When Alia pulled herself back to what was transpiring around her, most of Dorian's mages were eyeing her with distrust or open aggression. Rosalynn was chief among them, never turning her scowl from Alia.

Rosalynn leaned close so that only Alia could hear her, bringing the wind up around them to whisk her words away. "You may have ingratiated yourself to another Master Mage, but I know what you really are."

Alia released Dorian, preferring to stand on her own when it came to Rosalynn. "Is it wise to threaten an Undoing Mage?"

The adept had been Ruben's enforcer of order at the Tower, at his heels incessantly and all too eager to fulfill every one of his requests. Rosalynn had taken exception to the attention Alia had received, her private lessons from the Master Mage. But she was so intrusive, so ever-present that Alia had difficulty believing that Rosalynn was ignorant of Master Ruben's ways.

That he had been refining the inculcation by using it on Alia, subjecting her to his vile experiments.

"We can go see Lena now," Dorian broke in, reaching for her shoulders again.

Within moments, she was back in her quarters in the Olden Wing, Dorian steadying her as she adjusted to the abrupt travel. "Is everything well with Lady Rosalynn?"

"Mmhmm," Alia murmured, avoiding explanation.

"Mother?" Lena came out of her room.

"There's been another incursion. Dorian and I have to go now, but you'll come along with the other mages," Alia explained, trying to cast off the scourge of the Tower and avoid another argument with Lena.

"Madeline can explain where you should report to," Dorian added.

Lena looked between them. "I'm coming with you."

"Not yet," Alia said. "You're still learning."

"You haven't even started your lessons."

"Lena," Dorian laced his voice with authority. "You will lead plenty of offensives in your time, I am certain of it. But what is asked of you now is to aid your fellow mages."

Alia marveled at how quickly Lena softened at his words, the fuel for her rage exhausted. It sent a shiver of warning through her; if Lena came to trust Dorian and he proved to be loyal to Veillant, the girl would be devastated.

"Take care of her until I get there," Lena said to Dorian.

"Of course." Dorian bowed his head.

"Stay with Madeline," Alia added.

Lena stood back as Dorian readied to depart, arms folded and an odd glint in her eye. Alia tried to distinguish the novel expression as Lena stared back at her. It resembled pride.

Dorian flickered to the point where he had felt the disturbance in the veil, in the middle of the dense forest. It was quiet, almost tranquil. Alia took a deep breath, savoring the feeling of being out of the palace and holding onto the hope that, at least for a moment, her daughter had been proud of her.

"It's nearby," Dorian said, casting a glowing orb into the sky and spinning in a full circle to take in their surroundings. He moved slowly, intentionally, attuning his senses.

If an immortal was nearby, she shouldn't be here. Not to mention that if Dorian was indeed a traitor to Mandal, killing her would put the kingdom at the most risk.

"There's a tear in the veil where the Alasaran came to our realm." Dorian squinted upward.

"How did you feel it now, but not when the Oucura came through?"

Dorian's hands tightened into fists. "I did feel the Oucura. I just didn't know what it was. By the time I realized, it was already rampaging towards the palace."

Alia saw flashes of the villages she'd passed through, entire communities slaughtered, whether in the Oucura's hunger or their own madness. The knowledge that he might have been able to step in before the carnage must torture Dorian. Pushing him onward on this escapade, dragging her down with him.

"What does it feel like?"

"*Now* you want to talk." Dorian rubbed his temples. "Can you place a barrier while I look?"

Alia raised her arms, lifting a dome around them as Dorian took a meditation posture. If he were deceiving her and summoning the beast himself, the simple barrier would be her only defense. The reinforcements from the palace would be on their way by now and only hours behind them. But not in time to save her.

"Ah." Dorian finally opened his eyes and sprang to his feet. He crashed through the undergrowth, leaving Alia to scurry behind him.

A short walk later, Dorian stopped at a massive oak tree that reached to the sky. "Can you feel it?"

Alia didn't feel anything out of sorts. There certainly wasn't anything denoting a tear in the veil. "What should I be feeling?"

"It is right here. If we wanted to, we could walk through to Alasar," Dorian said with longing.

The thought of the Otherworld terrified her; she had seen enough of this realm not to want to venture into the evils of another. "You sound like you want to go."

Just like a Veillanti. Just like a traitor.

"You've never wondered?"

"I don't need to wonder. You would be just the latest in the long line of mortals to die at the Tiarcons' hands."

"You know, they didn't just kill every single mortal they saw. Some mortals served the Tiarcons willingly."

"Is that what you would do?"

"I might have." Dorian looked up to the sky. "I can hear the whispers."

"Whispers?"

Dorian flashed a smirk, which fell into a frown. "For a people tasked with protecting the veil, you know precious little about it. It is a void between the realms, Tribunal magic. Were you taught about mortal magic before the creation of Entien?"

"We didn't have any."

"Only what the Tiarcons loaned, to be returned once the purpose was fulfilled. And if the mortal died in the pursuit, the magic would revert to the Tiarcon."

It was a rosy explanation. Most of the stories Alia heard in her youth in Mandal had featured Tiarcons plying mortals with magic they could barely wield and sending them off to be slaughtered over a petty dispute. The magic wasn't so much given as it was thrust upon them to do the Tiarcon's will.

"But now, the veil prevents that magic from returning upon death."

"Good."

"That is what whispers to me. The magic that cannot return."

"Every mage ends up there?" Alia looked back up, imagining the veil, their protection.

"Just a piece."

"And now there's a tear."

"For me to fix." Dorian sat once more, muttering a spell, then his body gave off a golden glow. He cast off his robes, leaving only a plain tunic and breeches beneath. He pulled one sleeve up to his shoulder, revealing a series of markings just like the ones on his head. He swept one hand over his bicep, causing a small spark to ignite and cut its way through his arm, adding yet another mark.

Alia set aside her suspicions and moved forward to heal him, to close the cut and erase the scar.

He stopped her, holding up his hand. "I need to remember."

"Remember what?"

Dorian turned his back. "What I leave behind, what I've done." He raised his hands as the blood dripped down his arm. The sky above rippled, like it was a lake with raindrops falling up into it, creating a swirl of color. A golden light came from Dorian, filling in a place in the sky that hadn't lit up. Filling the gap, repairing the tear.

When he dropped his hands, Alia kept her eyes on the sky until the colors faded. "That's it?"

"I am Mandal's Master Mage for a reason." Dorian brushed a leaf off his shoulder. He donned his robes once more, the blood on his arm forgotten. "It takes high magic to do a binding spell like that. Lena will be able to one day."

"What are your affinities?"

"Sensing and seeing magic to start. But I can give you a full accounting another time." Dorian took off at a brisk pace through the underbrush. "Now, there is a community nearby that we must fortify."

"How do you know that?" Alia stomped through the undergrowth. She found it peculiar that Dorian was so well-acquainted with his surroundings, as if he had picked this very spot.

"If you bothered to practice meditation, you would know how it can heighten your senses. I heard them. Come on."

Dorian reached out, waiting for her to take his hand before flickering to the village. Outside of the forest canopy, the sun cast shadows, each one looking like a potential attacker to Alia as she broke away from the mage. The bustling villagers barely noticed the new arrivals.

Dorian looked around in alarm. “We need to get them inside their homes.”

“I can do that.” At this time of day, the villagers were hard at work in the fields or in the forest, but they shouldn’t stray far.

“I’ll place a barricade around the dwellings.” Dorian tensed in preparation to flicker. “I’ll need to set anchors along the perimeter.”

“You’re going to let me out of your sight?” Alia raised an eyebrow. “What about the emblem?” Dorian was either being reckless or trying to slip away from her.

“We established I wasn’t going to keep you anywhere you didn’t want to be.” Dorian smoothed his hair as the breeze ruffled it. With a flourish of his hand, the emblem, still encased in gold fabric, bobbed in the air beside her. “I haven’t figured a way to sever the connection completely, but it’ll stay with you, unseen.”

“How?”

“A shift,” Dorian said. “A space, unseen, but tied to you.”

Another twitch and the emblem vanished without harming her. Her shackles were removed. Gratitude surged through her; she no longer cared if Dorian was loyal to Mandal or not.

“Dorian,” Alia took his hands in hers. “Let’s leave.”

“Leave?”

“You can sense Lena, can’t you? Flicker to her, and then we can go. Leave Veillant and Mandal and let them wage their war.”

“Something is coming—”

“It is not our concern.” Alia tempered her fear, trying to appear resolute. “You promised.”

Extricating his hands from hers, Dorian took a step back. “I promised I would help you get away from Mandal. And I will if that is what you want. But I—I have to come back."

"You'll die."

He scratched the back of his neck. "Without you? Probably."

"You'd let me go and still come back, knowing you can't fight it?" The master mage must be the most idiotic man she'd ever met.

His fingers danced their pattern. "Believe me, I know how foolish this sounds."

"They don't deserve your sacrifice." Cormac didn't even think he was loyal.

"But perhaps it's the end I deserve."

"No one gets the end they deserve," Alia said. The powerful persisted, and everyone else suffocated beneath them. "You betrayed your kingdom, and so have I. But maybe it is because they aren't worth being loyal to, they aren't worth saving."

Defeat weighed on his shoulders. "I'll help you, but my reasons to return are my own."

"Take me to Lena. Then take us to Parth's southern border." Go north, just as Lena had wanted to when they arrived in Sheath.

Dorian drooped, as if the last bit of nerve keeping him upright withered. He looked so wretched that leaving him behind felt callous. Callous, but necessary.

"I'll take you to Lena, then Idrium." He reached out.

But his hand never touched hers.

A heaviness descended, a feeling of discord. Alia searched the treeline, trying to spot the attacker. A pulsing current sliced through the air, clashes echoing in Alia's head.

An aura of chaos.

The figure who emerged from the trees was just a man: a conspicuous, spindly figure in sunflower-colored robes moving toward them with unexpected grace. His light gray eyes would have been mesmerizing, were they not sunken and laced with red streaks. An extensive band of tattoos wrapped from his temples down around the base of his head, his pale hair cropped close. His magic was impossible to read, as his aura had been shattered into shards. But everything about him screamed Veillanti.

As he approached, Alia looked to Dorian to handle him. But Dorian was frozen beside her, a statue not even drawing breath, as if, for him, time had stopped altogether.

"*Master* Dorian found himself at least one capable mage," the man spat Dorian's title like a curse.

"And what would that make you?" Alia demanded. While Dorian projected warmth, this mage plunged her into an inferno.

"Merely a spectator," he said, gaunt cheeks tightening into a grin. "To Mandal's glorious demise."

"You're trespassing, Veillanti." Alia stepped into her threat, trying not to think of what it meant for a Veillanti mage to appear and render Dorian useless.

"What kind of mage are you?"

Beside her, Dorian was moving ever so slowly; he was beginning to break through the spell.

"I'm not a mage," Alia stalled, giving Dorian time.

The cruel smiled persisted as the new mage brought his palms to his chest before pushing them outward, then shooting black shadows directly at her. Alia lifted her hands, the Undoing bursting forward. The mist extended before her and devoured the shadows, knocking the mage back.

She looked to Dorian for help. His fingers twitched slightly; he was almost free.

The Veillanti mage laughed, a nightmarish chuckle, blood-curdling and pitched. "An Undoing Mage." The Veillanti savored each word, crossing the field. "How I've longed to find one of you."

The closer he got, the more he overwhelmed Alia's senses. Her ears were filled with a high-pitched whine, and the air seemed too thin.

With a yell, Dorian heaved a torrent of fire at the man. The mage easily blocked Dorian's attack, still grinning madly. "I see you've found another for me, Dorian. Well done."

Dorian's skin was aflame, his entire being consumed as he advanced on the Veillanti while the older mage cackled. Alia shielded herself, knowing this was one fight that didn't need the Undoing's volatility.

"Get away from her, Vincent." Malice spiked from Dorian's words as the fire spread. The marks on his head seemed to spark, growing more prominent as he fought.

"Haven't you learned not to interfere?" Vincent gathered shadows. "Did you enjoy my gift?"

Dorian launched fire, uncontrolled and scorching. Flames jumped to the trees. Cormac had called the skewered eagle a coronation gift from Queen Odessa, but perhaps it had another meaning for Dorian. "I won't let you kill anyone else."

Vincent came closer to where Alia sheltered, shadows pushing Dorian back.

"Come on, Dorian." Vincent's predatory grin was back. "Just one more. Hold her still for me, keep her calm. You're good at that."

Vincent held an amulet the size of his palm up in the light from Dorian's flames. Its edges were clawed, like pointed teeth. The mage sent a torrent of darkness towards Alia, knocking her onto her back, pressing her into the grass. She couldn't move, couldn't shield herself, as the force of Vincent's magic was too much. Screams tore out of her, the memories of inculcation sending her into a panic. The shadows rendered her helpless, preventing movement too similar to the way Ruben had commanded her limbs.

Vincent raised the amulet, hovering over her chest. Flame rippled; Dorian flickered to her side.

In a short jump, he flickered them to the shadow of the village cottages. "Stay, please, this is my fault." Dorian didn't stay to hear her agree, but the earnestness in his plea made her obey anyway.

There were clashes once more at the far end of the village, but Alia was only able to see the remnants of magic in the air as she tried to catch her breath. She wrapped her arms around herself; she could move, she was in control.

Until storm clouds began to swirl.

Alia broke into a run, the distinct magic pulling her in.

A whirlwind pinned Vincent's arms down at his sides, preventing him from attacking. Vincent cursed and struggled against the torrent. And it was Lena who emerged from the trees, hands outstretched.

Lena's whirlwind was precise, a level of focus that Alia hadn't seen her accomplish before. A strange mix of joy and terror overtook her.

Alia sent the Undoing to join the whirlwind which was picking Vincent apart. The mage tried to defend himself, but his shadows were swallowed by Dorian's light.

Confronted by the loss of his advantage, Vincent disappeared.

"I had him," Lena cried out in frustration.

"How are you here?" Alia asked.

Lena's cheeks burned. "I flickered. Just a little bit at a time."

And she'd managed her magic without devolving into an outburst. As much as Alia wanted to scold her, she held back. "Dorian," Alia gritted out his name.

He raised his arms and raised a barrier over them, covering the entire village.

"Who was that?" Lena demanded.

But the shadows in Dorian's eyes hadn't dissipated with Vincent's departure. They clung, deepening as Dorian bent to one knee.

"What happened?" Lena asked, her tone soft this time, looking at Alia.

Alia shook her head slightly, squeezing Lena's hand to reassure her before standing beside Dorian. "We were attacked. He's gone."

Dorian's chest heaved and caved in. "You don't understand. He isn't going to stop." He was shaking, clearly suffering a shattering pain that Alia recognized all too well. After wiping the tears from his eyes, Dorian regained his feet. "Idrium?" He offered his palms.

"What about Idrium?" Lena asked.

Running had flown from her mind. Weakness infected her, rage spurred by Vincent, by the anguish Dorian obviously carried.

"Vincent," Alia said. "He's the one doing all this? Tearing the veil? He's the one who imprisoned you?"

Dorian hung his head in confirmation.

It wasn't love for Mandal or care for her countrymen that kept her there. It was the knowledge that there was another mage out there who could overpower her, another who could make her helpless. And that, she couldn't allow.

"We need to warn the villagers then."

"We?" Dorian asked in shock.

Seeds of regret sprouted. "Yes. Lena?"

They turned their attention to the villagers. It was difficult not to look at them and see their family as they had been in Dihlmere. They walked down the path leading between the cottages, singling out a villager with a sword at his hip.

"May the sun stay high." Alia showed empty palms.

His hand tightened on his hilt before he spat at her feet. The villager likely wasn't a swordsman by trade; this was a performance. If Dihlmere had contained more fighters, perhaps it would be more than just ash.

"What do you call this place?" Lena's question was born out of true curiosity, her tone also admiring.

"Wrendlin."

"Do you have a haven?" Lena asked. Dihlmere had one, a location where the vulnerable were to gather at the first sign of threat. Theirs had been the first dwelling to burn.

The villager nodded.

"Use it. Danger in the forest." Lena spoke with authority.

The man scowled. "What kind of danger?"

"The Otherworld," Alia snapped. It would be easier for them to believe once the soldiers and mages draped in the Barton crest arrived. But she would have to be convincing enough. "Get to the haven."

Alia grabbed for his wrist to make a demonstration of the Undoing, but Lena pushed her away. Instead, Lena gathered garnet light in her hand, making his mouth part in a gasp rather than a scream.

It was effective; the man sent Wrendlin's inhabitants running to gather the last materials they would need and call others in from the fields and the river. When the activity settled a bit, Alia felt Dorian's protective dome settle around the village once more, stretching from one end of the clearing to another.

He joined them once the village quieted, tapping each finger to his thumbs in succession. "I hope we're enough."

"Enough?"

"To stop them."

Alia drew back, startled by Dorian's doubt. She studied his features, wondering if this was a deceptive ploy or if Dorian happened to be the most earnest inhabitant the palace of Mandal would ever have. "You know more about Alasar than anyone. If we all die, at least you gave us our best chance."

Dorian winced. "At least I've taught you to call Alasar by its proper name."

"If nothing else."

Mages and soldiers worked in units, fanning through the forest in search of the Alasaran under Dorian's command. A small contingent stayed near the village, which had quickly become the main camp. Thankfully, Lena was assigned to the second group, allowing Alia to watch over her.

Lena ran from post to post, flickering a foot or two at a time to deliver supplies. Madeline often ran beside her, making sure the mage and soldiers were well-equipped with arrows and spears. The Truath girl even tried to offer Alia a bow and quiver at one point, which she immediately declined. She'd more likely shoot herself in the foot than deal a blow to the enemy.

When trickles of soldiers began to return to the safety of the village with burns and wounds, Alia wrung her hands. They were ushered to the healers at the center of camp, their panicked voices carrying past those standing guard. Tales of a hulking beast with four heads.

A Traimine.

The beast had been depicted in Dorian's books; several creatures spliced together. It was rumored to be one of the Tiarcon of the Sea's experiments; she was known to create beings from carcasses, making them as powerful and ruthless as the Tiarcon herself.

"Undoing Mage!" a mage cried out to her from across the small stream. "North!"

It was innerving, feeling the creature's approach. The beast had four heads in all, its snouts smoking. Each head had a different likeness: tiger, boar, snake, and wolf. And from it came the same power the Oucura wielded, magic bursting outward through the ground, crackling through air and making everything else bend around it.

"Don't let it bite!" Dorian yelled at the advancing mages.

She tried to remember the danger of the Traimine's bite, memory hazy as it moved closer to Dorian's barrier. But an overzealous young mage stepped behind the barrier, wielding ice. The ice caught the snake's head, but the creature spun, and the boar's teeth closed on the man's forearm. His screams echoed, even after the boar let go and left him behind.

Alia couldn't look away from the fallen mage as his body shivered and crumpled. His form twisted, bones reforming, until a boar stood in mage robes. Whichever species of head dealt the bite, the victim would become.

She had no intention of spending the rest of her days crawling and snarling.

Whether imbued by bravery, duty, or pure stupidity, other mages stepped forward to tackle the beast, their attempts bouncing off the beast's thick pelt. It was as protected as the Traimine's legs, which were neither fur nor scales but somehow both. Thankfully, the others were drawing the ire of four jaws. Elemental magic did nothing to slow its progress, leaving mages scrambling out of the way as it slammed against Dorian's barrier.

It wouldn't hold.

The Undoing was there; it was always there. It itched, scratching its way out. Alia endured the revolting sensation, delaying it. She'd given up her chance to flee, and in doing so had committed herself to this path.

Alia let go. It was even easier this time, an instinctive unfurling of what she kept tightly wrapped, starved, and denied. There was more than enough anger to sustain it. Alia fed the Undoing darkness, the fury that she endeavored to keep caged beneath the surface. It was the shroud she liked to cast around herself, to hold herself in. Mist curled around her fingers, clawing across the grass to where the Traimine prowled.

It took focus to keep the Undoing away from the other mages. It crowded Alia's sight with ghostly outlines, maps of injuries that the sought Undoing to exploit, healing to be reversed, parts to be unmade. The Undoing wasn't spread too thin by multiple targets; it was delighted.

But Alia maintained the path, and the Undoing remained an extension of her, obeying her silent orders.

The Undoing was gone; she was free of it. It was no longer torturing her, but was off to become a threat to everyone else. It billowed around the Traimine, leaving a blissful emptiness behind.

The Traimine raged, shredding Dorian's barrier with teeth and claws. Heat reached her; she locked eyes with Dorian over the beast's writhing heads. He advanced, sparing the other mages the burden of battling the Traimine, his magic outpacing the rest. He bore the brunt of all four heads, whips of light lashing out from his hands and catching at their throats. He thrust the whips into the ground, anchoring the Traimine in place. For a moment, Alia watched him in awe, the entire clearing quaking with his power.

Mandal's Master Mage for a reason, indeed.

With the Traimine leashed to the ground, Alia moved forward through the remnants of the barrier. She could feel the wrongness of it, a mismatch of beasts crudely forced together. The Undoing mapped out each seam, where fur met scale, broken patterns and forced joining.

The mist of the Undoing gathered at each juncture.

The Traimine began to scream with all four mouths. With renewed vigor, Mandal's mages joined and reinforced the attack with weapons of their own. The Traimine's snake was doused in wave after wave of water, vines snaked around the snout of the boar, fire berated the snarling tiger, and the wolf was hacking for air. Mist burned up Alia's arms as she fought to leash the Undoing, the strain holding her wholly focused on the Traimine.

The Traimine was made for the Undoing to dismantle. It was poised to tear the beast's back apart, outpacing Alia's will as she continued to sustain it. Her skin began to burst, like invisible worms eating through her flesh, before it reformed in their wake. She wouldn't be able to push the Undoing for much longer before she was entirely consumed.

Urgency faded when a hand seized Alia's throat. Rosalynn's flat eyes wavered before her, narrowing as the mage's hand tightened. As an elemental mage with an affinity for air, Rosalynn was uniquely skilled at taking the breath from Alia's lungs.

Alia croaked and fumbled, the Undoing responding of its own accord. A festering burn erupted on the side of Rosalynn's face, making her drop her attack.

"The Traimine—" Alia tried to refocus Rosalynn's rage once she could breathe.

"Justice." Rosalynn didn't turn away.

Now free of the Undoing, the Traimine's surge of strength broke through Dorian's whips and gored several mages, Rosalynn's comrades.

Not that the mage even noticed, as she again grasped for Alia's throat. The mages transformed, beasts writhing in robes.

Alia shuffled out of Rosalynn's reach, wondering if she could chance weakening the mage with the Undoing without killing her. Killing a mage of the Tower would be met with punishment, and confinement would no longer be enough.

"You found out about the others, didn't you?" Rosalynn asked, trying to whisk the Undoing away with wind. "Found out that you weren't special."

"What are you talking about?" Alia struggled to hold back the Undoing as it desperately fought her to tear Rosalynn to pieces. It took even more effort to convince herself that she should hold it back at all.

"You thought you were the only one Ruben wanted," Rosalynn said.

"He's dead." She had known of Rosalynn's loyalty, expected her jealousy, but the fact that she could ever think that Alia had desired anything from Ruben in return was maddening.

Rosalynn was more than ten years older than Alia and trained by Ruben himself, raised to take the helm of the Tower. Her aspirations had waned with Ruben's health.

But with every wound the Undoing found, each burn, Alia recognized the same pattern. A realization struck Alia as viciously as Rosalynn's squall. Rosalynn had been molded, inculcated. She had suffered, just as Alia suffered. She hadn't had a choice before that monster got his hands on her mind.

"There can't be justice, not for us." Because it can't be undone, it couldn't be adequately healed. Ruben changed them, made them. And now they had to live.

"This is all I need, all the Queen needs." Rosalynn's fingers found her throat again. "The Undoing Mage won't survive the battle. Not with a trampled, crushed windpipe. And I will bring down the Traimine myself."

Alia searched for help, but the soldiers and mages had retreated in the wake of the Traimine's last attack. Dorian was struggling to keep the Traimine contained and away from the village. Alia heard him calling for her, but she could not respond. Rosalynn had whisked her into the trees, obscuring them from view as the Traimine charged at the barrier.

"For Ruben." Rosalynn's elemental magic tore through Alia. Her lungs screamed as her windpipe collapsed.

Alia rasped, the fight for breath blotting out everything else. Alia fell on her back, flailing for air. Her Undoing returned in full, coming back to its injured host, unfettered as she succumbed to her injuries. Even as she filled back up with its inky power, she feared it was not enough to stop the death coming for her.

Rosalynn's chest deflated; her rage seemed to desert her as she took in Alia's haggard rasps. The look in her eyes was reminiscent of how Alia had felt when released from inculcation, studying her fingers to see if they obeyed, holding her arms around her waist to prove she could shield herself. Ruben was gone, but he was still the one dictating Rosalynn's movements, his influence guiding her thoughts.

The trees trembled; the Traimine had turned its attention to the pair, bursting between trunks. A sensation of healing tickled her throat, a bit of the passageway opening and allowing a shallow intake of air. Alia lifted her hand, sending the Undoing back out. She spread her fingers, her arms nearly dissolved by the strain of high magic ravaging her mortal frame. Alia bent her fingers into fists, seeking to impose her will over the primitive desire of the dark mist, to seek out life to destroy.

The Traimine batted the dazed Rosalynn, knocking her to the ground with such force that she crumpled beside Alia. This couldn't be Rosalynn's last act, driven to murder by the lasting influence of that sadist. There had to be more to Rosalynn's life than killing in Ruben's name.

There had to be more to Alia's life, too. More than the Undoing.

The Undoing penetrated the Traimine once more, tearing at the pieces of the creature that had been stitched together. It swiftly lopped off the tiger's head. The clawed paw was next before all four pieces of the beast separated, still snapping and snarling.

The Undoing, still pouring out of Alia, scattered over the fallen Traimine. She tried to take deep breaths and call back to it, to urge the darkness to return, but her attempts were insufficient. She didn't want the Undoing; she didn't want to feel it and didn't want it to exist within her anymore. Even if she only had a short while left.

Then she heard it—a forlorn cry that she would never be immune to. Alia would have given her last breaths to take Lena's pain, but it was those same scant gasps that caused it. The tree quaked; Lena unleashed herself on Rosalynn as the mage lay beside Alia.

No, Lena.

The mage cowered to protect herself, as Lena's eyes glowed in anguish. Alia could feel the heat even as she lay gasping. Lena formed a cocoon around the two of them, the forest shaking.

Lena tried to pull Alia upright as her body fought for air. The sky overhead had darkened and rain began to fall around them. Alia felt a familiar pull as she recognized that Lena was attempting to heal, though it was not magic she was attuned to. The pain in Alia's throat lessened, but the burning from Lena's touch exploded. The Undoing returned once more, curving its way through Lena's whirlwind to take its place once again within her, stemming the feeling of slipping away. It was a kindness, or a symptom of just how close she was to death, that the Undoing did not demand its due. It returned, without torturing her.

Healing, rather than trying to kill her.

"Back away, Lena." Dorian appeared through the tumult, bathed in grime. Still, the sunlight streaming from him cut through Lena's storm. Calm wrapped around Alia. "Lena, you're hurting her."

Alia had never seen Lena regain self-awareness during an outburst. She flinched at Dorian's words, then lifted her hands and turned towards him. "That's it, like we practiced," Dorian soothed. The pelting rain subsided as Lena fell to her knees.

Dorian bent and placed his hand on Alia, fright edging into his tone. "I need a healer."

Armored men joined them in the trees, hacking away at the pieces of the still-breathing immortal. Harlan thrust his sword through the wolf's eye, Cormac scorched the tiger beyond recognition, and another man, one so familiar to Alia, tore the boar's head from its neck.

It was Lena who stamped out the snake, garnet light filling the head until it exploded, spewing blood and scales across the clearing.

Alia's lungs inflated with a deep breath, her body healing itself.

"So that is the Undoing," Cormac said, standing over her and looking at the hacked pile the Traimine had become.

In full armor, he was almost unrecognizable to Alia. And he was looking at her with the same emotion, as if he had never seen her before. He had heard of what she was capable of, but he had never seen it himself. Cormac took her from Dorian, lifting her up.

"I thought I—" Lena sputtered.

"Lena," Alia said with rasping breath. But her daughter had already stalked off, and she didn't have the strength to wrench herself from Cormac's arms.

"Rest," Cormac said, bracing her back.

"Help her," Alia murmured, meeting Dorian's gaze.

"I will," Dorian promised as Cormac, Harlan, and the third man obscured him from view.

IO

Cormac claimed victory, ordering the remnants of all four heads of the Traimine to be carried back to Mandal and sent to Odessa. The Mandals combed the forest for any other signs of Alasarans, wanting to be certain that no other creature had made it through the tear in the veil. The bulk of Mandal's mages and soldiers camped in the village to rest before the ride back to the palace. With Dorian preoccupied with hunting down and trying to revive the mages who had been transformed by the Traimine's bite, Alia stayed as well.

Alia was weak from the day before and now sore from the ordeal with Rosalynn. The disgraced mage was on her way back to the palace already, in bonds that Dorian had fashioned himself. As she sat now, hatred for Rosalynn was shockingly absent. Instead, her emotions bounced between betrayal and pity. Rosalynn hadn't broken free of Ruben, and she might never.

Persistent fantasies swirled: what could have been different if Rosalynn had stepped in between her and Ruben. If anyone had stepped in for her.

Bruises still covered every inch of Alia's body, her skin seemed stretched too tight, and her head felt too heavy to keep up. She bent her forehead to her knees, willing away the regret that if just one person had intervened, she might have been spared.

"The Alia Meador I knew would never deign to sleep on the ground."

She lifted her head slightly. A tall, well-built man, clothed in Mandal armor, stood before her. The same man who had dealt the boar the killing blow. His mussed black hair and dimples were unmistakable.

Lord Baldric Cole.

"That Alia had shame."

"Look at you. I never—" Guilt flashed across Baldric's fair face as he pressed his lips together.

"I never expected to see you again either."

Baldric frowned, and his fingertips brushed Alia's hand. "I'm sorry I didn't come see you earlier."

"Harlan said you were at the border?"

Baldric sat beside her and began removing pieces of his armor. "Cormac called all of us soldiers back." From the intensity of his green-flecked eyes, he wasn't too happy about the decision.

"You became one after all." When he was younger, Baldric had been in danger of being thrown out of training at the palace. He had never been able to resist a fight, even with his superiors. Alia had sat with him for countless hours as he toiled and trained, especially when he redirected his destructiveness to fights in the city streets, a welcome distraction from her obligations at the Tower.

"What else could I have been?" Baldric said, piling his armor beside him. "Not everyone can escape like you did."

"What have I missed?"

Baldric snorted. "Nothing." He pulled a small bottle of whiskey out of his pocket and took a drink. "Flora is an insufferable busybody, Cormac gets pricklier every second, and Harlan ... " Baldric paused. "I guess Harlan ended up having a bit more backbone than I thought. Just a bit, though. George being gone is the only thing that changed, fucking

Veillanti ambush."

Alia gave him a mournful look. "And you?"

"I'm the same miserable bastard as when you left." Baldric took another drink and offered it to Alia. "But you. You're some new kind of bleak, aren't you? Who will be there to talk me down now?"

Alia drank. "You never listened to me before."

"What happened to you, Ali?" Baldric's voice was raw as he grasped her hand. Alia didn't have an answer she was willing to give him.

He didn't wait for an answer. "Harlan told me that Cormac is forcing you to stay. Prick. The best thing about you leaving was getting away from him."

Alia looked at the fire to avoid disagreeing.

Baldric hacked a laugh. "You're still caught up on him? Even after he married Elowen, of all people?"

Alia lightly smacked his shoulder. "And this is what I come back to after all these years?"

Baldric scowled in response.

"Now, this is where I need to be," Harlan said as he snatched the whiskey out of Baldric's hand and joined them by the fire. "My ass is going to be sore for days from that ride."

"Maybe Cormac could kiss it better, change things up," Baldric grumbled.

"But then what would you do?" Harlan asked. They stood and sparred, taking lazy swipes at each other.

Cormac shook his head as he approached. "Imbeciles."

"Congratulations on your victory, Your Highness." Harlan stopped swinging long enough to take an exaggerated bow.

"Things unfolded as expected." Cormac was cloaked in arrogance as his attention settled on Alia. "I'm glad you've recovered."

Recovery was a tricky term.

To avoid Cormac, Alia turned toward the next fire where a group of mages sat. Lena was among them, her back set decidedly towards Alia. She had been keeping her distance from Alia since her outburst. Lena had been angry with Alia many times before, but Alia always knew there would be a time when it was just the two of them on the road. Lena would eventually opt to talk to her rather than to no one at all. But that was no longer a certainty. And this time, Alia had no idea why Lena's anger was being directed at her.

Lena was talking to Madeline and another mage roughly her age. Alia heard her daughter laugh and knew that the sound should make her happy. It only left Alia terrified.

Alia found herself in possession of the whiskey once more. "To George," she toasted and took a long draw. The three men around the fire murmured the same with shadowed eyes.

Over at the mages' fire, they had begun to play a game of sorts, conjuring the smoke and sparks from the fire into shapes and faces.

Dorian walked up to their fire, bowing his head to Cormac. "Your Highness, the last sweep was uneventful. All the changed are accounted for."

"Thank you, Master Dorian."

Even in the dark, Alia could see lines of exhaustion on Dorian's face. He was injured from his bout with the Traimine, or from trying to capture his mages. He would be the type to be too noble to ask for help from one of the healers, not wanting to burden anyone else.

"Dorian, wait." Alia stood up and followed him a few paces from the fire. She placed both of her hands around his so he couldn't yank them away from her. In a couple of moments, his physical ailments were gone. Healing Dorian disrupted addressing her own ailments, but he had earned it.

"You didn't have to—thank you," Dorian said once she had finished. "I see your healing talents have suddenly returned."

"They have." She raised her eyebrows. "What do you know about it?"

"I know when you suppress part of yourself, everything suffers."

"That's—" Alia bit her lip, staring into the dark rather than at the mage who knew too much. In refusing the wield the Undoing, she was stifling her healing magic. Ruben had told her otherwise, that the Undoing would take root and destroy everything within her.

She could heal again; she could do something other than hurt. Alia took in Dorian with narrowed eyes; he'd known. Since their first meeting, he had known. And he let her find it on her own.

"I guess you were enough."

"We were. Thank you." Dorian offered her a weak smile, looking over her head to where Cormac sat, keeping him from saying more. "I should take it back. Unless..."

The emblem, which had stayed tucked into the unseen shift. Where it would stay if Alia intended to flee Mandal lands. But if she stayed, Dorian had to reclaim it; Cormac would expect him to return it.

The mage waited until Alia gave a nod of ascent before recalling the emblem.

"Vincent ..." she began.

Dorian's aura pulsed like a wound, sapping all warmth from the air.

"What is he? What did he try to do?"

This time it was Dorian who evaded her questions, eyes dulling with guilt. "Lena is taking a turn." He shifted his attention to the mages' fire.

After considering pressing him, Alia allowed him to escape and followed his gaze. "What is this?"

"Torch-telling. Shaping a tale with fire and smoke. It is an exercise to improve precision and control."

"A Veillanti exercise?"

Wistfulness parted his lips, a sigh slipping through.

"Should she be using her magic so soon after...?"

"It is important for her. She has to learn to trust herself, to learn control. It is not good for her to dwell on what happened." His gaze lingered on Alia too long, like he intended his words to hold meaning for her as well.

"Is that why she won't speak to me?" As much as Alia hated asking the mage about her own daughter, she desperately wanted to know.

"She blames herself for losing control."

It tore at Alia to know that Lena had any guilt over the outburst, as Alia certainly didn't blame her. She knew the feeling intimately, the panic and powerlessness of not being in control of her own body. Alia had never wanted that for her daughter.

Alia watched as the shapes Lena conjured were beginning to look identifiable, drawing the attention of the mages and warriors alike. Lena made Dihlmere, a village not too dissimilar from the one they were camped in. A row of cottages backed up to towering trees, with the river running through the center of town. And at the end of the row stood their cottage. Lena even managed to put the likeness of Alia, Finn, her six-year-old self, and their massive hound, Tesira, at the front.

Alia couldn't look away as Lena told her silent tale. The family, arms draped around each other. The daughter clinging to her father's arm, drawing out a lightness from him that only she could. The mother, straight-backed, clutching to the doorway of the cottage as the rest paraded off to the field.

And then Lena darkened the smoke, signaling the arrival of men with swords and fire. Suddenly, the quaint cottages were in flames, and the family was running. Once they were in the safety of the trees, the father split off and went toward a burning cottage to help others escape, trailed by his loyal dog. But as soon as they disappeared inside, the roof caved in, and they were gone.

Lena showed the image of the mother holding the child's hand and running. As they ran, Lena grew bigger until she was running on her own. Always running, never able to find a safe place to rest. Lena led the two figures to a halt before an intricate recreation of Mandal's palace. There they stopped; Lena's story ended.

Dorian placed his hand on Alia's shoulder. Alia shrugged it off and trudged back to her fire, where she snatched the whiskey from Harlan and settled back down. She could feel her three friends staring at her, unsure of what to say.

Baldric reclaimed the bottle from her. "To your husband." He took a drink.

"To Finn," Alia repeated. Even Cormac joined in the toast.

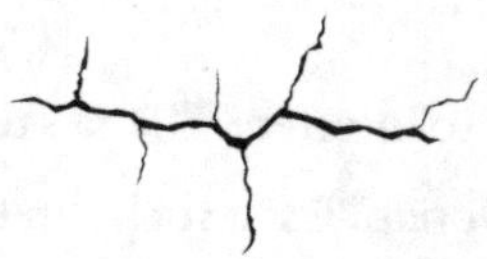

Figures of smoke lingered in Alia's mind all the way back to the palace. Lena's tale exposed what Alia preferred to deny: the memories she buried deeper with each year. And a truth that burned as if it had been shaped from the flames: the only thing Alia had taught her daughter was how to run.

Lena's magic drowned the balcony, reaching Alia where the railing met the cliff. Alia tried to find meaning in the feel of Lena's power. It wasn't the sinister creep of the Undoing or the crush of chaos. Rather, it flowed into everything, jolting life even into stone. It was reminiscent of the piercing power that had illuminated Dihlmere's destruction for only a moment. The power Alia wished had died with Finn.

Lena dropped the garnet sheet that had begun to expand far beyond their domain. "I'd like to work on healing."

Dorian risked a glance at Alia, noting her sharp opposition with a nod. "It is a difficult skill to master without an affinity. I've never managed it."

Alia remembered the litany of scars cut into Dorian's arm, hidden beneath his robes. The ones that he preserved with purpose, wanting to remember.

"I want to learn," Lena insisted.

"Well." Dorian sighed. "The simplest way to learn how to heal is to—"

"No." The tenuous tolerance Dorian had earned snapped. Alia knew which method produced the best results; she'd suffered it. "Don't you dare touch her."

Dorian flinched as Alia inserted herself between her daughter and the mage.

"You are not supposed to interfere." Lena's temper buzzed behind her. Alia stayed focused on Dorian, lest a spell slip from his lips.

"I would never." Dorian kept his hands low, backing away from them.

Alia drew back, her heartbeat thrumming as she exhaled. She expected resistance, for Dorian to defend the sacrifices that must be made to truly become a mage. Those who cloak themselves in titles so often cling to arcane rites.

"Alia." Dorian never looked away from her. "You can believe that. I would never hurt Lena."

"What is going on here?" A scrape of steel against a sheath sounded from the doorway, that of Baldric drawing his sword.

'The easiest way to learn how to heal is to heal yourself. Feel every bit of pain, the disruption.'

Alia froze, caught in echoes. Baldric seized on her pause and gripped Dorian's robes in his free fist. He slammed the mage against the rough edges of the palace walls. Dorian could have reached for his magic, leveled the quotidien soldier with minimal effort. But instead, he only pushed against Baldric's chest, trying to lessen the pressure of the soldier's forearm on his collarbone.

Lena slid out from behind Alia, sending a pulse of garnet light at Baldric. It was enough to make him drop his sword and send him skittering across the stones, sword sliding along with him.

Alia came back to herself, rushing to Baldric's side as he lay sprawled out on his stomach. He groaned and rolled over, trying to reclaim his weapon. "Stop," Alia bid her friend, looking back at Lena. Lena was ready to defend her teacher, magic crackling between her hands.

"What did he do?" Baldric grumbled.

"There was a misunderstanding." Alia stood, putting her hand on Baldric's chest as he regained his feet. "Enough, Lena."

Lena intensified her glare. "He attacked Master Dorian."

"It's fine." Dorian straightened his robes. He moved towards Baldric and extended his hand. "I don't believe we've met."

Baldric recoiled as if Dorian brandished a weapon. "This is Lord Baldric Cole," Alia offered as cover for Dorian to rescind his hand. "Baldric, I trust you're aware that this is Master Dorian. And my daughter, Lena."

"That was quite the blow," he said to Lena, ignoring Dorian. "Magic is a fine enough weapon, but it is no substitute for steel."

Lena snorted, but her shoulders relaxed. "Any oaf can wave a sword."

Baldric chucked and held out his hilt to Lena; she couldn't resist the taunt. The sword immediately clattered to the ground as Lena's arm buckled beneath its weight.

"How were you taught to heal?" Dorian kept his voice low so only the two of them could hear as Lena tried to retrieve Baldric's sword.

Alia shivered, crisscrossing her arms over her midsection. "He's been fighting Veillanti on the border for years."

"He is not the first Mandal to despise me on sight. And that is not what I asked."

"Cormac summoned us." Baldric sheathed his weapon and beckoned to Alia. "I am to escort you."

Alia looked between Lena and Dorian. "I can't leave."

"I'll go," Dorian said.

"The lesson isn't over," Lena protested.

"For today, it is. Fine work, Lena. Pleasure to meet you, Lord Baldric. Alia."

"Fucking leech," Baldric mumbled as he leapt the catch the emblem Dorian tossed at him before flickering away.

"He defected," Lena and Alia said in unison.

"But you don't trust him."

Lena retreated inside the suite. "She doesn't trust anyone."

Alia looked after her, helpless as Lena sulked to her room yet again.

"Let's go." Baldric pulled Alia's elbow.

"What does Cormac want?"

"You're being brought into the fold." Baldric flashed his dimples as he led her through the halls.

"What does that mean?"

"Are you going to tell me what the Veillanti did?"

"I told you."

"A misunderstanding." Baldric clicked his tongue. "How many times have his kind tried to return us to the Tiarcons? They will kill every last Mandal if they have to. Think of George."

"It must have been hard, losing George." Alia watched every tic in Baldric's expression as his emotions raged.

"I should have been with him."

Baldric's guilt over George dredged up thoughts of Finn and that fiery night. She'd pored over alternative outcomes, how she might have rushed into the burning building to drag him from the flames, but then would have perished alongside him.

Her self-professed quotidien husband.

"I'm sure he's glad you weren't." It was the same with Finn. As much as Alia cursed herself for not running after him, she knew he would have wanted her safe, would have wanted Lena safe.

Baldric muttered curses until they reached the door of the chancery. He tried the knob, leaning back against the door when it didn't turn.

Flora entered the hallway from the stairs. "Does this little conference need to happen right now? I was napping."

"Yes, do make the king wait while you laze about," Baldric snapped.

"You had just died, Baldric." Flora's smile didn't reach her eyes. "It was a happy dream."

"Come on." Harlan stepped up from behind Flora with an easy grin. He cast one arm around Flora's narrow shoulders and the other around Baldric. "All of us, together again."

"Not all of us." Baldric grimaced but didn't shake Harlan off. "Do you know what he wants?"

Harlan's smile vanished, brow creasing as he reached behind Baldric to knock on the door to the King's chancery. The door glowed with Barton magic before swinging open.

The chancery was more of a vault than a study. It was perfectly circular, the smooth limestone walls covered in cerulean tapestries. Cormac was within, seated behind a gleaming onyx desk with sharp angles. He twirled a dagger in his right hand, waving the group forward to four chairs arranged before him.

The door shut behind them. The king, the captain, the soldier, the courtier, and the Undoing Mage. Flora, Harlan, and Baldric obeyed Cormac's wordless direction; the room might be novel, but this type of audience was not. Alia had departed, but they continued on. The friendships held together, trust enduring the ascent to the throne.

"Well?" Flora said.

"We've dreamt of being here." Cormac looked at each of them in turn. "The king's chancery."

Alia's dream hadn't been the chancery, but the throne.

"I figured I'd be dead before I had to call you king," Baldric said.

"If only." Flora smoothed her hair. "You've done well, Your Highness."

"And now we have to hold the throne."

Alia flinched when Cormac unceremoniously sliced the dagger into his left palm. The king tore down the tapestry nearest to him, pressing his wound against the stone behind it. The wall split into a door without a sound.

"What in Orlast's—" Baldric began before Cormac interrupted him.

"Only the blood of Mandal's king can open the door. Now, give me your hands." He brandished the knife, still dripping with his blood.

"What is this, Cormac?" Flora demanded, clasping her hand to her chest.

"I can't tell you unless you swear a blood oath." Cormac proffered the knife again, expectantly.

Alia backed away, hitting the opposite wall from where Cormac stood.

Baldric drew nearer to her, his posture tense. "Orlast swore never to require a blood oath from his subjects. That kind of forced loyalty was why we escaped the Tiarcons."

"I'm not asking you to swear an oath to me." Alia could feel the pulse of Cormac's magic, strength projecting outward. "I'm asking you to swear it to the entire realm."

The weight of his words intensified the atmosphere of the chancery, stretching tight the bonds of fealty and friendship.

Flora's words were measured, for once. "What use is a blood oath among friends?"

"Flora." Cormac stepped towards her, his charm showing through his striking gaze. "This is not a test; it is protection, for all of us. Your loyalty is unquestioned."

The formidable noblewoman wilted under his flattery, but it was Harlan who stepped forward first. The captain had lost all sense of levity, resigned to do what was asked of him. Alia wondered whether the oaths he had already taken or his remorse over Elowen motivated him.

Cormac clasped the proffered wrist and drew the dagger across Harlan's palm. Cormac placed his open wound atop Harlan's, their blood mixing and dripping onto the stone floor. Cormac gave Harlan his oath, "I, Captain Harlan Gust, swear to protect and keep secret the Spear of Orlast with each breath, until my last."

The Spear of Orlast?

Shock held her still as the wound on Harlan's palm closed of its own accord, the blood oath marked and satisfied. A ball of light moved beneath Harlan's skin, travelling up his arm. He pulled at his tunic, baring his arm. It settled just beneath his shoulder; the Barton crest was etched on Harlan's skin.

Flora fled to the door before Alia could breathe. Baldric reacted with equal speed, slamming the door to the chancery shut as soon as she opened it. The warrior glared down at Flora, his imposing form making her shrink away from the doorknob. "Coward," he spat.

Baldric made his blood oath without hesitation, his chest swelling with pride to be given such an honor. Betrayal rankled within Alia; Baldric should have refused alongside her, but the mention of the Spear had clearly converted him.

"Cormac," Flora protested. "How could I possibly be of use here?"

"No one is quite as skilled in social warfare," Cormac explained. "No one knows the secrets of Mandal as well as you. To protect this one, I need you at my side."

"Please, Flora." Harlan enclosed her hand in his.

Flora blushed crimson, blurring away her fear. "Sleeved gowns are in fashion, I suppose." Flora sniffed. "But if you scar these hands that I've endeavored to keep idle, a debt will be owed." Haltingly, Flora swore the oath.

And then it was Alia's turn.

"Ali." Cormac turned her name into a command.

"The Spear of Orlast is lost." Alia held herself together.

Cormac just shook his head.

He had it. Odessa's demand hadn't been an impossible charge after all.

"Ali," Baldric urged, prodding her forward. "For Mandal." Harlan reached for her hand.

"I am not a loyal soldier." Alia jerked away from Baldric and Harlan. Flora had the right idea in running for the door. "I'm not one of you."

"But you are." Cormac's smile was tight. "No one has ever defended who they love with such ferocity. You've killed two immortals now; don't you want to know why?"

For a moment, they were the only two in the room. Cormac crafted a flattering portrait, fashioning Alia's rueful nature into a higher purpose. For she had protected him for years, with a certain fervor that could be interpreted as ferocity. Propping up Cormac, pushing back on his family, the expectations of his birth, and keeping space for him, a young man with so much thrust upon his shoulders. And wasn't she still doing that, even as he denied her freedom?

Ferocious. And flawed.

"Baldric," Cormac summoned.

Without his king needing to specify, Baldric pulled the emblem out of his vest. Cormac held it in his palm, thumb sweeping over the form he molded of her.

"If you swear an oath to me, you'll be free of this."

It wasn't release, it was a trade. A tether for an oath, confinement for allegiance.

Alia could only hope oaths were easier to break than sentences.

She extended her hand. Cormac's touch soothed her doubts as he made the incision.

Her skin prickled, rebelling. Cormac placed his palm to hers, slick with blood, just as he had done the night they were paired. Their blood mixed, sparking a reaction once more. Alia shielded her eyes from the flash, a pulse that would have leveled her to the floor if Cormac hadn't held fast. The others weren't as quick and were scattered by the explosion of light.

Cormac's knife clattered to the ground as sparks flew from their interlocked fingers, shades of warm gold and stinging violent. The heat from their intermingling blood was coursing through her body, every inch responding to Cormac.

"Say it," he commanded.

Alia couldn't hold on much longer, knees buckling under the strain. The reaction tore at her magic, pulling her in to feed the combustion. He was going to consume her, release the Undoing if he didn't let go first.

"Say it, Ali." Sweat beaded on Cormac's brow.

"I, Alia Meador, swear to protect and keep secret the Spear of Orlast with each breath, until my last."

Their hands flew apart, and in the resulting darkness, the only thing that shone was the golden crest now carved into her arm.

"I knew it," Flora exclaimed with delight from the floor.

"Knew what?" Baldric stood up with a surly grunt.

"Their pairing was never broken."

The sparks, the reaction. It was the same as it had been at their pairing ceremony all those years ago.

How could that be?

"Later." Cormac turned to the door he'd opened with blood. "Come."

Alia let Harlan and Baldric file eagerly behind Cormac. The stairway descended, the scent of the sea wafting up into the chancery. Torches in hand, the three men began their journey through the blood-smeared entry.

"Now we have to see if it was worth the blemish." Flora's attempt at humor was flat.

"I would have thought—"

"That I would want to know what was at the bottom of a dark, secret staircase?" Flora said as they walked side by side. "I know enough to know there are things I don't want to know."

Alia fought to maintain her footing on the winding, uneven stairs. Her legs tingled with remnants of the connection with Cormac. Flora's complaints echoed down the stairs, about the damp ruining her shoes and hem, and a collection of other inconveniences.

But instead of opening into a cavern, the stairs ended in a solid limestone wall. Relief dared to rise within her, hoping Cormac lied and the most powerful weapon in the realm wasn't beneath the palace. But Cormac again fed his blood to the stone, smearing crimson against the mottled chalk.

The stone cracked, yawning into an intimate cave.

The entire circular room was carved, whittled with faded words and leeched images. Reflected light slipped across the forgotten lines, shadows on the sea. The chamber was just large enough for the five Mandals to encircle what lay in the center. The Spear of Orlast was upright, wedged between two limestone posts.

The magic hadn't diminished with the passage of time. It reverberated through Alia, pounding a rhythm in her chest.

The killer of Tiarcons, the weapon of Mandal's first king.

"This is what Odessa wants." Cormac's eyes met hers from across the spear.

"No fucking shit," Baldric whispered.

"I thought it'd be bigger." Flora pursed her lips.

"This killed the Tiarcon of the Moon?" Alia stepped forward. Her stomach flipped, regarding the legendary spear with a mix of awe and terror.

"It did." Cormac paused with reverence. "Before my father died, he brought me down here and explained my responsibility. The Spear has been protected by the kings of Mandal since King Orlast. The task was entrusted to our kingdom as the dominion of Orlast."

"Are the Veillanti right about it?" Harlan asked. "The veil?"

"After Orlast killed the mad Tiarcon and severed the blood oath, he petitioned the Tribunal to create Entien. To sever Alasar into two realms, one for the immortals and the Tiarcons, and the other for mortalkind. The Spear is the mortal means of survival and the manifestation of the Tribunal's order to create the veil."

The Spear called to her, capturing her gaze and pulling her in. It was a void; her magic couldn't reach it. Alia compulsively moved forward, close enough to reach out and touch the weapon. The Undoing roiled, begging to be unleashed. To meet or destroy, it was impossible to tell which.

"Ali!" Baldric shouted, yanking her back from the blade.

Even as she was pulled away, the Spear came with her. The limestone cave gave way to a windswept glacier. The Spear of Orlast plunged into her stomach, cutting through flesh without resistance. She felt the sting of the blade, the shock of it, before the gushing of her own blood. Her hands dripped as she struggled to grasp the weapon inside her. And standing before her was a woman, beautiful and imposing, reclaiming the spear of steel, her ochre skin sprayed with blood.

Her killer was smiling.

The ice was gone as soon as it came.

"What happened?" Flora demanded, kneeling beside Baldric and Alia.

"It knows me," Alia whispered, still transfixed by the weapon. Her vision haunted her, the instrument of her end within her reach. "I need to touch—"

"Ali, the last thing we need is the veil coming crashing down because you were curious," Baldric said.

"You'll die if you touch it." Cormac shook a strand of dark blonde hair out of his eyes. "Countless kings have tried since Orlast. It took them all."

"You have to tell Dorian. He will—"

"You four are the only ones who can know. The responsibility falls on us to protect the Spear and Entien," Cormac said.

"We'd be foolish to trust that kind of information to a Veillanti." Baldric glared at Alia.

Dorian would have guidance for them; he would know why she was feeling this way upon discovering the spear. But he could also confirm its existence to Veillant. "If the Spear is destroyed, the veil goes with it?"

Cormac nodded. "And our power to kill a Tiarcon."

"Hide it." Baldric still held Alia. "Hide it where Veillant can't find it."

"The power of the Spear is concealed in this chamber. Protections were made by Orlast himself," Cormac explained. "It has not been moved in nearly five hundred years."

"Why tell us then?"

Cormac looked at Alia like she was a fool. "My son is too young for this weight. Should anything befall me, I want to know that the Spear will be protected by those I trust the most."

His words stung. A hopefulness clinging to the idea of the five of them, decades ago. Young, unencumbered, and mischievous. All they had now were burdens.

"We will protect it with our lives," Harlan reiterated the oath.

"We will not let the veil fall," Baldric promised.

"We will not let *you* fall," Flora specified, placing her hand on Cormac's bicep.

Alia was still drawn to the weapon, more concerned with the feeling of unease she felt around it than Cormac's expectant stare. She was both desperate to touch it and to leave the chamber behind, unsure if she wanted to court her death or prevent it.

"I will keep the secret," Alia said, an aggressiveness awakening in her as she desired to rebuke the blood oath, to tell Dorian and find out more. Her words were enough to satisfy her friends as Alia's mind churned.

Cormac led the way back up, followed by Harlan and Alia, with Flora and Baldric trudging behind. The climb was significantly more difficult than the descent, Baldric joining Flora in the chorus of complaints.

"What now?" Baldric asked once they had returned to the chancery.

"We ready ourselves for war." Cormac sat behind the desk. "Flora and Harlan, I need you to see to preparations for a summit with Parth and Royce in hopes that they'll stand with us when we respond to Veillant. And Baldric, make sure the soldiers are prepared."

Flora balked. "Shouldn't the queen—"

"Flora, make the arrangements," Cormac said curtly.

"Yes, my king." Flora bowed her head.

"But first," Cormac kept them hovering. "Report."

Flora, Baldric, and Harlan shared the same sharp inhale, looking at each other before Baldric stepped forward. "I've concluded the investigation into Lady Rosalynn."

"I still don't understand why we were forced to tolerate Rosalynn for as long as we did," Flora chattered.

"And?" Cormac asked.

"The Paxtons were made to see the benefits of confinement at their estate. If Lady Rosalynn leaves their lands, the entire family will face punishment."

"And your assessment?" Cormac invited.

"They'll come for the Crown at the slightest provocation." Baldric clenched his jaw. "And there's more. Rosalynn acted after consultation with your mother."

Cormac blinked and looked at the ground, his brow furrowing. "That poses a problem."

Alia chuckled. "Just give Rheta what she wants."

"She is the queen dowager. I cannot change what happened, cannot fault her need for vengeance, but I cannot let her succeed either."

"You cannot fault her for trying to kill me?"

"We'll need to put in place new procedures for your safety," Harlan cut in. "I'm increasing the guard and limiting your movements."

"Procedures?" Alia protested. "Isn't my confinement lifted?"

"Confinement, yes," Cormac pressed the heels of his hands into his temples. "But you'll require protection. Though I doubt she'd risk another public display."

"We can make sure that Baldric or I are always with her," Harlan offered.

"All of this because you won't stand up to your mother." Alia folded her arms and drew in a breath.

"Ali—" Flora grabbed her.

A flash in Cormac's eyes told Alia that she had stepped onto shaky ground. For a boy who had been largely ignored by his father except when inspiring his temper, Alia knew his mother took on an exceptional role in his life. The wedge that Alia's continued presence in Mandal created between Cormac and Rheta must be excruciating for them both.

"Harlan?"

"The Palmers remain dissatisfied after Lady Lillian's failed pairing—"

Cormac jerked forward. "It isn't like there are scores of magical noblemen to offer them."

"Lord Tristan knows. He has been asking if you'll reconsider your father's stance on Truath descendants. The girl, Madeline, apparently—"

"No."

"Of course not." Harlan agreed, cowed.

"Anything else? Any progress on finding who is leaking information from my council to my enemies? Who might have delivered Odessa's gift to this very room?"

Harlan, Baldric, and Flora became enticed by the floor.

"Harlan, Baldric, I'll call for you when you're needed. Flora, Alia, you stay."

Alia's head snapped up.

"Come on, Ali." Baldric reached for her, pretending to misunderstand his king.

"She stays."

The concern on her friends' faces made Alia wonder if she should be more worried. Harlan put his hand on Baldric's shoulder, nearly forcing the soldier out of the room.

Flora and Alia exchanged glances as Cormac settled into the chair behind his desk.

"Flora," Cormac began.

"Cormac?" She lifted her chin.

"What is it you were saying about our pairing?"

Alia had nearly forgotten in the revelations of ancient spears and looming war.

A grin spread across Flora's face as she settled herself into an armchair opposite Cormac. "When two people have a successful magical pairing, the spell has a memory. A connection forms and lives on in your veins."

"But he paired with my sister."

Cormac waved her off and focused back on Flora. "What does it mean?"

Flora looked over her shoulder at Alia. "It means that your pairing with Elowen wasn't valid in some way. In the eyes of your magic, Alia is your true pairing. Still."

Alia dug her fingers into her sides.

"Thank you, Flora. You can go," Cormac dismissed her, looking down at the papers on his desk.

Flora stood slowly, turning and clasping Alia's arm. "Stop fighting it," she whispered, before releasing Alia and shutting the door behind her.

Alia let out a loud sigh, but Cormac refused to look up from his work. "I think Dorian is loyal," she said to shake his concentration.

"Why do you think that?"

"A Veillanti mage came to us in the hinterland. They hated each other, fought even."

"Hatred can be faked."

"Just like love, apparently."

That captured his attention.

"What more do I have to do for you?" Cormac's fists weighed on his desk. "I've spurned my family, my duty for you. What more do you demand?"

She felt the overwhelming impulse to scream at him. To tell him all of it, the agony of losing him, the unrecognizable chasm her life had become, the hate she clutched so hard her hands couldn't hold anything else. To tell him while there was still time. She was well-acquainted with how fleeting her happiness often was, how quickly those whom she loved slipped away.

"Nothing you can give." Her hardened heart made her lie.

Cormac sighed and put his head in his hands. "I can't lose you again."

"She isn't going to stop." She expected nothing less from Rheta.

"I need you to follow orders." Cormac stood from his desk and walked around to the other side. "Your confinement is lifted, but I don't want to see you about the palace without Harlan or Baldric. You can do your training with Master Dorian in the Olden Wing, but no going to the Tower or somewhere out in the open like the garden. Mother has demanded you attend Court functions, so you must, but I will be there with you."

"You know she'll still find a way."

"Do you have such little faith in your king?" Cormac placed his hand on the side of her neck, thumb teasing her jawline.

Alia blushed at the way the touch of his hand made her feel. If she had faith in Cormac, she would tell him everything. What Ruben had done, why she attacked him. But as she regarded Cormac now, she knew that it was just another burden that he couldn't carry.

"There's oil in your blood again."

Cormac's hand stayed pressed to the side of her neck, the pressure of his fingers increasing. "It is none of your concern."

"You've never acknowledged your limitations."

"Is that why you left me? To teach me my limitations? You were supposed to be my wife, my queen. When you betrayed me—" Cormac's words caught.

"I couldn't stay."

"I needed you." Cormac's voice rang out, filling the whole room. His pain was plain, etched into his face, coursing through his body.

"Cormac..." Alia stood and put her palms on his chest, seeking to bring him calm.

They held onto each other, brimming with years of hurt that words couldn't fix. She had pushed away any hope of attachment with a man since Finn's death. The only way she had survived was through insisting on her independence.

But Cormac was hers.

"Our connection was never broken," Cormac whispered. "And I never stopped loving you."

She tasted the smoke on his lips when she guided his mouth down to hers. It was bitter and sharp, mixing with the charred cedar scent that the fire mage always carried. She was struck by how disparate Cormac and

Finn were. Finn's cinnamon smell was locked away in her memory. Finn had been gentle, purposeful with every touch, while being with Cormac was to tangle with flames.

The memory of Finn persisted as Cormac tore at the bodice of her dress, ripping through the gown. She tried to banish Finn's face as Cormac pinned her against his desk. Alia wished that her touch could erase the years of suffering from Cormac, wished it could turn him back into the hopeful young prince who had been so sure of himself. Maybe then she could reclaim a glimmer of who she had used to be.

"You still love me." Cormac broke their kiss long enough to demand.

She had loved enough to know that it was not a static declaration. That the void within her would persist, but she could let herself feel something for Cormac. In hopes that it could dampen her pain, that in resigning to passion, she could find relief.

"I still love you."

Her breaths came heavily as Cormac pushed her skirts out of the way, gripping her thighs and placing her on the desk. At the feeling of his hands on her hips, Alia's thoughts began to whirl. The memories of his touch came quickly. They had been good together. He wasn't Finn, but he loved her.

Cormac's sword clattered to the ground in its hilt as Alia unfastened his belt and began to unfasten his breeches. She felt the king quake at her touch, his lips emboldened.

And at last, they stopped fighting.

II

Wisps of the Undoing fluttered around her fingers, swirling against the ring she wore. She toyed with the sparkling crimson gemstone and smooth gold band, considering letting the Undoing tear it apart. Her wedding ring. She had stopped wearing it years ago in fear that someone would steal it, but she always kept it secured to her person.

So that Finn would never be far.

The Undoing showed no interest in dismantling the ring. Instead, it danced, gentle and benign.

Alia had been certain that bedding Cormac would make her feel better. That she would feel closer to him, to the woman she had been, to being loved again. But afterward, when she was sent back to what had served as her prison, she knew she was wrong.

She'd betrayed her sister, whether Elowen loved Cormac or not. And if Lena ever heard of it, Alia would only have shame to share with her. The woman she used to be could not be found in Cormac's arms; chasing her was folly.

The Undoing twisted into barely perceptible circlets as she wound her finger.

Lena pushed open her door, heaping clothing onto the chair. "Aunt Elowen sent us new dresses for Mabon. How was your bath?"

Alia wrung out her drying hair, noticing that Lena's curls were already bound in a coiled pattern at the nape of her neck. Lena held up a plum gown. "How about this one?"

"Lena." Alia clutched her robe closed at her throat. "I do not think it is wise—"

"We have never missed Mabon."

Her quiet insistence eroded Alia's determination to collapse into the sheets. They hadn't spoken of Lena's display in Wrendlin. Alia kept waiting for the right words to form, but they hadn't come.

Don't you want her to see you well, despite it all?

"Here." Lena snatched a brush from the armoire. "We used to talk about Father on Mabon."

It was a provocation, Lena needling to see how angry Alia was, what the consequences would be. Alia pulled her way through a tangle, wondering if the time had come. "We can talk about him."

Lena's eyes widened slightly, and only for a second before she recovered. "He used to make those baskets."

"He liked to make sure everyone had what they needed." Finn would pull in the last of the harvest, and she would carefully pack it into baskets. And then he would put Lena up on his shoulders and heft the packages up the road to gift to the rest of the village. Their way to honor Mabon.

"But no one ever did that for us."

Except for Harlan and the sack of bread and coin. "We had what we needed." Alia didn't fault the villagers; they'd never had the chance. She'd been sure to keep her and Lena apart, moving as soon as attachments began to form.

Lena fell silent, treading lightly. "That isn't true."

Alia turned; words caught in her throat. Her expression was too sharp, Lena dimmed.

"I needed more. I need more."

Of course she did. Pain rippled through Alia's chest, igniting her fears. They'd stayed too long, and Lena had seen too much. And now she knew exactly what her mother lacked, what she'd been deprived of.

"What do you need?"

"A home, friends, purpose. All things I could have here if..." Lena trailed off.

"Speak plainly," Alia snapped, unable to moderate her tone.

"There are days when you don't look at me. Like it hurts you to see me. And I've tried so hard. Wondering what was wrong with me that I couldn't make you happy, why it hurts you so much just to look at me."

Alia stilled. Empty phrases went through her head, assurances that she didn't believe herself. Lena yearned for what Alia lacked; the softness had been stomped out of her until only sharp edges remained. She'd left her daughter wanting for exactly what Alia had wanted from her parents. It had never been Lena she couldn't look at, and she was not the source of Alia's pain. She'd held herself away from Lena for her own protection, to stop the dark from spreading. She had protected Lena, kept her safe and free of influence. But she left her alone in the process.

"Nothing is wrong with you," Alia started. "I—"

"I want to live in the Tower." Lena trembled.

Alia knew that a few well-worded attacks would bring her daughter back into line. But even as they threatened to come out, she tried to be slow and moderate. "No, it isn't safe."

"An entire dormitory of mages is the safest place for me. Madeline said—"

"Do tell me what Madeline said." Alia sharpened her tone. "She'll have you requesting a pairing next."

Lena's cheeks flushed. The Truath had already raised it. It had been a common enough method of escape when Alia was young—seek a pairing, escape the family you'd been born into, build your own. But it was a trap.

"Father would—"

"It doesn't matter what your father would do. He isn't here. I am. And I am the only one concerned for your safety."

Tears began to make their way down Lena's cheeks. "I wish he was here instead of you."

"So do I."

Those were the final blows, given to hurt each other the most. Wretchedness stained her lips, but Alia didn't open them again. She couldn't look at Lena as she turned back to the mirror, afraid of what other manner of darkness might spill out.

Finn should be here. He'd always been better suited to parenthood, able to comfort even in his coldest moments. And then Alia would finally be able to take a breath without being consumed by worry. They could have shared that burden. It wouldn't be so terribly lonely.

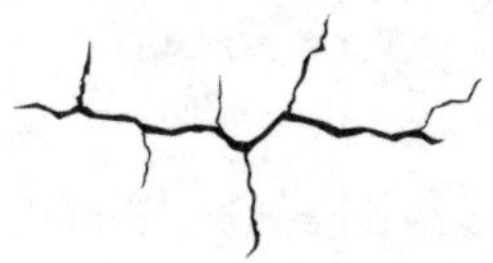

While Mabon was celebrated in every village across the continent, nowhere was quite as grand as Sheath. Candles dripped from every surface of the palace halls, hundreds of flickering beacons. The tables were cloaked in wine red and piled high with the yield of Mandal's fields. Baskets, woven with golden silk, overflowed with gourds, apples, and breads. The scent of cinnamon was overpowering, charred in bouquet centerpieces.

It was the scent that Finn had always carried, spiced and sweet.

Music played over the din of voices, drifting along the cooling air. Every curtain was pulled open. The assembly of nobility failed to note their arrival, already consumed with their indulgences.

"You can manage from here." Baldric sulked away, having fulfilled his duty to escort Alia and Lena in case Rheta tried to kill them on the walk from the Olden Wing.

While rows of tables stretched across the hall, most nobles still stood in clusters. The space left clear for dancing was full of twirling couples, the king and queen among them. Alia's stomach involuntarily lurched at their proximity. Cormac's gaze didn't meet hers once. And it wouldn't. Because if they weren't behind a locked door, she didn't exist to him. She couldn't.

She forced herself to look away before Lena noticed, only to lock on a pair of warm eyes. Master Dorian cut through the crowd to reach them, a slight smile on his lips. "May the sun rise this Mabon."

Alia squinted at his greeting. "Do you not commemorate Mabon in Veillant? There couldn't very well be a ceremony of lights without the dark."

"Master Dorian," Lena said gruffly. "I'll take my leave."

Madeline Truath approached, clad in her shapeless black dress. The Truath color had been pearl, and despite her vocation, it would have been appropriate for her to wear some sign of her origins. But it had been stripped from the entire family in the wake of their demise. Their only crime, the audacity to hold the throne and the misfortune to lose it.

"Master Dorian, Lady Alia," Madeline chirped, lowering herself into a curtsy.

"Lady Madeline," Dorian inclined his head, and Alia gave him a sharp look. Truaths weren't allowed to hold any titles of nobility.

"Let's go." Lena shuffled away, holding onto Madeline's arm. Lena only took a few steps, but she already felt so far away.

"What have I done to upset you now?" Dorian's eyes glimmered with humor.

Alia retreated to judgment, unable to look away from the back of Lena's head. "You aren't even trying to observe Mandal customs, are you?"

"Perhaps you can educate me on how one properly celebrates Mabon." Dorian shifted to stand beside Alia, a stone wall at their backs.

"Polite talk then?"

"What kind of talk would you prefer?"

Alia narrowed her eyes at the mage.

"Did something happen between you and Lena?" Dorian asked. "You both seem ... tense."

Alia's chest rose. The man dared to presume to know how she felt, how Lena felt. "I'm sure you're aware that Lena wants to move her quarters to the Tower."

Dorian cleared his throat. "A request was made, which I denied."

"Why?"

"Because it wasn't coming from you." Dorian chuckled. "And I've never seen you do anything without good reason."

Alia blinked at him. He noticed and knew so much, too much. But still, he looked at her as if there was no danger, no darkness, no shame in what she was. He always had.

Polite talk then.

"Do you see that group over by the throne?" Alia began, nodding towards the cluster of commoners. "Those are the farmers who produced the largest yield this harvest. It is a great honor, to be invited to the palace on Mabon. Even if the harvest yield is less than half it was a decade ago."

"Mandal isn't alone in that." Dorian peered at the commoners with curiosity, rather than the open disdain most nobles displayed.

"Mabon used to be the day when the daylight and nighttime held equal sway. The work to be done for the duration of the light, and then the celebration at night. The perfect balance, time to gather and be grateful before the dark of winter."

"A worthy sentiment still." Dorian's arm brushed against hers. "And the dancing?"

"The dancing?"

"What is its relevance to the occasion?"

Alia looked around at the spinning couples keeping pace with the upbeat music, though the king and queen had left them. "Does dancing need to be relevant?"

Dorian chuckled and looked down at his feet. "Would it surprise you that there isn't much dancing in Veillant? None outside of ceremony. The leaders temper every celebration, waiting for the elation that awaits when the realms are reunited."

"How dour."

"Care to teach me?" Dorian offered his hand.

Alia immediately recoiled, ignoring the part within her that leapt at the prospect. "I can't."

"A proper Mandal noblewoman who doesn't know how to dance?" Dorian lifted his eyebrows.

"I know how," Alia clarified. "But I don't anymore."

"A shame. For both of us." Dorian withdrew his hand, his arm touching hers lightly again.

Dorian's aura curled around her. He seemed wholly unbothered by her refusal. He must have expected it like everything else, but something in her response had emboldened him.

It was inconceivable that so light a touch affected her this way. Her body angled towards him of its own accord, responding to the feel of him. She closed her eyes, imagining that she was up in the meadow on a sunny afternoon, basking without a care. Her smile broadened.

"Ali?"

Alia's eyes blinked open, the clamor of the hall breaking through as she realized that Flora was standing before her. "What?"

"I asked if you'd walk with me." Flora looked from Alia to Dorian.

"Gladly." Alia grabbed for her arm. "Master Dorian." She bowed her head.

He cocked his head to the side at her hasty departure, returning her nod as he rubbed his lips together.

Flora's laughter started to sound when they were five paces away. "What was *that*?"

"I do not know what you're talking about."

"Cormac sent me over to collect you. What kind of tricks does that mage have to have you smiling and blushing?"

"Collect me?" Alia pulled back on Flora's arm, bringing her to a pause.

"He can suffer the dashing mage to teach you, but making you smile is a whole other matter." The corners of Flora's eyes crinkled.

Alia willed her heated cheeks to cool with the satisfaction that Cormac had noticed her presence.

Flora drew her aside to a tall table and summoned a servant with the snap of her fingers. Glasses of wine appeared soon after. "Now, where have you been hiding?"

"In her room." Harlan came to stand at her shoulder, a towering presence.

Alia stiffened. "That's not fair."

"But it is accurate." Baldric walked up with a tankard in each hand.

"I thought you might have made a run for it. What with the new tattoo and all," Flora said.

She'd thought about it. "And where would I run?"

"That didn't seem to stop you before."

"Get off it, Baldric."

Baldric grunted and took a turn around their table, sneering at anyone nearby to make them skirt away. When he returned, he plopped his elbows on the table. "What are we looking at?"

Harlan gave Alia a sideways apologetic glance. "The Palmers, to be sure. But we should keep an eye on the Paxtons as well. And naturally, the Wexworths and Meadors."

"The Palmers have yet to arrive, but they will be here," Flora added, scanning the room with her ever-present grin.

"What about them?" Alia looked at each of her friends.

"The most pressing internal threats to the Crown," Baldric said, his voice low. "This," he patted his shoulder where the Barton crest was hidden beneath his tunic, "is not our first assignment."

"And you're with us again. Finally, we have someone who can eliminate threats rather than just assess them," Flora said.

Both Baldric and Harlan huffed, bringing a chuckle out of Flora.

"My assessment is far more useful than your drivel," Baldric said.

"Then why does Cormac never seek it?"

"Do you two ever stop?" Alia was more interested in learning about Cormac's rivals than their bickering.

"Never," Harlan grumbled.

Baldric's jaw tightened, lowering his head. "She is the one who can't help herself from destroying everyone's lives."

Flora put her hand on her hip. "For the last time, Baldric, all I did was make an introduction. I had no part in George's decision to wed Quinn."

Baldric's hand tightened around his tankard, his gaze staying on the table rather than any of his friends.

"Lady Quinn? The healer?" Alia looked to Harlan for confirmation. "Lady Quinn is George's widow?" Alia pictured the noblewoman who had come to see Lena at the inn; she'd been at least ten years her junior. She would have made a young bride for George.

"She was barely his wife." Baldric slammed his cup on the table.

"Why would you coerce George's widow into helping Lena?" Alia demanded of Harlan.

"Coercion?" Flora flushed, hitting Harlan with the back of her hand. "I told you to leave her alone; she's been through enough."

"Hardly." Baldric's expression darkened. "George had to join the ranks just to get away from her."

"George went off to fight because he was chasing you!" Flora thrust her finger in Baldric's face, and he looked close to cutting it off.

"She's still doing it." Harlan leaned his shoulder into Flora, pushing her back. "Lady Quinn is supplying Cormac with opium from the infirmary."

Baldric's eyebrows ticked up as Flora folded her arms across her chest.

"How long?" Apparently, Cormac's dependency was problem enough for his friends to try intervening.

"How long do you think?" Baldric's brow was once again furrowed, and he was staring into his cup as if it were about to refill itself. "I thought you talked to Quinn, Flora."

"I'll talk to her again." Flora strummed her fingers on the table.

Their unease was contagious, too potent for Alia to prod any further. "Let's focus on the threats."

"Finally," Baldric muttered.

"Finally, what?" Flora asked.

"She finally sounds like the old Ali."

Alia let the assessment roll over her. They thought she could be brought back to life by Court warfare. They were wrong.

"You know about the Palmers," Flora began.

"And the Paxtons, because Rosalynn is imprisoned at the Paxton estate for her attack on you." Baldric quirked his lip, judging the severity of the sentence. "And the Wexworths because the whole lot of them are rotten gits."

"And the Meadors—" Harlan began.

"Because you suspect that Edgar will overthrow Cormac and declare Thomas the first Meador king," Alia finished for them.

"Precisely." Flora gave Alia a probing look.

"And lately." Harlan checked behind both shoulders. "We've also been taking note of threats to you."

"Mainly ..." Flora nodded over to where the royal family gathered, Rheta among them.

"And the leech." Baldric glowered.

"Dorian is hardly a threat to me." Alia turned to search for the mage in the crowd. He was easy to identify, standing out among the cluster of common farmers. He was engaging them, gesturing with his hands to emphasize his point. The commoners eyed him with guarded fascination, obviously wary of the Veillanti. Alia nearly laughed when a particularly wild gesture sent the commoners careening back a few steps.

"Or maybe he's just a threat to Cormac." Flora lifted her eyebrows.

Baldric sighed. "Your taste in men has not improved."

"We've also been trying to sort out an informant. Our emissaries in Parth, Royce, and even Veillant have been fed tales about Cormac's movements. Tales that they only could have heard from a Mandal traitor." Harlan's frown deepened.

"You don't still think it is Dorian?"

"Cormac has told us what you believe. We're still going to watch him." Flora winked.

"What do we have here?" Harlan shifted behind her, both he and Baldric abandoning their perches and moving toward the thrones.

There was a bloom of burgundy at the entrance of the hall, the Palmers' entrance to the Mabon banquet. Lady Lillian stood beside her proud father, Tristan, no longer cowed in disgrace. Her gown sparkled with Palmer gems, parting the crowd with its finery and sizable skirt.

"Upstaging the royals is never wise," Flora whispered. Alia looked back at Elowen, seeing the queen and Mariana ignoring the Palmers. A clear sign of a rift.

The pair watched as Lillian broke with her father and strode to join a gaggle of young noblewomen, the same ones that Alia had seen her with in the garden, including Lady Quinn. Lillian's friends. Except, as soon as Lillian approached, her friends fled, turning away to other pursuits as if their shift in attention was entirely natural.

"Why?" Alia asked Flora, who pursed her lips.

"Lillian is disgraced, toxic to any woman hoping to catch the Intercessor's favor."

Mariana was still terrorizing women who were barely past childhood. Lillian carried the disgrace well, barely reacting to the universal rejection.

Alia's stomach clenched, angered that Mariana was still having her way at Court. Before she was thinking of what she was doing, Alia grabbed Flora and dragged her across the hall, joining Lillian where she stood tall and alone.

"Ali!" Flora protested sharply, pulling away when Alia greeted Lillian.

"Lady Lillian." Alia allowed Flora to skulk away among the crowd, not losing her will to defy her mother.

The young woman's smile did not falter, but her eye twitched slightly. "Lady Alia. What reason could you have to approach me?"

Alia paused, drawing back from Lillian's sharp words. "Who else is clamoring for your company?" She had been mistaken in thinking Lillian crushed beneath Mariana's rule; the woman was very much still fighting.

"I don't need pity, especially from a Meador." Lillian lifted her chin and stepped forward, impressing her superior height on Alia.

Alia swallowed. "There is more to life than this Court and their favor."

"You won't see me slinking away to the hinterland."

"Of course not. Court memories are short—"

"What fault was there of mine?" Lillian took another step forward but kept her voice low. "I didn't deserve a botched pairing at the hands of your mother."

Alia's palms itched as she tried to rein in her annoyance. "I had nothing to do with that."

"Do you really expect me to believe that my misfortune wasn't orchestrated so that you could have Master Dorian? Everyone has seen you chasing after him, manipulating him with your magic."

"Is that what it is for?" Alia gathered the mist in her hand, her aim to support Lillian souring into aggression.

At last, Lillian backed away, fear cracking her confidence.

"Alia." The smooth, authoritative voice compelled her. Mariana appeared at her side, clothed in golden finery.

Alia closed her fist, scattering the Undoing and letting her shoulders fall.

"Lady Lillian, you would do well to watch your words." Her mother reached for her hand, pulling Alia to her side. It wasn't a show of protection, but control. A message to the Palmers that the Undoing Mage acted at the direction of the Intercessor. That Alia was, at her core, a Meador.

It was stifling.

The confrontation broadened as Tristan came to stand beside his daughter. Alia tried to walk away, but Mariana held her, digging her nails into Alia's arm through the sleeve of her gown. Edgar swept in front of them, his hand on his hilt.

"Tristan." Edgar clicked his tongue. "Why don't we enjoy the banquet? Surely you would relish the opportunity for celebration."

Tristan's face reddened, his hand shaking with anger as it neared his bejeweled hilt.

Alia looked over her shoulder. Harlan had positioned himself in front of Cormac and Elowen, the princes behind them. Cormac's gaze was sharp, but his hands were relaxed. This was to be a conflict between the Meadors and the Palmers, and the Crown had no interest in interfering.

"Always the hound on the Barton leash." Tristan spit at Edgar's feet. "Hiding behind your daughter now?" Tristan's hands crackled with sparks.

A public insult to a Meador would not be tolerated. Tristan knew that, courted it. Edgar drew his sword. It was his second favorite weapon, usually preferring the Meador battle axe. "The Meadors are of the same mind, despite your needling. Just a shame that your daughter doesn't have the strength to stand beside you."

Alia fought a laugh at the insinuation that she would ever stand beside Edgar.

The inflammatory comment was too much for the aggrieved lord, too riled to withstand the question to his bloodline. The lightning at his fingertips intensified. He would strike down Edgar in mere moments, and there was no way her father could defend himself from such an attack.

Mariana's fingernails bit into Alia's arm even deeper at her beloved husband's obvious peril. Lord Tristan Palmer's lightning grew, and Alia could see Baldric running from behind the Palmers, sword outstretched. But Baldric was too far away. Tristan pushed Lillian to the side and away from harm so that he could focus his deadly bolts on Edgar.

Before she thought about it, the Undoing snaked from her fingertips. With stunning discernment, the Undoing bypassed Edgar, curving around him to reach for Tristan. Her power whipped across the hall, a purposeful beam, snarling the lightning and burying itself in Tristan's chest.

The Undoing made a quick survey of Tristan, every stab he suffered on the battlefield, every singe. It moved through him so easily, far more quickly than the Alasarans. For all of Tristan's strength, for the threat that had kept his family safe for decades, barely any effort was needed for her high magic to overpower him.

The connection between her and the Undoing pulled taut, as Alia refused to allow more magic to leak out of her.

But she was too late.

Edgar buried his sword in Tristan's chest. And twisted.

Tristan was dead before he crumpled to the ground.

Alia fell to her knees, the Undoing overriding her attempt to corral it.

Lord Tristan Palmer was a mortal man, and she willfully attacked with control and precision. For the crime of being a threat to her father. A threat that her father had stoked and brought upon himself, knowing that he was a fool to stand against Tristan.

This is what all of them had wanted: her parents, Cormac. They wanted the Palmers to be silenced and all other challenges to the Crown stymied. They wanted the entirety of the Mandal Court to see what an Undoing Mage would do. To see what a menace she was. This was why they'd insisted she be here, at Court, especially on Mabon.

They didn't care what it would do to her.

What it *was* doing to her.

Alia barely felt the blade as it bit into her back. She was aware of it, could hear Lillian's screaming as she stabbed. But the depths of betrayal numbed her to any sort of bodily wound.

The Undoing pooled around her, in an uncontrolled current. Alia flinched as the blade was pulled out for the third time. Lillian raised her arm once more, and Alia turned to grab her wrist before the knife cut into the back of her skull.

The Undoing caught Lillian first.

It sliced through her like Palmer lightning. She was a quotidien woman, with barely a shadow of an injury for the Undoing to exploit, save for a pair of skinned knees. The injury every child boasted. And a single cut on her forearm, her failed pairing.

Lillian had barely lived.

But all the Undoing could see was the threat.

It pulled apart Lillian's heart faster than Alia could take a breath, unmaking her blood vessels and disrupting every connection. The ones needed to breathe, for her heart to beat. The gems on the bodice of Lillian's dress shattered as her body went limp, the knife sliding to the ground.

Alia reached for her, trying to summon her healing power. Her magic flashed over the young woman's fallen form, uselessly trying to find something to fix. She could repair what was broken, but she couldn't restore a life that had already gone to the next realm.

There were shouts and clashes of steel, a melee breaking out.

"Call it back, Alia." Dorian appeared before her.

The Undoing darkened as he drew near.

"It killed her." Alia blinked. "I killed her."

"Just call it back."

Darkness continued to pour from her, stretching like molasses. Alia began to wonder why she fought to keep it in at all. The more darkness left her, the less she had to battle.

Out, out, out, get out.

Fear faded away; she no longer cared if her magic turned on her. She reveled in its absence, basking in weightlessness. It was enough to block out the pained cries of the combatants closest to her.

She had been a fool for fighting the Undoing for this long. She had been the architect of her own misery by denying it. Alia felt the power exploding from her hands as it stretched through the hall.

Then her power bumped against something sturdy, a container keeping her in. The darkness climbed higher, searched the container for a crack and folded back on itself.

"You need to call it back." Dorian was still at her side, gritting his teeth as the Undoing tore into him. The air around her was too thick, and there was too much to wade through. She felt the barrier, which must be Dorian's, press in on her, forcing the Undoing back into her.

No.

Dorian had steered her in the wrong direction; he knew nothing of her power. There was no calling it back. Not when she was finally free. Alia brought her hands up, gathering the mist between her fingers and circling around her. The flurry of Undoing coursed around the two of them.

"Alia, please," Dorian pleaded.

Alia bid the Undoing to force the intruder back. Her will broke through Dorian's barrier, reaching inside of him. Alia could feel his racing heart, could feel the strength with which he was resisting her, but could also sense that the tide had turned. He knew that he could not stop her. The markings on Dorian's head glowed as he fought, his skin shimmering with gold. He was struggling to breathe as the Undoing tightened around his heart.

The Undoing broke him down, unleashing itself on all the wounds he had suffered before. Each and every mark carved into his body sliced open, blood streaming down his face.

"Mother!"

Alia's neck snapped towards the sound.

She could feel Lena move behind Dorian, sending waves through the Undoing. Lena's garnet light crackled around her, protecting her from Alia's darkness and banishing it where she stepped.

"Mother, please."

Alia heard her clearly, saw her amidst the decay she had created around her. And she saw Lena's face, the horror writ there. "Get away from me."

But she couldn't stop the Undoing from coursing over Lena, exposing the shadows of injuries. It was a story she knew, every scrape, the shadows of the affliction that had darkened her veins. It danced before her, the shadows on her daughter's skin, distracting from what was next.

The Undoing intensified, acting of its own volition, the singular need to destroy. It was going to tear Lena apart.

You can't contain the darkness inside of you.

She tried. She'd hid it, denied it. But it had all been for nothing. As the dark mist overtook Lena's frame, control failed, sending even more darkness outward. Alia's body buckled, hands eaten away by the mist, unable to call it back.

The strain overtook her, leaving her withering on the floor as the Undoing continued to ravage Dorian and swept over Lena.

The Undoing focused on Lena, trying to exploit her injuries. Except, the magic couldn't find its way in. It slipped along her skin, clawing at past injuries, but couldn't sink in. Something repelled it, elevated Lena past its influence.

Garnet surged. It burned so bright, it was all Alia could see as she cowered. It cut through the pool of Undoing, shooting through Alia's power. Lena stood against her, not losing control but in command. Lena's magic broke through, making the Undoing recoil from Dorian, sending it crawling back to Alia.

The garnet light didn't yield; it infused into the stone floor, shaking and cracking rock. Lena's magic infused into the air around her, bending and distorting. Just like the Oucura. Just like the Traimine.

Alia came down from her intoxication, focusing on Lena.

Alia called to the darkness, called her power to once again return and be bound within her. Pain tore through her as it filled the void, plaguing her once again. She struggled to breathe as the memories reared, being trapped within her body, powerless to control her own movements or thoughts. But she didn't have the power to fight it anyway.

You belong to me.

The delicate blade grazed her leg, metal cool on her skin. "The scholarship of what makes an Undoing Mage is pitifully lacking." Ruben brushed the hair out of her eyes so he could see them clearly. They were the only expression she was allowed, as every other muscle in her body held still by the inculcation. "Old Silas Meador was said to first show signs of the Undoing after watching his younger sister be torn apart by wolves. She died, of course, but he lived. Though I suppose it was the wolves that got him in the end." Ruben chuckled, amused by himself.

No, not Wen. Please.

"Don't look so alarmed, little Meador. If you do well here, there will be no need to involve others in our research. Let's see if this does the trick. Hold still." He laughed again, knowing she couldn't move an inch.

"Feel it," he instructed as the blade sliced down her shin. "Feel everything."

She still did.

Alia's face was buried in black robes. Dorian's arm was hooked around her, shielding her from the clashes around them.

"I'm sorry." He stroked her back as she shook.

Again, the Undoing sputtered beneath her skin, pinpricks of mist showing through, pulling her apart. "Get it out. Please."

"It'll settle. But you have to get out of here."

Alia grimaced as Baldric buried his sword deep in the torso of a household guard dressed in Palmer burgundy. The madness that plagued them now was not the Oucura, but the kind that made men kill to keep their power.

"Lena?"

"I lost sight of her after she—"

"Find her, please."

For a moment, he looked as if he wanted to protest, but gave her a nod instead. He vanished.

"Hold still, Undoing Mage." Flora's water magic swirled around her, creating a bubble over them. When a sword-wielding soldier broke through their barrier, Flora nearly drowned him before pulling back.

"I hadn't seen you in action before." Flora slowly pulled her toward the hall. "I thought there would be more blood."

"I killed her."

"She attacked you first." Flora pinched her arm.

Baldric shook the moisture from his hair as he stepped into Flora's water barrier. "I'll take her." He put his back to Flora, helping guard all of them from any attacks. "The Paxtons are joining the Palmers. I hate wind mages."

"Pricks," Flora agreed, undeterred as she sighed and pushed Alia towards Baldric.

"At least we can get rid of them on the same night."

The tension between Flora and Baldric had dissipated in the crisis, the two moving together as a wayward Palmer household guard dared to advance on them. Baldric moved Alia back against him, one arm pinning her and the other brandishing his sword. But it was Flora who felled the guard, shoving a palmful of water into his mouth and holding her palm over it until his lungs filled.

Flora grimaced and shook out her hand once the man was dead. Her chest heaved, and she looked like she was about to be sick. Flora's loyalty might have prompted her to use her magic, but she took no enjoyment in it. She was just as trapped.

Baldric edged backward, away from Flora and the crashing of swords. There were nobles running towards the fighting and those trying to flee it. "Where are the royals?" she asked.

"Safe with Harlan," Baldric assured as they entered the corridor. "Don't worry, Ali, you did well."

"Did well?" Alia wrenched away from him, careening into a pillar.

"Stop." Baldric snatched her arm, yanking her to him. His fingers pressed into her upper arm, where the Barton seal burned. "We all do as we must. For Mandal."

Alia fought his grip uselessly, wishing to break free of it all. "Why?" she asked. "Why do you fight for a kingdom that has done nothing but deny you? Deny you George."

Baldric checked the hallway, one of the handful of passages to the Olden Wing. It was empty of combatants, just a few stewards jogging towards the fighting. "You weren't here. You don't know what happened."

"It isn't hard to guess. The Mandal obsession with magical children, making you too quotidien and too male to be a proper match for George. So, they married him off to a girl with magic, made him lie until it forced him to the border just to find you."

The storm in Baldric's eyes made her want to reclaim the words. But her friend only soured and kept pulling her along. "We can't have disagreement among ourselves if we are to win a war against Veillant."

"Unity through blood." Alia shuffled behind him in her slippers, bordering on a run as she hoped Lena would be waiting for her when she arrived at their chambers.

"Exactly." Baldric rejected Alia's judgment. "You used to understand."

The guards at her chambers acknowledged Baldric when they approached, hopping up quickly to admit them. "She doesn't come out," Baldric instructed roughly, brandishing his bloodied sword for emphasis.

12

Alia slammed the door behind her, arms still rippling, the Undoing refusing to return without marking her. She ran to Lena's room expectantly, only to be disappointed. Instead of her daughter, Mariana Meador stood in Lena's doorway, arms folded.

"Are you hurt?" Mariana's arms opened, a concerned crease forming on her forehead.

The stab wounds in her back had been taken care of by the Undoing, but the marks left behind by Mariana were far deeper.

"Don't pretend to care now."

Mariana soured, clasping her hands together. "You did well. We're sheltering in the royal apartments until it's over. Let's go."

This was it. Being back in Cormac's confidence was one thing, but being invited back into the Meador family was unthinkable. But she'd done it, with blood and savagery. By appealing to her parents' idea of strength.

"Get out."

"What is this?" Mariana raged, her usually frozen face contorted with anger. She grasped Alia's forearm, nails digging into her skin once more. "This useless defiance."

"You manipulated me. To kill for you." Even if Alia knew how to describe the depth of her pain, she doubted her mother would hear a word of it.

"Violence is a tool, just like any other," Mariana said. "Our family is safer because of it."

But she hadn't been the one to do it. Mariana didn't know how it felt.

"Besides, it is a bit late to claim moral superiority; I know what you did." Mariana fixed Alia with a harsh look that still cut to her soul. "You were seen."

The hasty escort from the King's chancery to the Olden Wing, her dress hardly salvageable after Cormac's passions.

A pit opened in her stomach. "Seen?" Alia feigned innocence.

"Do you not remember anything I taught you?" Mariana sputtered. "There are always eyes. Always."

"I'm sorry if I wasn't hanging on every word while you were offering me up to every man with a title."

Mariana pulled back her lips to show teeth. "I had such plans for you."

Alia believed it. There had once been a time when her mother looked at her kindly, indulged her. Mariana was the daughter of a lesser family, whose beauty and ambition had landed her a Meador. Alia genuinely believed there was affection between her parents, bonded by being born quotidien in magical families. Their craving for status united them, made them a formidable team. And according to the stories, their pairing ceremony had been explosive.

"It is just as well you had Elowen to satisfy you."

"And what exactly do you think will happen now?" Her nails were still digging into Alia's arm. "Do you think that he'll want you, that he'll claim your daughter? If you get everything you desire, what do you think will happen to your sister? The Bartons have always done whatever suits their interest."

"A trait you know well."

"Everything I've done, I've done for my family." Mariana thrust her chin forward.

Alia's anger flared. She had said those words herself and actually meant them. For her mother to hide behind such an outright lie was intolerable. The very walls shuddered as she struggled to rein in her toxic magic.

"Everything you've done, you've done for yourself and your precious legacy."

Calm settled in over her mother—Mariana had struck with anger and could now look at Alia with cool contempt. "My children are my legacy. My grandchildren. Generations from now will know the strength of the Meadors."

"I'm sure that's what they will remember. But it will be a lie. A legacy built on betrayal, the sacrifice of your own child."

"I did what I could for you." Mariana's gleaming brown eyes locked on hers. "My firstborn. Stalwart and beautiful, even as a child. You were given everything your father and I had, anything you could imagine wanting. We thought for sure—" Mariana reached over and tucked a strand of wayward hair back into Alia's braid. "You had the makings of royalty." Mariana smiled, trapped in a memory.

The days of being in her parents' favor were almost too distant to grab onto now. When Alia looked into her past, Ruben had devoured her memories, one by one, until he was the only thing that remained.

"You didn't protect me." Alia's tone wavered.

Mariana shifted but quickly regained her composure. "And what exactly was I expected to do? How was I to know?"

"You should have listened to me when I begged you not to send me back to the Tower. When I begged to return to our lands. You should have listened to me when I told you what happened, instead of only believing what you wanted to be true." Alia felt her chest crack in half, unleashing haggard sobs and making her fight to catch her breath.

"You were hysterical, not exactly the portrait of legitimacy." Mariana squared her shoulders. "I learned differently, of course. Rheta's reaction told me that it was true."

"How absolving for you."

Mariana let out an aggravated sigh. "I thought perhaps, being a mother yourself now, that you'd understand."

Alia's hands shook with rage. "I would never, could never, treat Lena the way you treated me."

But her mother was still unaffected. "You always were selfish. I went against this kingdom in letting you escape; I risked everything for you."

"To be free of your tarnished daughter? Brave of you."

"You never listen," Mariana hissed. "The queen would have never let you live; she knew the truth about her brother's perversions and experiments. I gave you a chance at another life, albeit separated from me. It was the hardest thing I've ever done. And you squandered it."

Alia chewed on her fury. There was nothing her mother wouldn't warp to her benefit. She bound her arms around herself to ward off anyone who might pull at her, who might seek to hold her still. "How long did it take you to make yourself the victim? Blameless. Selfless. Did the narrative lodge itself immediately, or was it a couple of years before you came up with something that sounded right? Was it before or after you promised my sister to the man I loved?"

Another angry sigh. "Come with me, claim your place. Or keep grasping, laying waste to everyone around you to indulge the pain you caused yourself."

It felt like the Undoing might come forth again, ill-suited to the void it inhabited.

As Alia fought for control, Lena and Madeline flickered into the sitting room, clutching each other. When Madeline's eyes met Alia's she let out a scream, tears pouring out.

"Stay away," the grieving girl shrieked. "Lena, stay away from her."

Lena was caught between her scrambling friend and red-faced mother. Her clothes were torn, hair pulled from its bonds. Lord Tristan and Lady Lillian were the closest thing to family Madeline would have had, and both lay dead in the hall. At Alia's hand.

"I won't harm you, Madeline," Alia said softly.

"The threat to the Crown had to be handled." Mariana didn't falter.

Despite her grief, there was a quiet resolve in Madeline's eyes. She was the child of a fallen family; she knew more about the battle for the throne than any of them. It had already cost her everyone.

Lena stayed still, locking onto Mariana. "You and Aunt Elowen planned this. You used me to make sure my mother would attend, to make sure she would—"

Draw the first blood.

"And you did wonderfully," Mariana beamed. "I'm so proud of you."

"Get out."

Pride surged through Alia, her daughter standing firm before the woman who had always bested Alia.

With an aggrieved sigh, Mariana left their quarters, reclaiming the guards she'd left in the hall.

Alia bit into her cheek while Madeline still sobbed on the floor, and Lena remained frozen.

"Let's go to the Tower," Madeline said. "Lena, please."

But the girl didn't know the questions plaguing Lena. She must not have seen that Lena was the one to stymie the Undoing, to rebuke it in the way the Oucura and Traimine failed to. Questions mixed with exhaustion; Alia could see Lena's concern split.

Dorian staggered into the sitting room from the balcony, breaking Lena from her state.

"Did you get the commoners out?" Lena asked as they crowded around him.

Dorian nodded, twinges of pain ticking across his face. Alia could feel his injuries, see it in the way he stood.

"All of them?" Lena clasped Madeline's hand for comfort.

"All," Dorian confirmed, bending forward and wincing.

"You're hurt," Madeline said.

"I'll be fine." He faked a grin before turning to Alia. His face fell.

"You need to heal him," Lena said, harsh with urgency.

"I'll look after him," Alia said. "If you want to go, I won't stop you. But I think it might be safer here than the Tower tonight."

Lena backed away towards her room, Madeline trailing behind.

"You don't have to." Dorian grimaced.

"Your ribs are broken." Alia approached him. "Wind mage?"

Alia gripped Dorian's forearm, her magic snapping his bones into place. "I was supposed to lead them, not be forced to—"

Healing Dorian was a different experience, the tapestry unlike any other she had seen. The Undoing, the healing, once latched on, brought out the shadows of every injury ever suffered, ghostly memories that the skin and bone held. But on Dorian, there was not one inch left untouched, casting a glow all over him, like a second form lying atop him.

She placed her hands on either side of his face, healing the parts of him that she had reinjured, restoring the strength she had taken. She had nearly killed the mage in her desire to be free. As twisted as any motivation Mariana might have wielded.

He shut his eyes as she worked, taking short spurts of breath. His warmth strengthened as he healed, reminding her of the caress of sunbeams from earlier in the night.

His relief was audible. She broke contact as soon as she could, retreating into the crisp air of the dark balcony.

"I—" Dorian faltered, feeling along his repaired ribcage. "I should have been faster."

"The Meadors have a way of twisting any situation." Alia pressed her lips together. "You couldn't have known. This is what I was made for, it is what the Undoing does. Besides, I'm the one who nearly killed you."

Dorian's shoulder brushed hers, his subtle way of offering comfort. Or proving to her that he wasn't afraid to be near her. "I do not think the Undoing is as simple as that."

"Simple enough to be exploited."

"I'm sorry—"

"Don't." It came out with more malice than she intended, malice that should have been reserved.

He ignored her and reached for her, wrapping his arms around her as her crying intensified, every good feeling she ever had leaving her. She felt exactly as she had when Ruben experimented on her, helpless and empty. An undercurrent of dread for what would happen next, not wanting to have to withstand anything else.

"I saw what Lena did." There was no surprise from Dorian, as if it were another thing he'd always known.

Alia pulled away. "Do you think anyone else did?"

He shook his head. "It was chaotic."

"It's a relief that someone can stop me." Alia could feel Lena's magic breaking through the hall, the stones bending around her. "Just don't make her be the one to kill me. She won't recover."

"Alia." Pity softened Dorian's eyes.

She had nearly killed him, and he pitied her.

"Your husband. His magic."

"Don't." She didn't want to hear his theories, didn't want to hear evidence supporting what she didn't want to be true.

"I'm sorry," he murmured.

"Stop apologizing to me. You have nothing to do with it."

"That's not true." His magic oscillated, struggling to find a steady rhythm as his breath came quickly. "In the hinterland, you asked me about Vincent."

Alia nodded, eyebrows raised.

"It is difficult for me to think about the things I've done, let alone tell someone else."

"You're talking to me."

Dorian exhaled and nodded. "Vincent was different when I met him. He was brilliant, had an answer for every inquiry. Knowledge was his affinity, and he hated it. He only saw weakness."

His eyes captured starlight, shimmering despite the dark. Neither had bothered to light the sconces or bring a lantern.

"And then he discovered a bit of magic that allowed him to transfer magic from one mortal to another," Dorian continued. "It is a complex spell, and risky. But Vincent was determined to figure it out."

"Transfer?"

"Don't look so eager."

"He did it, didn't he? I could transfer the Undoing to someone else?" Alia leaned even closer to Dorian, laying her hand over his.

"No, Alia." Dorian cast her off. "Vincent managed the spell, but none of the mages ever survived having their magic stripped away."

"We could try—"

"I was there, every time. He would assure them that their strength would hold out. And every time ..." Dorian's fist tightened. "Do you know what it sounds like when someone is having their magic severed from their body? How quickly the light fades from their eyes once it's gone?"

The agony in Dorian's voice sent shivers through her. She remembered Lillian's body hitting the ground.

"I helped Vincent find mages. He wanted different kinds of Tiarcon magic. He promised each time he was changing the spell so they would survive, but they never did. I helped him kill them."

Alia tried to process Dorian's role. "He killed them. He took their magic for himself."

"It has made him the most powerful mortal mage in Entien. But he won't stop. He won't stop until he can rival the Tiarcons."

"Can he?"

"I don't know." Dorian's shoulders fell.

"And in Wrendlin, he wanted to take the Undoing."

Dorian nodded, swallowing down his guilt. He paced down the edge of the balcony and disappeared into the dark.

"Dorian?"

"Sorry." She heard from the shadows. "There is more to explain. By the time I realized that Vincent didn't care that he was killing mages as he stole their magic..." In his pause, she heard him sigh. "It was too late."

Alia felt along the balcony railing, trying to find him.

"I tried to make the spell rebound on him, to take his magic instead of the hapless mage we had ensnared," Dorian said. "I failed."

"That was your betrayal."

"And for my crime, I was caged," Dorian whispered, standing beside her now. "Trapped in my other form."

Alia felt the ripples of Dorian's magic through the air as a flash of gold and a searing heat went past her. It was a bird, but not one of the seabirds that frequented Mandal's cliffs. It was a shimmering, golden eagle, catching the meager light of the shrouded moon on its wings. Alia had never seen such a creature, so incredibly beautiful that it must be of the Otherworld. It continued its flight around the towers of the palace, skirting around the cliff and passing over the city dwellings, visible by the torchlight.

The eagle circled higher, gliding on the same breeze that called to the waves. Alia almost lost it in the dark until it perched on the balcony just before her. She held her breath as the creature stared at her, thinking of turning in the direction Dorian had disappeared to. But instead, she just remained fixed in the eagle's probing gaze, drawn in. As she watched the eagle's eyes shifted, widening until it was Dorian perched on the railing before her.

Alia reached up without thinking, touching the etched pattern on Dorian's head. "They're feathers," she whispered, as Dorian stilled under her touch.

"Not something I share readily." Dorian watched for her reaction.

"The Tiarcon of the Sun can change his shape."

"High magic. One of my affinities," Dorian confirmed.

"And Vincent." Alia's finger trailed down Dorian's cheek. "He trapped you as an eagle."

Dorian leaned his head into her hand, closing his eyes. "For years. My memory of that time was taken, but I remember how it felt. I still fear changing forms, that I won't be able to come back to myself. And to share that side of myself with others, I still find it very difficult. It hasn't yet been a year since I escaped that place."

"Dorian." The right words fled Alia, leaving her to gape at him. It was suddenly so obvious how Dorian had managed to endear himself to her despite her attempts to block him out.

They both knew what it felt like to be trapped, their bodies used against them. The eagle was the shadow she had seen in Dorian's form, two bodies together as one, two sets of wounds.

"Odessa's gift." The thought burst to the forefront.

"As much of a message to me as it was to the King."

Alia's horror made her grab hold of him, pulling him down from the railing and against her chest. Dorian shook against her, his breath uneven as he held back sobs. "Was it—"

"I don't know who, as I've never met someone with my affinity. But whoever they were, they must have been of my blood."

Alia held him closer, trying not to imagine the dead eyes of the eagle, that it had been the body of a mage on the king's table. Vincent had taunted Dorian about the gift—he and Odessa had murdered one of their own just to torment Dorian. Even if Dorian's loyalty to Mandal was in question, there was no possibility that he still held ties to Veillant.

"I brought Vincent mages to kill. And now, I've led him to you."

Alia could feel his tension beneath her palms, his grief and grudges. "No one could blame you for what he's done. Not then. Not now."

Dorian softened at her words, but his words remained fraught. "He'll come for the Undoing again."

"He won't be the first." She pulled back from his embrace, and they stood shoulder to shoulder at the railing.

She trembled in the wake of Dorian's confessions, depths he'd divulged to lighten her burden, to make her feel less ghastly, or perhaps just not alone. Her gratitude drove her onward, wanting to alleviate his guilt in the same way.

"Do you still want to know how I became an Undoing Mage?"

Dorian nodded, his head inching up and down at a snail's pace in her periphery.

Alia looked up at the stars and controlled her breathing. "My parents were overjoyed when I showed magical inclinations as a young girl. I became the prize of my family, sure to fetch a coveted pairing. And to do just that, they sent me to train with your predecessor."

Dorian didn't take his eyes off her, and she stared ahead.

"Except Master Ruben was more interested in making me an Undoing Mage than training me to be a healer. That, and honing the inculcation." Alia blinked tears out of her eyes, remembering when her body was no longer her own. "Have you met an Inculcation Mage?"

Dorian shook his head, still unwilling to speak.

"Once an Inculcation Mage is inside your head, once you let them in, it is nearly impossible to get them out. I was a child when he convinced me, when he enticed the permission that I didn't even know I was giving. Once inside, Ruben was powerful enough to take hold of my body, to make it move as he intended. And he had the extra influence—to whisper poison into my ear, phrases repeated over and over again until I believed them myself," Alia recounted.

'No one else would want you if they knew.'

'You belong to me.'

'Without me, you can't contain that darkness inside of you.'

"I was trapped, while he did as he wanted, while he made me do as he wanted. He hurt me in all the ways he could think of to grow the Undoing. It took me years to get the courage to tell my mother. Years of torture. And when I finally did, she called me a liar."

Dorian flinched.

"She called me a liar and told the queen. Master Ruben was Rheta's brother after all. Rheta decided that lies were too treacherous to her position for me to live. That night, Ruben cornered me in his office. He was trying to control me, to convince me that I was insane, that I had orchestrated the idea in my head. They needed me to be silent, the queen, the Master Mage, my mother, so that is exactly what they tried to make happen."

It was the short version of a long story that Alia had harbored, fearing judgment, fearing that even when they knew, nothing would be done. Her own mother hadn't protected her, had only laid her bare for more suffering. Everyone had coalesced around Ruben to make sure that he wasn't to be tarnished by Alia's accusations. The damage done to her was swept aside, not worth enough to topple such a powerful mage.

"And now, Cormac is facing threats from within for the Crown. My father picked a fight with a mage that he couldn't beat. My mother held me there, knowing what I would do. And the rest of them let them do it, wanted it to happen. To show everyone that the Undoing Mage was a Meador and loyal to the Crown. I played my part perfectly; I did exactly what they wanted. They didn't even need the inculcation."

When Dorian didn't respond, Alia shifted her attention back to the sea, trying to summon calm. It was odd to her that the Undoing was quiet, not threatening to show itself despite its origins being revealed.

He finally cleared his throat. "When you use the Undoing—"

"I feel all of it again, what he did to me. I hear him again, rifling around in my mind. Something else controlling my actions. It's only a matter of time before my mind is gone. That's what happened to every other Undoing Mage in the Meador bloodline."

Dorian's habitual warmth bordered on scalding as his aura fluctuated. Anger, just like she had seen from him in the hinterland, tainted him. "You used the Undoing against Ruben to break free of inculcation. You were defending yourself," Dorian said. "You were not at fault. You were a child, Alia. Why don't you tell them?"

She didn't want to see the look on Cormac's face if he ever found out what had been done to her. "I don't want to tell them that was how I was made. What I am."

"Does Lena know any of this?" Dorian asked.

Alia shook her head. She had never been able to bring herself to expose Lena to that horror.

"Alia," he said her name softly, like a plea to the next realm. "I'm sorry. That I pushed you to use the Undoing, that I brought that pain upon you."

"Don't," Alia repeated, placing her hand over Dorian's.

"Has any of it helped? The time that has passed, Ruben's death?"

Alia could hear the desperation in his voice, wanting her to give him hope. "I have tried to forget, to move beyond, but it is always there, waiting for me to fall just enough to be firmly in its grasp again. The Undoing, that darkness. I am what he made me."

13

There was nothing left to say, but burgeoning bonds held Alia in place, leaving her unable to part from Dorian just yet. She eyed Dorian warily, trying to see if he would look at her differently now. He gave her the same appraisal, searching her face perhaps to see if a man who became an eagle would terrify her, if his involvement in Vincent's exploitation tarnished him, or if the weight of what he had suffered made her shy away.

He didn't. It didn't.

She couldn't see how Dorian could stand to be in Mandal, to smile in the faces of the petty nobles who reviled him. He hid his true feelings away and somehow mustered the strength to withstand them. Alia had nothing but venom to offer.

"The fighting has stopped," Dorian whispered as the bells tolled and marked the early morning despite the dark.

"The dissenters have been silenced." Alia sighed, still picturing how the Undoing had ripped away Lillian's life. She clasped her hand over her arm, where the Barton brand was hidden.

Dorian placed his hand on her back, heat permeating her gown. She didn't deserve the comfort his touch gave her, but she didn't move away.

"Have either of you slept?" Lena had a blanket wrapped around her shoulders as she stepped out onto the balcony.

"I've overstayed." Dorian summoned a smile for her daughter.

Lena's tight lips barely moved. "Mother, you must be tired." She spun away, retreating back inside.

Dorian bowed his head and disappeared, flickering away. Alia looked at the space he had just been standing in, missing the warmth that he took with him. She stepped inside to find Lena prodding the fire.

Alia settled herself on the couch. She felt like she had been hollowed out, blood seeping out of her hands. The pain was fresh, persistent, a pulsing chorus making it impossible for her to think clearly.

"Well?"

Alia took in Lena's tightly curled fists. "What?" Alia feigned ignorance. It was a Meador trait to retreat inward, to cut oneself off from anything that could hurt. To deceive.

"You're going to leave." Lena's eyebrows knit together.

Alia's teeth bit into her cheek. Lena always had a way of anticipating her moods and decisions, learned over the years. "It is too dangerous here."

"If you go, you're the one leaving me." Lena's eyes were glowing, burning. She was losing control, ready to erupt.

Her magic grated against Alia's, a novel sensation rippling through her. It was like he was there, staring through her daughter's eyes.

Nothing explained the power Lena wielded, the power that Alia had felt the night Finn died. And Dorian, who could see magic, knew.

It was not of this realm.

"Do you remember Tesira?" Alia plucked out the memory of the hound that was always at Finn's side. Tesira had immediately warmed to Alia, but it had taken her years to get used to the mongrel.

Lena balked. "Of course, I do."

"He talked to her."

"Constantly," Lena agreed.

"No. He talked to her. Like she was talking back."

Lena bit her lip.

"He said he was quotidien. I never saw him use magic. I never sensed it." Alia pulled her arms tighter. "But the night he died ... he was fighting back against the marauders, and he changed. And then he was gone."

Lena's shoulders caved. "I know."

Flashes of Finn went through Alia's mind. The haunted mood that he would never fully explain, and how he was terrified that she would leave him alone. The signs that Alia hadn't had the capacity to understand at the time but had plagued her in the years since his death.

"I don't have answers for you." Alia grasped Lena's hands. "I don't know who, what he was."

"But someone here might."

It was an impossible position. If she stayed, the Undoing would be provoked to further others' ambitions. But if they left, Lena would suffer.

"Go rest," Alia granted, conceding to Lena for the moment.

"And you'll stay?"

Despite her exhaustion and reluctance, Alia forced a smile. "I'll stay."

She waited until Lena shut the door of her room behind her. The bed within creaked as Lena lay down, hopefully now able to find the sleep that eluded her.

The palace bells rang out the morning hour, but dawn showed no signs of arriving. Alia knew she must be a sight, splattered with blood from the hall, but she didn't bother with washing, changing, or even fixing her hair.

The Undoing churned within her, demanding her attention. The roaring that subsided after Lillian returned had been fueled by the layers of betrayal. Finn's lies. Her family's manipulation. And while Finn's ashes had been left in the ruins of their village, only a few passageways separated her from her family.

Both guards jumped when she thrust the apartment door open, their armor clattering against stone as they tried to restrain her. Alia moved past both, stomping down the corridor.

"My lady—" one tried to appeal to her as they rushed to catch up.

"I'm going to see the Meadors." Alia attempted the feeble explanation, noting that the guards stopped short of making physical contact with her. Either out of fear or orders.

"You must return to your chambers." The other was less proper.

Wisps of Undoing escaped her hold, following separate designs and latching onto both guards at once. A row of broken ribs, a stab wound to the thigh.

Neither guard managed to follow her after that.

The Undoing swelled in Alia's chest, guiding each step she took. And she certainly knew the way—she knew every turn of these halls.

The Meador palace apartments had been her first home.

There were no guards at the doors, as the Meadors had never needed them. The horned golden doorknocker shone in the glow of the hallway torchlight. The rest of the wooden door was smooth; no handle to be found.

The Meadors never allowed anything, not even entrance, easily. And she knew no matter how much her parents despised her, they wouldn't have tampered with the generations-old spells that bound the door. She felt along the horns, the Undoing prickling against it as she pressed harder. The tips of the horns were sharp enough to cut through the skin of her fingertip and draw out the sacrifice demanded.

Meador blood.

The door groaned as it admitted her. Signs of the Meador's growing fortune were apparent as she stepped inside. The foyer dripped with crimson, an unsurprising fascination in a bloodline renowned for violence. Glowing rubies were encased in golden fixtures and white pillars framed elaborate tapestries; it was almost awe-inspiring.

Alia bypassed the finery, walking deeper within through a tight passageway. It had taken some getting used to when she was young, as the air was heavier here and the ceiling low, a trial that each person entering the Meador rooms had to pass. But even more disconcerting than the gloom of the close walls was what hung on them. A double row of axes stretched the length of the hall, gleaming like rows of teeth.

The other houses liked to joke that Meadors were born with axes in their grasping hands, birthed from the very forges the Meador lands were famous for. There were plaques nailed under each axe, a list of names. But these were not the names of the past Meador lords and ladies. Instead, they bore names of nearly every great house in Mandal, and many more from Royce, Parth, and Veillant.

For these axes had been preserved, spelled always to be stained with blood. Bright, fresh blood never to fade, blood belonging to each name listed under. The blood spilled by Meadors over the centuries.

And that is how one was greeted into the Meador apartments.

The rooms were quiet, each holding a perverse interest for Alia to distinguish what was the same and what had changed, to remember the scenes from a childhood she had purged from her mind. Mariana and Edgar weren't there—likely still on the royal floors—but Alia pressed on. Past the entertaining rooms, the elaborate couches, and wide tables were the winding corridors of the Meador bedchambers.

The door that had once been cloaked with spells, any manner of cruel sensations that Alia could dream up to avoid interruption. But now it was quiet, dead, and without the spark of magic. She pushed it open and was met with darkness. Moving back to the hall, Alia claimed a lamp, holding it out before her to take a look into her old room.

It was clean, cared for. She might have softened at the realization, but it was too close to the blood on untarnished axes, a crafted depiction, a portrait of a time marked with so much pain. The lie that her parents were so enamored with that they couldn't break free of it to save her.

Before she could even take an inventory of each dress, scrap of parchment, or jewel, she cast the lamp onto the bed, spewing oil and flame. Alia waited, chest heaving, as the flames caught. There was no magical encouragement, no interference from the Undoing.

Just fire.

After the bed erupted, the table and the closet followed, licking over the stone floor and walls. The heat made Alia draw back, the black smoke choking out the stale air.

She then slammed the door shut, stealing away into the hall once more. She stayed there, listening to the hiss of the fire, hoping to hear the crack of stone as she knew what raged just behind the door. It wouldn't be able to be ignored as she had been. Eventually, the fire would consume the door itself and spill into the hallway, infecting each room with the stench of soot and, if she was lucky, burning its way through the whole of the Meador apartment. Reducing it as she had been reduced, at last making them feel one twinge of what she had suffered. A sliver of justice that she claimed for herself.

Alia stayed there, in the hall, a smile of satisfaction plastered on her face as the door splintered and buckled. The smoke spilled out, filling her lungs, and still she stayed.

It wasn't long before her parents rounded the corner to the passage that their daughters had shared, the poison dripping from their mouths more toxic than what fire could muster.

Edgar's first move was to run for water, while Mariana went to demand help from the servants. The flames licked the walls, searching for something else to consume.

"What have you—" Elowen stopped, pulling cloth over her nose and mouth to ward off the putrid air. When she tugged on Alia's arm, Alia followed her, still grinning, all the way out of the Meador apartments and into the palace hall.

Cloaked guards gathered outside, and Elowen directed them to fetch the mages to sort out the incident; water and air would make quick work of Alia's disturbance.

"Do come on." Elowen did not relinquish her hold on Alia until they had trekked across to the royal apartments and were settled within. "You reek."

At Elowen's urging, Alia stripped down to her shift, not minding the smoke that clung to her clothes and hair. The queen had a robe brought for her and tea for her throat before sending her attendants away and leaving them staring at each other across from Elowen's lavish table.

"I suppose thanks are in order first." Elowen cupped her mug. "The Palmers were planning to murder my sons; I owe you a debt for what you did last night. We've been up all night sorting through everything. Cormac and I."

Alia flinched at the sound of his name. Cormac had likely been the one to put those words in Elowen's mouth, the idea that the destruction of another house was warranted. This was the way Cormac would keep his Meador hounds loyal.

"Lillian should have never been allowed near you," Elowen continued. "They were supposed to be protecting you."

"They've never protected me." Alia folded her arms and leaned away from the comfort of the tea. "They've only ever used me."

Elowen scoffed, staring ahead to avoid looking at her. "Not just you. You're easy to hate, do you know that?"

She did.

"This is your life; this is what you were supposed to become."

Alia let her sister's anger wash over her.

"I hate you for what you did to Cormac. We thought you were dead, and still you were always there, between us. I could never do enough because I was never you. And then when you came back ..." Elowen's hands were shaking. "I hated you for being out there this whole time while I was stuck here living your life. And now you're the damn savior of Mandal, the only one who can battle the Otherworld. And instead of mending your wrongs, you seem determined to expound them, refusing to help unless under duress.

"And I've wondered why. Why you absolutely refuse to fulfill your duty. To honor your family." Tears made lazy paths down Elowen's cheeks. "But it was all right there in front of me all this time, wasn't it? This life was taken from you."

Alia opened her mouth to speak, faltering several times before Elowen continued, "I didn't realize it until Queen Rheta threatened you. Mother filled in the rest. But I should have known what Master Ruben did to you. I should have seen."

"We were children." It was stunning to be faced with Ruben's memory so soon after speaking it aloud to Dorian, the first time she had told someone of it since Finn.

"We aren't anymore." Elowen wiped her face.

"It is fine to hate me." Alia didn't want to think about what kind of a sister bedding Cormac made her.

"Last night was too far, too much. I can't watch you suffer anymore, so I told Cormac." Elowen reached for her hand.

The teacup slipped from Alia's fingers and clattered to its saucer, somehow managing not to spill its contents. "What do you mean? What did you tell him?"

"You're to be reinstated as a noble of the Court. Lena will officially be granted the Meador name and title." Elowen's face regained a bit of color, as if she was delivering grand news.

"I don't understand."

"I told Cormac about Ruben," Elowen said.

There was no name for the sensation that overtook Alia. Her joints locked; she couldn't feel her face, let alone form words.

"He needed to know, and you needed him to know."

A scream gathered in her throat, flames dancing before her eyes as she stifled both. Alia had carried the truth about Ruben and had hidden it from Cormac, only for it to be divulged by her sister. Her whole body went cold, failing to function.

But when she looked at Elowen, there was only earnest intent etched in her features. She didn't know, didn't understand, what it meant for her to divulge a secret that wasn't hers.

"We can set it right. But I need you." Elowen hunched her shoulders in an unfitting posture for a queen.

Questions formed and died in her mind before Alia gave up. "You have me," Alia choked out, unable to offer any other assurances in her state.

More tears gathered in Elowen's eyes, accompanying the doubt that lurked there. "I know Flora told you about Harlan."

"She did." Alia was relieved for the shift away from Cormac.

"Do you think I'm terrible?"

"Not at all." Alia knew her voice was too wooden, but it was all she could manage.

Elowen needed little encouragement to continue, her confessions rolling like a stone toppled from a peak. "Cormac was attentive during both pregnancies, so pleased with me. But then, after they were born, all he had for me was indifference. As if he didn't even see me. I held no interest to him now that he had two male heirs."

The heartbreak was evident in Elowen, the cruelty that Cormac had shown her.

"I figured that since I would not have a chance to be a good wife, I would at least be a good mother. I sent the maids and nurses away to leave me alone with Owen. And I was a miserable mess at taking care of him on my own." Elowen rubbed her hands together. "One night, I was begging Owen to go to sleep in the nursery." A light shone in Elowen's face from the memory. She wasn't even looking at Alia but staring off into the distance. "Harlan barged in, wearing full armor, as if he were attacking an intruder and not beholding a devastated woman and a child. And then he took Owen from me, and, with a gentleness that I had never seen from a man, rocked him to sleep. When Owen was asleep enough to lie down, I found myself in Harlan's arms. Cormac had never held me like that."

Alia nodded. For so long, it had been all she wanted, too. To be held, to be loved, to be cared for. In the way Meadors could never bring themselves to love. She and Elowen had become so intoxicated by nurturing kindness because it was something they had never known, never learned.

"And after that, I didn't give him a moment's peace." Elowen finished her story with a smile on her lips. "I need him. He doesn't look at me and wish I was someone else."

Her sister's raw confession eased Alia's anger. She couldn't begin to unravel her emotions with the weight of everything else pressing in on her.

An apology would be wasted, as nothing Alia could impart now could change what Elowen had already survived. “I ... Cormac—”

Elowen dismissed the beginnings of an apology with a wave of her hand. “I wish things were different. That I could pledge my love to Harlan before the entire hall. If not for the boys, I think I’d do it. I would rather be ruined than royal, as long as I had him.”

The morning after Mabon was dark, mocking ideals of balance with its persistence. The guards stationed at the door during the fighting melted away with each tolling. Torches were refreshed, stewards delivered breakfast, and no one appeared to make Alia answer for setting fire to the Meador apartments. Or murdering a noblewoman in the middle of the hall.

Nothing was amiss. Lena sat across from her at the table, not quaking with immortal magic but drawn from too little sleep.

“How is Madeline?”

A biscuit bore the brunt of Lena’s frustration. “My family killed hers.”

Another casualty. “That is how these rivalries perpetuate, binding us to the actions of our kin.”

“Is that why you pretended not to have family?”

“One of the reasons.” Alia took a bite. “I hope Madeline can see through this.”

Both flinched at a knock on the door, their silverware clattering against the plates.

Flora shook her head as she bustled in, hair flying and skirts swirling.

"You leave the door unlocked? Time to go, Ali."

"Why?" Alia asked. Flora was certain to have known about the Meador plot, had probably been a part of it herself.

Lena pretended to be absorbed in her food, but her eyes rose to shift between Alia and Flora.

"Because the sun is about to rise. And your complexion could use a little warmth." Flora let out a mocking laugh as she teetered down the hall to Alia's room.

Lena snorted.

"Do you have something to add?" Alia scowled.

The smile on Lena's face was worth a thousand of Flora's insults. "She's not wrong."

When Alia swept past to make sure Flora wasn't making a mess of her room, she flipped Lena's book out of her hands.

Flora had thrown open her closet and was shuffling through its contents. "Ah, here." She selected a red gown.

"Flora, leave me be."

"You know very well that I can't leave anything be. And you owe me; it took me nearly an hour to cleanse the Meador rooms after your fire." Flora busied herself with the armoire. "Ah, look, just your shade of red. It took years after you left for the ladies of Court to be bold enough to wear *your* color again. I don't think Wylann ever has."

Flora alluded to Alia setting Wylann's dress on fire because she dared to wear a color that Alia had claimed as hers. The flames had reached her hair, setting her entire head aflame before the tutors put it out. Alia remembered Wylann's scream and how pleased she had been with herself for the display, her delight only heightened when Wylann claimed the whole incident was an accident, her own graceless mistake. Now the mere memory made Alia's stomach churn.

Flora grabbed Alia by both arms and lifted her into a seated position. "Now I haven't done this in a while so ..." Flora snapped her fingers, and a torrent of water appeared above Alia's head and crashed down on her with stunning force.

Alia cursed, and Flora cackled. "Just a bit rusty," Flora said as she laughed so hard that she struggled to breathe. "Let me try again."

Snap.

Alia found herself thankfully dry and surprisingly clean, except now she was completely naked. "Flora," Alia exclaimed, covering herself with her hands.

"Oh, please." Flora rolled her eyes. "You had the chance to dress yourself, but here we are."

Snap.

Now clothed in the crimson dress that Flora selected, Alia dropped her hands and let out a furious hiss.

"And now to fix that hair." Flora lifted her fingers to snap.

"No, no, no." Alia sprang up and closed her hand around Flora's thumb. "You're not going to touch my hair."

"Dramatic, but fine." Flora folded her arms and stepped out of Alia's way to let her sit before the mirror. Flora's spell had thankfully removed her plaits before soaking her hair, easing the tangles slightly. Alia brushed it out and fixed it in a single braid for speed, before Flora became impatient and tried her hand at another spell.

"What now?" Alia asked when she was satisfied.

"Well, last night was eventful. Which means we have plans to make." Flora spun, grabbing Alia's hand and pulling her towards the door.

"Plans? Like the one you didn't tell me about?"

"Come now, Undoing Mage. You wouldn't have cooperated otherwise." Flora was a whirlwind as she looped Alia's hand around her arm, nearly yanking Alia forward onto her face.

One of the things about Flora that Alia used to appreciate the most was that she required very little encouragement or response to carry on a conversation. Alia was again content to let her friend go on, picking up and dropping threads as she went. It lulled her into a comfortable space, companionship without the burden of performance.

"And Lady Gwen had to claim rivers, no torrents, of blood. So, of course, I had to step in and fill them in on what really happened. That Lord Tristan nearly burned the life out of Lord Meador before you were forced to retaliate—"

"Retaliate, Flora?"

"He would have if you hadn't subdued him so quickly. My throat is going to go raw from having to tell the tale so many times. And Baldric, that insufferable ass, was no help at all. I swear his bluster over being quotidien gets worse with every year. Harlan doesn't have any magic, and you don't see him pouting about it at every turn."

Alia pursed her lips.

"And that Lillian," Flora continued. "I have no tolerance for that kind of behavior. She couldn't accept what she was."

"She's dead, Flora."

"A fitting punishment."

They climbed the stairs towards Harlan's quarters, reminding Alia of Elowen's confession and Lillian's accusation the night before. "Why didn't Cormac and Elowen's pairing supersede mine?"

Flora snapped out of her rambling. "Don't you know anything?"

"You know that you're going to tell me, so do you really need to bother with insulting me first?"

Flora heaved a sigh. "Fine. But don't go all dark and misty on me." Flora pulled her down to sit on a bench for the added effect of looking straight at her while she divulged her gossip. "Elowen cheated during her pairing ceremony with Cormac. She even had Queen Rheta fooled."

"Cheated?" Alia narrowed her eyes. "You can't cheat a pairing."

"You can if you tamper with the elixir," Flora whispered, lifting an eyebrow.

"What are you saying?"

"I'm saying that Elowen, with all of her concoctions, made the elixir so that it would yield a successful pairing when Cormac's blood was mixed in." Flora's eyes were wide, her elation clear.

Alia shook her head. "Elowen wouldn't." And if she had, she would have confessed it to Alia along with everything else.

"The princes are magical, yes." Flora kept prodding. "But not nearly as powerful as a reaction like that would indicate."

"What does it matter now, Flora, all these years later?"

"Because you remain Cormac's proper pairing. If Mariana were any sort of Intercessor, she would enforce it," Flora said, speaking slowly to note the gravity of her words.

"You just want to see everything burn."

"Rich, coming from you. I want to see you be yourself again. Take back what is yours. Cormac, the crown. With an Undoing Queen, no one would dare stand against the fourth Barton king." Flora was trying not to draw attention to herself, but her furious whispering was far from inconspicuous.

"The woman who wanted those things is gone."

"Don't let him win, Ali," Flora said. "Ruben is dead; you can live the life that you were meant to."

The Undoing fluttered, Flora's words the only provocation it required. Alia had said something similar to herself over the years—she was out from under his magic, he couldn't hurt her anymore—and yet, the damage remained. She couldn't expect Flora to understand.

"Does everyone know?"

"Cormac told us."

"Us?"

"Baldric and Harlan. He's a mess about it, Ali. And I—" She paused. "I find everyone's secrets. You weren't the only one, Ali."

"Rosalynn."

Flora nodded. "And others."

Of course there were.

Alia's heart pounded, her face hot and tears all too close.

"You're stronger than this."

"You don't know what the fuck you're talking about."

Flora had really meant, Y*ou* should *be stronger than this.*

Alia wasn't.

Flora inched back, expression curious. She looked down at the ground, swallowed, and then sucked in another breath. "Ali, I just want to bring you back."

Harlan's door swung open. "Ali!" His smile was too wide to be genuine.

Baldric was all harsh angles, jaw quivering as if he didn't know what to say. Flora remained frozen, as if staring could bring back the person she'd known.

Alia's skin was too tight.

"We have much to discuss." Harlan ushered them in, directing them to a table already littered with papers.

"We need an accounting of the remaining living Palmers and Paxtons and decide if they can be left alone. I'd rather not have Wexworth grabbing for their lands," Baldric began.

More targets on the list. Mages that she would have to deal with.

"And the summit. The invitations have been dealt with, but we haven't even begun to prepare for the delegations or the bouts."

An influx of nobles, more Court events to endure. Everyone looking at her and wondering if she was about to kill again.

"I can't."

"You can't turn your back on this." Baldric was obviously still angry about her comments about George. "Need I remind you." He gestured towards his shoulder, where all of them bore proof of their blood oath to protect the Spear of Orlast.

"Leave her be," Harlan interceded.

Alia was still boiling over Flora's words. "As if we can stand against the power of Veillant and Alasar."

"What is the alternative?" Baldric pressed.

Alia drew away from them as mist escaped her hands. The memory of how simple it had been to drain away Lillian's life made her turn away.

"You two see to the accounting of the remaining family members, Cormac will expect an outline of the summit. Alia and I are going to check on the progress with the ships," Harlan said.

Baldric and Flora tried to protest, mostly about being tasked to work with each other, but Harlan wouldn't hear any of it.

The captain didn't speak as he took Alia's arm and intertwined it with his, escorting her through the palace halls. The silence was a welcome change as Alia scrambled to recover.

Meadors didn't entertain sentiment; strength was the highest pursuit. She had been driven mad by it, interpreting it as brutality. As the years went on, she became more consumed by mere survival. Flora's goading may have been well-intentioned, but it was a searing stab into her armor.

Harlan nodded to the guards as they left the palace grounds, moving out into the sundrenched square.

"I would have thought you'd be tired of escorting me."

The burly man smiled. "Only of being ordered to."

"To the docks then?"

"No, though we'll catch a glimpse. We're going to the Wall." Harlan's smile vanished.

The Wall was abjured by most Mandals, revered by a small few. Mandals sent their dead to the Sunset Realm in flames, pushed out to sea on boats, lit by a flaming arrow, their bodies to become one with the sea and air, to be lifted onward to the realms beyond. Still, a subsect of Mandals had desired a piece of the dead to remain behind with Entien, proof of their existence after so many years of toil and death in Alasar at the hands of the Tiarcons.

If those left behind willed it, the names of the dead were carved into the cliffs of Mandal, where the sea met the mountain.

Harlan kept a slow pace to allow Alia to keep up with him. It wasn't long before Alia saw wooden structures erected along the shoreline. Half-constructed ships for the war with Veillant, a siege of an isle that had never been breached.

Alia sank deeper into her mood, not wanting to face the scene before her. Each ship would carry hundreds to their deaths, common soldiers sure to be broken against the might of Veillanti magic.

The low tide allowed them to access the Wall on foot, skirting along the surf, leaving behind footprints in the sand that faded quickly and covered their presence. Harlan paid no mind to his damp boots or Alia's dragging hem as he looked overhead at the names. Somewhere up there, Daphne and Howard Gust were etched, Harlan's parents.

"Baldric nearly throttled me for carving George's name. One would think he'd be the last one to have superstition about the Sunset Realm. But I find him down here sometimes, talking to him."

"Baldric has never known what was good for him," Alia said, searching the names for one she recognized. There had been no passage to the Sunset Realm for Finn.

"Grief," Harlan said. "When my mother died so soon after my father, I was in its clutches. And nothing anyone said could make it better. There was nothing to say." He paused. "I wonder if it is the same for your situation."

Alia rubbed the back of her neck. It was difficult to unravel her emotions when they were weighing her down.

Harlan settled himself on a rock. "Do you remember what you told me then?"

"Orlast knows I won't own to it now." Alia sat beside him.

"You said you would never play another trick on me for as long as you lived." Harlan chuckled. "A lie if I ever heard one."

Alia laughed with him, surprising herself.

"And good thing it was a lie," Harlan said. "Because weeks later, when you put honey in my boots, I remember it being the first time I felt like myself again. Not Harlan Gust, the tragic orphan. But just Harlan, the boy with the absolute worst friends in the realm."

"If I recall correctly, it was you and Cormac who put taffy in my hair first," Alia said, her laugh shaking her shoulders.

"I don't doubt it." Harlan sighed and looked back at the Wall. "Do you want to talk about it? Just you and I."

Alia shrugged. "At times, I feel like speaking of nothing else. And then other times, I want to pretend as if it never occurred. As if Ruben never existed."

"And now?"

Alia closed her eyes, letting the waves quiet her mind before tears surfaced. "I know you all look at me and see a ghost. That you're searching for the person I was. I miss her, too."

Harlan murmured in agreement.

"But I want you all to still love me, even though it hurts to find me changed." They were words Alia had never spoken, a plea she had never been strong enough to make. To be valued as she was now, not as a memory or out of respect for ties forged long ago.

"Ali." Harlan cleared his throat. "I'll never try to convince you that any of us know the proper way to love. Flora always has something to share about others but rarely chooses to divulge the truth about herself. Baldric battles with those closest to him, daring us to reject him just like others have. And Cormac. He thinks he's sparing us, protecting us from the worst of it by carrying all the weight alone."

"And you love so many things, so many people, that it is impossible to be true to all of them at once."

"Aye. My point in all of that ..." Harlan paused to collect himself, rubbing his clammy hands together. "Is that you can be certain that we all love you the best we can. And you aren't alone."

She clasped Harlan's shoulder, letting time pass and her emotions settle. Harlan was transfixed on the Wall, the heft of his words holding him in place.

"I suppose I can stop hassling you over Elowen."

"Thank Orlast." Harlan looked to the sky. "You must know, Elowen is the sun."

"She better be."

"I tried to fight it." Harlan sighed. "But then I would come out here. Eventually, all of us will become this, just a name on the Wall. And shouldn't we try to hold onto anything we can until then?"

14

Harlan delivered her back to her quarters, leaving her with one more crushing embrace. "Now to make sure Baldric and Flora haven't murdered each other. May the sun stay high."

"And the moon forever fallen." She paused in the doorway, looking down the hall and savoring the quiet. She wiped her tears on her sleeve and smoothed her hair, a strange lightness taking root.

When she turned around, Lena and Dorian crowded the balcony entrance.

"Where have you been?" Lena's scolding was blunted by the softness in Dorian's eyes.

Alia let a small smile peek through. "Enjoying my freedom."

Lena looked down at Alia's hem. "You're soaked."

"Allow me." Dorian waved his hand to conjure a steaming pot of tea and several cups, in the same breath, showering Alia with his warming magic.

Comfort. Abandoning her sullen instincts, Alia sank into it. "Thank you."

Lena shook her head and turned back to the balcony. Alia snatched up a cup, watching as satisfaction graced Dorian's features and his shoulders relaxed; he was clearly pleased that she had taken something he offered. For once.

"What is that spell?"

"Spell?" Dorian's brows knitted together.

"When you feel like sunshine."

"Sunshine?" Dorian's confusion gave way to amusement.

She snapped her head back towards him. "You know what I mean."

"The magic in my bloodline was taken from the Tiarcon of the Sun. I have learned how to extend my aura to bring comfort and calm. I've been told it feels like rays of sunshine before."

Once, she had seen only horror in his ability, but there was so much beauty. "So, it's just ... you?"

"You have drawn it out of me before. When you needed me." Dorian's deep eyes brimmed with emotion. He liked being someone she needed.

"It is rare, isn't it?" Alia frowned. Unease settling in her—wanting, needing someone had never ended well for her.

"Only high magic can create an aura potent enough to be shared this way."

"What about mine?"

"Ah." Dorian scratched his brow. "I suspected that you weren't aware of your effect."

"My effect?" Alia rounded on him, both desperate for him to explain and unsure if she wanted to know. With a power like the Undoing, she was terrified to think what her aura felt like. "It's dark, isn't it?"

Dorian put his hand on her shoulder, and Alia breathed in his warmth. "You already know. The Undoing and the healing are shades of both at times. The other night, when you learned the truth of Odessa's gift, your aura came to me as healing *and* as a need for vengeance." Dorian's eyes shifted away from hers, and he withdrew his hand. "I can teach you to choose to extend your aura, but it should be intuitive now that you're aware. It isn't a bad thing; it is who you are."

She wished those words could be inculcated, scratched into her mind. Not warnings about how the Undoing would destroy her, but that she could exist alongside it. That even with the poison of her bloodline and how thoroughly she'd been beaten down, there was still a bit of herself left.

For the first time, she was jealous of Dorian's sight, wanting to know what she looked like to him. "You've said before you can see magic. You can see the Undoing?"

"Yes," Dorian's voice was barely above a whisper. "I can see it, see you. Every shade."

Dorian stayed still and quiet beside her. Alia wondered if he was sensing her power, trying to see if the Undoing was going to show itself again.

"Are you warm enough?" He reached for her hands wrapped around her teacup.

Alia knew she shouldn't encourage him; she should step away. But his touch, attentive and soft with a shiver of nervousness, felt good. She wanted so badly to feel good.

"I'm going to reach the roof this time," Lena called out.

Dorian turned, severing contact as they both went out on the balcony. Lena coaxed a vine all the way up the palace walls, passing the balcony above and clinging to the rough stones. Alia had spent her youth climbing those stones, sneaking from floor to floor where no one could see.

"This time?" Alia whispered to Dorian.

"Her skills are progressing." Dorian tipped his head back and shielded his eyes to watch the vine continue to creep up the outer wall.

They pressed their backs against the railing as Lena outstretched her hand, extending her control. The progress of the vine slowed as it neared the top of the Olden Wing. A sheen of sweat broke out on Lena's forehead.

"That is far enough," Dorian declared. "Well done."

Lena ignored him, grimacing as she reached even higher. She at last dropped her hand, a few feet short of her goal, and a burst of garnet light careened into the sky as she let go. The light crackled like lightning, temporarily darkening the sunlit sky.

"Now, the signal," Dorian instructed.

Lena bent over, bracing her hands on her hips as she panted. She cast her hand back up into the sky, a swirl of garnet spheres traveling up as far as Alia could see.

"Signal?"

"To let the rest of the Tower know we're not under attack," Dorian said with a sheepish grin.

"And I suppose there was an incident to prompt the development of this signal?"

"A very minor one." Dorian coughed.

"Did you see how close I was?" Lena approached.

"Incredibly." Alia looked back up. "And the cloud is stunning."

"Cloud?" Lena and Dorian's heads both snapped towards the sky.

Hovering near the space where Lena's spheres had swirled was a crimson cloud, crackling with orange and golden beams.

"That's not mine." Lena gaped.

"Nor mine." Dorian's fingers began to twitch.

The cloud began to descend, hurtling towards them.

"Take your mother and go." Dorian put a barrier around them.

Lena seized Alia's arm. "I can't move." Lena's face reddened.

All they could do was watch as the cloud descended from the sky, hovering over the balcony before transforming into a human figure.

A scowling older woman, with wrinkles marking numerous lifetimes, stepped forward. At first look, Alia assumed this was another immortal, come to infiltrate their realm. But she didn't feel like the Oucura or the Traimine. Not even like Lena. Alia couldn't feel the being's magic at all. She was a void.

"I told you not to take too long," she said to Dorian, her coal black eyes burning with intensity.

Dorian tensed for a moment, hands fidgeting. "Has it been long?"

The older woman just grunted in response. "Aren't you going to invite me inside?"

"I would be honored to host you in my office, it is just—"

"I'll remain here."

Alia shot Dorian a glare as the woman walked past her and inside the suite. They were released from the spell that held them in place. Lena dashed into the sitting room after the woman. "What are you?"

The woman snorted. "Someone should teach you manners."

Dorion interjected, "This is Lady—"

The woman scowled when he spoke her title with uncertainty.

"... Effe. May I present Lady Lena and Lady Alia?"

"A friend from Veillant?" Alia stepped slowly around the back of the couch Lady Effe settled on, staying close enough for the Undoing to reach her if necessary.

"Uh ..." Dorian twitched, his attempt to appear nonchalant transparent as he leaned against the wall.

"I am not a part of any mortal kingdom," Effe said, lifting her head high.

Alia moved closer, wanting to be able to intercept the mysterious woman if she moved towards Lena. The emptiness that Effe was shrouded in was perplexing.

Effe must be Alasaran. And her magic was cloaked.

"Go back," Alia said. The Undoing gathered at her fingertips.

Effe twisted to look at Alia, her bottomless eyes capturing her. "You're the last one who should be making threats." She reached for Lena's hand; Lena recoiled slightly but let Effe take it. "We've been waiting for you."

The Undoing spilled out of Alia, seeking the woman and aching to bring her to heel. But the Undoing breezed over her, glancing off without effect. It was as if there was nothing where the woman sat.

"Undoing Mage," Effe said through clenched teeth. "I have no use for you." With unseen force, Effe pushed the Undoing back at Alia, locking it up inside of her.

Lena looked between her mother and Effe, but something about the older woman had her cowed. "Are you like my father?"

"Hardly," Effe said. "You're the one who carries his magic."

"What was he?"

Effe dropped Lena's hand in a rage. "I sent you here to educate her!" she bellowed at Dorian.

For a moment, Alia forgot about Effe. Her vision homed in on Dorian as the Master Mage flinched and stammered. She had known from the beginning that a Veillanti couldn't be trusted and that any leader of the Tower had to be corrupt. She had known, and yet she had been unnerved by him. She had come to rely on him, come to care for him, even.

She was going to kill the leech.

"Alia..." Dorian's tone was a warning as he began to back away.

"How fucking dare you!" Alia edged around the couch, her fury crackling before her, a deluge of the Undoing lancing its way across the room.

"Alia, wait," Dorian said, holding off the Undoing.

"You lied to me!" Hot tears rushed down her cheeks. "To Lena!"

Dorian strengthened his defense and started tearing at his robes, pulling at them until he was down to his tunic and breeches. He unlaced his tunic, bearing the right side of his chest.

Alia dropped her hands.

Etched across Dorian's chest was a circular mark, a wheel.

"You swore a blood oath?"

"It's an accord." Effe cackled from the couch. "He needed something from me, and I needed something from him. It can't be spoken, only fulfilled." The woman reached out her hand, and the brand on Dorian's chest burned. Dorian cried out and clutched his hand to his chest. "Fulfilled or it would cost his life."

"Stop, please." Lena jumped to her feet as Alia tried in vain to extend her healing to Dorian and ease his agony.

The older woman huffed and reclined, releasing Dorian. "But now that I am here, I suppose our accord has ended." She stood, palm outstretched.

Dorian was lifted into the air, his limbs spread wide as Effe mumbled. When her hand closed, he fell to his knees, and the mark vanished from Dorian's chest.

"Dorian?" Alia edged closer, keeping an eye on Effe's proximity to Lena.

"You may speak," the Alasaran granted.

"She freed me from Veillant." Dorian coughed as he struggled to catch his breath on his hands and knees. "I made the accord to get out."

"And in return, he promised to come to Mandal and await the arrival of a mage born of both realms. And he was supposed to bring her to me when he found her."

Effe had used Dorian as a tool to get closer to Lena. "Get away from her, Lena," Alia said.

"Why did you send him here?" Lena asked, disregarding her mother's warning.

"Because you will reunite the realms, my dear," Effe said.

Alia stilled. Reuniting the realms would put mortals back under the rule of the Tiarcons, forcing them to bind their blood to the tyrants for scraps of magic.

"Reunite?" Lena said slowly, clearly having pieced the implications together.

"She won't."

"You can't stop fate, Undoing Mage." Effe grasped Alia's face. Alia refused to recoil. Close up, Effe's black eyes were even more unsettling. "She knew Finnian would take to you," Effe whispered, searching for something in Alia's eyes. "But I never saw you."

At the woman's touch, Alia was no longer standing in the palace of Mandal. She was on the ice. And the Spear of Orlast was lodged in her midsection. The Undoing fettered about, trying to repair the wound. And directly in front of her, the same woman she had seen before, covered in blood.

"Mother!" Lena shook Alia's shoulders as Effe pounced.

"What did you see?" Effe said.

Not a single part of her wanted to divulge the vision to the intruder. Effe's words repeated in Alia's mind, with no sense to be found in the older woman's babbling. The only word that Alia comprehended was *Finnian.* Finn, her Finn.

"You knew my father," Lena said.

The woman's smile was cruel. "Yes."

"You're Alasaran, like him?" Lena asked. Alia couldn't share in Lena's curiosity.

"I'm nothing like him." Effe huffed. "I'm not a Tiarcon."

Alia looked to Dorian, begging the mage to recover and do something to remove Effe. He had caught his breath but appeared as transfixed as Lena. Alia couldn't let this creature keep speaking nonsense, insinuating that Finn was a Tiarcon of all things.

"You need to go!" Alia shouted in exasperation. "I don't care what you came for or who you are or who you think you know—"

"My father was a Tiarcon? Not just an Alasaran, but a Tiarcon?"

"Lena, she is delusional. She doesn't know anything."

Lena's fingers tightened on Alia's arm, holding her back.

"Your father is the Tiarcon of the Harvest." Effe's grin twisted her features.

"You really think your father hid being a Tiarcon from us?" Alia challenged Lena.

"How is that possible?" Lena asked Effe.

"Your father was not a Tiarcon," Alia insisted. "He hated them."

Alia could hear Finn's voice, cursing the Veillanti and their allegiance to the Tiarcon of the Mountains. When a Veillanti merchant had stumbled through Dihlmere, Finn had chased him out, sword in hand. His list of insults for the Veillanti had been endless: *leeches, traitors, swine ...* He had blamed every long night on them, every threat to his fields.

Effe showed off a set of rotting teeth. "The Tiarcons have been at war with one another for some time now."

Alia sighed deeply, not letting herself believe Effe.

"The Tiarcons are the stewards of both realms, the realms that used to be one. They are the source of all magic in Alasar, and now Entien." Effe pressed her hands together.

Lena stepped in front of Alia, pushing her back. "Does that make me a Tiarcon?"

"No." Effe was stern. "There were eight Tiarcons, never more. Harvest and Frost, Moon and Sun, then Mountains, Forest, Sea, and Desert.

Each is critical to supporting life, their absence devastating."

"The Tiarcon of the Moon was killed by King Orlast." Lena knew that part of their history.

"And Frost and Desert no longer dwell in Alasar. Five Tiarcons where there should be eight, two realms where there should be one. And you mortals wonder why the nights never end."

"The Tribunal created Entien." Alia's fists clenched at her sides. "Are you challenging their authority?"

Effe's laughter was infuriating. "The Tribunal is powerful enough to create a veil the Tiarcons could not penetrate, but they are not all-knowing. If they had foreseen the chaos that their ruling would cause..."

"How are you here then?"

Effe's magic surged forward, taking all the air around Alia and sucking it out, leaving her gasping and retching for breath. But the onslaught lifted, Effe advancing with a furrowed brow. "What do you have?" Effe demanded. She turned to Dorian. "Have you seen it?"

Dorian's grim expression didn't confirm Effe's sudden suspicion, but he didn't put her off either.

Her eyes were full of smoldering dark fire as she advanced on Alia again. She snatched the pouch that Alia always carried at her waist and dumped the contents on the table. In amongst a precious few coins was Finn's ring. Effe brought it close to her face and peered at its crimson gem, which glinted like an autumn sunset.

"What is this?"

"My wedding ring." Alia splayed her left hand, her skin burgeoning with speckles of light in the wake of the Undoing.

The crone snorted. "It is no mere ring. It is a talisman of the Tiarcon of the Harvest, made by his own hand. If you wore it, you would draw power from him, even across the veil." She looked like she might close her wrinkled hands around it and keep it. But eventually she handed it back to Alia. "It sings to you," she said grumpily. "It was given to you and with you it must remain. It can never be taken, only given. Wear it, never take it off your finger. Never."

Alia took the ring back and considered putting it back in the pouch just to vex Effe. As much as she didn't want to believe the older woman's musings, Alia wasn't daft. The ring that Finn had given to her was a piece of himself, the only thing he had left behind. If she could access Finn's magic, perhaps that could rival the Undoing. She placed the ring back onto her left ring finger, where she had worn it years ago.

"There were eight Tiarcons, and you said that now there are five," Lena looked intently at Effe. "So, Sun, Mountains, Forest, Sea, and Harvest are still alive?"

"If the Tiarcon of the Harvest wasn't still in Alasar, your realm would have no seasons to speak of."

"My father is alive in Alasar?"

Alia's heart leapt. It was a dream she hadn't let take hold. That, somehow, Finn could come back to her. But now, that realized hope rang hollow with the knowledge that Finn had left them alone for ten years.

He hadn't died—he had left. And he'd lied.

"And you must go to him." Effe placed a gnarled hand on Lena's shoulder. "He has much to teach you."

Lena frowned, clearly making the same calculation Alia had.

"This is useless." Alia stepped between Lena and Effe. "Lena isn't going anywhere. And she isn't going to fix a mistake made by Alasar."

"As useless as an Undoing Mage with no understanding of what the Undoing is."

Alia sensed both Dorian and Lena draw back as she and Effe faced one another again, likely expecting another magical confrontation. "I know what it is and why it's there."

"You know nothing. And the longer you treat it like your enemy rather than your strength, the more you will suffer," Effe scolded her.

"I know how I was made."

Effe threw her head back and laughed again. "Precisely. The Undoing only awakens in mages who have an understanding of its darkness, the truth of it. It is how you survived, not a manifestation of what was done. And it is your recourse. Magic seeks balance—a weapon of darkness to combat the like. You're supposed to use it."

Alia felt the Undoing stir within her. Effe didn't know her, didn't know what she had suffered, didn't know what the Undoing had put her through. She didn't know its hunger.

Effe turned to Lena. "I can take you to your father."

Lena reached for Alia's hand. "Can we go?"

"The Undoing Mage cannot go to Alasar." Effe folded her arms.

"Lady Effe." Dorian rooted himself to the ground. "You cannot take Lena."

Effe raised her eyebrows, clicking her tongue as she saw Alia and Dorian positioned protectively, while Lena clung to her mother. Then she broke into a slow smile, her posture relaxing. "I've missed mortals," she said.

The change in her demeanor sent a sigh of relief through Dorian and Lena, but Alia remained on alert.

"If the realms remain separated, both will fall." Effe gave a truly terrible smile, then blinked out of view.

In the wake of Effe's departure, Lena began to glow, filling the room with heat. "Lena!" Alia and Dorian called in unison, feeling an outburst brewing. Alia reached Lena first, putting her body between Lena and Dorian.

"Stay away from her." Alia didn't have time to care about Dorian's anguish as she turned to her daughter. "Everything is going to be fine, Lena," Alia lied reflexively. "We don't even know who or what that creature was. Alasarans have always employed trickery to bring us misery. Don't think on a single thing she said."

Lena clenched her teeth, fighting the outburst. "It is true, I can feel it. Father, my purpose, all of it."

"No, Lena," Alia insisted, projecting healing as Lena's skin turned molten.

"I'm going to get every mortal killed. You heard what she said. The realms will combine."

"You won't." Alia tried to capture Lena's attention. "We'll tell no one and never think on it again. It will not happen."

"Like you pretending you weren't an Undoing Mage?"

Alia bit her lips, shying away. She had feared for so long that Lena would become an Undoing Mage that she hadn't contemplated that she was something else entirely. "They can't have you, he can't. You're mine." Wisps of Undoing slipped through Alia's fingers.

Dorian's sunlight magic struck her as he pried Alia off Lena, pushing her aside. "You are the master of your power," Dorian said to Lena. "Fate and blood be damned, you decide."

"I don't want to give it over to Alasar. I want to fix Entien." Lena's chest heaved.

"Then you will."

At Dorian's unfailing assurance, Lena diminished, the garnet leeching from her skin.

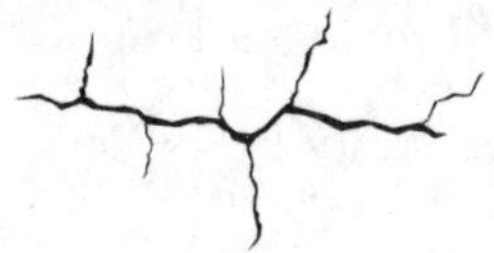

Alia shut Lena's bedroom door quietly, trying not to wake her now that she had finally fallen asleep.

"Why are you still here?" Alia asked the Master Mage as she wrapped a cloak around her shoulders.

"I can fetch someone else if you'd like." Dorian stood from the couch, face creased with exhaustion. "I don't think you should be alone."

"Did you lie to everyone about why you came to Mandal, or just to us?"

"That is not what we need to focus on right—"

"What was your plan? To get close to us, make us trust you, and then turn Lena over to Alasar?" Trust, he had once asked her for, and she'd allowed it to build.

"You're lashing out at me to distract yourself." Dorian's logic was infuriating.

"You need to go."

Dorian's fingers twitched as he looked at the ground. "No. You can say what you want, but I'm not leaving you alone."

Alia narrowed her eyes.

"Your husband is the Tiarcon of the Harvest." Dorian took an ill-advised step closer. "He's alive."

Alia shrugged. "He's still dead to me."

"The Alasarans think Lena can reunite the realms."

"She won't."

"The Undoing is you. Not Ruben, not evil. You."

"Purportedly."

He stood before her. "I told you; I can see your magic. It isn't what you fear. I think if you find a way to embrace it, you'll be able to wield it without so much pain."

Alia's lips twitched downward as her feet shifted. She hardly dared to believe the words of that woman, that she might be able to find something other than shame in the Undoing. Be able to see it as something other than a malicious force.

"Show me what you see."

Lines of worry deepened on his forehead. Dorian held out his palms, inviting Alia to rest her hands on them. She closed her eyes as Dorian's fingers tightened around hers. She'd become accustomed to his touch, even come to enjoy it, but now the Undoing searched where their skin touched, ready to defend.

Dorian's sight overtook her immediately, and a door swung wide open. She could see herself, the violet light surrounding her. And concentrated below her ribcage, the deep purple mist. She tried to look into it, sense it. To find a shade of inculcation, a shadow of Ruben.

But it looked as if it belonged—a part of her, rather than a remnant of someone else.

When she opened her eyes and returned to herself, she felt almost hopeful. It was a unique sensation, a dangerous thought for someone like her. Her lips parted as she looked back up at Dorian.

"Alia." Dorian cupped her cheek. "I entered into that accord because I had to."

Alia wrenched out of his hands. Alasarans were notorious for taking advantage of mortals in need. Effe had preyed on Dorian, forcing him into choosing between imprisonment and giving her someone he didn't even know.

"I knew when they brought Lena into the council chamber that she was the one Effe wanted. That she was the mage born of both realms. But I also knew I could help her."

Alia thought back to how ill Lena had been, unable to use her magic without an outburst. She had been a danger to herself and anyone who happened to be near her.

"And then they brought you in." Dorian rubbed his temples.

"Oh, did I make it difficult for you to rip my daughter away to Alasar? Am I supposed to sympathize?" Alia interrupted Dorian's confession. There was too much circulating through her mind already without adding his guilt.

"I didn't do it, though." Dorian's eyes glistened. "I couldn't."

Alia scowled, unmoved by his emotion. "Effe is going to come back for her, isn't she?"

"She will." Dorian nodded slowly. "Alia, your aura—"

"Fine then." Alia pulled her shoulders back, closing herself off from Dorian, stifling everything other than her most dire purpose. She had to protect Lena.

If Finn insisted on being a realm away, if he wasn't going to fulfill his duty to her or Lena, then Alia would have to. Just as she had for the decade that he had been supposedly dead. The powers of Alasar wanted to use her daughter to destroy the veil for them, to force her to subject mortalkind to the tyranny of immortals and their Tiarcon rulers.

Alia didn't care if the sun ever rose again; no one was going to control her or her daughter.

"You are not forgiven. And if you hint at trying to take my daughter from me, I will kill you. You know I can at least do that." Alia felt the Undoing leap at the threat. "But since there is no other high mage waltzing around Mandal, you'll have to do." Alia held out her palms. "Teach me how to govern the Undoing."

15

Strain blotted Alia's hands, pinpoints of light shimmering beneath her skin. As she caught her breath, they began to fade, the signs of her body healing and the high magic rescinding. The reaction was controllable in small expressions, preventing the Undoing from eating away at her hands.

A flash of flame made Alia jerk to the right, her barrier reflexive at this point. Lena had begun working with fire, part of her attempt to master every type of elemental magic. Her intensity continued to be imprecise.

After Lena mumbled an apology and extinguished her palms, Alia dropped her hands. Finn's ring still felt too heavy, pestering her with its presence even though she refused to draw from it. She refocused, leaving the Undoing alone to call instead for magic to restore life. It entered the vines before her, each leaf, stalk, and bud. The starcrest unfurled before her, five petals and a plumed center. While the blooms in the royal garden had been lavender, hers took on a deeper shade of purple as they wove through the railing of the limestone balcony.

"The Tiarcon of the Harvest is known for a number of affinities," Dorian answered another of Lena's questions. "Control of the seasons and weather, the ability to make the ground hospitable to any sort of living creature, plant or beast."

Her daughter was rapt with attention. Lena refused to blame Dorian for the episode with Effe. If Lena wanted to pretend the Master Mage was as kindly as he seemed, she had the freedom to do so. Because Alia was watching his every move once more.

Dorian instructed Lena to create a patch of snow in the middle of the Mandal autumn. He turned to Alia, delighted to see the flowers blooming under her hand. "Think of healing and the Undoing as a spectrum rather than two opposite forces." Dorian encouraged Alia. He offered her a small smile, as if that could chip away at the wall that had snapped down between them. "You've made them bloom, now take it away."

Alia obliged; Dorian was taking pains not to needlessly force her to release the Undoing in large bursts. Rather, he was allowing her to become reacquainted with it, to treat it as an extension of herself rather than an infestation. She turned her hand like a dial, spinning right to bring life and left to take it away. The flower blinked out of existence only to come back again.

"How does the veil work?" Lena asked, sending snowflakes swirling in her palm.

"The veil was designed by the Tribunal to keep the Tiarcons out of Entien." Dorian walked towards Lena to share his attention. "In one ruling, they snatched every mortal from Alasar, entire communities, and brought them to Entien. The veil is particularly attuned to keeping the Tiarcons in Alasar; the more powerful a being's magic is, the more difficult it would be to try and traverse the veil."

"How could they expect anyone other than the Tribunal to remove it?" Lena asked.

Because it all hinges upon the Spear of Orlast beneath our feet.

"Effe seems to think that it is possible." Dorian shrugged. "Vincent has been able to summon Alasarans into Entien."

"What about traveling the other way?" Lena took a drop of water, freezing it midair and crystallizing it into a snowflake. "How does one go from Entien to Alasar?"

"I don't know for certain. I've been studying how to create tears in the veil, doors."

"There has to be a way. My father came and went."

It still seemed too implausible for a Tiarcon, so fearsome that mortalkind needed to be a realm away, to be sulking in a village, taking in wayward noblewomen. Except that every kind of magic Dorian had Lena try because of her supposed relation to the Tiarcon of the Harvest … she excelled at.

Alia had heard enough. "Lena, you should change before dinner. The Meadors do not tolerate lateness." Elowen had campaigned tirelessly for her family to share a single meal, resorting to tears until Alia relented.

Lena chewed her lip like she might argue before retreating inside.

"You are no longer required," Alia dismissed Dorian.

Dorian drew to his full height and nodded towards the starcrest vine. "You are making progress."

"And you are making me late." Alia folded her arms across her chest.

He pressed his lips together, holding back his next comment. Alia turned her back on him, the absence of his aura jabbing her a few seconds later as he flickered away. Alia followed her recommendation to Lena, washing and preening to avoid giving Mariana a chance to critique her.

It had become apparent that Dorian began their classes each day hoping Alia might soften towards him, and she took pleasure in draining the optimism out of him. Punishing him, holding him at arm's length, gave her peace. She fed off his disappointment, exacting her own brand of justice despite the irritating need to interact with him.

Lena appeared in the hall in a tunic and breeches, daring Alia to make her change.

Alia smoothed her own dress. "It is your grandmother you'll have to deal with."

"I can handle her." Lena grinned. "*I* didn't set her home on fire."

With the Meador apartments still reportedly in disarray, Mariana had seen fit to demand use of the royal dining room for her dinner, requiring both of her daughters and their children to come together for what promised to be a grating affair.

Mariana assessed them when they arrived. "You're early."

Alia stiffened, not out of fear, but with hate. "It was bound to be something," Alia grumbled under her breath.

Alia prodded a snickering Lena farther into the chamber before Mariana caught on. Elowen and the princes were within, Owen rushing forward to embrace Lena while Thomas focused on a puzzle box.

Elowen's cheeks were flushed. "You look well," she greeted before looking to Thomas, disappointed when he failed to acknowledge his aunt and cousin.

"Where is Edgar?"

"The men are reading over the latest reports from Veillant."

"Men?"

"Father, Master Dorian, and Cormac, but they'll be along soon enough."

Alia's appetite vanished. Even though the inclusion of Cormac as Elowen's husband was to be expected, she hadn't anticipated the king would deign to sit through a Meador affair. He would have had ample excuses to decline: the impending war, the fate of the kingdom. She hadn't seen him since Elowen had told him the truth about Ruben. Nor had she expected Dorian's presence; it was draining enough to share the days with him. Sitting down at a table with Cormac and Dorian would make the Meador dinner even more of a torment.

"What is the impetus behind this dinner?" Alia attempted to hide her discomfort. It wasn't possible that they knew about Finn or Effe. Not even Mariana could have pulled that secret together so quickly.

"Father has an announcement." Elowen waved her hand, making light of Edgar's penchant for drama.

Mariana ushered her daughters and grandchildren into the dining room. She bid one of the stewards to fetch Lord Edgar and arranged her guests for his arrival. She pinched Alia's arm, placing her to the left of the head of the table, presumably where Edgar would sit. The King was given the seat of honor opposite Edgar, Elowen to sit at his right, Thomas on his left. Lena was steered to the position across from Alia with Mariana beside her. The seat beside Alia was left vacant, Owen a chair away.

They stood behind their chairs until the three men entered, Mariana orchestrating their movements as well. Once Cormac took his seat between Elowen and Thomas, the rest of them were given leave to sit. Alia didn't let herself look at Cormac long enough to read his expression, and she did not greet Dorian when he sat beside her.

The mage had tied his hair back for the occasion and even trimmed his short beard. It made it impossible not to admire his angular jawline, nor notice his furtive glance her way. Dorian tugged at the strap restraining his hair, clearly uncomfortable with the way his feather scars were more visible.

The arrival of the first course relieved the need to converse. When the servants had completed the delivery of each plate and filed out, Edgar cleared his throat.

"I have gathered all of you here today to discuss the fate of the Meador family."

The room seemed to shrink with each passing second, the preponderance of Meador blood in a single place crowded out the very air.

"War is at our doorsteps," Edgar began with harsh practicality. "I will be honored to represent the Meador line in battle, but that means that our affairs must be in order." He nodded to his king.

Elowen gasped and looked between her father and her husband. "Father, you can't. Cormac, you cannot permit this."

"I fought the evil of Veillant before, and I will do so again, Elowen," Edgar said evenly.

His pride was going to drive him to his death. A family trait. Alia pressed her tongue to the top of her mouth, keeping from saying as much. Her opinion wouldn't matter to him, and she wasn't moved enough by the prospect of his death to try.

Cormac dodged his wife's hand as she reached for him. "Mandal is lucky to have warriors of Lord Edgar's caliber, and we will require all of our strength for the trials ahead."

"Your father is one of the finest warriors Mandal has ever known. He will be victorious." Mariana regarded Edgar with adoration. "Still, we must prepare."

"Meador is a strong, proud bloodline," Edgar announced, and Alia arched an eyebrow and looked to Elowen. There wasn't much to be proud of in the violent Meador family history. "And it will continue to be for generations to come."

Alia noticed Mariana had fixed her eyes on her while Edgar spoke. She began to dread what was going to be said next. "With dear Elowen on the throne and her son poised to ascend to the highest title in the kingdom, I must look elsewhere for my heir."

Now, both of Alia's parents were focused on her. Alia couldn't believe that this collection of noble blood had been assembled to pressure her into accepting the mantle of the Meador household in the event of

Edgar's demise. She refused to accept being tied to the life she had hoped to leave behind.

"Mariana and I have decided that we will claim Lena as our child and heir," Edgar announced.

Alia started, having expected instead to hear her name come from her father's mouth. Lena went into a coughing fit.

"Lena is my child." Alia let her fingernails dig into the edge of the table, as Dorian's aura coated her fury.

"The question of her parentage is detrimental to her prospects." Mariana was maintaining calm in the face of Alia's distress. "If she is affirmed as our daughter in the eyes of the Crown, there will be no further stench of speculation."

Alia had determined that the truth about Lena's father would stay between Dorian and Lena for now. Dorian had sworn on his life, but Lena was less committal.

"The question of my parentage?" Lena wrenched away from her grandmother. "I have a mother. I have a father."

"A Roycan commoner with no other relations to claim is not a father," Edgar dismissed.

"My father is—"

"A request of that nature requires royal ascent." Cormac placed his elbows on the table heavily. Mariana had orchestrated a dinner designed to force the king to choose between Edgar and Alia in full view of Elowen and his sons.

"Which we humbly seek, Your Highness." Mariana bowed her head.

"Why not name Alia as your heir?" Cormac massaged his knuckles like he was preparing to use his fists.

Both Edgar and Mariana frowned. They had to be furious about the fire, but this decision was far more calculated than retaliation. "Alia will take another path to serve the family."

"Another path?" Alia hated how her voice wavered.

Edgar heaved a condescending sigh. "Your mother, the Intercessor of Mandal, has divined a new pairing for you."

Alia's blood boiled. She would not be forced into marriage, especially not while her husband still drew breath. Alia looked down the table, meeting the eyes of the man that she was currently paired to. "I do not accept."

"It is not for you to accept." Mariana's smile returned.

"But, again, it is for me to approve." Cormac's hands were now in fists.

"Mother is already mar—" Lena began.

Lena was once again drowned out by wills even stronger than hers. "My King." Mariana stood. "As the Intercessor charged with providing Mandal the strongest magical pairings, I have determined it is in the kingdom's interest for Alia to be joined with another of powerful magical blood. I am asking you to look beyond her disgrace and her crimes and think of our future."

"Ali, look at me," Elowen said quickly, sensing Alia's growing rage.

It would be better to ship Lena off to Alasar than be left with Meadors. "I will die before I subject my daughter to you as parents," Alia said forcefully, feeling the Undoing coming to the surface. "I refuse to accept a pairing."

Dorian was calm beside her. "You command the Undoing," he reminded softly.

This is not that kind of threat, she told herself, retaining the Undoing not by force but with reason. Her magic soothed, the urge to expel it subsided.

"Ali, just listen. This could be good for Lena." Elowen stood to join

Mariana. "She would have status, her own lands. And I believe we can all agree that Dorian is a fine man."

Dorian had been in the process of taking a bite, but he froze as his mouth clamped down on the fork.

Alia got to her feet. After all that she and Elowen had shared and confessed, her betrayal was particularly potent. "What does Dorian have to do with this?"

"I have determined that the most fitting pairing for you is Master Dorian." Mariana pursed her lips before turning to Cormac. "Think of the mage their union would yield."

Cormac's knuckles cracked; his glare fixed on Mariana. "I refuse."

"Thomas, Owen, you are excused." Elowen hurriedly sought to remove her children from the dining room. Perhaps in their plot, they imagined that their presence would quell Alia's anger. Their calculations had been woefully misinformed in every respect. Thomas begrudgingly obeyed his mother, smiling at the level of conflict, but Owen was in tears.

"Lena, you too," Alia said.

Lena gaped. "I have a right to—"

"Lena, listen to your mother," Dorian enforced from beside Alia.

Lena swore but stomped out of the room.

"I do not need your help," Alia hissed at Dorian.

Once the door was shut behind the children, Cormac rapped his fist on the table, his rings colliding with such force Alia thought they might shatter. "Sit," he commanded, forcing the four Meadors and the Master Mage down.

"My King—" Edgar began.

"That is enough, Lord Edgar," Cormac barked. He directed his ire at Elowen. "I do not take kindly to being cornered."

The Meadors fell silent before the menacing king, waiting for a crack to slither their way back into a position of influence.

"Nor do I relish having two members of my Council conspiring." Cormac glared between Edgar and Dorian.

"The Intercessor's determination is novel to me, Your Highness." Dorian clasped his hands.

"But you did not dispute it." Cormac's fists were still clenched, heat wafting from him. Alia could see the vein in his neck pulsing, as if he were just barely containing himself from leaping across the table and striking Dorian.

Dorian bought himself a few seconds by clearing his throat before responding to Cormac's charge. "I am unpracticed in Mandal customs, sire. You tell me what you demand of me. I will say that I have not, nor would I ever, seek a pairing with an unwilling partner, which Lady Alia clearly is."

Alia's chest constricted involuntarily at Dorian's words and the shake of his voice at the end of his statement. But her hands remained fastened to the edge of the table.

"I entrusted you to see to her magical education." Fire danced across Cormac's palms. "But you've had other intentions."

If only Cormac knew what Dorian really intended.

"Your Highness, my only intention has been to aid Lady Lena and Lady Alia in using their magic to serve Entien." There was no tremble in Dorian's voice this time. "To support them in battle each time an immortal threatens your kingdom."

Cormac clenched his jaw, his quest to make Dorian cower before him rebounding.

"A noble sentiment." Mariana checked to make sure Cormac wasn't about to silence her before continuing, "But you have sworn an oath to Mandal, an oath to share in our sacred responsibility to the veil. You cannot deny your obligation to pass on your magic, just as Alia cannot. We are all bound to this one duty."

"Is that what you told yourself when you tampered with Elowen's pairing ceremony?" Alia launched the accusation out of desperation.

And it landed.

Mariana's eyes widened with fury, her chest heaved, and Alia knew that if there was an ounce of magical ability within her mother, Alia would be dead.

"Mother?" Elowen looked at Mariana, her eyes narrowing in disbelief.

"Your sister is a liar, always has been," Mariana assured her queen.

Cormac leaned back in his chair, resigned. He already knew that Alia's charge was true.

"I am a Meador, after all." Alia moved for the door, leaving the Meadors to tear themselves apart.

As Alia moved to find Lena and distance herself from the royal dining room, she cursed her family once again. They had cornered her, twisted her to their ends. And now they were trying to take her daughter.

Dorian was the only one who had given her the respect of determining her own fate.

The fate held firmly in King Cormac's clutches.

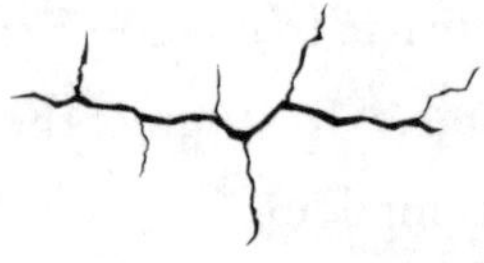

The King didn't chastise her until the next day.

She had expected the summons, dreading a confrontation over her proposed pairing more so than discussing Ruben.

Alia was delivered to the council chambers, empty save for the grim king. He stood over the map of Entien, both palms flattened on the table as he surveyed the landscape, as if his intense contemplation could make fortunes shift.

The guard shut the door behind him, leaving them alone. She had hoped that one of their friends would also be present, but whether they had already deserted her or weren't aware, there was no one to blunt the king's anger.

Staying a few paces away, Alia looked down at the same scene that was consuming Cormac. Mandal encompassed the southern portion of the continent, including an impressive coastline, large swaths of forest, and a network of fields. To the northeast lay Royce, a kingdom as harsh as its rocky terrain and treacherous rivers.

Royce and Mandal had a tenuous relationship that went back to the establishment of the four kingdoms five hundred years ago. Queen Joan had continuously contested the strength of King Orlast, even after he slew the Tiarcon of the Moon. The land they had claimed was as unforgiving as she was, but she established an unmatched reputation for warriors. Prizing battle prowess over magic had a price, as Royce had very few strong mages left as the bloodlines dried out. They placed ability over all else, even blood. Royce had been Alia's favorite place to hide over the years due to the lack of mages to identify her and Lena.

Parth jutted into the sea to the north, a labyrinth of mountains and ice. From the time of King Alfric, Parth had maintained close, albeit guarded, relations with Mandal. Still, it was unclear if they would be trusted to stand with Mandal now, as Parthians abhorred leaving their own borders. There were whispers of some talented mages in the north, those who knew the way to break through ice and find a way to survive in those harsh conditions.

Back south, across the sea, was the Isle of Veillant. The last major war between Mandal and Veillant had erupted when Alia was a child. She only vaguely remembered her father leaving and the long days of Court with just the children and women. Many noblemen hadn't returned, including Flora's older brother and Harlan's father. Bloodshed without resolution.

She looked to the pensive king, sensing the flecks of opium in his body. It wasn't enough to be a danger to him, but enough for Alia's worry to flare.

"Do you ever wonder what it must have been like to be one of the First Monarchs?" Cormac finally spoke, still searching the map for a desperate solution. "They were unified against the Tiarcons, imbued with magic of the Otherworld, the only four survivors of an entire mortal army. Do you think they knew what was to come when the fight began?"

"There was nothing inherently remarkable about the First Monarchs except their ability to survive the Battle of the Moonlands."

"You're unimpressed by the strongest mortals to ever live." Cormac leaned his hip against the table.

"I am extremely talented at not dying. Should that earn me a crown?"

"I would have given you one."

Alia suppressed a groan and let Cormac's response fade through the room.

"Why didn't you tell me?"

There was no fitting response to provide him, nothing that would encompass every feeling.

"I would have protected you." His hands were clamped into fists, flashing with flame. "I would have—"

She did not doubt Cormac would have tried violence. Maybe now he was a match for his uncle, but back then, he would have been finished.

"You were protecting me," Cormac spoke as if he could see in her mind.

From Ruben. From that ugliness. From ever seeing you look at me the way you are right now.

He leaned back and rubbed his hands through his disheveled hair. "My mother—" he cursed. "She will not be permitted to leave the Barton estate for the remainder of her life. She is not to return to the palace and will not be allowed to communicate with anyone at Court. She won't be able to hurt you anymore."

A stillness settled over her. It could not have been simple for Cormac to banish Queen Rheta. In effect, Cormac had just lost both of his parents. One to an illness of the body and the other to a wickedness of the mind.

"Thank you," Alia whispered.

"She let me hate you." Cormac's fist tightened around her fingers as he grasped her hand. "She let me lose faith in the woman I loved."

Alia wanted to apologize. For the years alone, for the worry he must have felt. But a stronger part of her mind rebuked the impulse. Because Cormac had finally learned the truth of what had happened to her, and yet was agonizing about the pain it had caused *him.*

"Ali." Cormac's breath came quickly. "I wish you had told me."

"I couldn't."

Cormac's gaze bored into hers, both of them adamant and testing each other's strength. It had been much the same when they were together—a battle of wills.

He looked so wretched that guilt festered. She had found Finn, but Cormac hadn't had anyone to put him back together or, worse still, he hadn't allowed anyone to get close. The scars were out as he sat before her. The newly crowned king was laid bare by the decades alone, isolated.

Cormac's breath hissed out as he put his head in his hands. "I never really had you, did I? You were never mine," Cormac finally said, taking what was left of her heart and grinding it beneath his boots. It was just as she feared, the pain when he regarded her, the refusal to meet her eyes. She had never told him, not out of shame, but because she knew he would only make her feel worse. His hands went slack, dropping hers.

Alia turned away from him, knowing the facade had shattered in its entirety now. The specter of the love they once shared tortured them, but it would never materialize, never grow. The versions of themselves who had loved each other had been ripped out, replaced by parts better equipped to survive. She couldn't distinguish whether the feeling in her chest was defeat or relief, leaving her panting as she focused back on the map.

"What would you do if you were me?" Cormac drew near enough to touch her again. "About Veillant."

Alia was glad for the clarification. "Find a way to kill Vincent."

"Dorian counseled the same." Cormac strummed his fingers on the table. "Declaring war could draw him out, could stop the next Otherworld attack."

"Or he'll attack us here while the soldiers are across the sea. From what Dorian says, Vincent has been plotting the destruction of Mandal for quite some time. Open war may be just what he expects."

Silence descended yet again.

"You're awfully familiar with Dorian." Cormac's biceps flexed as he rested on the table.

"I've watched him, as you ordered." Alia watched for flames as the king smoldered. Cormac had a fraction of the power that Dorian had and somehow couldn't manage to control his magic when his temper flared. "I told you he isn't in league with Veillant. I think he hates them more than you do."

Cormac snorted. "But is he loyal to Mandal?"

Alia bit back from divulging Dorian's treachery to Cormac. If she explained that, she would have to explain Lena's parentage and how her daughter was supposedly going to be the end of Entien. That is information she couldn't trust Cormac with.

He could have Lena killed.

"Have you made your decision?"

Cormac's jaw clenched. "About your pairing?"

"And Lena."

Cormac gripped her chin and turned her face towards his. "What do you want from me?"

Alia didn't drop his gaze. "Don't let them take my daughter from me."

"I told Edgar that you remain his heir."

Alia let out a breath, interlacing her fingers with his to draw his hand away from her face. He wasn't through with being tortured; he never did know how to let go. Before she could sever contact, the doors of the chambers crashed open.

"Alia!" Dorian shouted, face dripping with sweat. "Lena."

"What is it?" Alia asked, pushing Cormac away.

"There's something—something in the Tower. With Lena." Dorian's eyes were wide.

"Take us—"

Cormac didn't finish his order because Dorian was already transporting both of them to the Tower. She didn't recognize the room, but from the look of it, it was one of the classrooms at the mages' complex. Four young mages, including Madeline, were gathered in a circle and at the center of the circle stood Lena, bathed in garnet light.

"Tiarcons of the realms, I call you forth," Lena chanted, her power humming around her. "Open a door between Alasar and Entien. I call on the Tiarcon of the Harvest. Come to me, show yourself."

Her hands were coated in her own blood, two deep cuts made just below her elbow. Her spell created an irresistible draw, like a whirlpool sucking everything else inward.

"Lena, stop!" Dorian shouted as he launched himself towards the circle, breaking it by pulling back Madeline and dragging her away.

Lena was unfazed. "Tiarcons—"

"Lena!" Alia shrieked, using every bit of authority she could muster. "Stop this at once!"

Lena paused, looking at Alia through the garnet swirls. "—of the realms, I call you forth."

Cormac brought flames to his fingers. "I command you to stop."

Dorian was fueling his golden light into Lena's spell now, trying to overpower her. "Stop, please," he pleaded.

Lena was resolute as ever. Alia inched towards her, magic thick in the air. She nearly reached the circle when she was pulled back. Cormac seized Alia around her waist, lifting her into the air and hauling her backward, away from danger.

Alia's scream pierced the room, shaking Lena and Dorian's concentration as an angry flood of the Undoing latched onto Cormac. Alia unleashed the Undoing, letting it hack away at the king, forcing him to let go of her. She once again sprang forward.

There was a flash, sending Alia toppling to the ground. When she recovered, her daughter was on her back, garnet light put out. Dorian, Cormac, and the other students had similarly been leveled.

Magic rippled through the room as Lena sat up. "You're not my father." Lena stared up at an empty space.

"Get away from there." Alia struggled towards Lena.

"No." Lena shook her head, transfixed on the same space. It wasn't Alia she was answering. Her face contorted in horror.

"Lena," Dorian called out. His light reached towards Lena, but it never made it. There was a barrier around Lena, keeping the rest of the room out. "Something came through." Dorian was looking at the same spot Lena was.

"You have no power here." Lena was doing an admirable show of defiance for whatever creature had been summoned from Alasar.

Dorian attacked again, an onslaught of flame and light aimed right at the void.

Alia moved towards Lena, meeting a sturdy barrier.

"Mother!" Lena screamed. "Mother, help!"

And then Lena was gone.

Lena's terrified face was burned into Alia's mind as she stared at the place where her daughter had been only moments before. Lena's last cries echoed in her mind.

The Undoing left her in droves, seeking out an opponent to land her anguish. Madeline screamed as the Undoing invaded. Cormac was already writhing in agony. Dorian moved towards her with determination, blood once again seeping from his scars and covering his features.

"Forgive me," Dorian begged as he placed his hand above her heart, launching a reluctant attack with his magic that had the Undoing rushing back to her and her mind descending into darkness.

16

Alia woke to a void.

Every muscle in her body was spent, the strain of her vain attempts dulling to an ache. Her head throbbed; mist clawed its way up her shoulders. But she didn't have the time to take inventory of her poor state.

Lena needed her.

"Ali," Elowen murmured as Alia's feet gave way beneath her, leaving her sprawled on the floor. They were in a bedroom that was not her own but too quiet to be the infirmary.

Powerful hands grasped under her arms and hauled her back to the bed. Harlan. Alia opened her mouth to speak, but only a whine came forward.

"What did Lena do?" Cormac pushed Harlan aside, fingers digging into Alia's skin with impatience.

"Cormac." Elowen cast herself between her husband and her sister. "She just lost her daughter."

Cormac's eyes glowed, the weakness exposed by the Undoing grating on him.

"Lena is not lost." Alia found her voice, albeit shaky and thin.

"Dorian said she was taken by the Tiarcon of the Mountains," Harlan said. "You know what happens to mortals in the Otherworld."

"But Lena isn't mortal, is she?" Cormac's eyes narrowed. "You lied to me. To all of us."

Neither Elowen nor Harlan chided the king this time, eyes downcast.

"And now my Master Mage has disappeared with the summit with Parth and Royce approaching. A Tiarcon, summoned to my palace."

"Disappeared?" Alia managed a whisper. She needed Dorian if she hoped to follow Lena.

"Shortly after ..." Elowen clasped her hands.

"Harlan, you will not let her out of your sight. She is not to go anywhere. Those are my orders." Cormac straightened.

"Please." It wasn't in Alia's nature to beg, but it was all she could think of.

Cormac turned back to her before he reached the door. A sobering realization crept into his icy eyes. "You're the only defense Mandal has left."

When the King left, Flora and Baldric entered.

Flora strode up to Elowen, daring to be ordered away. "You should go, Your Highness."

Elowen glared, a surprisingly potent flare of magic coming off her.

Flora stepped back and blinked.

"I will go reason with him."

Once the door had shut firmly behind Elowen, Alia's three friends exchanged glances.

"I swore an oath." Harlan balked under Flora and Baldric's harsh gazes.

"If your oath is the only thing that concerns you, then by all means ..." Flora gestured towards the door.

Harlan swore and paced back and forth. He weighed his loyalties, his love.

"We're going to help you get Lena back," Baldric said, dressed in full armor with weapons at his hip and strapped across his chest.

"There isn't much time. The sun is rising," Flora said calmly. "We have to get you out of the palace."

"Cormac ordered—"

Baldric clicked his tongue. "We serve the king's interests, not his every whim. Especially when he makes rash decisions out of fear."

"Out of love," Flora corrected. "But still, no one should keep a mother from her child."

"We need all of our high mages back before the next incursion," Baldric reasoned. "Lena is family."

Somehow in the wake of Lena's absence, gratitude bloomed, and an ache formed in her chest. Alia didn't have to face this alone. Finally. "The Tiarcon of the Mountains has her?" Alia looked at Harlan.

When Harlan nodded confirmation, Alia stopped breathing, stopped thinking. She knew about the Tiarcon of the Mountains, the patron of Veillant and ally of the wretched Tiarcon of the Moon. The pit in her stomach grew into a chasm, dragging her down.

Flora knelt before Alia, holding her head between her hands. Alia's body slumped into her.

"It's true, then, that Lena's father is a Tiarcon?" Baldric toyed with a dagger. Harlan held out his arm to stop Baldric from getting too close to Alia.

Alia's silence was answer enough.

"I could wring your neck for not telling me." Flora gripped the fabric of Alia's dress. "Dorian traveled to the Otherworld two days ago to get her back." Flora thrust a letter into Alia's hands. "He left instructions on how to follow."

Two days. Lena has been in Alasar for two days. A prisoner of the

Tiarcon of the Mountains for two days.

"I don't think she is ready." Harlan put a hand on Flora's back.

"She'll have to be," Flora snapped before grasping Alia's shaking hands. "You need to put these on." Flora gestured towards a dress and cloak identical to her own. "There needs to be two of us."

Alia's limbs barely obeyed direction as she struggled to comprehend the plan to smuggle her out of the palace. Flora was to leave the royal apartments first, disguising herself as Alia and leading the guards on a chase. Then Baldric and Harlan would get her to the meadow and into the forest where Dorian had opened a door to Alasar.

Flora looked convincing enough, her fiery hair hidden beneath the cloak and her fashion dull in one of Alia's nondescript dresses. "Get your girl and come back to me."

In her heart, Alia knew Lena would be coming back or no one at all.

Harlan scouted their escape, and Baldric stayed at Alia's side, lifting her when her steps faltered. The climb to the meadow had never been so strenuous.

Lord Jaremiah Wexworth stood at the opening of the meadow when they reached the top. His son, Gawain, stood with him. "I'm sure the King would be desperate to know why his Captain of the Guard was helping a threat to the Crown escape."

"You know better than to put faith in rumors." Harlan placed his broad shoulders between Alia and Wexworth.

"When there is this much talk, there is usually some truth to it." Jaremiah sneered. "And there is a fair amount of talk about you too, Captain."

Harlan unsheathed his sword. "Step aside."

"Do your duty and arrest the menace."

Harlan cast one glance over his shoulder at Alia and Baldric before lunging for Jaremiah with his swords. The clang of metal resounded as Harlan took on both men. Baldric flipped Alia over his shoulder and broke into a sprint, making for the tree line as the sun began to rise. Baldric ran until they reached the location in Dorian's letter.

Even in her weakened state, Alia could hear the whispers Dorian had heard in the woods after the Tramine incursion. The door he had fashioned must be a larger tear in the veil, that or Alia was more attuned to it now.

It wasn't actually a door at all. Just a space between two trees that Dorian must have offered his blood for, to which he carved yet another feather into his skin. It wasn't the first time that he had bled for her.

There was just enough light for Alia to make out the words Dorian scribbled down in the letter.

I will go make a plea to the Tiarcon of the Sun. Use your blood to open the door, let the ring guide you.

Baldric held her arm firmly. "I'm going with you."

"Alasar is no place for a quotidien soldier." It was no place for her either.

"Oh, believe me, I will hate each moment. But I'm going with you."

Alia turned to the door; there was no time to argue. "Do you have a knife?"

Baldric produced a blade from the strap across his chest.

She grasped Finn's ring and reached out towards the whispers, where she could sense the disruption bridging this realm to the next. She felt Finn's magic mixing with hers, shimmering within, as she traced the outline of the door. She sliced the knife into her palm, reaching through the door. Baldric kept his grip on her as they both stepped through.

The whispers intensified, pieces of mortal mages crowding around. Her hand dripped with blood, held out before them to satisfy the Tribunal's veil, to prove her mortality. The ferocity of the murmurs dimmed as they flowed past her, brushes of magic across her skin.

The gatekeepers paid little mind to Baldric, his quotidien nature allowing him to slip through. Baldric's hand tightened as he grunted; the same pressure would be building in his head as was hers until they broke through to the other side.

The Otherworld smelled like cinnamon, firewitch, clove, and cranberry. Alia breathed in deeply as she acclimated to her surroundings. Baldric, who had braced for an immediate attack, blinked in the warm sunlight.

They were in an orchard, with neat rows of apple trees giving way to a large sparkling lake dotted with cranberries floating near the surface. Everything looked still, tranquil. Nothing sought to harm them as they stepped forward, the shimmering door disappearing behind them. Alia and Baldric surveyed the pleasant landscape before turning to each other in bewilderment.

Her fatigue faded as she drew newfound strength from the orchard channeled through the ring on her finger. Beyond the orchard stood a towering, vine-covered estate, gray stone and white trim consuming the horizon.

Finn.

Alia lurched toward the house, but an animal crept into her path. It was a vixen, standing taller than either of them. It eyed her and Baldric, sniffing the air and pawing the ground, ready to pounce. The expression on her face was too perceptible for a simple beast and she must be assessing if they belonged to Alasar or not. Alia stood in front of Baldric, ready to put up a barrier to protect them.

The vixen circled them, showing off a crown of bark and fur intertwined with wildflowers. Where a plumed tail would be, sprouted a tangle of stalks, each one tipped with a different color. The giant vixen lifted her head and shook her glistening red coat before letting out an ear-piercing howl.

"Fucking Otherworld." Baldric dropped her sword and put his hands over his ears.

The orchard around them quaked. The trees pressed in around them, obscuring the path to the house. Baldric reclaimed his sword and senselessly hacked at branches with his sword as Alia tried to keep the apple trees from coming any closer with a flimsy barrier. She managed to open a gap to find the path forward, pulling Baldric to follow her as they ran towards the lake.

The water had been still when they arrived, but now tossed and lapped up against the path. As they rounded it, a pair of screeching black ravens intercepted them. Alia tried to dodge, but in a blink, the ravens were replaced by warriors dressed in fine black armor.

Alia cursed as an entire skulk of Alasaran foxes joined the warriors. Baldric stepped in front of Alia with his sword, as if it could do anything against horse-sized foxes and beings powerful enough to change forms. The warriors took him in stone-faced, unamused by his feeble show of protection. They surrounded the pair, making it impossible to see anything beyond auburn coats and black armor.

"You are trespassing on the lands of the Tiarcon of the Harvest," a female warrior said, squaring her broad shoulders.

At least they were in the right place. When Alia didn't drop to her knees, the vixen nipped the air near the back of her head.

"Mortals," a male warrior assessed with disgust, looking down at them with a scowl.

The immortals were an imposing, nearly identical pair, imbued with the beauty of the Otherworld. The man had a scar cutting across his temple from his close-cropped black hair to his high cheekbone.

"A lurcher." The woman's dark eyes flashed. "And carrion," she said, surveying Baldric.

Alia stepped in front of Baldric with her arm braced against his chest. "The Tiarcon of the Harvest. We demand an audience. Immediately."

Baldric swung around, drawing Alia away from the armed warrior. One of the foxes snapped its jaws, faster than any mortal could move, and snatched Baldric's sword from him. A cruel smile brightened the male warrior's face. "Mortals do not see the Tiarcon of the Harvest."

"You will make an exception!" Alia shouted. She brandished her ring, a surge of Undoing bolstered by garnet light, knocking him back.

Immediately, Alia was seized, the back of her dress lodged in the vixen's mouth. Terror gripped her. Baldric was apprehended just as easily, sword forgotten in the dirt. The man got back on his feet in one smooth motion, dusting off his armor. He advanced on Alia, grabbing her left hand and stretching it out.

"How do you have his ring?"

"We demand an audience."

"Twice a thief." The woman pulled the ring from her finger. "Drop her," she ordered the vixen. When the vixen didn't immediately comply, the warrior sighed, "I'll tell Tiarcon Finnian you were the one who apprehended them, Sabie."

Finn.

Sabie was satisfied, dropping Alia to the ground to be bound in magic. Baldric was similarly trussed, and while Alia wanted to summon the Undoing, she allowed them to be dragged towards the estate. The landscape parted before the warriors, but the Alasarans made the two Entiens feel each rock in the path on the way.

The interior of the estate was just as stunning as the grounds. Intricately carved wood and gold fixtures adorned every surface, and the ivy from the exterior carried on to the inside. "The Tiarcon of the Harvest has guests. You will wait." The warriors pulled them down a stairway to a dank corridor. The skulk followed as if it were customary for foxes to storm through a lavish estate.

Alia struggled against her captor. "I need to see him now." Alia struck the ground pitifully, her bound hands failing to catch her as she was pushed into a cell. Baldric fared only slightly better, pitching forward to brace himself on the back wall of the prison. The bars slammed shut before she managed to scramble to her feet.

"Did you hear what they called me? Carrion! I'll show them carrion." Baldric tried to wriggle out of his bindings. "They didn't even bother to search me."

Alia tuned out Baldric's bluster as she peered through the bars. There were no guards to speak of and no other prisoners. Tiarcons must find justice another way. The warriors and beasts must not have thought much of their capacity to escape. She tortured herself with the thought that Lena was similarly imprisoned, alone.

"I need you to get as far away from me as possible."

Baldric gestured wildly around the cell, which was hardly large enough for the two of them to lie down. "Where exactly do you suggest I go?"

"There." Alia pointed to the far corner before turning her back and stepping into the opposite corner. Alia focused as she brought the now-familiar glow to her hands, tendrils of mist escaping her fingertips. She willed the Undoing to attack the bonds around her wrists, just a small amount of force. It did her bidding, staying close to her palms.

When she was confident in her control, she turned to Baldric. "Give me your hands."

"Fuck." Baldric grudgingly thrust his bound hands in her direction, turning his head away as if that would save him.

The Undoing obeyed her, pulling apart the spell that kept Baldric tied. He shuddered as it curled around him. Alia could feel Baldric's rapid heartbeat, see the shadows of his battle scars.

"Ali—" Fear crept into his eyes as the Undoing fluttered over him.

Alia grasped the bars of their prison. She indulged the Undoing, the corrosive light from her palms sinking into the metal bars and wearing them away. Alia fed the Undoing her distress over Lena, the sound of Lena screaming for her before fading away from sight.

"Stay there." Alia closed her eyes and motioned Baldric back as the Undoing pooled at her, looking for the next thing to devour. She clenched her jaw and started reeling the Undoing back in. Dorian had told her to treat it like a spool of thread, to keep wrapping it upon itself until it fit inside her once more.

She braced herself for images that did not come. Relief surged through her.

Baldric relaxed in the Undoing's absence. "We need to get out of here."

"We need to find the Tiarcon."

"Ali, they are going to kill us before we can ever get to the Tiarcon." Baldric's chest heaved. "Our only hope is to escape. Figure out something else."

"We need Finn." She needed to see him. She needed confirmation of his treachery with her own eyes. And then she needed him to find Lena.

Baldric took the first step to freedom, reaching back to make sure Alia's skirts didn't catch as she moved into the hall. She waited at the top of the stairs as Baldric peeked out into the main floor. They emerged from the lower level, hugging the wall to escape notice.

The estate was a maze. Greenery adorned nearly every surface and absorbed the sound of their steps on the stone floor. They moved down a hall, passing a room bustling like a kitchen. Alia was still weak from her flight from the palace and the smell of food ground into her stomach.

The din of the kitchens allowed them to move quickly through a series of small living quarters, which Alia assumed were reserved for the servants. As they turned a corner, Baldric threw Alia back, pinning her against the wall and covering her mouth with his hand. He held her in place while loud footsteps sounded down the corridor.

Alia could barely see over Baldric's shoulder. She saw a flash of antlers, but they were standing too tall to belong to a stag. Alia slammed her eyes shut as a strangled gasp threatened to escape her lips, the memory of the Oucura surfacing. When the footsteps faded, Baldric released her, her knees shaking.

He gave her a foreboding look before pulling her in the direction of where the antlered being had just come. Alia was anxious to put as much space as possible between her and that thing. They tiptoed down the hall, no other servants or guards in sight. No one must be foolish enough to try to escape.

Alia tensed, wishing Dorian were with her. He would know what to expect, he could prepare her. Her heart alighted at the thought of him; he could have already reached Lena. She could be safe already. They both could be.

A reverberating bark made her freeze. The beast behind her yipped as Baldric turned, then started pulling Alia back behind him. She faced a hound, jaws dripping with drool as it huffed. It was so large it nearly reached her chest. The slobbering beast tossed Baldric aside with a swipe of its claws, sending him careening into the wall, before leaping at Alia.

Alia crashed to the floor beneath the monster, pinned and waiting for it to snap its jaws around her neck. Instead, Alia was flattened by the slap of its sticky tongue as it licked her. While the revolting sensation was a welcome alternative to being eaten, Alia was unable to open her eyes or breathe as the hound feverishly licked her. She finally managed to block her face with both arms, pushing the creature away enough to scramble out from under it.

The obsidian-furred hound whined, giving Alia a sorrowful look before defaulting to a happy pant. Alia stared at the beast. "Tesira?" Finn's ever-present hound had disappeared into the flames with him. Alia had seen it. This dog was a great deal larger than Tesira had been, and the fur around her neck furled out like a mane, framing impossible, sharp fangs. But still, there was no mistaking the acknowledgment in her eyes.

Alia reached out, needing both hands to scratch one ear. "Is he here, Tesira?"

Tesira barked happily.

"Can you take me to him?"

Another bark of affirmation.

Baldric had retrieved a dagger from his boot and was positioning to launch himself at Tesira. "No." Alia stopped him. "She's going to take me to Finn."

"Ali—" Baldric looked sideways at Tesira. He grabbed Alia's arm, eliciting a growl from Tesira.

"Come on," Alia said. Tesira's jaws closed around Alia's upper arm, holding her with a soft mouth, leading her onward. Baldric had no choice but to follow Alia and the oversized dog back into the belly of the estate.

Alia was dragged, with Baldric on her heels, into a grand chamber only slightly smaller than Mandal's hall. Alia could have believed she was back at the palace if the room hadn't been filled with such odd beings. Some of the revelers looked just like mortals, others looked more beast, and some were just *other.*

There was a woman completely covered in shimmering scales, her hair floating outward as if she were immersed in water. Another's form quivered like he was made of wisps of smoke and flame. Their conversations died as the mortals entered, frozen in equal astonishment.

Tesira's pace was quick as she bounded up to the golden throne where presumably the Tiarcon of the Harvest languished. The Tiarcon's fine gold tunic matched his throne, trimmed deep crimson. The Tiarcon was beautiful, with russet hair bound at the nape of his neck, fine garnet eyes, and porcelain skin that seemed to glow.

Alia was unceremoniously released, dripping in Tesira's saliva, onto her knees before him.

When she lifted her head to meet his eyes, her heart seized.

While the man sitting before her was every bit a thunderous Tiarcon, an immortal ruler, he was also her husband.

"Finn." Alia reached for him, only to be held back by Baldric. Tesira nuzzled into her master, seeking her reward for fetching Alia.

"Tesira, what have you brought me?" Finn asked, stroking the hound's head.

In an instant, the two warriors from before were on top of them, appearing from the air. The woman gripped Alia by the collarbone, keeping her on her knees. "Trespassers from the mortal realm, Tiarcon."

"Prisoners, while we have guests?" The Tiarcon looked slightly annoyed.

Alia could barely string words together. The man was certainly Finn, but he acted as if he had never seen her before. His gaze swept over her without settling. "He has Lena. Finn, he has Lena."

The Tiarcon's eyes narrowed. "Is it a riddle?"

The onlookers began to laugh.

"Our daughter," Alia raved as her captors pulled her arms back so hard she thought they would snap. "The Tiarcon of the Mountains has our daughter."

"So, it is true." A woman standing before the throne crossed her arms. She was mundane in comparison to the rest of the Alasarans, dressed in a simple, black dress clasped at the neck. But her beauty was a marvel, with her caramel-colored hair tumbling free and luminescent eyes like embers of stars. Alia openly gasped. The Alasaran standing before her was the same woman who plagued Alia's visions. The woman wielding a spear. The woman who was going to kill her.

"Tiarcon Bergan claims to have a child of yours in his dungeons."

The room went quiet. Finn stood, drawing near to Alia. "Our daughter, you say?" he scrutinized her face before turning to the woman with the molten eyes. "Are you sure, Deanna?"

"Finn, it's Lena." Alia lunged in his direction.

He simply side-stepped her. "Now I wished I remembered such spirit."

Beside her, Baldric thrashed against his captor. The entire room was laughing, mocking Alia. No matter how he appeared, this was obviously not the man she had loved.

"Thank you, Cara," the Tiarcon addressed the woman holding Alia. "Why don't you leave this one in my rooms so we may be reacquainted later?"

The smirk on Finn's face was cruel. That was not how her husband smiled.

"Wait," the woman from Alia's visions protested. "This one you can have." Deanna waved her hand at Baldric. "This one." She bent down to be eye level with Alia. "The lurcher belongs to the Tiarcon of the Forest; her magic must be returned to its rightful place."

"You presume to tell me who I can have? I'll send her to Rowthra when I'm finished with her." Finn returned to his throne, an imposing figure even while he sat.

Deanna held her head high. "The Tiarcon of the Forest will not suffer one more moment without what was stolen from her."

Alia snuck a glance at the onlookers. The scaled woman had shifted to stand behind Deanna. Another man, whose alabaster skin gave off a pearly light, stepped closer to the throne to defend Finn. The wispy man didn't move at all.

"Cara, Ossian. Take the mortals to my chambers." Finn's voice was low, dangerous. His antlered guards stepped forward.

Cara and Ossian bowed and did as the Tiarcon ordered.

Alia was led through one ornate room to the next, finally settling in a private chamber. Cara splayed her fingers, sinking Alia and Baldric into the wall, the stone itself encasing them.

"Stay here, Ossian," Cara instructed. "Obviously, the lurcher is more resourceful than she appears."

Ossian crossed his arms across his chest as Cara left the room. "You should have stayed where we put you."

"Why don't we settle this with steel?" Baldric taunted.

The Alasaran's cold laugh filled the room. "I suppose you are fearsome for a mortal warrior. Your challenge is beneath my dignity to accept, but it does amuse me."

Baldric's eyes bulged in fury.

Ossian rubbed his square jaw, scratching the shadow of a beard. "What are you to the Tiarcon?"

"His wife," Baldric answered for her.

Alia trembled. Somewhere inside the Tiarcon was the man she had loved, Lena's father, who, after a decade, no longer knew her face or his daughter's name. He had deceived her, left her and Lena with nothing.

And in this chamber, stronger than anywhere else in Alasar, was the smell of cinnamon. The Otherworld smelled of cinnamon, of Finn.

17

When Cara rejoined Ossian, they swept over the room, inspecting each item within. When they had finished their search, a flash emanated from Cara's sepia-toned hands, a light touching every crevice.

Seeing Finn was just as jarring as it had been the first time. Already, he seemed diminished from the Tiarcon she had met in the hall, more mortal as he stood before her. The harshness was gone from his face, the mocking mask abated.

He crooked his finger, summoning her forth from the stone prison. His magic set her on her feet, freed her. "You shouldn't be here, Alia."

There was nowhere she should be.

"Now you recognize me?" Alia steadied herself, not giving in to the despair that rippled through her.

"I didn't want them to know," Finn explained. "It isn't safe."

"I don't care. You have to get Lena back."

Finn's unworldly face twisted. "How do you know he has her?"

"She was trying to summon you, and he came for her instead." Alia's voice broke. "I tried to—"

Finn beckoned for his warriors. "Go see what you can find out, and do it quietly," he ordered. They vanished.

"You trust them?"

"They've commanded my forces for centuries." His mouth tightened after he spoke.

Centuries.

Alia's stomach churned, trying to fathom the chasm of time between them. When Finn moved closer, Alia flinched back to the wall.

"Alia." Finn stopped, softening his tone. "You must be tired, hungry."

The roaring in her ears intensified. "You have to get her back."

Finn dimmed even more, lifting his hand to let Baldric down from the wall. "We'll know more once Cara and Ossian return. Tesira will show you where you can rest."

His retreat from his own quarters was slow, but Alia couldn't formulate a response. And then he was gone.

That was it. That was all he had for her after ten years apart.

"He deserves worse than your silence." Baldric shook with rage as Tesira panted in the doorway.

Her mind was flashing through each moment she spent with Finn, each memory leaving her wondering how she hadn't known who he was, what he was.

And that she still didn't.

"I'm tired." It was a deep ache, one that had persisted since Entien. Seeing Finn again only exacerbated it, brought it to the surface to grate against her.

Baldric pressed a kiss to her temple, allowing her to curl into his chest before following the hound.

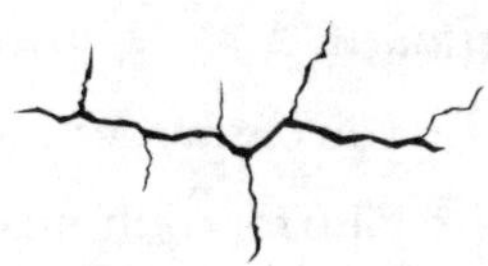

Alia decided to draw comfort from her helplessness. If Finn was going to allow harm to come to her, there was nothing she could do. There was no purpose in refusing his hospitality as they waited.

Alia was twisting her wet hair into a hasty braid when Cara came to fetch her. "Did you find her?"

Cara gave a slight nod. "Tiarcon Finnian will see you."

The warrior led Alia from the simple quarters back into the main halls of the estate, stopping at a small study.

Finn sat behind a walnut desk, flanked by Ossian; greenery permeated nearly every inch of his study. His expression tightened when they approached. "Cara and Ossian confirmed Lena is indeed well and being held in the Moutainlands. Bergan has her tethered to the castle. For her to leave, he has to allow it, or it'll kill her."

Alia's relief was shallow. "Get him to release her then."

"He is only holding her to get to me. If I show any interest at all in her fate, he'll never let her go."

"I don't care why he took her—just go get her."

"It has to be done delicately."

"Lena doesn't have time for this."

Finn flattened his hand on his desk. "Cara and Ossian will be at your disposal until Lena is returned to you."

Cara's eyebrows ticked up, and Ossian shifted his stance.

"Fine." Alia refocused her attention on the two Alasarans. "Take me to Lena."

"Take you?" Cara questioned.

"It would be advisable for you to stay here, where you are protected," Ossian suggested, looking to Finn for confirmation. "The Tiarcon of the Forest will not relinquish her claim."

"What is her claim?"

"The Undoing." Finn coaxed the Undoing to him. Mist spun in the air between her chest and his fingers. "It originates from the Tiarcon of the Forest. Your ancestors fled Alasar with her magic in their possession, her oath on their lips." His fingers tangled with the Undoing, as if shaking hands with an old friend. He had no fear of it; Alia couldn't hurt him.

"Why should that give her a claim?"

Finn released the Undoing. "Every bit of magic in Entien was taken without permission from Alasar. Stolen from a Tiarcon."

"It was owed to us," Alia disputed. "And I don't even want it."

"Magic as powerful as yours will make her stronger; she wants it back." Finn looked more fatigued by the moment.

"She can have it. Our daughter needs us." She turned to Cara and Ossian. "You will take me to the Mountainlands."

"You can't just—"

"I will ask Tiarcon Bergan to release her, seeing that she is no one of importance to this Tiarcon here. And if he refuses, you two will have to find a way to get her out by other means."

Both commanders looked at their Tiarcon to rebuke her order and started to panic when Finn remained impassive.

"Mandal's Master Mage is also here—to recover Lena—he was to go to the Tiarcon of the Sun. Have you heard anything of him?"

Finn shook his head. "Haziel has stayed clear of the conflict with Bergan and will not be sympathetic."

"And if a mortal with his magic sought his audience?" Alia dared to ask.

Finn's forehead creased. He gave a silent order to his commanders, dismissing them. "Alia, this is not your world."

Tears sprang once more from her eyes, cutting an angry path down her face. "Of course, this is not my fucking world!" Alia exploded, showering Finn with sparks of Undoing. "And it isn't Lena's."

It was a recognizable dynamic, her rage and his unflappable countenance. She didn't know how she had ever found him caring, stable. He was infuriating.

"If the mortal mage went to Haziel, then Haziel will have reclaimed his magic and killed the shell." Finn fought to hold her stare, pulling her in.

Alia couldn't mask the torment of the thought of losing Dorian. Not with all that was left unfinished between them; it couldn't be. "The shell? Is that all we are to you?"

"Alia." Finn got to his feet. "You are my wife."

"And when you're done with me, you'll send me to the Tiarcon of the Forest."

"I said that to satisfy the emissaries."

"Emissaries?"

"The Alasarans you saw in the hall. Emissaries from each of the remaining Tiarcons, Sun, Forest, Mountains, and Sea. No doubt Lena's capture was the true reason for their arrival." Finn rubbed his jaw. "They are dangerous, Alia. Despite my performance, they're going to want to use you, hurt you, to get to me."

"I'm sure it won't be difficult to convince them of your indifference. They already have Lena, how could they hurt me more?"

Finn's garnet eyes transformed into pits as he slipped back to his other persona. It was a look he had gotten from time to time in Dihlmere, when he would draw away from her but refuse to explain. "They can. They always can. Please, Alia, don't go."

She hadn't the strength left to shield her emotions; everything rose to the surface. This was a side of her Finn knew well, that he had saved her from. And now he was the cause.

Finn grasped her left hand. Alia looked down as he slid the red-jeweled ring onto her finger. "This belongs to you."

"I doubt I will have use of it." Alia fixed the hapless Tiarcon with one last glare before snatching her hand away.

He lingered long enough to watch her move his ring over to her right hand.

After several more attempts to dissuade her, Ossian and Cara agreed to take Alia to the Mountainlands. Baldric insisted on joining, refusing to stay behind despite Alia's urging. She didn't have time to convince a stubborn soldier that this was a fight he couldn't cut his way through.

"You're going to stroll into Tiarcon Bergan's keep and ask for your daughter back?" Ossian questioned her one last time.

"Take it as an opportunity for you to get to Lena while he's distracted."

Ossian turned to Baldric, grumbling about taking orders from a mortal. Cara was far calmer than her brother. "I did wonder where the Tiarcon went all of those years," she said, eyeing Alia. "And when he came back, he was ... changed."

"I doubt that."

Cara turned her dark eyes to Ossian and Baldric. "Once we take you to the entrance of the holdfast, you will be on your own. Ossian and I are known to Tiarcon Bergan's guard. If we are successful in procuring your daughter, we will try to send you a sign."

"And if you are unsuccessful?" Baldric asked.

"No doubt Bergan would display his kill for you," Ossian said. "Remember, your mortal weapons are nothing compared Alasarans. You are nothing." Then he focused in on Baldric. "Are you sure you want to follow her to your death?"

Baldric gave him a curt nod. Alia caught a hint of respect in Ossian's features.

Brave for carrion.

"If it comes to that, we'll be with you," Cara assured. "The Tiarcon won't receive either of us warmly if we return without his wife and daughter."

"I'm not his wife."

"Take the protection, Ali," Baldric said. He'd moderated his hatred for Alasarans now that his survival may depend on them.

"Let's hope your woman's bravado doesn't run out when she faces Tiarcon Bergan," Ossian drawled.

"It hasn't yet." Baldric took her hand. "And even if it does, I'll defend her with each breath."

"Until my last." Alia finished the Mandal phrase.

Cara gritted her teeth. "Let's do this quickly and without bringing Tiarcon Finnian into a war."

Alia made no such vow as Cara put her hand on Alia's shoulder.

Ossian approached Baldric, hesitantly extending his hand, unsure of where to touch the mortal. With a sharp intake of breath, Baldric clasped Ossian's forearm.

The commanders took them to the center of the Mountainlands. Baldric stumbled into Ossian's arms when their feet touched stone.

"We'll be watching," Cara said as Ossian untangled himself from

Baldric. They turned into a pair of glistening ravens, flying off towards the mountains.

Baldric took a few unsure steps. "Fucking Otherworld," he muttered, sticking close to Alia's elbow.

Bergan's holdfast stood in the slight depression between mountain peaks. The morning air was thick, sulfur overpowering her senses. The entire mountain chain smoked, blocking out any light from the sun. Flashes of fire lined the path, guiding them onward.

Her daughter was stuck in this wasteland.

Alia tried to draw strength from the knowledge that Lena was close. Her daughter was waiting for her; she needed *her*, not Finn.

"No one would blame you if you went back," Alia offered. Ossian had been right; she couldn't guarantee Baldric's safety.

Baldric wiped sweat from his brow, walking ahead of her toward the looming pillars. "I would blame myself."

He hadn't been with George when the Veillanti came upon him, but he could follow her into the Otherworld.

"The things I said on Mabon, about you and George..."

"Nothing I haven't thought of before." Baldric trudged ahead. "Here they come."

She didn't struggle when the Tiarcon of the Mountains' guards apprehended them. The guards were just as threatening as Finn's antlered sentinels, like they had been carved right out of the mountain. There was no demand for an audience, just vicious silence as they were dragged into a cavern-like hall.

They were taken from the stifling fires into a tomb. The ground was shimmering obsidian, making Alia think of the Tower each time her feet slipped against the glassy surface. The entrance poured into a circular chamber where Alasarans lurked in the maw-like opening, gathered around scant tables.

An elevated outcropping lay at the far end of the chamber, with a solitary black throne silhouetted before a fire. Other than the fire, the only light came from a slight glow on the ceiling, luminescent stalactites. A single figure cast shadows.

"Ah, Lady Harvest."

There was no need to wonder who he was. His beauty was arresting, his face sculpted in angular slate planes with an obsidian gaze. His soot-colored hair flowed to his shoulders, matching the pressed cape that pooled at his feet.

Alia was desperate to run.

"Tiarcon," she responded, hands balled into fists. She leaned on her anger; she was a Meador.

Tiarcon Bergan descended, stooping to stand level with them. Shadows moved with him, swallowing the firelight. Alongside the shadows stalked a giant feline with protruding fangs.

The chamber seemed to shrink, shadows massing at every corner. Tiarcon Bergan's subjects gathered closer, most with the pallid look of creatures who never saw the sun. Others were like the man from Finn's estate whose form shimmered like wisps of smoke. Alia tried not to focus on any of them, lest her nerve desert her.

"Welcome to the Mountainlands." Bergan gave her a gleaming smile as his simmering aura reached for her. He wasn't quite as tall or broad as Finn, but his lithe form moved with grace. "I hear you carried news of my latest acquisition to our dear Finnian." His smile twisted.

Alia clenched her jaw. "I came for my daughter."

Bergan's gaze sharpened. "I gathered as much." He formed three chairs out of shadow, offering them to Alia and Baldric with a wave of his hand. "Join me, we don't receive many visitors."

It had to be a trick. The ease with which they'd been granted entry to the holdfast, the welcome from the Tiarcon himself. Alia had expected to be thrown into a cell upon arrival. But she had hoped that cell would be near enough to Lena to find a way out together.

But this genial reception was even more threatening. The longer Tiarcon Bergan held his mask, the more certain Alia became that they wouldn't live long enough to be imprisoned.

Shadows nipped at her, herding her into the chair.

"So, enlighten me, Lady Harvest," Bergan spoke softly as he sat, resting his elbows on his knees as he leaned forward. "How did your lover receive you?"

The Tiarcon of the Mountains wanted to toy with them. Baldric flinched in the chair, grimacing as the shadows bit into him as well.

"Tiarcon Bergan—" Alia looked around the chamber, trying to spot Cara and Ossian.

"I was told mortals still spoke our tongue." Bergan looked over his shoulder at his attendants with narrowed eyes. "Was I misinformed?" His skin, which had been slate gray, rippled with violent swirls of blue.

"No, Tiarcon. But I—"

"Good, I would have hated to make the wrong impression." His skin settled once more. "Well, then I asked you a question."

She was out of her depth. She'd stood against a number of mortal lords, even a king, but the creature before her with the alluring smile had centuries of preying on mortals. "He didn't remember me. Or my daughter."

Her hands trembled of their own accord when Bergan took them in his. His skin was cool to the touch, too stiff to be comforting. "How could he not remember you? Noble Finnian, dulled by contentment. The feeble favored." The hand on her surged with burning blue.

Beside her, Baldric seemed to have sunk into his chair, barely breathing.

Bergan rolled his neck, murmuring to himself. Heat receded, the Tiarcon's anger fading. "I remember all of them."

Shadows gathered around him before dividing into forms to sit beside them. Women, with empty indents for eyes turned towards Alia with gaping mouths. As if they were screaming.

Alia started to pull her hands away, desperate to sever contact. "My daughter has no value to you now. We will be on our way, back to our realm."

Bergan squeezed her fingers, refusing to let her go. "I wouldn't say that. I have to admit I hoped for more of a ... reaction from Finnian. But I'll just have to be clearer this time."

The Tiarcon was only inches from her—he'd pulled her closer without her knowing, sucking her into his shadows. He raised one hand to tug at a strand of curling dark hair that had escaped her plait.

"Please." Alia committed to appearing helpless, hoping he would deem it beneath him to kill her.

The Tiarcon ignored her struggle, undisturbed by her thrashing. "A mortal wife is one thing, but to have one still alive ..." Bergan twisted the lock of hair around his finger and pulled, jerking Alia's head back and exposing her neck. "Finn found a way to Entien." He wrapped his hand around her throat. "Tell me how."

Bergan let his molten power burn. His subjects still watched, unbothered by the volatility of their Tiarcon.

Alia weighed lying, making herself seem useful enough to barter with. But Bergan had likely been trying to get across the veil for so long that he'd be difficult to deceive. "I don't know anything about that. I just want my daughter back."

"Lena." Bergan's perfectly shaped lips curved. His grip on her neck tightened, but she could still breathe. "We've grown quite fond of her; I think I'll let my sons keep her as a pet."

The Undoing sparked from her palms, arching towards Bergan. He dispersed it with a glimmer of shadow.

"There it is, your value." Bergan's breath whispered across her cheek. "What would Rowthra give to have you in her grasp? To take back what you stole."

Shadows pushed against every bit of her exposed skin, feeling like hands fastening around her. She was sinking into the chair, trapped just as Baldric was.

"She can have it," Alia rasped. "Just let Lena go."

"Your death is just another thing he'll malign me with, even though he's the one who let you come here. Unprotected." He cast a disparaging look at Baldric.

Baldric couldn't let the taunt go unanswered. "If any harm comes to us or Lena, the Kingdom of Mandal will—"

"Mandal?" Bergan stood over them, enjoying watching them try to free themselves. "You invoke a mortal kingdom? Hovels that would not exist without our generosity. You were given everything, but could not be satisfied to serve. When the realms become one once more, your kingdoms won't last a single night."

There was something familiar in Bergan's face as he mocked them. He wanted to see them suffer, to see their fear. It was as Ruben had been when he attacked her; he had wanted her to resist the inculcation, to challenge him, only to sweeten the complete victory over her when she proved she could not break free.

Alia stopped struggling. She leaned her head back into the chair, letting the shadows bite into the back of her head. "If you knew how to unite the realms, you would have already."

"I'm working on it." Bergan rocked his head side to side as his skin cooled. "One of your own is proving useful. He was hoping you'd arrive soon."

A golden eagle appeared beside Bergan.

Alia's stomach dropped and bile rose in her throat when she beheld Dorian. He was alive, but barely. The eagle had been beaten and bloodied; it quivered down on the ground with its wings outstretched, each bent at unnatural angles.

And worse, the eagle wasn't alone.

Standing over him was a man just as chilling as the first time Alia had seen him. From his pallor to his crimson stare, Vincent belonged here. With his fractured aura, he was more of this realm than hers. In the oppression of Bergan's presence, Alia couldn't feel his aura of discord, but she knew it was there, lurking beneath the surface.

"I understand you're acquainted with Haziel's hatchling. I couldn't afford to let Haziel kill him. Not after I promised him to my most loyal mortal servant."

Vincent glowed under Bergan's praise, placing his hand on Dorian's crested head.

Alia ignored the burning in her throat. "Dorian."

The heap that was once Dorian didn't stir.

Her heart thundered, a hollow beat.

"Don't worry, I'm taking him back home," Vincent said. "You can join him if you'd like."

A cold fury brewed within her. Dorian had become a prisoner again, for Lena, for her. After all Dorian did to be free, he was in Vincent's hands once more. That monster was going to lock him away, trap him again.

"As you can see, he wasn't able to provide enough useful information to please me," Bergan said. "But my guards did tell you that he calls for you."

"Why would you give Vincent anything?" Alia questioned the Tiarcon, still hoping that Dorian would stir.

"Because he is going to deliver your entire realm to me." Alia could see Bergan's teeth, his hunger. Finn's words came back to her. The Tiarcons wanted their magic back. And if the veil were no more, they'd be free to take it.

"You're sending the Alasarans through the veil."

"Just a choice few, only the lowliest." Bergan's arrogance dampened his beauty.

Alia would hardly describe the Oucura and Traimine as lowly, but to Bergan, their beastly natures must make them so. This must be what allowed them to fool the Tribunal's veil.

Alia willed her healing power into Dorian, wishing she could pull free of the shadows. "I'm going to get you out of here," she promised, a healing light spreading over the eagle and beginning to put life back into his limbs, luster in his feathers.

"If I were you, I would save my energy," Bergan chided, stepping between them. He turned his attention to Baldric next. "And think about how you might be more useful than your friend. How about you?" Bergan drew closer to Baldric.

"Mortals have shed Tiarcon blood before." Baldric puffed out his chest.

"Not mine," Bergan responded, placing his hand on Baldric's. "What is it like to be the lowest form of mortalkind?"

Baldric yanked free of the shadows, grasping the dagger at his hip faster than Alia could track, and he stabbed it into the side of Bergan's neck.

The Tiarcon didn't even bleed.

Bergan flicked the dagger from his neck, sending it scattering across the floor. Baldric's screams echoed across the chamber as each of his limbs cracked with a sickening snap. She should never have let him come here; she should have fought harder.

"Tiarcon!" Alia screamed, turning her attention from Dorian to try to distract Bergan from killing Baldric. Dorian's head rested on the floor, not healed, but no longer in agony.

Baldric was still screaming. He lay on the floor now, the shadowed chair evaporated. Bergan twitched his fingers like he was playing an instrument rather than breaking mortal bones. It was a dance for the Tiarcon, a performance. He was enjoying it.

Where are those fucking crows?

The chamber echoed with laughter, Bergan's subjects joining in his delight.

The Undoing had begun to work on the chair, eating away at where shadows latched onto her skin. She fueled her magic, urging it to work faster.

When Alia was able to scramble to her feet, she ran to where Baldric lay. She put her body between the Tiarcon and her friend, disrupting the torture.

The Undoing pooled around her, branching out to obscure Baldric from view.

"How impressive, you've bested a mortal." A sarcastic voice broke into the struggle and distracted Bergan just enough. A towering woman stepped out of the crowd of onlookers. It was the woman Alia had seen before, in Finn's hall, in her visions.

Baldric's screams had dimmed into whimpers of agony as he tried to lift his mangled limbs. While Alia kept her eyes on the Tiarcon, she placed her hand on Baldric's chest. The Undoing swept down over the soldier, mapping out his injuries. Healing, rather than exploiting.

"Back from the Forestlands so soon, Deanna?"

"I should have stayed there. Better entertainment." A smirk graced her plump lips.

Bergan leered at Deanna as she filled a glass with a red substance that bubbled out of a crack in the stone wall.

The distraction wouldn't last forever. Baldric's whimpers died into merciful silence, his body stilling as the Undoing numbed his wounds. Several paces away, Vincent knelt over Dorian, stroking his tarnished feathers. Alia couldn't bear it.

She gathered the Undoing away from Baldric, sending it to Vincent. She turned the dial, changing her power from a healing cloud to a poisonous swarm.

"What news?" Bergan ignored the plight of his servant as the Undoing surrounded Vincent, sinking in before he could summon shadows.

"Rowthra rejects your terms," Deanna announced unceremoniously. "She has no interest in retreat, even in exchange for the lurcher. She hopes to see you on the battlefield."

The onlookers jeered, and Bergan's hands balled into fists.

"And this show of strength will do nothing to convince her otherwise."

The Undoing's attack on Vincent was fleeting. He recovered, chasing the violet mist away with shadow. He defended himself, but pressed no further, looking to the Tiarcon for permission.

Her hands shimmered and shook, the Undoing leeching flesh from her bones as she struggled to sustain it. She didn't have much longer.

"Where is my daughter?" Alia demanded.

Bergan whirled on her, his dark shadows scorching. Drawing on Finn's power from the ring to support a barrier was the only thing that saved her, but she still fell to the ground.

"If you can't be of use to me, then at least you can be amusing."

The time for the crows had ended.

"Just let me see her, please," Alia pleaded. She needed to be sure he had her for the next step.

"She can watch you die." Bergan smoldered.

Lena appeared.

Alia's mouth went dry; seeing her daughter again had been what she had clung to. Lena's cheeks were flushed, reddening every moment as she took in the scene around her. Alia slowly crawled across the glassy floor towards her, leaving Baldric lying flat on his back. Lena was still wearing the same tunic and breeches she had worn in Entien, now torn and muddied. Her face was streaked with grime, but her eyes glowed with a captive power.

Tears took the already worn paths down Lena's cheeks. "Leave me." Lena's strength faltered. "This is my fault."

Bergan's boots invaded Alia's line of sight, obscuring Lena completely. "This is what I've been trying to explain to you. Your father isn't coming. He doesn't even care enough to save her." Bergan gripped Alia by her hair, dragging her upright.

"Put her down." Lena got to her feet, hands trembling with rage. It was the posture Lena took before an outburst, before her power exploded.

Except, nothing happened.

"Your attachment is endearing." Bergan's voice was smooth as he tried to twist her daughter's ear. "I've even had affection for a few of them. But you need to understand that you are so much more."

Lena's eyes widened as shadows gathered around Alia. Bergan enveloped her in darkness, the swift-moving shadows piercing where they touched. Alia focused on breathing rather than on the pain, mustering the remainder of her power for a final attempt at escaping the Tiarcon.

"My lord Tiarcon," Vincent cut in. "If Tiarcon Rowthra has refused the Undoing, perhaps I might—"

"You can have the power I allow you to have," Bergan said sharply, silencing Vincent. Bergan refocused on Lena. "You'd be far better off aligning with me."

"Killing my mother won't win me to your side."

Bergan's laugh echoed through the chamber, in concert with his subjects. "Your father killed her the moment he allowed her to come here."

Alia struggled against Bergan's hold, her scalp protesting. As the shadows whipped around her, she saw flashes of Lena's face and watched her posture tighten. She could see it in the shifting, muscle by muscle: Lena had made a decision. The Tiarcon of the Mountains sought Lena's allegiance, and he held the price of it in his hands.

Lena was about to make a deal to save her. And Alia couldn't allow it.

Alia retreated within herself, calling to the Undoing. While she summoned her power, she made sure to focus on the ring on her hand, Finn's power channeling through her. A torrent of garnet met with the Undoing, circling and fusing with it. Alia delved into the pit that had formed when Lena was taken from her, the depths of her torment, and summoned the strength there, the magic that had taken root in darkness but needed to be dragged out in order to save her from it.

The deep purple mist leaked from her fingertips and set to work on the gathered shadows. It swirled through them, scattering them in the air above them. The Undoing pressed forward, invigorated by Finn's magic, searching out vulnerabilities in the Tiarcon.

Bergan's hands shifted from her hair to her neck, cutting off the air to her lungs as the Undoing drifted around him. Alia reflexively tried to pry at his hands, her fingers striped with strain, tuning out the sound of Lena's yell. Bergan wasn't even bothering to use his magic to kill her. He was going to show Lena just how frail mortals were and choke the life out of her with his bare hands.

Even with Finn's magic, Alia couldn't dampen Bergan. The Undoing was a meaningless haze. She clawed at his hand and her throat, opening her eyes to meet Bergan's triumphant gaze.

"You'll understand one day," Bergan said to Lena as Alia's vision clouded and her hands fell down at her sides.

Alia swung her legs, trying to shift Bergan enough to let her look at her daughter one last time.

But instead, a searing light ripped through the chamber, blinding her. Alia fell, crumpling to the ground. But among the agony, there was breath. Her chest rose and glorious air filled her. She braced herself up on her elbows, seeing Bergan focus his shadows on the source of the light. And as it had after Rosalynn's attack, the Undoing returned to heal her instead of dragging her down with memories of torment.

The light had to be Finn beating Bergan back. The Tiarcon of the Mountain's cavernous chamber exploded with garnet rays. But as Alia's eyes adjusted, she realized the warmth emanating from the light and the familiar feel of it.

Not garnet, gold.

Not Finn, Dorian.

She saw the eagle, hovering high above. Rather than the golden sheen she had seen before, Dorian's feathers burned with the heat of the sun, impossible to stare at. From his wings, the pure golden light bore down on the shadows that Bergan had to offer, clashing with the Tiarcon.

Before Alia could start to wonder how Dorian possibly had the strength to rival Bergan, she wrapped her arms around Lena. She wasn't sure which one of them was trembling, but she reveled in the feeling of embracing her daughter.

"You have to go," Lena said tearfully into her shoulder. "He wants to use me to hurt Father. He isn't going to let me go."

"He'll have to." Alia pulled both Baldric and Lena behind her, facing Bergan, who was slowly chipping away at Dorian's beams with Vincent at his side.

"Vincent, you've lost your prize," Bergan muttered. The shadows cut through to Dorian in a flash, dousing his light. The golden eagle quaked, turning gray as the Tiarcon's magic encircled him.

Then the eagle fell.

The ground cracked; the force of Dorian hitting the floor shattered the surface. His feathers had gone ashen, dead. Stone.

A scream tore through her.

Dorian had sacrificed himself, put forth the power to stop a Tiarcon, only to be trapped once more. The statue horrified her; she wasn't even able to look upon his face or try to see if he could be healed. She couldn't sense anything. Vincent fell to his knees beside the stone eagle, his movements frantic and his expression pinched in sorrow.

Bergan rolled his shoulders as Alia panicked, trying to rouse the Undoing once more. Her magic responded with a meek puff, like a final breath. She had nothing left to fight with, nothing left to give.

"What do you want?" Alia shrieked as Bergan stepped closer to the three of them. "You want Finn?"

Bergan's nostrils flared. "I want him to serve me. To relinquish his lands to me."

"I can help you." Alia tried to keep strength in her voice. "I can help you defeat him."

Bergan lifted his eyebrows. "How?"

"I will give you a way to weaken him, if you release Lena—and the eagle—and let my guard and me go with them." Alia held onto hope that there was some way to revive Dorian.

The room went quiet at the offer. Bergan rested a hand on his chin, considering. "If you give me a way to weaken Finnian, all of you can go."

"Tiarcon, please," Vincent pleaded on his knees.

"You can't," Lena hissed from behind her.

Alia stared back at Lena, into those eyes she inherited from her father. Lena hadn't even seen him yet, but she was so desperate to find him that she had ended up here. And now, Alia was about to take him from her. Alia tested her resolve, agonizing over whether she could do that to Lena and if she could give her husband to his enemies.

If that's what it takes to save my daughter.

They had lost Finn once, and they survived. They could do it again. And if Lena never spoke to her again, at least she'd be safe.

"Release the tether you have on her, and his talisman is yours." Alia turned her back on Lena. "It was given to me, and I am the only one who can give it to another." She held up Finn's ring, and Bergan's lips parted in shock.

"Tiarcon, please. I will kill her for you, and you can take it off her corpse." Vincent rose to his feet.

Bergan raised a hand to silence the mortal mage. "How did you come by a talisman of Finnian's?"

Alia shrugged. "You're right about him. Noble. Feeble. He couldn't leave me without leaving a piece of himself behind."

Bergan grinned, turning to Vincent. "You'll have to find another way to claim your eagle and the woman's magic." Bergan snapped his fingers at Lena, destroying the invisible tether keeping her bound.

A raven perched high in the rafters caught Alia's eye. This was the time. Alia pulled her arm back and cast the ring over at Bergan. As he grasped to get a hold of it, the ravens were already swooping down. Garnet ropes encircled Baldric and the eagle, securing them to one raven while Lena and Alia reached for the talons of the other.

And then, they were gone.

18

"What did you do?" Ossian pounced on her once they flickered back to the orchard. "What did you do?"

Cara pulled her brother back, allowing Alia to stand.

"How could you?" Lena grabbed Alia's arm.

Alia couldn't convey how simple the decision had been. "You're safe." She took her first full breath in days, the parts of her that had fractured in Lena's absence melding back together. Her mind emptied of all else, each beat of her heart elated. "You're safe."

She touched Lena's cheek, wiping the tears and dirt away. Alia searched for harm, letting the last wisps of her power unravel over Lena. Relief surged through her when the Undoing didn't find a single wound. She cradled Lena's head into her chest, uncertain if she was ever going to be able to let her go.

Lena was safe, but it had come with a cost.

From over Lena's head, Alia watched Cara heft the ashen eagle in her arms. Ossian knelt over Baldric's prone form. The commander had his hand on Baldric's chest, which was rising with breath.

Alia tucked Lena to her side, looking between the commanders and the fallen.

"He'll live." Ossian's voice was less hostile now. "I'm not sure how, but the mortal will live."

When Baldric woke up, he would never stop telling the story of withstanding a Tiarcon. The thought brought a slight smile to Alia's lips, but the assurance couldn't quite settle in, not while Dorian was locked in stone. "And him?" Alia looked at Cara.

His feathers were rigid, biting into Alia's fingers. She felt nothing, but didn't know if it was because her magic was spent or because Dorian was gone.

"The Tiarcon's healers are very skilled," Cara answered, failing to give the same certainty as her brother.

Alia couldn't accept it. "He has another form. Perhaps it wasn't affected."

The shapeshifting Alasaran shook her head. "What happens to one happens to both."

"But he fought a Tiarcon. He's one of the most powerful mortals—"

"If something can be done for him, it will be."

Energy coursed through her, anger spurring her on. "You don't understand. If Dorian doesn't come back—"

Alia couldn't finish the thought.

"That's Dorian?" Lena's lips quivered. Alia hadn't divulged his other form to anyone, not even when she'd wanted to hurt him. "They said there was another mortal prisoner, but they never let me see him. This is my fault."

"Please." The pressure rose in Alia's chest again. The ache was deeper than she expected, mixed with guilt and gratitude.

Cara gave a knowing nod. "Creatures of Haziel are more suited to transformation than the rest of us. There is hope for his return."

Hope had never sustained Alia. But Dorian had, with his sunlight aura and soft eyes that saw every shade.

Ossian lifted Baldric into his arms, careful not to harm the ailing mortal. "We should hurry. The Tiarcon is nearly here."

The orchard trembled, reacting to Finn's presence even before he appeared. The branches parted, the grass preened, every living thing determined to please him. His passive exterior melted away as soon as he saw Lena. The autumn sunset deepened overhead, casting a glow over the entire land.

Lena rushed into his arms, catching the Tiarcon off guard with the ferocity of her embrace.

"My Lena." Finn bent down to look into her eyes. "Look at you."

Lena flattened her palm on the side of his face, as if committing each inch to memory. "I was trying to find you."

"I'm here." He fell to one knee. "I'm so sorry I didn't hear your call."

"I called for you so many times." Lena wrapped her arms around her father's neck, tears streaming down her face once more.

"I'm here," he repeated.

Bitterness rose, smothering any remorse Alia might have felt. The Tiarcon had done nothing to save her, he had done nothing to raise her. He had left them alone.

Tesira bounded from the estate, tackling Lena to the ground as her daughter cried out with joy. Finn became guarded once more when he looked away from Lena. He took in Alia's disheveled appearance, the singed fabric of her dress, hair torn from her braids, mist swirling beneath her skin. "Thank you," he said heavily, reaching out to clasp her shoulder.

"They need healers."

Cara and Ossian had been waiting for the Tiarcon's approval, the injured mortals still in their arms.

"Go," he bid his commanders, before turning back to Alia. His fingers brushed against the darkening bruises on her neck. "You aren't healing."

His touch was cold, just like Bergan's at first. Numbness spread through her body. Exhaustion ebbed away, the ache dimmed, and the Undoing settled.

"I'm fine." Alia tried to jerk away. "I need to—"

Finn's voice was gentle, but insistent. "I'll see that they are all taken care of. You can rest, Alia."

Finn dismissed most of his household and turned the estate into a haven. Only the guards multiplied, and they were still far too reminiscent of the Oucura for Alia to feel comforted by their presence. Alia wasn't sure if the guards were there to keep Finn's subjects away or to protect against the forces of one of the Tiarcons.

The scorching moon had been her only companion when she woke. It seemed that while Entien lived in darkness, Alasar was subjected to endless light, never to truly rest. Beams had guided her through the estate, and she shouted demands to see her companions at any guard who passed.

A bleary-eyed Ossian responded to her demands first. After telling her Baldric would be fully recovered with rest and Lena was already abed, he took her to Dorian.

While the healers had managed to restore the golden hue of Dorian's feathers, softened the stone that had bound him, he remained in his eagle form. His wings were tucked flat against his body, orderly now that he had thawed.

He breathed, but he wasn't there. Alia couldn't stand to see him perched in the room, reduced to silence, stillness where there should be earnest warmth. So, by the scorching light of the moon, she carried him outside with her own hands.

He hated enclosed spaces.

The courtyard was peaceful, cloaked in the same wild beauty that burst from the rest of the Harvestlands. Alia waited with him as the moon was replaced by the sun, watching the hues of Alasar shift but never dim. And still, his eyes were cold, staring vacantly ahead.

Leaves had gathered over Dorian's talons; he hadn't moved.

Alia willed her influence over him, all the strength she possessed, to pull him out of wherever he had gone.

They had their own realm to return to.

She needed him back. Bergan would continue to use Vincent as a pawn in Entien to destroy it. Dorian was the only one who could make sense of it.

"You don't get to leave me alone in this."

But he spent days in Bergan's dungeons with Vincent. With the man who had once been Dorian's friend but had turned into his torturer. And Dorian, who had made a deal with an immortal to free himself from this form, was trapped once more.

There were no promises she could make if he came back. She'd shown cruelty, hid behind spikes when she'd felt threatened. Assuming the worst of him, never giving him a moment of grace.

"I know." Alia twisted a fallen leaf, still clinging to life, between her fingers. "I know you wouldn't have taken Lena to Effe. That you put her life above yours then, and again in coming here."

The eagle didn't move a feather.

"There is more than this," Alia mumbled at the impassive eagle, despite her inability to truly believe it. Despite Effe's musing about the Undoing, she feared it was still inspired by Ruben's control. "More than Vincent, more than Ruben. We are more."

Empty words weren't going to summon the man from the eagle. Dorian deserved more from her; he'd earned it.

Tears were easy, on hand the instant she let them free. The Undoing was there, feeding off her pain. But she didn't need it now. She needed something deeper than darkness. Truth.

"I need you." She wiped the tears away, the words finally feeling honest. "When everyone else fled, you stepped closer. You haven't left me alone, not even when you should have. Please, I need you."

"He can't hear you." Alia looked up to see Cara at the entrance of the courtyard, leaning against the doorframe. She was an imposing figure, with the soaring height Alia now associated with the Alasarans. Her features were delicate, entrancing, but often obscured by her grim aggression. "The healer sent me to try to reach him."

Cara began to remove her clothes, stripping off her cuirass and the long-sleeved tunic beneath.

In doing so, Cara revealed markings covering her shoulders and collarbone. Alia was immediately drawn to a pattern of white contrasts on her brown skin, beginning where her neck met her shoulder.

Feathers.

Just like Dorian.

"What are they?" Alia dared to ask.

"The mark of one's true form." All that remained above her waist was the tight band strapping down her breasts.

Alia stood as Cara neared Dorian, positioning herself protectively over him.

"Lady Alia." Cara bit her lip. "My life is sworn to Tiarcon Finnian."

She gestured to the crest just below her collarbone. It was a small circle with crimson antlers. "And to you as well, as his wife. I will not harm the brave mortal who came to the defense of the Tiarcon's wife and daughter."

Alia let Cara's oath lull her into leaning back. "What are you going to do?" Alia shuffled back to her feet as the Alasaran peered down at Dorian's unseeing eyes.

"Call to him in my true form."

"A raven."

"Ossian and I can take just about any animal form we choose. But yes, ravens are sacred to our bloodline, considered our true form."

"Can Dorian become forms other than an eagle?"

Cara chuckled and shook her head. "He's just an eagle." Cara bent over the Master Mage and placed her hands on his folded wings.

From where her fingertips touched him, Dorian's gleaming golden feathers rippled. At the same time, Cara's skin shifted, churning with dark feathers but not transforming. It was a bizarre sight, Cara slipping in between forms while sparks of change showed in Dorian. Alia's head throbbed as the air became thick with magic.

Cara finally pulled back, skin stilled. She left behind the eagle, though now the sharp eyes were closed. "He will wake soon," Cara said, rising to her feet.

"What did you do to him?"

"The mortal's consciousness had given way. Because of what we are, I can still speak to him even when he is not in control. I let him know it is safe to come out."

"How? Where did he go?"

"I don't have much experience with mortals, but sometimes our magic cares for what the mind cannot."

When Alia's frown deepened, Cara heaved a sigh.

"It might be difficult for someone with your magic to consider. Your darkness is always right under the surface. For others, like those of us who can change form, the impulse is to bury it deep. There is the form we present, and the face we hide. That self can be just as real, just as strong, but more trying to see."

Dorian always made such an effort to appear calm, genial, even when things went awry. That composure had cracked from time to time, but he always found a way to reclaim it. By burying everything else.

"Keen insight for a warrior," Alia deflected.

"In Alasar, we value balance." Cara smirked before slipping out of the courtyard, cuirass in hand. "Tiarcon Finnian wants to see you in the garden."

Alia was about to take issue with Cara's order when she saw Dorian flex his wings. In a blink, the eagle melted away, and the man returned. From the ground of the courtyard, Dorian's eyelids fluttered and a groan escaped his lips.

Alia bent beside him, smoothing his unkempt copper curls out of his eyes. She held her breath as he blinked, trying to dispel his daze. "I have you," she whispered, the knots untwisting in her stomach.

His eyes shimmered as he clutched onto her sleeves, sitting up and pulling her into a tight embrace. "You're real?" he asked with a gravelly voice.

She put her arms around him as his head rested on her shoulder. "Yes, Dorian."

"Vincent..." he muttered.

"I have you," Alia repeated. "Not him. I'll never let him have you."

It was what she had needed to hear.

Dorian relaxed against her. His fingers twitched against her spine. Just as she always had the impulse to tuck her arms around herself to prove that she was in control of her own body, that she could shield herself, Dorian was reminding himself that he had hands, fingers. Not wings.

"Lena?"

"She's here. Safe."

"Where?"

"Alasar still." Alia sighed. "In the Harvestlands now."

"And Vincent?" Dorian asked again.

Alia shook her head. "He can't reach us here."

Dorian looked up to survey the courtyard, taking in the crimson leaves that surrounded them. He grimaced; his body must be weak from days without nourishment.

"Let me get you some water." Alia went to stand, but Dorian caught her hand.

"Stay with me." A shiver went through Dorian's body and his pupils surged, as if he was going to slip away again.

"I'm here." She didn't want to leave him either. "And I'm sorry."

"You're sorry?" His dark eyes flashed, focusing on her.

"You went after Lena when I couldn't. And Vincent was able to hurt you again because of it."

He squeezed her hand. "I chose to come; I knew what could happen."

"Why did you then?" Alia spat out. She knew about his guilt, his need to make up for the lives Vincent had taken. But going to the immortal realm on his own had been asinine.

"Imagine what you would have done to me if I hadn't." Dorian pulled her hand onto his chest.

She could feel his heartbeat through his torn tunic. If he hadn't gone after Lena, if he had still been in Mandal when she woke, she would have subjected him to her fury. Alia turned her head away from him as she flattened her palm on his chest, trying not to shake.

"Alia, I didn't mean ..." His fingers grazed her cheek, tilting her chin to face him once more. His eyes were kind and searching. Despite what he'd suffered, his expression was light, as if he was on the verge of a grin. "I have never been the type to risk my life. But for you, I don't even think. I don't hesitate."

Sunlight burned through the short distance between them. His words repeated in her head, sparking light in the dark. Warmth spread, alleviating the strain that bound her. Alia wanted to look anywhere other than into his earnest eyes, tried to focus on something other than the way his hand felt on her cheek.

The feathers cut across his forehead drew her in. Cara's musings echoed, true forms and hidden selves. The carved feathers, so clearly marking him as a Veillanti, and merging his two forms together. Bringing the self he had to hide to the fore. And each feather he carved on his body left to scar, a reminder of what his magic had done but also who he was.

It suddenly struck her, not as misguided, but as a particular show of bravery. Bearing what he feared so plainly. Alia had never managed to do anything but hide, but to run. But there was none of that weakness in Dorian, especially not as he faced her and confessed his heart.

"You should," Alia said. There was danger in the words she could sense coming, made all the more perilous by the way her heart lifted. "Think. Hesitate."

The heartbeat beneath her palm sped up.

Dorian broke into his easy smile, making Alia's chest ache. "I'd rather not." His gaze slipped between her eyes and lips before he pulled away. "But I know you don't—"

Alia slid her hand upward from Dorian's chest, curving around the back of his neck. Her nails dug in, holding him in place. He stopped speaking, he stopped breathing. Dorian stilled completely under her touch.

He waited. He'd spoken the words, made his affection known, and now he waited for her. As if he could see that, as formidable as she was, she was still a wounded creature. Of course, he knew. He'd shown that with his gentle patience, his unfailing support, even when she dismissed him.

After all she'd done to push him away, she didn't want him to move another inch.

"What do you know?" She was close enough to brush her lips against his if she chose to.

"I know—" he tried and failed, gulping down his words. "I know I'd give you anything. Everything. And you'd still deserve more."

His face was between her hands. She moved slowly, haltingly, as if her mind might change. As if the fear of wanting, needing, loving someone else might win.

It didn't.

His lips were stilled with shock at first, his breath stolen in the first moment she kissed him. And sunlight, warmer than the Alasaran morning, swept across her skin. The barrier between them broke, overcome by the softest touch until every space between them demanded to be closed, to be conquered.

Dorian's fingers threaded through her bound hair, bringing her even closer.

A spectrum of color burst behind her closed eyelids. It was Dorian's sight, the way he saw magic when others could not, becoming hers. The lights danced before her, banishing the darkness, lifting the shroud she always carried. There was proof there, that someone like him could want her, could find something worth loving.

The sound of boots on fallen leaves disrupted them, Dorian's warmth fading as he was ripped from Alia's arms. Alia looked up to see Baldric's fist twisted in the front of Dorian's tunic, the soldier's shoulders lifting and falling as he took deep breaths.

"Baldric." Alia gave him a sharp warning.

Baldric's fist tightened on the fabric before his hand opened and released Dorian. His teeth unclenched and he took a step back. His brow furrowed, but he extended his hand to Dorian. "Thank you for what you did. With the light," Baldric gritted out awkwardly.

Dorian smiled and let out a straggled breath. "Of course."

The soldier relaxed his shoulders. "You're a bird, then?"

"From time to time." Dorian pressed his lips together.

"The garden." Baldric looked at Alia, a twinge of red topping his ears. "He wants you to meet him in the garden."

"I've heard." Alia let her annoyance edge into her voice.

"He?" Dorian asked.

Baldric had the courtesy to look apologetic. "Her husband."

"Right." Dorian's jaw quivered before he scratched the back of his neck.

Alia reached for Dorian's hand. "I'm not going."

"Lena is waiting there too." Baldric folded his arms across his chest.

"Go." Dorian reached for her hand, pressing her palm to his lips. "I'll be here."

"He needs to eat," Alia instructed Baldric. If he was brash enough to intrude, he could at least be useful.

Baldric balked before giving her a nod. "I'll look after him."

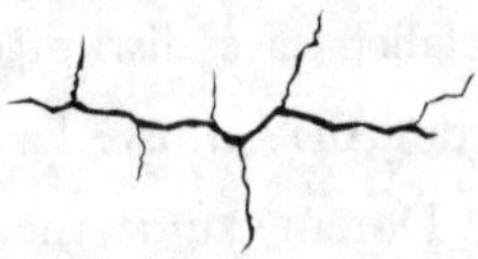

Alia made her way across the estate with Dorian's magic swirling before her eyes, the sensation of his lips on hers staying with her. She'd been foolish to encourage him, pretending as if she were capable of returning his affection. If it was love that drove him, it had already almost gotten him killed. She was toxic.

She walked to the back of the estate. Finn's garden was a departure from the manicured designs of Mandal. Deep plum flowers intertwined with sunset hues against a lush green backdrop. It was warm, a bit wild, and absolutely beautiful.

Lena began to run towards her as she approached. The color had returned to Lena's face, the crimson of the Harvest uniform matching her flushed cheeks. "How is Dorian?"

"He is himself again." Alia couldn't help but smile.

Lena's expression relaxed, but her shoulders were still tight. "Good."

"He'll be fine. We're all fine."

Lena took a few steps to the side, holding up her hand to warn Alia away. "I knew you would come," she said. "I never doubted for a moment you were going to come for me."

The light Dorian imparted dissipated. "Do you want to tell me about it? What happened to you?"

Alia crossed the distance between them, and this time Lena didn't move away. Alia put her hands on Lena's shoulders, holding her daughter as she began to cry.

"It was ..." Lena pressed her cheek into Alia's shoulder. "It was terrifying. Bergan wanted me to swear an oath to him and was confident that one day I would. But one of his sons wasn't like the others. Xavier. He didn't let anything happen to me."

Alia held Lena even tighter. They stayed that way for a time, holding onto each other. They needed a rest from words, as the worries melted away now that they were together. "You can tell me. You don't have to pretend to be well if you're not. I want to know; I want to help if I can."

"Because you're always so forthcoming." There was a tired sadness in Lena's voice, rather than a cruel bite.

"There are other things—" Alia's throat ran dry, her body fighting her from continuing. "You were right to be angry with me for keeping things from you. I want to explain while there is time. I want you to understand." Alia searched her daughter's eyes.

"I want to understand."

"'Undoing Mages are created in darkness," Alia said quickly.

Alia let it all tumble out. She told Lena about the abuse, that they had tried to silence her, Mariana's betrayal, and the deep, grinding depression that ensued. That lingered even now. "His voice is still in my head, the inculcation. I struggle with it. I don't want you to know that kind of evil, ever. But I do want you to know me."

Tears fell down Lena's face anew. Alia could feel her aura pulse, rage expanding.

"The thought of anyone hurting my mother." Lena began to shake, grappling with having nothing to direct her anguish towards.

"I'm still trying to understand what it is, what I've become."

Lena frowned, turning away as her emotion overcame her. "It isn't your fault," Lena seethed. "It's the rest of them."

"Lena—"

"That man knew he could hurt you and no one would punish him." Lena slammed the back of her hand into her opposite palm. "Because he was the queen's brother. It doesn't matter if they're wrong when they're royal. We need to stop them."

"They'll always win, Lena." Alia took a sharp breath in to stave off more tears. It was a lesson she had taught Lena herself, perpetuated with her own words after Lena defended Madeline against Thomas and Gawain. No matter what a royal did, it was Lena's retaliation that would yield consequences.

Alia had taken the lashes. She had instructed Lena, constructed her confines herself brick by brick. Because challenging the dynamics of the powerful in Mandal was something she had only tried once and failed at completely.

I should have torn it all down for her.

She should have fought her way back to Mandal years ago, to destroy it from the top. To give her daughter a better kingdom to grow up in.

Lena reached forward, grabbing Alia by the shoulders. Her fingers dug in painfully for a moment before Lena knit her eyebrows together. The pressure from Lena's grip lessened as she pulled Alia in for a feverish hug.

"I'll protect you," Lena whispered.

Alia's shoulders quaked, wracked with dry sobs, as she contemplated how disappointed Lena must be in her. Angry that her mother hadn't been able to expand the confines that she found herself in.

Alia's shoulders tightened when Finn came to stand beside them.

"There is something I want to show both of you."

Lena broke away from Alia but clasped her hand. Alia gave a sharp nod, accepting his invitation.

"Follow me," Finn bid, stepping into the towering hedges. Alia felt Finn's magic as she followed behind him, a spell working its way through the garden. His magic transformed their surroundings into a grassy expanse.

They were in a field, leading to a small, fire-lit cottage. On one side of the cottage, a tame river burbled. Alia knew on the far side of the cottage there would be a small garden, bursting with every color and shape that existed in nature.

"Dihlmere," Lena said with delight.

Finn nodded. "Our home."

"It's an illusion." Alia bit into her cheek.

"A memory." Finn straightened his plain tunic. "I thought we could share a meal here."

The Dihlmere cottage was the only place Alia truly loved. The years here, spent healing, spent learning about what it meant to be in love, spent learning what it was to be a mother. The emotions were overwhelming, so intensely wonderful and painful at the same time.

How dare he.

Alia turned her back and stalked off towards the garden, leaving Finn and Lena in her wake. She sank into the grass, trying to summon tranquility. She could hear Finn and Lena as they let her be and went into the cottage.

"You should have anticipated that." Lena's voice came through the window overlooking the garden.

"I'm out of practice when it comes to your mother." Alia could almost hear him shaking his head.

"Because you left us. Why did you go?"

"I expected you to have questions."

Alia wanted to slap him. He had been absent for the majority of his daughter's life.

Of course, she has questions.

"I never intended to stay in Entien. I used to be allowed to visit Entien once a year on Mabon to ensure the harvest yield. One year, at the end of

Mabon, the Tribunal didn't call me back. So, I stayed. Without magic, without my title, just like a mortal."

"Why?"

"The Tribunal does not account for their actions, not even to a Tiarcon." There was a bitterness in Finn's tone that captured Alia's interest. "What has your mother told you? About what you are?"

"You didn't exactly leave her with answers."

"My people—our people—we have lived in Alasar since the beginning of memory. Our magics are part of the fabric that dictates each aspect of the natural order. We are stewards of these lands; our responsibility is to protect and manage life in every expression."

Bergan isn't too preoccupied with protecting life.

"Some of us have moved on to different realms. There used to be more: Pustin, Gedalla, Yahear..." Finn trailed off, a wistfulness coming through. "And when we lose a Tiarcon, that responsibility to the land remains and is passed on to the others. I am the remaining seasonal Tiarcon."

"You create the seasons?" Lena blurted out.

"I *manage* the seasons. Haziel, the Tiarcon of the Sun, looks after the passing of the days in the absence of his counterpart, the Tiarcon of the Moon. Which neither of us has been able to do sufficiently for both realms."

"You're managing the seasons, at this moment?"

Lena's pitch drew a chuckle from Finn. "At least in Alasar. I haven't been granted proper access to Entien for over a decade, not since I last saw you and your mother. The veil limits my influence there."

"Why haven't you done anything to fix it?"

Finn heaved a great sigh, so exaggerated that Alia could hear it. "Many of the Tiarcons don't want it fixed; they want the mortal realm to suffer until the Tribunal agrees to remove the veil. That, and we can hardly spare a thought to your realm when ours is at war. Bergan, Mire, and Rowthra have been at each other's throats since Entien was created. They contemplate the worst in each other and often born it to be true. Haziel and I try to stay apart from it, but that seems less and less possible with each day."

"So, the Tribunal left you in Dihlmere. With Mother."

"Far enough away from any seats of power to not be detected or drawn into the struggles of an independent realm, a place where I could live quietly."

"How did you meet?"

"I pulled her out of the river. She had fallen, nearly starved in her escape from Mandal."

Finn knew well that Alia had entered that river by her own power.

"You saved her." Lena's voice was faint.

"She was starving and sick. I took her in, thinking that when she got strong enough, she would move on." Finn paused, and Alia wished again that she could see his expression.

"But she didn't."

"She never left. She didn't know, didn't care about who I was. To her, I was just a man who had taken pity on her. And as she began to heal, she loved me for it."

"And you never thought to tell her?"

"It was selfish. I wanted so badly to be loved for ... I let her love someone who didn't exist. I never intended to leave either of you."

"Then why did you?"

"When Dihlmere was attacked, I used magic." Finn sighed again. "The Tribunal must have felt it and called me back. I thought it would be better not to fight them, better for you and your mother if they never found you."

"It wasn't better."

"I'm sorry, Lena."

"I'd like to learn more," Lena said. "About Alasar, about the Tiarcons, about what I might be capable of." Alia knew that Lena was thinking of Effe's words and the threat that her existence could pose to the veil.

"That's why we're here. I think you should stay in Alasar with me."

Alia had heard enough. She picked herself off the ground to head inside the house, her house. She found Lena and Finn sitting at the table in their tiny kitchen. She leaned against a beam.

Alia looked between her husband and daughter, waiting for one of them to speak.

"I can protect her, Alia." He stood, taking Lena's hand into his. "Bergan's mortal puppet will tear Entien apart. I haven't been able to care for my daughter, let me at least help her now."

The Undoing flourished as her husband contemplated ripping away the person Alia loved the most, as he dangled Alasar in front of her daughter, promising Lena could finally discover who she was, rather than toiling away with the mortals.

Alia willed the edge out of her voice. "It is Lena's decision."

Lena stood from the table and pressed her palms on it. "This isn't—" Lena swore and slammed her hand on the table before disappearing into her old bedroom and slamming the door behind her.

"She's certainly your daughter." Finn lifted his eyebrows.

"There is nothing wrong with seeking solitude to think." Alia sat opposite her husband. "She has already chosen Entien once. Your friend tried to persuade her."

"My friend?"

"The crone who came for Lena. Effe," Alia said. "She was one of your kind."

"Effe?" A tremor went through Finn's controlled expression. "She came for Lena? When? Where?"

"A few days ago." Alia watched him closely, intrigued by how Effe could scare a Tiarcon. "Who is she?"

"What else did she say?" He ignored Alia's question.

Alia weighed telling Finn a lie. Despite what he had done to them, Alia had no doubts that he cared for Lena. She just wasn't convinced when it came to the veil between realms that she and Finn would be of the same mind. "She told Lena who her father really was."

"Alia, Effe is not a friend," Finn said. "Please, you need to listen to me—"

"How can I believe you?" Alia's back was straight.

Finn's eyebrows drew together. "Your safety, Lena's safety ... trust that I value both."

Alia waved her hand, dismissing Finn's forced passion. "What is the real reason behind Bergan's war with Rowthra and Mire?"

Finn dusted off his breeches. "Bergan is a scoundrel."

Alia propped her elbows on the table. "Elaborate."

"Yahear discovered that he favored a mortal over her, and her mortal subjects suffered. That was the last of many transgressions against mortalkind, the one that finally united your people and turned the Tribunal to your side. The loss of Yahear, the departure of our mortal subjects and the magics they retained, the chasm between our realms ... it has ruined the Tiarcons."

"And everything else apparently." Alia refused to grant Finn pity.

"Alia, please. We need to focus on our daughter."

"How many children do you have anyway?"

His eyes went dark. "I've lived more than a thousand years."

"And how many wives?"

Finn leaned forward. "Two."

"Why is that?"

"Kenina."

Alia held his gaze and lifted her eyebrows, an invitation for Finn to continue.

"Kenina and I were married for a long time," Finn began, his shoulders slumping and a deep suffering shining through his eyes.

"What happened?"

Finn's shoes scraped against the floor. "She left me. She had had enough of our life, enough of the churn of time. She severed our marriage and left my lands." Tears were flowing freely down Finn's cheeks now, causing Alia to grasp his hand. "Years later, I met you. That is why when I saw you—" She knew immediately that he was referring to that day in the river. "I thought that if I could help you, somehow, that would make up for not being able to help her."

"You did help me."

"I had to leave you; I had to follow the Tribunal's call. I know the cost—when you realized that I had left rather than died, I saw in your eyes the same anguish I carry."

Alia sat back in her chair, taking her hand back. "We understand each other then."

Finn's fingers fluttered, coaxing the Undoing and calling it to him. Once more, it curled around him without the impulse to harm. "You've changed. I used to feel your magic suppressed within you. Now it is enforcing you," Finn assessed. "You've done well."

Alia was rescued from responding by Lena emerging from her room. She took Alia's previous position, leaning against the support beam with her arms folded across her chest. "What do you think?" she asked Alia.

Alia's entire being was fighting what she knew she had to say. "I think you should stay with your father. War is coming to Entien, and he is better able to protect you here."

"And leave you?"

"It doesn't have to be forever," Finn said.

Alia nodded in support. "Just until Vincent is no longer a threat."

Lena looked from Finn to Alia. "I'm in crisis, and now you two patch things up?"

"We happen to agree on this point." Alia tried to speak calmly and get Lena to think straight.

"You are hoping that I listen to you."

"Since when do you care about what I hope for?"

Lena bit her lip. "Can't you stay in Alasar with me?

Alia's head throbbed. If she stayed in Alasar, the Tiarcon of the Forest would hunt her down and reclaim her magic. "If it is the only way to convince you, I'll stay with you."

"No," Finn rejected outright, flaring dissension between them once more. "Lena is my blood; I can protect her. If you stay, and Rowthra finds you, she'll claim you, command you. You can't deny her. Not even I can."

"And what will Mandal do without you? They'll be overcome by Veillant," Lena stated. "What about our family?" Alia knew that she was thinking of the collection of friends and relatives that they had cobbled together over the past few months.

"That is not your concern."

Lena glared at both of them, stomped back to her room, and slammed the door once more.

"I suppose we should settle in." Cups and plates appeared on their table, far more than they had ever been able to afford when they lived here. Alia reached for the wine first, pouring herself a hefty glass before sitting back.

"Family. Your parents have made amends?" Finn asked.

"Of course not." Alia began to fill a plate. "But Elowen, my younger sister, has become very close with Lena. And we have our friends."

"Baldric. And your mage."

"Dorian," Alia corrected. "And Harlan and Flora. Lena has her own friends, too."

"Harlan and Flora? From your childhood?"

"The same ones." Alia nodded. "Some people were happy to have me back."

"And Cormac?"

"Married my sister."

Finn shook his head. "I never thought you would go back there."

"I thought Lena was sick. When she came into her high magic, I thought it was a disease. They kept asking me what kind of mage Lena's father was, and I assured them that he was a talentless commoner."

Finn almost choked on his wine.

"They assumed I was lying, of course. Cormac thought he was her father. Dorian was the only one who figured out who she was."

"Dorian is Mandal's Master Mage?"

Alia nodded. "Ruben died years ago."

"Oh, I know that."

"Oh?"

"Cara visited him. It was a short trip."

Alia should have known. His early passing had been too much of a kindness to be a coincidence. "Have you figured out what to do about Bergan and your talisman?"

"I know Bergan. He will save the talisman to use against me when it most benefits him. He is patient, devious. Which means I have time to find a way to get it back from him, or to break the link."

"I'd do it again."

Finn almost grinned. "I have no doubt."

"Why did you give it to me to begin with?"

"It was the only protection I thought you would accept. I knew as long as you had my ring, you could protect yourself and Lena. If you would let me gift you magic, I would."

"Deanna was in Bergan's hall," Alia deflected his offer. "Who is she?"

"Deanna serves as Rowthra's emissary; she has many connections to the various lands and is able to move freely despite the war. What was her message to Bergan?"

"Rowthra refused his peace offer of handing me over to her."

Finn's flat expression shook, showing a bit of emotion for a moment. "She refused?"

"Apparently, the Undoing isn't that enticing of a prize."

Lena's door slammed open. Alia examined her expression and knew what she had decided to do. Lena looked past her mother, fixated on her father. He returned her apologetic look with a tight smile. "Come, join us," he beckoned, and Lena sat beside him.

"I admire that you won't leave your mother, that you want to help the mortals."

Lena bloomed at his words, throwing her arms around his neck.

"Father." Lena looked to Alia for permission to continue.

Alia knew what she wanted to say and fought her instinct not to trust Finn. He was Lena's father, and if she wanted to confide in him, Alia wouldn't stop her. She inclined her head. "Do you think that the realms need to be reunited?"

Finn's brows furrowed, taking in Lena's trepidation as she spoke.

"Twenty years ago, I would have said absolutely, for all our sakes. But I didn't understand, didn't appreciate ..." Finn took a heavy breath.

"What it was to be mortal," Alia finished for him. "Powerless."

"I fear if the veil were to fall, that my fellow Tiarcons would revisit the same brutality that spurred its creation."

It was Finn's way of saying that they would murder indiscriminately and demand blood oaths from those who survived.

When Lena dimmed, Finn seized her shoulders. "My love for you crosses realms. There is no power that will change that."

Lena buried her face in her father's chest, shaking with sobs.

Finn locked eyes with Alia over Lena's shoulder, trying to tell her that the same went for her. She felt nothing at the admission, searching deep within herself and finding that her love had been drained away by betrayal. By years alone, by deceit.

She didn't need Finn to put her back together; she stood on her own.

And the Tiarcon had nothing else to offer her.

19

Dawn coated the Harvestlands, but Alia preferred Entien's empty sky to Alasar's harsh routine. Still, this land hummed around her, docile now that she was leaving it. Or perhaps because Finn walked beside her. Every languid movement belied his weariness and restraint as he led the mortals back to the door. His commanders walked with them, ever watchful.

As they passed through the orchard, a familiar vixen stepped into their path. She approached Alia, garnet eyes wide and repentant, before nuzzling her head into Alia's chest. The vixen's wooden helmet pressed uncomfortably into Alia's collarbone.

Finn observed for a moment before continuing on with a nod to Cara.

"Sabie apologizes for apprehending you when you arrived," Cara whispered to Alia. "But she is honored to have carried the Tiarcon's wife in her jaws."

"She speaks to you?" Alia asked as Sabie drew away.

"She speaks. Your mortal ears cannot hear."

Alia pressed on, catching Dorian's eye as he glanced back. He was ahead of her now, Baldric and Lena at his side, should he stumble. The signs of what he had suffered still shone in the lines on his face, the hunch of his shoulders.

"He's worried," Cara said. Her eyes were on her sworn Tiarcon.

"So am I." Alia knew what awaited; in returning home, there would be no relief. They still had to stop the incursions, prevent Vincent and the Veillantis from disrupting the veil.

Soon, Finn stood between the mortals and the door to their realm, commanding their attention. "Your accounts of the conditions in Entien are disquieting," he said, looking from Lena to Alia. "I'm sending Ossian along with you."

"No," Alia refused. "He will not be welcomed." By the mortals, or by her.

"He has agreed to accompany you at great risk to himself."

Alia couldn't restrain herself. "How brave of you to let him."

Ossian removed his tunic, a crack forming in the warrior's façade.

"Are you sure?" Finn asked his commander.

Ossian looked up, gazing beyond Alia to where Baldric stood. Alia assumed Baldric would be itching to vanish through the door. Instead, Baldric was still, transfixed by the Alasaran.

"Yes, Tiarcon." Ossian fell to his knees.

Finn pressed his palm against Ossian's bare chest, where the crest of the Tiarcon of the Harvest was carved. Garnet light emanated from Finn's hand as Ossian writhed beneath his touch, trying to hold back a scream. Cara reinforced her brother as light coursed up Finn's arm. The transfer went on for several moments before Ossian collapsed on the ground.

"What did you do to him?" Lena asked.

"To pass into Entien, Ossian had to relinquish his Alasaran attributes, his magics."

Ossian stumbled, bracing his hand on the ground before shuffling to his feet. He immediately turned back around and expelled the contents of his stomach. Baldric brushed past Alia to help the Alasaran up as he listed to the side, his limbs too burdensome for the newly-made mortal to manage.

"He gave up his magic?"

"It will be returned to him once his time in Entien is done." Alia glanced at Cara—she would have undergone a similar procedure to travel to Entien to kill Ruben at Finn's order. Gratitude surged through Alia, seeing what Cara had withstood to achieve that bit of justice.

Baldric, the man who only a few days before had been cursing everything that existed in this realm, steadied Ossian. The Alasaran shrugged his tunic back on, and Cara summoned his armor and weapons from the air. She methodically fastened the armor on her brother, doing her part to blunt his newfound vulnerability.

"Alia." Finn beckoned her to him. "I could gift you magic to protect you in Entien."

Alia recoiled. "No. I regret the vow I made to you. I am not going to hazard an oath."

Finn drew his eyebrows together, heaviness settling on him. He gripped Alia's wrist. "To replace what you lost in the Mountainlands, then." The same garnet light glowed where their skin touched. When he took his hand away, a golden bracelet encircled her wrist. The smooth metal was notched at the top, with curving tendrils up her arm resembling flower petals.

He stepped back without another word, saving his farewells for Lena.

Alia stared ahead at the door while they cried, unsuccessfully trying to banish the feeling of Finn's hand on her arm.

They left Alasar through the same door they entered. All three mages offered blood to the whispers, withstood the inspection, and dragged the two quotidiens behind them. Once through the door, they spilled out into the dark of the Mandal Forest.

There was a dullness about it, as if the realm itself was only a shadow.

Ossian stumbled. "Why is it so dark?"

"The moon fell," Alia answered. "You'll acclimate."

"Now we just have to convince half of the palace that we aren't traitors and save our realm from the Veillanti." Baldric gave Dorian a sideways glance.

"Traitors?" Lena asked.

"You are the daughter of a Tiarcon." Baldric tried to smile as he led the way through the trees.

"Don't worry, Lena." Dorian glared ahead at the soldier. "If they can get used to a Veillanti for a Master Mage, no one will flinch at your parentage."

"Have we gotten used to you?" Baldric didn't bother turning around to see Dorian's reaction.

"Anyone who seeks to defame the Tiarcon's daughter will be dealt with," Ossian promised.

"Says the magicless Alasaran."

"Baldric, did the veil addle your brain?" Alia snapped, stomping through the undergrowth.

Baldric paused, running a hand through his hair. "I'm sure it'll be fine, Lena."

Lena turned to Alia with wide eyes.

"If anyone gives you trouble for who you are, I'll stop their hearts," Alia said.

"A more formidable threat." Baldric grinned at Ossian.

A shriek came from where the forest gave way to the meadows, followed by, "Finally!" A fuming, disheveled Flora awaited them. Alia's friend, caked in the dirt and leaves, pushed her aside to embrace Lena. "My dear, you're back, oh thank Orlast."

"Did you sleep out here?" Baldric asked with a grin. "Rolling around in the dirt?"

"Someone had to keep watch. You all certainly took your time," Flora sputtered once she had released Lena. Her eyes caught on Ossian, and immediately her hands went to smooth her hair and her dress. "And you brought a friend."

Ossian regarded her with a raised eyebrow before Baldric waved her off. "How is Cormac?"

Flora stilled. "There's been another incursion. The city has been breached."

"Vincent knew Mandal was undefended," Dorian cursed. "I have to see," he said before flickering away.

"Where is the breach?" Baldric demanded.

"We've already lost half of the Fen."

The neighborhood sat in the northernmost section of the city, close to the sea, at the low point in the land before it rose to cliffs. It was the most exposed to the waves, characterized by decades of neglect.

Lena clasped Flora's hand. "Do you know what it is?"

"A woman with a terrible scream." Flora's face twisted. "She screamed and buildings crumbled into the waves."

Ossian lurked at Lena's elbow. "Withran. You should stay away from the sea."

Lena turned away from the Alasaran. "They need us."

Alia didn't want to rush into another cage. "Flora, what did Cormac do to you for helping us?"

"Let's just say that if you manage to get us out of this, it will improve our standing," Flora said through clenched teeth. "I'll need to inform him of your return and intention to join the defense immediately."

"I won't be a prisoner again," Alia imparted before Flora split off.

"You should stay away from the sea," Ossian repeated.

Alia was in no mood to deal with the warrior chaperone. "We've faced Alasaran monsters before."

"You are mine to protect." Ossian pulled her back.

Baldric stepped in. "All you can do is go with them."

"What good will I be against a Withran now that I'm—"

"Mortal?" Baldric's smirk caused Ossian to flush. If Baldric had dared to go against a Tiarcon as a quotidien mortal, Ossian couldn't beg his way out of confronting the Withran.

They reached the top of the stair leading down to the palace, catching the first glimpse of the devastation. Torches lit every window throughout the curving streets, except that an entire section, the Fen, had gone dark. Only sparks of magic along the shore could be seen.

"They need us now," Lena whispered, stepping out of Alia's reach, and flickering away.

"Lena!" Alia screamed at the place where she had just stood. Her daughter was determined to throw herself in front of every possible hazard.

"Why would they leave the only one who can actually kill these things behind?" Baldric grumbled.

"You can't even flicker?" Ossian groaned.

Irritation made her shiver as she contemplated the distance on foot. "We need to get there, fast. Vincent has been drawn out during an attack before. He might appear."

Ossian flashed his teeth.

"Can you run?" Baldric asked Alia.

"All the way to the shore?" Alia snapped. Her dark mood fueled her Undoing, which rushed like a river about to jump its banks. As if it knew Alia was finally back in an arena where her magic could have influence.

"I'm going to hate this as much as you will," Ossian said before hefting

Alia over his shoulder and running beside Baldric.

Alia felt each footfall as she was jostled against the warrior's shoulder. She cursed Dorian for not taking her with him; he was usually the one pushing her into the fray. Lena hadn't protested Alia putting herself in the center of the fight before. But now that they knew what the Undoing was and what she had gone through to awaken it, it seemed they were thrusting themselves out ahead of her. The realization bit—she'd wanted to be understood, not coddled.

They passed evacuating nobles on the way, too panicked to notice the towering Alasaran warrior in their midst. The palace courtyard was awash with commoners seeking refuge from the city. They were denied entrance to the palace gates, armed guards holding them off. Alia fumed, taking a moment to send the Undoing to disrupt one of the gates, taking down the guard and allowing a rush of commoners to stream in.

They were clear of the gates, running into the gap left behind, when a scream rang out, piercing the dark. "That's her," Ossian said, running ahead of Baldric. The ground beneath them shook forcefully. The buildings around them swayed and groaned, straining to stay upright as the ground quaked.

"Alia!"

She lifted her head at Dorian's call. The mage had found them, flickering back to retrieve her. Ossian discarded her at his feet.

"Running is so," Ossian let out a frustrated grunt, "*slow.*"

"Shall I carry you the rest of the way?" Baldric offered.

Ossian scowled down at him. "I matched your pace even with her on my back."

Baldric grinned, dimples deepening. "That wasn't my fastest. I just didn't know how this form would hold up." His eyes traced down Ossian's chest. "Especially if you shift every time it gets difficult."

Alia tuned their bickering out, focusing on the Master Mage. "How bad is it?"

"We need the Undoing." There was an apology in his eyes, a resignation. He didn't want to ask this of her, but he knew he must.

"Any sign of Vincent?"

"Not yet." Dorian shook his head.

"Don't—" Ossian lurched towards her.

Alia wrapped her arms around Dorian before the commander could stop her. Ossian and Baldric disappeared, replaced by signs of the attack, as Dorian flickered to the Fen.

It was gone. The maze of stacked wooden structures that narrowed the streets into alleyways had collapsed into rubble. Dorian and Alia flickered into a maelstrom; soldiers and commoners caked in sand and filth, blood mixed with dust, stumbling away from the shore.

When Alia separated from Dorian, she braced herself against the remnants of a collapsed wall, taking deep, shuddering breaths. This was why Cormac hadn't wanted her to go after Lena. She'd left Sheath unprotected. Alia tried to shake off the burden, but it persisted.

As she panted, the ground beneath her trembled. She waited for a moment, wondering if it was just the numbness in her legs or her racing mind. The tremor came once more.

The Withran.

Alia followed Dorian down the ruined street, moving towards the water with each step. She didn't have to struggle far before encountering Mandal's defense, a row of mages, archers, and soldiers with spears.

The sea tossed, waves pounding at the footings of the remaining buildings. Alia's hair and clothes were already damp from the spray as she kept moving onward.

Lena was farther out, crafting a barrier. Dorian surged forward, passing Alia to assist Lena.

"What do you need?" Harlan approached from the front line, already bleeding profusely from a wound on his temple.

"Keep your men clear." Alia squeezed his arm. "Keep yourself clear."

Harlan's order to Sheath's defenders was drowned out by the waves.

Alia gained control of her heartbeat as she went to join Lena and Dorian. The Withran stood just beyond Lena's barrier. It was a woman, her skin too gray to resemble life, dull olive hair hanging in lumps to her waist. She was dressed in rags, fabric blowing in the torrent. The beast could have passed for a mortal woman in stature, but she looked like a corpse that had been lost at sea for weeks.

Alia pulled at the Undoing, imagining Bergan and Vincent and letting her fury fuel her power. The violet glow returned; the same rush of the Undoing being unleashed within her. She felt threads of Finn channeling through her bracelet, adding reach and ferocity to the Undoing as it hovered above the sand towards the Withran.

The creature began to advance, rows of sharp teeth visible as the gash in her face opened. Her mouth gaped horrifically wide, funneling seawater at them with a shattering shriek. The Undoing scattered in the wake of the attack; Alia had to harness it with both hands, pulling the mist back into a cloud.

She lashed out at the Withran again with the Undoing, but its body was already so far decomposed that there was no past injury to exploit; every previous condition the Withran held was far better than its current state. The Undoing danced over the beast, trying to reach for its heart. But as the Undoing searched, it healed the Withran, returning its open wounds to healthy flesh, strengthening it.

Another piercing scream tore apart the Undoing.

"What is wrong?!" Dorian screamed as Lena buckled under the strain of reinforcing entire city blocks.

A tug on the Undoing prevented Alia from responding, sending her stumbling forward. The Withran had opened its mouth again, but this time sucked air in. The Undoing was pulled into its mouth, feeding the creature. Alia scrambled on her knees, failing to stop the Withran from pulling her closer. Her arms surged with mist, sections of her skin fading into nothing.

"Take the Undoing back!" Ossian called as he and Baldric made it to the shore. Ossian hooked his arm around Baldric's neck, holding the soldier back from coming to her side.

The Withran reeled Alia in.

Dorian and Lena flickered between her and the Withran, attacking with light and fire. The Withran overcame it all, moving forward still. Lena's garnet eyes glowed in the onslaught, fear leaking out. The scream of the Withran ripped through the shoreline, sending the earth shaking. Alia was yanked ever closer to its gaping mouth.

Hands grasped her around the waist, hauling her back.

"Get out of here!" Alia shouted as Harlan put his body between her and the beast.

He couldn't respond as the force of the Withran blasted him. His armor began to rip apart. The quotidien captain would not be able to withstand the immortal; she was going to break him apart.

"Stop!"

Harlan bowed over, bracing his hands and knees. The shaking subsided, the shriek fading away into the wind.

"Stop," Lena repeated; her eyes pressed shut. "What do you want?"

She was talking *to* the Withran.

Alia crumpled back to the sand, bracing herself with her arms as the battle between Lena and the Withran unfolded before her. Harlan lay beside her, his injuries healing under her hand.

"They're mortals!" Lena screamed.

The creature reared up, backing off the barrier and then abruptly shut its mouth and peered curiously over at Lena. Another screech shattered their meager line, almost too shrill for the Mandals to remain standing. Then its gaze settled on Alia.

"No." Lena walked forward, only a few feet from the creature. "That is my mother. Mortal." The Withran gagged, coughing up seaweed and black liquid the consistency of oil. Alia felt the Undoing spirit back to her, flashes of Ruben taking hold as she dug her fingers into the sand.

"I don't understand." It was one of the rare times he actually expressed emotion, frustration that she had yet to exhibit any signs of the Undoing. "I've tried everything."

And he had. Every way he could think to hurt her, to put her in so much agony that the power in her blood would be sure to twist. Inculcation held her immobile, staring out at the sea, as he referenced his notes.

Hope fluttered in Alia despite the mental shackles. Nothing had worked. He could stop, he could leave her alone. Ruben stacked his journals on his desk, his glasses discarded beside them as he laboriously got to his feet. He came to stand over her, as if looking at her could make a magic she'd never seen, or felt, come forward. Part of her yearned for it, if only to make him stop.

"Perhaps I've been too soft." He smoothed her hair, trying to untangle it from her plaits. She'd tried to braid her hair so tightly that he wouldn't be able to pull at it, but he was not deterred. "We'll go through it all again, try again. And this time, I won't let my heart interfere."

Another lie, one designed to smother any relief.

"Do you want to go home?" Lena asked the Withran, her voice gentle. The roaring of the waves died down. The creature must have given her a response because Lena sliced open her palm, lifting it into the air. A garnet door appeared, cut into the waves. The Withran stood over the door, looking between Lena and it in disbelief.

"Go on," Lena said. The creature shrank down, disappearing through the door and back into its own realm.

The ground beneath her stilled, and the sea calmed. Alia scrambled back to her feet, not quite believing her eyes. Ossian sprinted past, steadying Lena by the shoulders as she pitched backward.

"What happened?"

"I-I-I ..." Lena stammered. "I asked her to leave."

"You did what?"

"She didn't know she was in Entien. She thought she was attacking the Mountainlands." Lena panted as the rush of the sea faded away. Ossian let out a creative stream of curses. "She just wanted to go home."

"Lena, that is—" Dorian shook his head in disbelief.

"They think they are part of Alasar's war, but they are fighting us."

The Oucura and Traimine and now the Withran, beasts by nature. Taken from their lands and set upon another without their knowing.

Lena turned to Alia. "She called to you. She wanted you to go with her."

"A Withran feeds on vengeance and those who seek it," Ossian said, not meeting Alia's eyes. "You must have been enticing."

Alia sighed, understanding. "The Undoing didn't hurt her; it made her stronger."

Baldric grabbed her arm, pulling Alia closer as if they were still under attack. "Vincent knows. He knows how to overcome your magic."

Vincent had been denied Dorian and the Undoing in one defeat, and now he was tailoring his attack to weaken her.

"It's exactly what he said would happen. Our kingdoms will be crushed." Baldric released her, gesturing towards what once was the Fen. It had been leveled, senselessly.

When no one answered him, Baldric turned back to the sea and fell to his knees. Ossian put his hand on Baldric's shoulder, which was promptly shaken off. Ossian reached for Baldric again, this time grasping his arm. Ossian held Baldric against his hip, braced by the arm wrapped around him.

Lena threaded her fingers in Alia's. Despite the strain on the Undoing, having been emptied out and reclaimed, Alia jolted a bit of healing magic through Lena, repairing the cut on her palm.

Dorian was giving orders to his mages a few paces away. The palace healers had flocked to the shore and were helping as many of the fallen as they could.

King Cormac stepped onto the sand, his royal armor speckled with mist. "You came back." Alia had been prepared for anger, punishment. But instead, she found softness in his gaze as he tried to see how the journey to Alasar had marked her. "You're home."

Alia nodded, mist extending up her arms as her body slumped. It ate away at her skin, pulsing and rebuilding.

Cormac wrapped a cloak around her, staving off the cold of the Fen.

"Is Mandal lost?" he whispered his fears.

She didn't have the will to answer him.

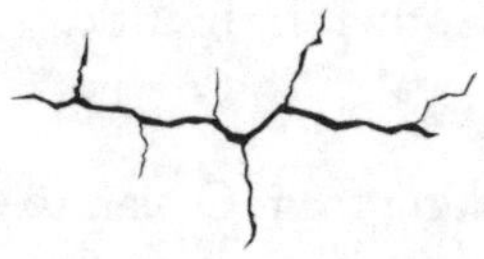

Any comfort taken in returning to Mandal crumbled in the Fen, broken on the shore in the wake of an attack that they'd only barely been able to deflect. Cormac had ordered an audience in the council chambers to hear an accounting of what happened in Alasar. While Alia and Baldric stumbled through the tale, Flora sulked silently in the corner, and Harlan stood at his liege's side. Ossian was a silent sentinel at the door. Elowen, who had been waiting for them when they returned, had been as quick to embrace her sister and niece as Alia was to draw away from her. Now the queen sat alone, rapt with attention. Dorian hovered just behind Alia, while Lena sat beside her.

The king leaned over his map, soot covering his hands where flames had escaped while Alia and Baldric spoke.

"The Tiarcon deceived you." All was now right in Cormac's mind, Alia figured. She hadn't chosen to leave him; she had run away from his treacherous uncle. And she had been taken at the mercy of a powerful being; she hadn't willingly cast Cormac aside and fallen in love with another. He still couldn't see that none of that mattered, not why or how their love had withered, only that it had. A doomed echo of youthful desires.

Alia took a long look at Lena before replying to Cormac. "We were married and had a daughter. Being of two different realms has separated us, but it does not break our bond." She couldn't equivocate for Dorian's sake.

"And he is not a threat to you or your kingdom." Ossian held his head high, refusing to address Cormac by his title. "As long as you don't mean his wife and daughter harm."

Cormac glowered, looking from Ossian to Alia. The Alasaran overshadowed every other man in the room by at least a head, but still Cormac sought to challenge him. The twitch of Dorian's fingers caught Alia's attention; he was willing to whisk them away at the slightest urging.

"Ossian is here to assist. If you all could suppress your agonistic tendencies for a moment ..." Alia said.

"They are the enemy," Cormac asserted, moving close enough to reach out and touch her. Ossian moved fast, positioning himself between Cormac and Alia.

Alia stepped out of Ossian's shadow. "We need to focus on Vincent." The silence stretched on once more, Cormac's face inscrutable.

Flora tapped her heel. "The delegations from Parth and Royce arrive tomorrow."

"We'll need their support if we are to rival Vincent," Dorian said.

"And for that, you'll need mine," Cormac said. It was his move, his piece to play. "Vincent knows how to transfer magic from one mortal to another?" Cormac looked to Dorian. "He has successfully completed the transfer?"

"He does," Alia's mind quieted, knowing that she would have to find her way back into Cormac's confidences to learn his plans. Where Alia would expect to see horror, she saw only excitement in Cormac's eyes.

Ossian clenched his fists. "He wants to become a locumten." When he was faced with blank stares, he swore. "A locumten," he repeated. "The Oucura, Traimine, and Withran are all locumten."

"Locumten?" Baldric shrugged.

"There is a reason why Tiarcon Bergan and your mortal mage can pull certain immortals through the veil. Locumten were once one of you."

Alia sat up in her chair, looking back at Dorian, who had gone still. "I have you," she whispered.

"It used to happen from time to time," Ossian continued. "A mortal gifted with too much magic transforms, but your bodies cannot contain it, your minds do not survive. You become little more than beasts."

Dorian gulped. “Vincent has no care for his mind.”

“Could it happen to any mortal?” Lena asked, rising to face Ossian across the table.

Ossian controlled his expression, locking away the impatience he had for the rest of them when speaking to Lena. “Yes, my lady.”

Flora was pacing at the back of the room. “Even more reason to attack Veillant.”

“Alia has killed two locumten already.” Harlan’s tongue fumbled over the Alasaran term. “Should we not wait until Vincent loses his mind? Won’t he be more vulnerable then?”

Alia shuddered as Dorian shook his head. “Vincent, restrained by what little mortality he has left, is vicious. Imagine the destruction if he becomes one of them.” Dorian didn’t have to elaborate; the rest knew all too well how much mortal blood had been shed already.

“The summit will have to work.” Cormac toyed with the rings on his fingers. “They’ll need to see the Undoing Mage stand with Mandal. We’ll keep the origins of Lena’s magic between us for now.”

“Are we going to ignore what just occurred on the shore?” Lena’s passion outpaced her tact. “Vincent lost his chance at the Undoing in Alasar, so he sent that creature to rip it out of my mother. And we’re just going to let him try again, hoping she isn’t killed this time?”

The chamber echoed with shifting footsteps. A bit of Alia’s zeal fled at Lena’s questioning.

“Lena is right,” Elowen spoke for the first time. “If Vincent can do as you say, Alia needs to be protected.”

Elowen’s words overcame Alia, but the time to seek protection had long passed. It had once been the only thing she wished for, but now protection was tinged with a feeling of uselessness, of being pushed aside. Alia searched the room for supporters, but Baldric and Flora shifted away from her gaze, and Harlan had a look of open pity. There would be no help from her friends. Cormac's mind was on other matters, as he still fumbled with his rings and stared down at the map. Dorian's fidgeting brought her little calm, and Ossian's level stare was infuriating. Alia bypassed Elowen's concern to settle on Lena.

Lena, who had just left her father behind in another realm, had to tangle with a beast to tear her mother from its grip. A young woman who had only just been released from a Tiarcon's prison. Who could only see the weakness in her mother, the vulnerability.

I should have torn it all down for her.

Alia should have been stronger, able to assuage the fears Lena now carried. To free Lena from worrying over her. Perhaps darkness was preferable to being a liability.

Because if Alia could not withstand this, there was no doubt in her mind who Mandal would turn to. They would turn to the daughter of the Tiarcon, both of this realm and the other, the one with magics beyond comprehension. And then Lena would be shackled, either to fulfilling an unspeakable fate at the behest of the Alasarans or to constantly bear the weight of mortal survival on her shoulders.

Alia couldn't allow either.

20

When Cormac dismissed them, Dorian flickered away before Alia could say a word. His departure left her standing alone, while Lena and Baldric peppered Ossian with more questions about locumten and Flora and Harlan spoke in hushed tones.

"Ali." Elowen reached for her hand. "I'm so glad you're home."

"So you can try to take my daughter from me?" Alia snapped, still not able to look at her younger sister without fuming. "Or chain me in a pairing?"

"Her father is a Tiarcon." There was a hint of bitterness in her tone. "I don't know if Father will decide that this is the end of the Meadors or our finest moment."

"I don't care either way." Alia turned her back on Elowen.

The chamber doors had never looked more inviting.

"Find me once you've rested," Flora called after her as Alia made her way out.

Rest? Her mind was still on Dorian, her first intention to seek him out. But as Alia stole into the hall, Ossian and Lena followed. She shifted her course to the Olden Wing, back to the prison that had become home.

"You can go now," Alia said to Ossian when they crossed into the Olden Wing. "You've successfully delivered Finn's message to Mandal."

"Although I don't understand Tiarcon Finnian's attachment to you,

I could not allow you to pretend it didn't exist."

"How trite."

"Enough." Lena pushed through the door of their apartment.

Alia breathed in the stale air and felt calm spread over her. She looked over the frayed furnishings of the sitting room, wanting to run out onto the dark balcony. But Dorian wasn't there either.

"This is where you live?" Ossian poked at the couch, rousing a puff of dust. "You gave up a place in the Tiarcon's estate for this?"

Lena snorted. "You should have seen some of the other places." Lena followed Alia to her room.

"Do not let him in here," Alia said, bringing a chuckle out of Lena.

"You look terrible." Lena hovered as Alia settled into her bed.

"I feel terrible."

Lena took a few steps towards the door before sighing, turning back to the bed, and lying beside her mother.

Alia propped her head up on her hand, trying to fight off sleep. She knew that Lena wouldn't have lingered unless she had something to say. "I'm listening."

Lena just stared up at the ceiling.

"It must feel different being here now." Alia tried to pull the meaning behind Lena's frustration.

"You were the one who always insisted that we didn't have a home. But this is the first time I've really believed you."

"I didn't want a home," Alia said. "It wasn't that we couldn't have had one. It was a choice. My choice."

"Because of what he took from us."

Alia rubbed her forehead and sat up.

Lena avoided her gaze, still looking upwards as she blinked away tears. "He didn't even try to find a way back to us. He's just been sitting on his throne as if I never existed."

The anguish in her words found a companion in Alia's heart, as they shared that same echoing emptiness. Finn's insistence on his own helplessness was insufficient, an excuse that not even his daughter could accept.

"I used to think that if I had been a more obedient daughter, then perhaps Edgar wouldn't have treated me that way he did, the way he still does." Alia took Lena's hand in hers. "It took becoming a parent to understand that his failures as a father were due to his shortcomings, not mine."

Lena's bottom lip trembled. "He's a Tiarcon. Why would he care about me?"

"Because you are his child; there doesn't need to be another reason. I can't even begin to try to understand your father, but no matter how many lifetimes or how much power he possesses, he's deeply troubled. You are not responsible for his absence."

"Do you think, if he wanted to, he could come to Entien like Ossian did? Give up his magic and stay here?"

It hadn't emerged as a possibility to Alia; Finn had made his choice clear. He was a Tiarcon first. "I don't know." It was the truth. Finn had been the one to remove Ossian's magic through his mark. She had no idea if Tiarcon bore marks in the same fashion or if any being was strong enough to strip a Tiarcon of their power.

"I want to be with you," Lena said. "When you face Vincent."

"Let's worry about winning over the other kingdoms now, Vincent, after."

Lena nodded, settling in. "Can I rest with you?"

Lena's wide eyes made her seem younger, more like the girl Alia wished she still was.

"Of course." Alia slid back under the blankets. "Thank you for stopping the Withran."

"She was sad." Lena nestled her head into her mother's shoulder. "Like she had forgotten who she was."

"How did you know you could reason with her?"

"She was sad," Lena repeated. "Like you."

Flora's rooms were in the heart of the palace. She had bragged once that she made them displace an entire family so she could stay in a huge apartment, even with her husband and children back at Waterston.

A frantic servant brushed past Alia as she walked into the drawing room. "You'd think a palace maid would be able to follow basic instructions," Flora complained when she saw Alia. "I specifically told them to have wine placed on this table at all times."

Flora stomped off into the other room while Alia settled in one of the armchairs. Her friend soon returned, triumphant, with a bottle and glasses in hand. Like she had before, she tested the wine by dipping her finger before she poured their glasses. "Talk."

Alia raised her eyebrows at Flora.

"About all of it," Flora instructed, trying to draw Alia out.

Alia's breath caught in her throat, the events of the last few days replaying in her memory. She couldn't grab onto any one place to start.

Flora clapped her hands together. "Alia Meador, I can only take so much suspense."

"As if you haven't already discovered the whole of it."

"Baldric actually has his uses from time to time."

Alia scoffed.

"So, your husband is a ruler of the Otherworld." Flora rolled her eyes. "Aren't you special?"

"Get off it." Alia waved her wine glass, coming dangerously close to spilling it.

"Oh, I understand. I can only imagine bedding a Tiarcon. The *knowledge* he must have acquired over the years ..."

"Flora," Alia grumbled.

"You could at least indulge me. I risked my standing to assist your escape."

The pouting noblewoman seemed just fine. "What is all of this?" Alia attempted a distraction, focusing on Flora's table. There were five different place settings strewn about the table, gold and silver clashing.

"The quality of the palace staff is sorely lacking; Elowen has let their skills languish. They can't even select silver for the summit on their own."

"Cormac is fortunate to have an etiquette maven at his disposal."

"Elowen gets the crown, you get his heart, and I get the chores."

"His heart." Alia thought back to the entanglement she had fostered with Cormac, guilt and fury sparking. "Don't delude me that it is love anymore. Cormac's version is to overwhelm and manipulate until he gets what he wants."

"He knows." Flora regarded her through her lashes.

Alia wanted to drown in peppery red wine. "Knows what?"

"That it'll never be the way it was before," Flora said with a deep sigh, cradling her glass to her chest. "He knows he can't have you. But he'll never let you go, not completely. He doesn't know how."

Alia snorted. "And how do you know that?"

Flora lifted her eyes to Alia's, looking for a challenge. "He told me."

"Cormac confides in you," Alia commented, settling back into the armchair.

"It isn't as if he can talk to Harlan or that bastard Baldric." Flora tapped her fingernails on her glass.

Alia studied her friend for a moment. "Did you ever—"

"Once. Only once," Flora confirmed her suspicions. "Somewhere between you and Elowen, Cormac bedded half of the palace. And he cried afterwards because he missed you. I refused to be a placeholder." She flipped her hair behind her shoulder.

It was Alia's turn to chuckle. Once she started, the laughter overtook her at the sheer ridiculousness of it. In the past, the knowledge of Cormac and Flora together would have made her murderous, but now it was comical.

Flora took exception. "I would never begrudge you from seeking pleasure wherever you could find it."

Alia set her glass down and opened her palms, still laughing. "I needed that."

"As always, the rest of us are here for your amusement." Flora looked at her with narrowed eyes.

There was a bitterness in her voice that hushed Alia's laughter. "What is it?"

"Nothing." Flora shook her head.

"Flora."

Flora worked her lips into a pout before deciding to talk. "Geoff wants me home," Flora said dismally.

Alia leaned forward; Flora hardly spoke about her family. "Do you want to go?"

Flora put down her glass. "What would you all do without my exquisite taste?" Her voice broke. "I love my family, I really do. But I don't feel suited for any of it. This, Court, this is what I am skilled at, all I am made for."

"Why don't you bring the lot here? Take a cue from Mariana."

"I would make a far better Intercessor."

"Easily. What does Geoff think?"

"He protests any length of time spent at the palace. He thinks I'm grasping onto your notoriety. Or having an affair with Cormac."

Alia resisted the urge to disintegrate into laughter once more. "Shall I have a talk with him?"

"You stay far from my husband." Flora wagged her finger. "You don't need another man seeking to heal that tortured soul of yours. You have enough."

"Please," Alia protested.

"I do miss my children." Flora's eyes glimmered.

"There has to be a way to have the life you want."

Flora allowed herself an uncouth snort. "What kind of life do you want?"

Alia thought for a moment. "An idle one. One where there's nothing to worry over and nothing to be done."

"Idle?" Flora smiled. "My darling, you will never be. You went to the Otherworld, you found a husband, saved your daughter, and even found time to find Baldric someone to keep his bed warm, quite the trip."

Alia had sensed something brewing between Baldric and Ossian. "Of course, Baldric is interested in Ossian; he's the worst."

"Who else would care to understand Baldric?" Flora said dismissively.

"What are we going to do, Flora?" Alia's light mood quickly dissipated. "How can we shoulder all of this? Lena is absolutely gutted that her father abandoned her. I have no answers for her, nothing to take the pain away. I am all she has, and I am complete shit."

Flora pursed her lips again. "Do you want to hear what I think?"

"Since when have you been slow with your opinion?" Alia took another drink.

"You don't have to tell her anything. You survived more than most could, Ali. Lena sees that. You've shown her how to survive this. And you aren't complete shit, you are going to kill that damned Veillanti and end this. You are going to protect your family."

"I am going to kill Vincent," Alia confirmed. "I never thanked you. You knew that I needed to go to Lena. You knew it was the only way."

"Is this your thank you?" Flora joked with a coy smile. "Some jewels from the Meador treasury should do." Her fingernails clicked on the table. "You would have found a way eventually; it was just a matter of how many bodies you left in your wake. I did the palace a favor."

Alia wanted to deny her words, but couldn't honestly dispute what she would have done if Cormac had been successful in caging her.

"What do you know of the delegations?" Alia asked instead of dwelling.

Another scoff. "I've had far more correspondence about the bouts than anything else."

"The bouts during a war summit?"

"Never discount the value a bit of sport can have when men are contemplating war."

"Just men?"

"All of us, really." Flora shrugged. "King Reglund himself is leading the Parthians. Royce is sending young Prince Everett. A fetching young man, I am told, true."

"Just what we need, another handsome young prince."

"Not everyone has a handsome mage to keep their attention."

"So Evris can't be bothered to attend himself." Alia glossed over Flora's mention of Dorian.

"No." Flora sighed. "But I did hear that his niece is joining the party."

"Brida?" Alia raised her eyebrows.

"Brida." Flora glowered. "She killed her way into King Evris' confidences."

"I met her when we were young. During the last summit with Royce." Alia could picture the Roycan she had been tasked with showing around the palace during her visit. Brida had been far more interested in swordplay than Court. "What if they don't join us?"

"We all have our tasks." Flora swirled her wine. "Cormac will try to draw them to his side with appeals from decades past and veiled threats. I will find which secrets they hold. And you."

"I am his threat." Alia finished her glass.

The addition of foreign delegations infused even more forced pageantry into Mandal's Court gatherings. Alia's presence was permitted for the adoration of the royals, now extended to include King Reglund of Parth and Prince Everett of Royce. She was to be seen, Mandal's Undoing Mage, but not heard from in any official capacity.

It was impossible for Alia not to feel the pervasive fear that at any moment, Vincent could unleash a murderous rampage on Mandal. The knowledge of the Spear of Orlast grated on her, the very existence of such a vulnerability.

"Aren't you supposed to be intimidating our allies?" Baldric walked up with a sneer. "You look miserable."

Alia gave Baldric a sidelong glance. "I've killed in this hall before, don't tempt me." She regretted the words as soon as she said them, the shattering of gemstones on Lillian's dress echoing in her memory.

"Save your threats for them." Baldric surveyed the room. "Where's Ossian?"

Alia shrugged. "He's patrolling the perimeter. He could not be bothered to attend this mortal frivolity."

Baldric frowned at his glass.

"Should I tell him you missed him?" Alia raised an eyebrow.

The soldier held her stare. "He already knows."

"Of all people—"

"As if you can judge me," Baldric snapped.

If a bit of respite could be found in the vexing commander, Alia could understand the impulse.

"What do you make of them?" Alia gestured over at the group of Parthians.

There were a dozen stout, gray-cloaked Parthians. Their cloaks were heavier than the autumn evening demanded, but may well have been the lightest they saw fit to fashion in the glacial mountains. King Reglund was dressed humbly compared to his royal counterparts; the king of the ever-secretive Parth was adorned with a crown of steel.

"They are content to hide from Veillant in their mountains, convinced the terrain alone is enough to save them," Baldric grumbled.

"And the Roycans?" Unlike the clump of Parthians, the Roycans were scattered about the hall, distinguishable by their desert-brown armor, which could not be set aside even for a banquet. Their delegation was slightly larger and a great deal more armed. Alia turned to look at each of the Roycans, positioned near the exits of the hall, more in a battle formation than a banquet.

Before Baldric could respond, King Cormac stepped to the front of the gathering, climbing the steps to stand before his throne. Elowen was draped over his arm, a smile plastered on her face.

Cormac raised his hands, silencing the pack of nobles and prompting everyone to turn towards him. "When the First Monarchs brought us to Entien, brought mortalkind from beneath the oppression of the Tiarcons, there were no kingdoms, no borders, just one people united. They founded the four kingdoms and allowed all former subjects of the Tiarcons to choose their new homes, their new kingdoms, regardless of which Tiarcon's land they escaped from."

"The call I put to our friends from Royce and Parth is the same call that the First Monarchs answered: to fight and sacrifice to be free from the horrors of the Otherworld. The fourth kingdom has turned away from that call, trodden down a path that would have mortals crushed beneath the Tiarcons. It is time for us to act as one people once more, this time united against the treachery of Veillant, lest they try to rip this realm away from us."

"Hear, hear." King Reglund raised his glass to Cormac, eliciting a murmur of approval from his attendants. He'd ruled Parth for decades, and streaks of white had crept into the black braids at his temples. The genial grin he now wore seemed genuine, even brightening his spelled eyes. His features were reminiscent of Madeline's, prompting Alia's faint recollection that Reglund's family had kinship ties to the Truaths. Prince Everett's response was more measured, as the young prince simply nodded, his face devoid of expression.

Cormac stepped down from his throne, and conversation bloomed once more.

"Not exactly an encouraging reaction," Baldric said, nudging Alia with his elbow before nodding towards an approaching Roycan. The woman wore armor instead of a gown, matching Baldric in height and build.

Alia pieced a smile together. "Brida Osterbury."

"Ali Meador, the years have been kind to you." Brida grinned broadly as she clasped Alia's hand, light green eyes sparkling.

"You'll remember Lord Baldric Cole from your previous visit."

"And from our joint border patrols," Brida greeted Baldric.

"How was your journey from Royce?" He managed a dimpled grin.

"Uneventful—no immortals and not a hint of sunlight." Brida tucked her shoulder-length wheat-colored hair behind her ears. "But enlightening, nonetheless. Seems the drought has extended to Mandal lands; the fields were not as full as I remembered."

"We'll make do. I haven't seen you since—"

"Since the last summit between Royce and Mandal ended in disaster," Brida said with a smirk.

Alia fished out the memory of King Isaac drunkenly calling King Evris a coward. "I'm surprised you came back."

"I had heard you were dead. Imagine my surprise to hear that you had come back to life. Had to see it myself."

Alia flashed another smile. "Not dead, although my mother might have tried to make everyone believe so." Brida knew enough about the Meadors not to appear surprised by mention of a rift between mother and daughter. Alia just hoped that the truth of Lena's father still remained contained among Mandals.

Brida looked at Baldric as if his mere presence was an interruption. "May we speak?" she asked Alia.

Alia tossed a tight smile at Baldric, who was all too pleased to excuse himself.

"I fear that with such a brief summit, I am forced to be bold. My uncle sent me with an offer for you," Brida said, shifting her broad shoulders.

"What does he want?"

"We heard that your homecoming was ... arduous."

Harlan had spoken of detailed information about the palace making its way to other courts. "And?"

"We heard that you've defeated the immortals. You and your daughter, whose parentage sets her ... apart."

Only Mariana's training kept Alia's expression neutral. "What does King Evris want?"

"He wants to offer you and your daughter a home in Royce. You would be given a protected position, without the entanglements of Mandal. You would be free. All we ask in returned is that you and Lena assist us when called upon."

"We're not up for negotiation." No one would own her or Lena.

Brida donned a predatory grin. "We are all on the table when the kings sit down. Mandal is fortunate in its protectors."

There was no hiding her tone. Veillant and Mandal attracted magical talent and maintained their bloodlines, while Parth and Royce ran dry. "Are you familiar with any of the visitors from Parth?" Alia changed the subject.

"Parthians keep to themselves." She shrugged. "And they don't let women fight."

Lena sauntered up to join them. "Mandal could do better in that regard. Women are permitted in our ranks, but discouraged to the point where we barely have any. Perhaps you could mention it to our new king?"

Brida brightened and nodded. "You must be Lena." Brida introduced herself. "Tell me, Ali, will we ever see you wield a sword?"

Lena gave an uncouth snicker. "My mother would never. She can barely hold a dagger."

"I have never desired the skill." Alia shook her head.

"And how about you, Lena?" Brida pressed.

"Baldric is teaching me," Lena announced, lifting her chin with pride.

Alia schooled her expression once more.

"We'll have to test what you've learned in the bouts tomorrow." Brida patted Lena's shoulder. "You'll be there?"

"I'll be there." Alia nodded, trying not to visibly gnash her teeth.

Brida patted Alia's arm before moving on to another circle of nobles.

"I like her," Lena said.

"Stay away from her," Alia said. "Baldric is teaching you what?"

"She seemed to like you." Lena smiled, decidedly ignoring her mother's question. "Ah, there's Madeline." Lena shuffled off, proving that she had learned to walk in her aunt's slippers after all.

Alia glowered after her daughter.

"Lady Alia."

Alia turned to find a Parthian standing before her, one who had wandered from the pack. He was an older man with a pointed white beard.

"I don't believe we've been introduced." Alia settled into pleasantries as she offered the man her hand.

"Octavius, the Master Mage of Parth." He bowed before her, taking her hand. A small jolt seized her hand when they touched, a sign of his magic. He had nowhere near the power of Dorian, but enough to achieve his station. He bore the telltale sign of a Parthian, glowing eyes that had been spelled to see in the darkness. Even before the sun had neglected

Mandal, the Parthians had become accustomed to months without light. Now, in the presence of so much firelight, Octavius's eyes blazed with the flames in contrast to his cool skin.

"I've been wanting to meet Mandal's Undoing Mage." The Parthian's other hand clasped her forearm, pulling her in close. The jolt expanded, holding her immobile as the awful sensation of someone rifling through her mind tickled the back of her neck. Alia responded with the Undoing, finding Octavius's invisible magic and pushing it from her mind until she could take a breath.

Alia withdrew her hand, her manners souring. "What do you want?"

"Just to take a look at you." His stare was shrewd.

"And since you've achieved your aim, you must have other matters to attend to."

"We'll speak again soon."

Alia drew away from the shifting nobles, seeking solitude in the archways that lined the hall and led out onto the balconies. She wrapped her arms around herself, a reminder that her body was her own. Octavius hadn't wielded inculcation, but he had done something to her mind.

It was then that she saw a sight that chilled her even more. Over on the other side of the banquet hall, she heard Lena's distinct laugh, the one she used when something was truly funny. Her daughter was talking to the young Prince Everett. Alia only needed a moment to take in their expressions and the tone of their voices for an unease to settle over her.

Lena laughed again, and Alia shuddered. Her garnet eyes glowed as Everett held his hand to her, leading her to a dance. Flora's assessment of Everett was accurate: young and handsome with his shining golden complexion and dark eyes. How Alia itched to rip out each one of his gleaming teeth.

Dorian approached to hover by her side. "Am I interrupting?"

She settled herself against a pillar and looked out on the balcony, letting the cold air keep her held to the present. "No."

"I would say you're brooding." Dorian paced from one side of the archway to the other. "But can I say that a lady of the Court broods?"

"A lady ruminates." A spark chased away her dark mood.

"Of course, I should have known." Dorian stepped beside her to share the view of the hall. As the next wave of night air wafted in and the glow of sunlight spread through her. "What are you ruminating on?"

Alia closed her eyes to block out the hall and the charming smiles that Roycan was giving her daughter. She just wanted to feel Dorian. "The repercussions of murdering a royal." Alia's spirit dipped once more. Alia only heard a small sigh from Dorian in response. "Or Parth's Master Mage. He has mind magic. Or the Roycan king's niece. She knows too much."

"Is that what stirred the Undoing?" Dorian asked with concern. He'd felt it; he'd felt *her*.

"The mage did something to me."

Dorian turned, searching the hall for Octavius. "I'll bind him; the Parthians could hardly protest after what he did."

"Don't." Alia didn't want Dorian to have to use his strength in her defense. Again. Besides, Mandal needed Parth even if they were boorish guests. "You've been avoiding me." She had scarcely seen him since their return from Alasar.

Dorian let out a dull chuckle. "And how spectacularly I've failed at that." He ran a hand through his hair, which he had failed to make orderly, and spoke with an abnormally sardonic tone. "I've never been able to stay away from you."

Another wave of warmth went through Alia as she suppressed the urge to reach for his hand. He seemed conflicted, like an overt show of affection would make him draw away. She didn't want him to go. "What is bothering you?"

A pause rippled through Dorian's aura. "You haven't asked to leave."

"Leave Mandal?" Alia slipped into a mocking tone. "Now you want to run away with me?"

His sharp jaw trembled, but he stilled it with a smirk. "Wherever you want to go. The hinterland?"

"Or farther." Alia cast another look around the hall. "I expect there would be a more thorough search this time. We're valuable."

"The mountains then. I have to warn you, the cold makes me irritable." Dorian feigned a shiver.

"Is that what it takes? I was wondering what it would take to really set you off."

"The mere sight of snow makes me completely miserable."

"I'll be sure to keep you warm then." Alia risked a touch, brushing his hand with hers.

This time, his shiver was real. His eyes were back on the hall, darting around to make sure no one had seen.

Alia's patience dissolved.

The balcony beckoned; Alia traded princes and mages for the open air. She courted the chill, letting it soothe. Dorian followed with halting steps, his shoes dragging along the stones.

"If you fear reprisal from Cormac." Alia's skin prickled, and the Undoing simmered. "I understand."

She didn't want to understand. She'd successfully doused her affection for Dorian until she kissed him, but the way she yearned for him now had become undeniable. Because he looked at her, saw everything, and still reached for her. He'd never pretended she wasn't what she was, instead encouraged her to confront her magic, to command it.

But still, there was little she could do for him in return. He could seek healing instead, someone who could balance his scars rather than add to them. So, if he wanted to stop, to starve a bond that had only just begun to form, she would let it die. For him, she would.

"What does Mandal etiquette demand?" Dorian rested his arm against hers, looking out onto the torchlit city. "The Veillanti have practices, but I fear I hadn't even hoped you might want ..."

Propriety, not fear, bound him. Of course, she'd even encouraged him to adopt the rigidity of Mandal society. The structure that demanded everything and yielded nothing.

"If you're asking how to court me, you can't. You've promised your bloodline to the Intercessor's determination. As a Meador, I've never had control of mine." Alia turned to him, watching the city's firelight dance across his face alongside growing horror.

If she were a kinder person, she would end it here. To tell him that there was no path forward. Besides, it had been nothing; she'd merely felt gratitude and had acted on impulse. If his unsettled tapping on the railing were any indication, it wouldn't take much to convince him to walk away. Then this loss could fuel her, just as all the others had.

She placed her hand on Dorian's chest where Effe's accord had been carved. Dorian fixated on the Finn's bracelet on her wrist and then on the exposed Barton crest on her upper arm.

It had been so long since she truly allowed herself to want someone. To choose, not out of duty or circumstance, but because of what she felt.

"Tell me what the Veillanti do."

His heart pounded beneath her palm, hope brightening his eyes. "Well, if one wanted to ... show interest ... it would not be uncommon to carve their partner's affinity into their skin. To show devotion." He winced, waiting for her revulsion.

"Of course you would." Alia wrinkled her nose. "Please tell me you didn't dot any of your skin with the Undoing."

"No—no," Dorian said rapidly, taking a step back. "But I did ..." He fished into the pocket of his robes. "I know you don't have an assigned affinity, but I thought this might do."

Alia's teeth clenched as Dorian spoke, dread sprouting in her stomach. Whatever affinity could be assigned to the Undoing, she wasn't sure she'd want to claim it.

She braced herself as Dorian pulled out a small object, holding his palm open so she could see.

Of all the twisted representations she imagined, Dorian presented a flower, a single bloom encased in glass. The familiar shade of deep purple with its soft, plumed center and pointed petals. Starcrest.

"I read about starcrest after I saw how much you like practicing with it." The words tumbled out of his mouth. "It's adaptable, skilled at surviving, and apparently quite poisonous. I thought this might suffice for our purposes."

Alia's dread turned into something far more dangerous, the ache in her chest expanding.

"May I carry it?" Dorian still held his hand out, waiting for her approval.

It was a favor, a sign of intent. That the connection between them would not die out after a single kiss in another realm.

"You may." The response came quickly, without hesitation.

"Good." His voice cracked as he closed the distance between them. Dorian's hand cupped Alia's chin, lifting her face to his. "I hope—"

Alia grasped the front of his robes and brought Dorian's mouth down on hers. The balcony exploded into light as golden rays emanated from Dorian. His magic flowed through her, transforming the world around her into a swirl of colors and light. Like the sun itself exploding through the sky, he banished any thought of night.

A stumbling Parthian joined them on the balcony, forcing Alia to spring away from Dorian. When the kiss was severed, the sky once again became dark, empty. The buffoon mumbled a greeting before leaning over the balcony to vomit.

Dorian pitched forward to catch her hand. The night sky gave way to an ornate room filled to the brim with books. His quarters.

She'd assumed that Dorian slept in the Tower, but this was a palace sitting room. Or, at least, it was supposed to be. The entire room was littered with books, papers, and bottles of ink. The furniture was gone, replaced by a simple, narrow desk and a single chair. Half-empty teacups were perched on every surface.

Alia stifled a laugh as Dorian stumbled and upended an entire stack of books, sending them clattering to the ground. He dodged the fallen volumes, intertwining his fingers with hers.

"What is all of this?"

"My work," he responded quickly, guiding her through the clutter. "This bit here is every record Mandal has of Alasar." He lurched forward to snatch a book from another precarious heap. "The accounting of magical inheritance of every noble family. I've been trying to trace all the bloodlines, make sense of the shifts in elemental magic across generations."

"You've been drawn into the Mandal obsession," Alia said, stepping around a discarded platter towards a glimmer of light.

There was something in the next room, cutting through the dark stronger than flame. "What is over there?"

"Oh, that's nothing." Dorian resisted her slightly as she pulled him by the hand.

Alia turned, looking up at him. "I want to see."

His hand tightened on hers, but he nodded. "I'll have you know it isn't finished. I was making progress, but the time away was ... disruptive."

Alia stepped into the sunlight.

The ball of light hung suspended in the center of the room, which was intended for dining, but had become something else entirely. Pots of various sizes were scattered about the room, and dirt caked into the rugs. And in them, a few spindly stalks that had begun to decay.

"What are you trying to grow?" It seemed pointless for him to struggle with this endeavor when Alia and Lena had the power to coax any seed to life. Alia spread her hand, ready to resurrect the dead sprouts.

"No," Dorian placed his hands over both of hers, pulling them to his chest. "Your magic would alter the results."

Meador magic could make anything grow, but it couldn't sustain it without sunlight. "You made a sun."

The sunlight cast a golden glow across Dorian's copper curls, pride sparking a smile. "Not quite a sun. A manifestation of the Tiarcon of the Sun's magic that I hope I can make self-sustaining. So far, if I am too far away, it fails. Not even the hardiest grain can survive without it." He gestured to the pots of dead plants.

The Tower had only ever pursued magic in support of war. But in Dorian's hands, it was something else altogether.

"Actually, it was the farmers at Mabon who gave me the proper instructions on watering. Before then, I hadn't made a single thing sprout."

He'd nearly died getting those families to safety.

There was a touch of color among the dirt, plum petals hovering over. "More starcrest. At least something survived your absence."

"Of course it did. They're yours."

"What do you mean?"

"Testing a theory. I think the things, the people, you touch with your magic retain a bit of their effect. That you impart strength."

Alia scoffed. "Not as often as I destroy it."

"Strength can take many forms."

Being here, seeing the passions of Dorian scattered about, made her believe him. It seemed that there was more strength in trying to feed the realm than in raising armies to seeking knowledge over power.

In trying to understand and remember, rather than longing to forget.

They came together again in the sunlight, Dorian's hands resting on her hips while she raised her hands to his face. The feather scars were rough ridges under her fingers as she traced them. "I want to see all of these."

Dorian removed his robes, exposing a defined torso and chest marked by feathered scars. Her fingers traced the lines as Dorian trembled beneath her touch. He was nervous, a fact that made her heart beat even faster.

"Each of these is a spell?" The scars extended across Dorian's chest and shoulders, and down one arm to the elbow.

Dorian nodded. "Some lose themselves to blood magic. I've lost enough of myself to want to remember. When Vincent imprisoned me, he continued my tradition, calling me back to this form to take my blood to serve whatever purpose he had, and leaving a feather behind."

Alia was again overcome with the need to dispel Dorian's suffering, to carve Vincent's skin until nothing remained. The Undoing soared within her, itching for retribution.

Dorian stayed still as her hands explored, only moving when she reached down towards his breeches. His hands grasped her hips, spinning her and pressing her back against him. He craned his head to place urgent kisses along her neck as he unlaced the back of her gown. Dorian had her down to her slip quickly, and she stepped out of the shell of her dress.

She turned around to face him, watching him taking in the glimpses of her skin that the sheer slip allowed. It had been so long since she bared herself to a man for the first time, and Dorian looked at her with such wonder.

"Have you forgotten yourself, Master Mage?" Alia beckoned him to come closer.

"Tell me what you want of me." Dorian's fingers trailed along her short hem.

Alia pinched his wrist, directing his hand upward and underneath. "I want you to take me to bed."

21

The bouts were an Entien custom, tracing back to the days of the First Monarchs. They had begun as a training exercise, a way for the kingdoms to hone their skills in warfare should the Tiarcons come for them. When the threat of Alasar dimmed, the bouts continued, shifting from camaraderie to rivalry.

The meadow had been transformed; rings had been burned into the grass, reminiscent of the training yards the soldiers used. It would have been up to Dorian, as Master Mage, to orchestrate it all and ensure that the rules were observed. His obligations had forced Dorian to return Alia to her own bed far earlier than she would have liked.

"Each ring is for a different skill," Baldric explained to Ossian and Lena as Alia trailed behind them. "Don't step into one unless you plan to challenge."

They jostled among the Mandal nobles, mages, and soldiers, mixing with the delegations to form an impassioned crowd.

"A diversion while the royals deliberate," Alia added, keeping her skirts from touching the frosted ground.

"What does a challenge entail?" Ossian asked.

"A bout." Baldric's eyes sparkled. "Until one yields, without serious injury or death."

In the ring to their left, a Mandal soldier traded blows with a Roycan.

The determination of what constituted serious injury was lenient, as both men were bloodied and looked to have several cracked bones. Alia crossed her arms beneath her cloak, trying not to let the spraying blood remind her of Mabon and Lillian's vacant eyes.

The Alasaran grunted beside her. "What is he doing?"

Baldric had disrobed down to his breeches and boots. His well-defined chest and thick biceps were littered with scars, jagged lines where weapons had almost cut him down. Beside her, Ossian was transfixed.

"It appears he is about to challenge."

Ossian shifted, about to stomp forward to stop him.

Alia grasped his arm. "You do realize that Baldric is a formidable opponent by Entien standards. Besides, the circle is sealed by a magical barrier until one of them drops it." Alia pointed up to the robed mages pacing along the platform that encircled the meadow.

"What if the fighters use magic?"

"Magic isn't allowed in combat bouts," Alia said as Baldric entered the ring with the bloodied Roycan who had won out over a Mandal soldier.

Ossian barely breathed as Baldric's fight began, though his eyes darted back and forth with every move. When Baldric quickly dispatched the Roycan into an unconscious lump, Ossian leapt forward to cheer with the rest of the onlookers. Baldric gave him a dimpled smile as he helped remove the Roycan from the ring and awaited the next challenger.

"How many opponents will he face?" Ossian asked.

"When we were young, he would stay in the circle until no one else would step inside or he had to be carried out."

Ossian crossed his arms across his chest. He stayed focused on Baldric through the next bout, scarcely blinking.

"At least he has someone else to fret over," Lena joked, nudging Alia to step away from Ossian.

"I'll be glad when it's all over and he's back in Alasar."

Lena frowned, looking down at her boots before blinking into the cloudy sky. "I've been thinking about what happens after. Where will we go?"

Alia had actively avoided entertaining the prospect. "Where do you want to go?"

"The Roycans said that their ranks need filling."

"We have to be careful around the Roycans," Alia blurted reflexively.

Lena's eyes narrowed. "Prince Everett, you mean?"

"All of them."

"There is honor to their way of living that is lacking in Mandal," Lena argued, though she glanced around to make sure she wasn't overheard. "Everyone has to prove their worth, their ability to hold lofty positions. And Brida earned a high rank and title without having to get married. They don't let blind deference to male royal blood rule their kingdom."

"Awarding power based on the proclivity for violence makes for a brutal society. Royce may have the illusion that a commoner can become king with the correct training, but in five hundred years, it has always been noble blood in the battles for the crown."

"I think Parth has an interesting—"

"What is so interesting about petitioning a mountain to give them a shared delusion of who their next leader will be? Do you really think that there is a pure result from communing with frost bears, or whatever they claim it to be now?" Alia fought to keep her voice low.

"They deliberate until streaks of sun appear in a dark sky—is that a feat you can manage?" Lena's expression darkened.

"Hallucinating lights is no accomplishment," Alia grumbled under her breath.

"I'd think you, out of everyone, would embrace a change from Mandal."

Alia rubbed her forehead, urging healing magic through her own skull. It had taken them mere days to be at odds once again, the truce they had reached in Alasar vanishing under the stress of Lena's contemplation. Any calm that Alia endeavored to have evaporated when Lena started talking about leaving her behind for another court.

Her fingernails dug into her palms, chest heaving with each breath as she prepared a lecture. She wanted to scream at Lena, regale her with all she had ever done her, and crush the nasty bit of dissent. To lambast her until the only feelings that mattered were Alia's, and she didn't have to feel the guilt of hearing about Lena's.

But that would make her Mariana.

"You're right," Alia conceded, tension pouring out with a shiver. "You have the belief that you can shape this realm to your will. I never did."

Lena narrowed her eyes, confusion bidding Alia to continue.

"You are almost a woman now. You can decide what kind of life to seek."

"You saw Prince Everett speaking to me," Lena stated. "You're scared I'll leave you."

Alia took a deep breath. "I am worried that Prince Everett is seeking you out to possess you, your power. What did you talk about?"

"Dihlmere." Lena grinned. "About how the Crown needed to take more care with the villages on the border."

"And how did he take being challenged?"

"He struck me as someone who had never been blamed for a thing in his life." Lena smirked.

"Did he have to fight for his position?"

Lena bit her lip. "Not yet. To become king, yes, but not to become prince. But that doesn't seem quite right, does it?"

"It doesn't." Alia put her arm around Lena as a group passed by too close.

She spotted Flora across a knife-fighting bout, standing beside a member of the Parthian delegation. Her smile was a tad too wide to be genuine, and her painted face couldn't hide the sheen on her skin.

"I have to see to Flora." Alia patted Lena's shoulder. "We'll talk about this after. Soon."

"Are you going to be angry if I join a bout?"

Alia looked over her shoulder at her daughter. "Like that would stop you."

Alia skirted her way across the field, careful not to disturb the throngs crowding each ring.

"There you are!" Flora hooked her arm.

Alia clasped her hand over Flora's, seeking out what was amiss with her. The Undoing hovered at Alia's fingertips, its healing force pouring into Flora.

"One frost and I catch a cold," Flora said.

"Why didn't you come find me?"

Flora was vibrating with anxious energy. "I've been busy."

"Cormac demands too much of you."

"He doesn't." Flora rubbed her nose. "He's in such a state about the summit."

"Let Harlan handle it," Alia said.

"It is my responsibility." Flora's eyes watered. "I'm supposed to know everything."

Alia turned Flora away from the other spectators. "You're doing all you can."

"Hush, Brida's coming." Flora cast off her gloom, fixing the façade of the delighted hostess firmly in place.

The Roycan approached, hand on the hilt of her sword. "Lady Alia, Lady Flora."

"I thought you would have been in a circle by now." Alia faked familiarity as Flora blanched.

"About to be." Brida tapped her hilt. "And you? Shall I look to see you in one of the magical circles?"

"The Undoing is not a magic you play with." Flora reserved a glacial tone for Brida.

"I suppose not. We wouldn't want anyone killed."

"Alia felled the Oucura right in this field." Flora's chest swelled.

"Ah, yes, that is the claim."

"Claim?" Alia eyed the Roycan. "Is that Royce's excuse? Mandals can't be believed?"

"If it was, could you fault us for it? It wasn't too long ago that the port at Waterston was Roycan."

Beside Alia, Flora bristled. Waterston had been one of King Isaac's conquests, a strategic outpost. "Until Royce conceded it," Flora said with clenched teeth.

"Concessions under threat of further aggression do not make the losing party develop fondness. The way I see it, Mandal and Veillant are the same, and your aspirations are pursued at the expense of Royce and Parth."

"Except that none of that will matter when the Tiarcons come for us. Kingdoms, borders..." Alia shook her head. "They'll mean nothing."

Brida's control slipped, a spark of anger showing through. "Royce will never be nothing."

Every syllable grated on Alia, the Undoing jumping its gate and racing to her aid. She held it back with sheer force as Brida moved on to find a challenger.

"How dare she." Flora vibrated with anger.

Alia shook out her hands to soothe the Undoing. "Do you think I could entice her into a magical bout?"

A cold smile graced Flora's lips. "If only."

Alia took Flora's hand. "Your father's fleet must have been an asset to deter Roycan aggression." She regretted the words as soon as she spoke them, because Flora's grin immediately turned grim. It was a truth that most would not dare speak to Flora. That, beyond wealth, her marriage was based on the power to hold off Royce.

"You've given everything," Alia whispered. "At least take your leave to go to your children."

"Oh, Ali," Flora recovered. "If there was ever a time to turn back, it is far past." She dropped Alia's hand, walking into the crowd.

Alia took a few short breaths to stave off tears. An unbidden image of Flora agreeing to the proposal, forsaking dreams of passion to do her duty. Alone. She'd left Flora alone.

I should have torn it all down for her, too.

"My lady." Octavius invaded her company.

"Leave me alone." Alia was in no mood to deal with another attack.

"Still angry?" Octavius chortled softly, stroking his pointed beard. "It was necessary. I had to find out what kind of Undoing Mage you are."

"What kind of mage are you?"

"Not an inculcator," Octavius assured her, confirming that when he had been inside her mind, he had seen Ruben.

"Where does King Reglund stand?" Alia swerved away from discussion of Ruben, trying to contain the violation she felt.

"That is for him to say."

"Did you see Alasar when you broke into my mind? Did you see what awaits there?"

Octavius's bright eyes flashed. "I was in your mind for mere moments; I only saw glimpses."

"Which Tiarcon will come for your magic?"

Octavius looked to the sky, where the sun was barely projecting light through the clouds. "I can see memories, thoughts, if granted proper access. I do not manipulate the mind. I respect it."

"I felt very respected when you were rifling through mine without permission."

"There is no Tiarcon to come for my magic." Octavius fiddled with the cuffs of his cloak. "Mind magic is derived from the Tiarcon of the Moon, Yahear, who your King Orlast dispatched."

"The mad Tiarcon."

"Aye." Octavius went back to gazing at the sky. "Tiarcon Yahear. So called the Mad Tiarcon, not for her lack of sanity, but for the torture she wrought upon her mortal subjects, holding sway over their consciousness, making it so that they never knew what they saw before their eyes was real or just a dream. Kept them docile while they did her bidding, completely pliable. But at that point, somewhat only partly living. A ghastly existence, don't you think, Lady Alia?"

Alia shivered at the description, brought back to the moments of powerlessness under the influence of the inculcation. "So Parth cares not if the Tiarcons come to claim the rest of us?"

"There are more than mind mages in Parth." Octavius stiffened. "And those of us who descend from mortals sworn to the Tiarcon of the Moon have not forgotten what they suffered. What they sacrificed."

"You'll stand with Mandal against Veillant?"

Octavius stepped past her and began to walk towards the group. "That, of course, is for my king to announce, Undoing Mage."

"What did you mean by what kind of Undoing Mage I am?"

Octavius turned with a smirk. "I meant that the Undoing is shaped by the mage, yielding different kinds, different expressions."

"What does that mean? How do you know of the Undoing?"

"The Meador line is not the only bloodline in Entien that produces Undoing mages."

"Master Octavius." Dorian appeared at Alia's side, upsetting the Parthians' mocking.

"Master Dorian." Octavius bowed his head, already moving away.

"Did he try to get into your head again?" Dorian brushed against her cheek, bringing back the memory of how his hands felt on her skin.

Alia furrowed her brow and stared after the retreating mage. "I think he's on our side."

He grasped her hand under her cloak.

"I'm fine," she assured him. "I'm sure you have bouts to get to. The Master Mage has to defend his title, after all." Alia smoothed the front of his robes as they stood in the shadow of the royal boxes.

"I don't care about any of it." Dorian bent down to rest his forehead on hers. "Can I find you tonight?"

"Yes," Alia said hastily. She wished she could throw herself into his arms now, but held back as he flickered away.

"Mother will be ecstatic." Elowen's voice made her turn.

"I'm not going to give her a pairing."

Elowen kept her frozen composure. "I like him for you. Now, come with me."

"I have no interest in another ambush."

Elowen didn't flinch. "There is something you need to see."

Alia sighed and took her sister's arm, accompanying the queen back to the palace. They didn't speak as they moved through the halls, graciously greeting those who bowed to Elowen.

"I never intended to harm her."

"Harm who?" Alia pulled back on Elowen's arm in alarm.

"I wanted her to confess."

Elowen finally stopped in a small workshop. The smell struck Alia immediately, the assemblage of herbs overwhelming. Elowen had maintained an impressive collection, shelves upon shelves of labeled bottles of concoctions and preserved herbs. There was a small window with a collection of potted greenery. On the table in the center of the room was a collection of empty flasks, bowls, shears, and gadgets of the like. There was no fire lit, the embers cold and dark. Sitting out on the counter was a single vial of clear liquid.

Slumped over in the corner of the room was a young woman. Her dark hair obscured her face where she lay. Her clothes were rumpled as if she had been dragged. Alia pulled away from Elowen, dropping down to her knees to brush the hair from the woman's face.

Madeline Truath.

"I can't bother Harlan with this; he has so much to manage," Elowen said, clasping her hands in front of her and glaring down at the young woman. "Is she dead?"

"Her heartbeat is faint, but she is alive." Alia placed her hand over Madeline's chest. "Why did you do this?"

"She is a spy." Elowen snatched the small vial of clear liquid from the table. "This should have made her tell the truth. She had a reaction."

Alia pulled Madeline up. "How do you know that it even works?"

"Mother tampered with my pairing." Elowen's hands shook. "A few drops of this, and she admitted to everything."

Alia narrowed her eyes; Elowen had it in her to use her magic for anything other than healing. Feelings of pride and concern battled within Alia as she watched her sister place the box back on the shelf.

Elowen was not without her weapons.

"It all could have been so different if Cormac and I had never paired well."

The layers of her mother's betrayal were endless.

I should have torn it all down for her as well.

"She used the knowledge of what Master Ruben did to you to pressure Rheta into the pairing in the first place. Then she switched out the elixir so even Rheta couldn't deny it. She even used your misfortune to force Rheta into naming her as Intercessor."

The information rolled over Alia. She felt numb to the treachery of Mariana, finding it almost couldn't hurt her anymore. "Do you finally see what she is?" Alia asked.

Elowen nodded, her lips twitching downward.

"You're the Queen. You shouldn't let her hold sway over you anymore."

Elowen looked away from her sister. "I'm much more than she'll ever be."

"You are," Alia agreed, even though she was beginning to reassess the lengths Elowen would go to for what she wanted.

Elowen's gaze was hard still; she wasn't overly relieved she hadn't killed Madeline. "Wake her up."

Alia turned back to Madeline, extracting bit by bit of serum. A twinge of guilt tortured Alia as she continued to the extraction, clearing the hold that Elowen's brew had on Madeline. As desperately as she wanted to discover the traitor, Alia hoped Elowen was mistaken. Madeline was Lena's friend; it would destroy her.

"Don't remove it all." Elowen hovered over Alia's shoulder.

"Why is the queen trying to capture a traitor?" Alia cast the bits of serum into Elowen's empty pot.

"I can do more than look the part."

Alia didn't need to wonder where her sweet sister had gone; she was a queen now.

The young mage stirred, groaning as Alia seized her and hauled her into a chair. Madeline's night-sky eyes looked between the Queen and the Undoing Mage before dropping them to the ground. "What do you want with me?"

"We have questions." Elowen kept her voice soft, but firm.

Alia doubted the shivering leaf before her was capable of any sort of treachery. But she was a Truath.

"Lena promised you weren't like the rest of them." Madeline looked at Alia. "Even after what you did."

"As long as you answer our questions, you can go on your way." Alia paced in front of her, trying not to show her guilt.

"About what?"

"Your loyalty."

Her wide dark eyes glistened with tears for a moment before they narrowed. "A Meador is questioning *me* about loyalty."

Despite being the target of Madeline's hostility, Alia was impressed by her nerve. Or perhaps it was just the effects of Elowen's serum.

"Do you know how Silas Meador was able to massacre my family all at once?" Madeline focused on Alia. When Alia didn't respond, she went on. "My family had gathered in the King's chambers to celebrate the birth of my great-grandfather's son. There was drink and celebration—every Truath living at the palace came to meet the baby. And then Silas Meador came to the door with a gift. A prized battle-axe, fresh from the Meador forges. A weapon for the new father that he would never yield."

Alia hadn't heard the story in such detail and dreaded its inevitable conclusion.

"They welcomed Silas like one of their own, invited him to join the celebration. No one knows exactly what transpired after the door shut behind him and the guard remained in the hall. But every man, woman, and child in those rooms was found cold less than an hour later—every Truath, every maid, even the healers. Even the baby. And there was no one left alive to tell the name of the newborn boy—no record in the palace history except a line that ends the day it began."

"None of them received a journey to the next realm, as they were burned on this very ground, trapped in Mandal for eternity. Just as I am," Madeline spat. "That is how loyal Meadors are. He was welcomed like family, and he murdered them."

Alia fought to keep her expression blank, battled not to show Madeline she was affected by her story. Madeline may not have been able to tell Alia what transpired behind the door, but Alia could see it as if she were there. She could hear the baby crying, she could picture the dark mist filling the room, the laughter turning to screams.

And then silence. An eerie silence accompanied by the stench of death.

The Meador legacy.

Enough to consume Silas Meador.

How long until the Undoing turned on her?

"It must make you furious to serve a Barton king," Alia prodded, wanting to get the questioning over with as soon as possible.

Madeline's eye roll was so reminiscent of Lena's that Alia's chest tightened. "It is how things are."

"Are you loyal to King Cormac?"

"I have no choice in the matter."

"And Mandal?"

Madeline sniffed and folded her arms.

"Madeline. How well do you know Brida Osterbury?"

Fear flashed like lightning in her eyes. "I don't know her."

"But you know of her." Alia drew closer.

Madeline gulped and nodded. "Don't tell her who I am, please." Madeline's teeth were chattering.

"Why not?"

"The Truaths and the Osterburys have a history." Elowen squinted, angry at not remembering sooner. "Kendel Truath tried to overthrow the Osterburys and hold both thrones. There were losses, and Osterburys do not forget a loss."

"Are they threatening you?"

"The Roycans? No." Madeline looked at Alia in confusion. "They don't know a Truath still lives, or they would have already taken my head."

"Have you been passing along information about Mandal to the Roycans?"

"That is what you wanted to ask me? If I'm a spy?"

Alia let out a sigh of relief. "What did you think I wanted to ask you?"

"About Lena."

Elowen grabbed for one of her potions, slamming it to the ground with such force that it exploded on the stones. "Who is it then?!"

"Wen." Alia caught her sister's arms, holding her. "We're going to find them."

"How?"

Alia drew back. "I'll handle it." She could at least do that for her sister. "Madeline, you can go." She didn't have time to worry over how quickly Madeline would run to Lena and what the recourse would be.

22

Pain pounded in Alia's head, beleaguering each step she took back to the meadow. It was past midday; the bouts would be intensifying as the afternoon wore on. And while she didn't think her absence among the spectators would be noticed, she wanted as much distance as possible between her and Elowen's den.

Alia took a lap around the meadow, searching for Lena, Flora, Harlan, or even Ossian among the onlookers. She tried not to notice the pull of the Undoing towards the circles of carnage, nor the wounds that cried out for a healer.

If Baldric was still fighting, he had moved circles. Alia found her way onto a platform to search him out, sure to find at least the surly Alasaran to dull the guilt of what she had just done to Lena's friend.

"My dear daughter."

Alia flinched at the voice. She slowly spun on her heels, looking back to see Mariana seated on the platform. The Intercessor was draped in a fur-lined cloak, her jewels visible at her throat.

"So nice to see you after your foray into the Otherworld. Have you finally come to tell me of your adventures?" Mariana's smile was too poised for her not to know every detail of what transpired in Alasar.

"I owe you nothing."

"Clearly." Mariana smoothed her skirts. "But I will tell you that if a child results from your activities with the mage, you should disappear again. The king isn't likely to tolerate that kind of challenge."

Alia didn't want to think about how she could possibly already know about Dorian. "There will be no—" She paused, swallowing her explanation as she looked at her mother. "Nothing happens in this palace without you knowing it. The eyes always watching are yours."

Mariana inclined her head, pride shining through. "And you want to know something."

"Who is feeding the Roycans their information?"

Mariana's smile vanished. "Sit."

Alia obliged and joined her mother on the platform.

"Who is the real leader of the Roycan delegation?"

"Brida."

"Good, at least you're not a complete simpleton. Who here in the palace does Brida have control over?"

"That is what I am asking you."

"Think."

"I'm not in the mood." Alia set her jaw.

Mariana looked put out. "You know which household is closest to the Roycan border."

"Waterston."

"And whose husband and children would be first under threat if the peace between Royce and Mandal were to evaporate?"

"No." Alia got back to her feet. "I came here thinking we could have a civil exchange, but—"

"Flora and Brida have met over the last two days. Alone."

Alia took a few sharp breaths, weighing the possibility of her mother telling the truth. Flora, who had stood by her side during the Palmer attack, could not possibly participate in betraying her. Brida knew too much personal information about her and Lena, information that Flora knew.

But Flora has risked herself to help Alia get away to rescue Lena.

"You're lying."

"You asked, I answered. What more do you want from me?" Mariana shrugged. Alia couldn't even begin to tell her how much more she wanted from her.

"If you knew, why didn't you tell anyone? Why didn't you tell Elowen?"

Mariana's eyes narrowed, sweeping over Alia as she lifted her nose in the air. "Sometimes the best thing to do is watch. It is not yet clear what this development will mean for our family."

Alia strained to keep the Undoing back, fighting ever harder not to scream at Mariana. "You'd side with Royce over your King?"

"The King who is insistent that your father go to war. Insistent that his paramour is the one to inherit the Meador lands and fortune."

"That is treason."

"Treason." Mariana's voice took on a sinister depth. "Has your time away dulled your senses? Have you forgotten what we taught you?"

Part of her wanted to run to Elowen, to tell her that she had discovered the informant and put her mind at ease. But a stronger part refused to believe her selfish mother, putting the welfare of the kingdom in the hands of someone who couldn't be trusted with its best interest.

She had to talk to Flora herself.

As she stood and skewered Mariana with a glare, all she could think of was the words she wouldn't say aloud.

I haven't forgotten.

A dark cloud followed Alia on her way across the meadow. She hadn't found Baldric between Mariana's barbs, but Harlan was easy enough to spot among the crowd. He wore a simple tunic and breeches, with his sword in hand and ready to join the bouts.

Alia elbowed her way past Harlan's admirers. "Where is Flora?"

Harlan clasped her forearms, dropping to one knee to look into her eyes. "What's wrong?"

Accusing her oldest friend of treachery was not something she had the strength for. "Just tell me where she is."

"The last I saw her, she was headed for a bout. Over in the magical circles." Harlan's forehead creased. "Can I help?"

Alia turned away without answering him, the roaring in her ears preventing her from focusing on anything other than finding Flora, finding the truth.

Flora was in a shimmering circle, encased in a barrier to keep magic from spilling out. She was engaging a Parthian mage with earth magic. She was sinking into the ground at the mage's direction, a trap she should have been able to pull herself out of.

Alia skirted around the circle, wanting to break through the barrier if only to spare Flora. She willed Flora to dispatch the earth mage quickly so that they could tear down Mariana's accusations, and she wished the bout would never end to never have them confirmed.

Flora pulled herself out of the muck, sweeping around the circle with a torrent. The Parthian fell, and Flora refused to relent. She stacked the pressure of every bit of water she could summon on top of the mage, squeezing the breath out of him until he shouted a yield.

Alia stalked the barrier until it relented, catching Flora's eye. Her friend was squeezing out her hem, snapping her fingers to instantly render her clothes clean and dry.

"Step out," Alia said, forcing Flora to focus on her.

Flora's face fell. There was something in her expression that cut into

Alia, a confirmation in it. “I don’t think I will.”

“Step out or I’ll step in.”

Flora shook out her skirts, digging in.

Alia crossed the circle, joining Flora within as the Parthian stepped out. It sealed shut behind her, locking the two of them into a challenge. There were shouts from outside, but Alia could only see her friend.

“You told them about me, about Lena.” Alia strained to meet Flora’s watering eyes.

“You’re challenging me?” Flora lifted her chin.

“Tell me it isn’t true.” It was a plea from a moment that already passed.

“Yield.” Flora rubbed her hands together.

Alia barely noticed the spectators that gathered at the edge of the circle, faces melding into nothing. The Undoing spilled from her hands, filling the air and obscuring their view just enough. Flora flinched as it flowed around her, ready for it to bite.

“Brida,” Alia said so that only Flora could hear.

Flora raised her hand a swiped at her, the lash of water catching Alia off guard as it struck her face. “You entered the circle.”

“What did she do to you?” Alia tried to break through Flora’s flustered defense.

Alia was ready for the second blow, raising a barrier in time to block it.

“Aren’t you going to attack?” Flora goaded. “Make use of that power you hate so much.”

Looking at Flora now, Alia was overcome with pity. Alia should have noticed that her friend was in peril right in front of her.

“She threatened Waterston, didn’t she?” Alia kept letting the Undoing out, clouding the circle and keeping the others out.

Flora's eyes blazed in response, both hands raising to whip a whirlpool around Alia. But while the waters coursed around her, twisting around the circle, she was unharmed. Flora stepped forward, standing face to face with Alia amidst the current. Her waters blocked them from view, blocked anyone who would try to hear.

"Cormac pulled the soldiers back from the borders and left us vulnerable. When Cormac called the summit, they took them."

"Your children." Alia's silence stretched on as she surveyed her friend. She loved Flora, needed Flora, but if Lena were in danger, she'd kill Flora herself. She would have done the same thing Flora had for Lena.

Flora put her hand on Alia's cheek, right on the place her attack had landed. It was already healing, the Undoing barely needing direction. "It's worse than Brida, Ali. Royce, they're entangled with the Veillanti."

Alia gripped Flora's wrist, keeping her close as she took deep breaths.

"Vincent is the one who has my family."

Alia gasped, processing the information with growing panic. The Undoing reached through her, creeping towards Flora's distress. "What are they planning?"

"I don't know."

"Do they know about the Spear?"

"Yes." She pulled down the sleeve of her cloak. Her upper arm was bound in a bandage. She unraveled the bandage, showing a gaping wound where the Barton crest had been.

"Vincent broke your blood oath." Alia didn't even know it could be done.

Flora nodded. "What are you going to do?"

"I'm going to get your family back."

"He'll kill me, Ali. When he finds out, Cormac will kill me for what I've done."

"We'll sort it out." Alia couldn't disagree; this kind of treachery was often met with death in Mandal. "You have to win the bout. Drown me or whatever you do."

"I can't." Flora threw her arms around Alia, holding her tightly. "I don't understand. You should expose me."

Alia hugged her back, wishing she could take on Flora's strain. "No one should keep a mother from her child," she whispered.

Flora's gleaming eyes were wide as they untangled. "So much has been taken from us."

Alia dropped Flora's hands as the whirlpool closed in on her, stealing her breath and sweeping her off her feet. The Undoing rushed back to her, unsure of how to defend herself from Flora's attack. Alia barely registered the pain as she was slammed to the ground, left retching up water as Flora stood over her, cloaked in false fury. But since the Undoing hadn't killed, hadn't harmed, it didn't make her suffer Ruben.

"I yield," Alia croaked, the faces of the spectators crowding in now that their magic no longer blocked them out. She rolled to her side, shakily standing, and stepping outside of the circle.

"My lady." Ossian was less than reverent as he put his arm around her shoulders. "What has possessed you?"

Alia turned in time to see Flora snap at Harlan before melting into the crowd. Harlan looked after her with a deep frown before looking over to Alia. Warmth found Alia—Dorian's magic reaching out to her from across the meadow. She searched for him in the crowd, but didn't find his soft eyes.

"What just happened?" Harlan demanded, attempting to pull her away from Ossian. The Alasaran held on.

"I will tell you," Alia gathered her now-dry cloak around herself. "But I need your help first."

Harlan gritted his teeth, looking back over his shoulder to where Flora had gone.

"Challenge Brida." Alia gripped Harlan's arm. "Challenge her. And hurt her." When he immediately bristled at the idea, Alia continued, "Don't worry, I'll be here to heal her."

Harlan's shoulders fell. "And then you'll tell me?"

"Yes," Alia promised.

"I do not like that look." Ossian kept her close as they followed Harlan through the meadow. "You're seized by the same madness that drove you to the Mountainlands."

"Then you should endeavor to be more helpful to me this time."

"How?"

"The Roycan is far too heavy for me to carry all the way back to the Olden Wing."

Comprehension trickled across Ossian's face, shrewd approval showing through.

Brida beamed when Harlan bent to whisper his challenge, honored to be asked by Mandal's Captain. Her pride would prevent her from refusing him. Being seen as an equal was too enticing.

The Undoing rumbled within her as Harlan led Brida into a circle, swords drawn. She could feel it curving up her abdomen, into her chest and stoking a fire there. It was most restless than Alia had ever felt it, watching each parry intently. Every time she focused in on Brida, the heat in her chest flared.

"Steady," Ossian whispered as she put her hand over her heart. "Wait."

Both of Ossian's charges seemed equally impossible as the Undoing continued to goad her. It conjured images in her mind: Brida's threats to Flora, her standing shoulder to shoulder with Vincent. A roar formed, a pressure that continued to build as the swords flashed until Alia didn't know if she could keep the mist from escaping her.

A flash of relief spread through her when Harlan plunged his sword into Brida's side. The Roycan's eyes bulged in surprise, her inadequate defenses falling away. Harlan feigned surprise, catching the Roycan before she could fall to the grass.

"Yield," he urged her.

The word came from Brida's lips and erased the barrier that stood between them.

Ossian surged forward. "We'll take her to the infirmary," he promised, scooping the Roycan up into his arms as she writhed in pain, and a dazed look filled her eyes.

The intensity of the Undoing surged as Alia followed Ossian as he cut through the meadow, Brida's blood dripping onto the ground. It prickled against her hands, itching. She could already see Brida's ghostly form, the memories of injuries that a warrior was sure to accumulate.

Alia raced ahead of Ossian, leading him through the palace and to the Olden Wing, although not back to her suite. Rather, she led him one floor higher to the abandoned rooms covered in filth.

Ossian set the bleeding Roycan down on a decaying couch, shutting the door behind him and sealing the room.

"Ali," Brida panted, pressing her hand against the wound. "Heal me."

Alia knelt on the ground before her, lifting her hand to watch the progress of the wound. "What did Vincent promise to make you betray your realm?"

Brida's expression didn't change. "All of you Mandals are infected with the same paranoia—" She stopped speaking as the Undoing leaked out of Alia, closing the distance between them. Alia could feel each haggard breath Brida took, sensed each way to make her hurt.

"Answer me." Alia barely recognized the sound of her own voice as she let the Undoing start to rip open Brida's old injuries.

"You've been lied to," Brida protested.

"Tell me and it'll stop."

Brida's chest heaved as whimpers escaped her lips, the pain from her wounds rushing back to her as fast as her blood poured out. "Do you think the Mandals will suffer you to live when the Otherworld threat is extinguished? Will they let your daughter live?"

It was a fair question, one that Alia had begun to contemplate. "I've seen what awaits in Alasar. I'll take mortal quarrels."

Blood started to drip from Brida's mouth. "I thought, after all you've been through, the Meador might have been torn out. But there you are, ruthless and bent on self-destruction. You must make your parents so proud."

"Your time to talk is waning." Alia held fast, knowing that in this act she was wholly consigning herself to the tarnished legacy.

"He's coming." Brida coughed. "You won't be able to stand against him."

"When?" Alia pressed.

Brida's agony drew out her response. "Tomorrow."

Tomorrow.

The Undoing danced, alighting at the prospect.

A soft scrap of shoes on stone came from behind her, and the familiar burst of sun reached her. Dorian.

"Pull it back." Dorian's arm snaked around her waist, trying to move her away from Brida.

"No." Alia didn't look away from her foe. Dorian loosened his hold and but stayed close.

"You said you'd make it stop." Brida's choking cough sprayed blood across Alia's face.

"You gave Flora over to Vincent. You separated her from her children."

The Undoing continued to slice, and Brida's blood continued to pour out. An odd calm settled over Alia, allowing her to look upon Brida with neither fury nor malice. Just the knowledge that she could not continue to live.

The beating of Brida's heart was already faint by the time the Undoing reached it. Her dying gasps turned to whispers as she reached out, fingers scratching against Alia's cloak before falling limp.

The Undoing lifted from the dead Roycan, flowing out of her and back into Alia's arms. Ruben's voice grated against her, the scene playing in her mind.

The darkness was consuming. The only sound Alia could hear was Ruben's voice.

"You're late."

Alia bowed her head and knelt, trying to delay inculcation by doing exactly what he wanted. She fumbled together an apology but didn't let it escape her mouth; he didn't like excuses. And the truth would only make him angrier, that she'd spent the night in the city with Cormac and Baldric. Embracing recklessness.

"If you are not going to fulfill your duty, I am going to have to direct my teaching elsewhere." Ruben circled her. "I hear Flora Szartinen is a promising mage."

He hadn't stolen her control away yet, enjoying watching her flinch. It was a threat he often made, usually directed at Elowen. That if Alia were to slip away from him, he'd find someone she loved to suffer instead.

"You'd be wasting your time." Alia defaulted to the Meador way, arrogance to cover fear. "The Szartinens are a young house; their blood is weak. And I'm making progress." A lie.

Ruben latched onto her then; his influence crept between them, filling her head with a rushing whine. "I would hate to think you're trying to deceive me. There is nothing in your mind that I can't see."

If Ruben could see into her mind, she wouldn't have a chance. But inculcators couldn't read minds, only influence them. A feeble mercy.

"Hear me," Dorian's voice broke through, banishing the pitch of Ruben's control and the crippling fear that came with it. "Your mind is your own."

Dorian knelt before her, using the sleeve of his robes to wipe Brida's blood from her face. Alia stayed still as he appraised her, wondering if he would be driven away by her violence.

He wasn't.

"Vincent will be here tomorrow." Alia looked between Ossian and Dorian. "We have to warn them."

Despite the faraway look in his eyes, Dorian nodded. "I'll seek the King." He flickered away.

Alia turned back to Brida's body, the stench of death already starting to fill the stale room. Brida's blood inched along the floor, reaching for Alia.

She turned to the Alasaran. "You spoke of the Undoing before. You knew others with it?"

Ossian paused, waiting until she looked away from the corpse. "A few."

"It's changing." Alia could feel in settling inside her, content to have taken a life. "It wanted me to kill her."

"Our magic changes with us." Ossian's demeanor was almost gentle. "Something I appreciate now more than at any other point in my life. The Undoing is rarely gifted. As powerful as it can be, it is a defensive magic. It needs a balance, a grievance connected to the wielder or else ... it turns inward."

"A grievance," Alia murmured, rolling over the thought as Dorian reappeared, not alone. She was littered with grievances.

Harlan's sword was still unsheathed, blood still dripping from its tip. Brida's blood. Baldric stood beside him, covered in the grime of his bouts.

"The King could not be disturbed," Dorian explained as Harlan silently took in the scene, fixing his gaze on Brida's body.

Baldric scoffed. "You could have waited until I won the day."

"We can fix this." Harlan's whole body shook as he moved to clean off his blade. "It'll be handled, Ali."

Alia almost smiled at the earnestness of his shocked response. He didn't ask what she had done or why she had done it. He gave her his trust, his support. "She was aligned with Vincent. He attacks tomorrow."

Harlan nodded frenetically, as if scanning the room once more could change the sight before him or the words that Alia had just said. He turned to Dorian. "I can prepare the guard, but we'll need the Tower."

"We'll be by your side," Dorian promised, placing his hand over his heart.

"I suppose you can't have any of her countrymen coming upon her." Baldric jerked his thumb in the direction of Brida's body, his callousness outpacing Alia's. "Come on, Commander." He beckoned towards Ossian as he neared the corpse.

Ossian blinked, assessing Alia before bending to grip Brida's ankles, aiding Baldric in his task.

Once Baldric and Ossian were in the hallway, Harlan turned back to Alia. "Flora—" He trailed off and locked on Alia. "You were fighting Flora."

"A misunderstanding," Alia implored, as if the strength in her voice could make it true.

"And then—" Harlan gaped in realization of Flora's deceit, clutching his stomach. Alia clasped his shoulder, taking on a fraction of the giant man's weight.

"We need to deal with the threat in front of us. There is no use," Alia pleaded. "Baldric cannot know. Cormac can never know; do you hear me?"

Harlan stilled under her hands. He'd have to keep his silence to keep Flora safe.

"Tomorrow," Dorian whispered, tapping his fingers together. "He'll attack the signing."

"The signing?"

"The royals will sign an agreement of joint defense tomorrow night. At the closing banquet."

"He won't be able to resist the spectacle," Dorian whispered.

Alia thought of Vincent's appearance in Bergan's holdfast, his lurking in the hinterland. "Go then." Alia trembled only slightly as she commanded both men. "Ready Mandal's defenses."

"And you?" Dorian asked.

"I have to tell Lena that she's going back to the Harvestlands."

Weight pressed down on her chest as she said the words. Her Meador instincts had saved Lena in the Mountainlands and throughout their lives. The hardness, the strength lodged within her, mingled with the darkness of the Undoing. The overflow of gratitude at recovering Lena had lulled Alia into the wrong decision, her desire to have her daughter at her side outpacing reason, and even considerations for Lena's safety.

In the wake of Flora's betrayal and Brida's demise, clarity found her.

Neither Harlan nor Dorian dared to contradict her, but Dorian let out a pained sigh.

Alia passed by them and sought the solitude of the hall, the freedom that the dusty air provided her. It was a quick walk down the stairs to her rooms. Her steps were slow, stalled by the prospect of convincing Lena that she had to leave.

Alia stepped into the suite, her fuming daughter leaping to her feet to advance on her.

"How dare you—"

Alia had almost forgotten Madeline's ordeal. "Lena, there is no time."

"There was time for you to interrogate Madeline, but not enough to be held accountable?" Lena pushed her sleeves to her elbows, ready for a fight.

Alia fought the impulse to shout back at Lena. She filled her lungs with air, letting the breath reach her toes before speaking. She needed to diffuse Lena's attack, prepare for the next phase of the argument.

"Elowen was wrong to suspect Madeline," Alia admitted. "And I shouldn't have helped her."

"I've been trying to tell her that you aren't like the rest of the Meadors, and then you do this."

"I am a Meador." Alia had been brought up to find a way to gain the advantage, ruthless enough to pursue her interest despite the cost. "You aren't."

"You know what I mean." Lena hunched her shoulders.

"I do," Alia said. She raised her hand to reach out to Lena, but drew back before touching her. Fear restrained her, the knowledge of the darkness roiling within. Lena didn't need to feel it again.

Lena watched Alia rescind her hand and bring it to her chest. "What is it?"

"I am sorry." Alia took a step back. "You are right to be angry. Your friend was hurt." Flora's face flashed across her mind, a vibrant woman reduced to misery.

"By you." Lena frowned, looking at the floor before narrowing in on Alia.

"By me." Alia sank into the couch.

Lena sat opposite her, back straight with anticipation.

"Brida is dead." Alia didn't regret letting the Undoing have her, but she still couldn't bring herself to tell her daughter the details. "She had information. Vincent will attack Mandal tomorrow."

Lena paused. "Vincent is coming to us?"

"Yes."

"Then he is a fool." A smile crept across Lena's face. "There is no way that he can stand against all of us."

"Lena," Alia cut in. "You're going back to your father."

Lena's thirst for confrontation rekindled. "Not now." Lena shook her head.

"In the morning. With Ossian."

"You can't. You don't command me."

"I'm your mother." There was cold spiking through her veins, releasing the hope that Lena would agree without more manipulative methods.

Betrayal was rife in Lena's watering eyes. "Then you should know that I can't leave now. This is my realm."

"No, Lena." Alia let the icy sheen of anger curdle, keeping weakness at bay. "Vincent is trying to tear down the veil." Alia's voice shook. "What if he discovers that you hold that power? We're safer with you on the other side of the veil."

"You don't mean that," Lena spat out, but her lips twitched into a frown that revealed her doubt.

Alia didn't mean it. Or rather, if there was truth in her words, but it was not a truth that propelled her. But she held Lena's probing gaze, fixing her with the same cold stare that Mariana and Edgar had inflicted upon her.

"You have the night to prepare." Alia stood, stealing away towards her room before her control slipped.

She could only hope that after Vincent was dead, she could undo the damage she had done to her daughter. She could only hope that there was an after.

Alia had already given up on sleep when she heard footsteps at the door. She'd stopped waiting for Dorian and knew Lena wouldn't seek her company. She blinked into the darkness as a man came and sat on the edge of her bed.

It wasn't Dorian.

"You shouldn't be here." Alia pulled her sheets up to her chest as Cormac hovered over her.

Cormac's expression was unreadable, his movement slow as he touched an unbound curl. "Do you ever think about how many nights were stolen from us?"

Alia sighed, sitting up and bracing her back against the bedframe. "You've spoken to Harlan."

"We're ready for them," Cormac gritted out. He laced his fingers with hers.

"Then what purpose can you have here?"

Cormac pulled her hand to his chest. "Do you feel the connection between us? The persistence of our pairing?"

Alia felt nothing except the desire for him to leave. "We have more important things to worry about tonight."

Cormac glowered, wounded. "What could possibly be more important?"

His question rang false, contrived. The King would not be driven to visit her bedchamber on the eve of an attack to reminisce.

"Out with it, Cormac." With all that stormed within her, patience had departed.

"I feel it." He ignored her directness. "A link that cannot be broken. The drops of my blood that flow through you." His other hand reached up her bare arm, running his thumb over his crest.

Alia bit her lip to hold back from shouting at him over Flora. If he had felt when Vincent broke her and tore the oath from her skin.

"There is a pressing matter." Cormac kept his hands on her. "Vincent is not to be killed."

"What?"

"I want him captured. Alive."

"Why?"

"There would be no better way to lay Odessa low than to hold the life of her mage in my hands."

"What makes you think you can hold someone like him? He is a risk to the entire realm."

"Because I have an Undoing Mage, a formidable Master Mage of my own, and the daughter of a Tiarcon."

Alia yanked her hand away and massaged her temples. "You try to use affection to keep me at your side. And when that doesn't serve you, a threat."

"He lives, Ali." Cormac stood and straightened his tunic; message delivered.

Alia swore when he shut the door, cursing the entire Barton bloodline. She almost didn't hear the soft shuffle and steps over her sputtering; Dorian emerged from the shadows of the dark room.

She couldn't make out his expression and waited for him to launch a round of accusations at her. Instead, he bent and tended to the fire she'd let go out.

"How did Lena react?"

"Poorly." Alia braced for the next question. They hadn't spoken about Cormac in detail, and Dorian didn't know how she felt about him now. Imagining what Dorian must think, how it would feel to have overheard their conversation, turned her stomach.

"Did you have a chance to eat? I didn't see you in the hall." Dorian stood, brushing his hands as the flames leapt. "I can summon—"

"I didn't ask him to come here. I didn't let him in," Alia interrupted, not wanting to delay any longer. "I was confused when I first came back to Mandal, but not anymore." Being with Cormac had only shown her how much they had diverged, how he could hurt her in every way he could think of and still call it love.

A slight smile graced Dorian's lips as he knelt in front of her. From where she sat on the edge of her bed, his gaze was nearly level with hers. "Your magic is paired with his. And you haven't made me any promises."

"We were paired a long time ago. And when I swore this—" Alia rubbed her arm as if it could make the mark disappear "—we found that it was still intact."

"I could break it," Dorian mused, inspecting the oath. "The pairing, not the oath."

"Please," Alia urged, reaching out to him. "I want it gone."

Dorian pressed his lips to her temple, making her curl into him. "But

I shouldn't."

"Why not?"

"I've been curious about your immunity to the King's mind magic. How he can influence an entire room of men and yet you remain unaffected? I thought at first that the Undoing made you impervious, but after Octavius' attack, I know that is not the case. The pairing provides a more fitting explanation."

"Cormac doesn't have mind magic." It had been a fear of hers after being exposed to Ruben's affinities. But Cormac was a fire mage like his father, showing no talents akin to the powers of his mother and uncle.

"It isn't very strong, but it is there," Dorian said. "And if the pairing makes him recognize you as his own, unable to be influenced, then I suppose I should leave it alone."

Alia couldn't begin to process the horror that filled her at the thought of Cormac having such capabilities. "How would you break a pairing?"

"There are several ways. The most common would be to pair you with another. And of course, killing him would always work. It would address both issues, actually."

"If Cormac dies, my oath dies with him?"

"Yes," Dorian confirmed.

"And other than that, how does one break a blood oath?" Alia thought of Flora's gaping wound.

Dorian lifted his eyebrows in alarm, then his customary academic tone took hold. "A blood oath can be *removed* by the one it was sworn to otherwise, it can only be broken by death."

"But the First Monarchs. They defied their oaths to the Tiarcons, didn't they? That is how they escaped to Entien and retained the Tiarcon magic?"

"They fooled it. It is a tricky bit of magic, but with the right mage, it is possible. The First Monarchs must have had help from a powerful Alasaran to overcome it. It was never written who helped them, probably to protect them from retribution."

"How does it work?"

Dorian seemed caught between his love of rattling off his magical knowledge and his desire to refocus the conversation as his fingers trailed along her neck and shoulders. "The spell gives one the appearance of death, tricking the oath. It is an arduous process, as the blood is drained from one's body to the point that their heart stops and breaks the oath, then life must be restored."

"How does one restore life?"

"By taking another's." Dorian's forehead creased.

"So, the First Monarchs—"

"There were sacrifices, as the story goes. This," he rubbed his thumb over the Barton mark on her arm, "you will have to honor it, or it could do you harm."

"It is the most asinine—" a blinding stab went through Alia's body, the brand reigniting as she defied its most basic rule.

"Don't." Dorian covered the oath with his hand. "It'll only hurt more."

"What does Cormac want with Vincent?" Alia clasped her hand over his.

His hands fought to be free of her, wanting to start the tapping pattern. Alia refused to release him, tapping the tip of each finger with her own in the way that she had seen Dorian do countless times.

"I don't even realize I'm doing it anymore," he murmured.

"I understand." Alia pulled him closer.

"I know you do." Dorian's palm rested on her hip, disrupting the compulsion. "I knew it when I saw you. And I tried to leave. The day the Oucura came, I had left Mandal. I knew Vincent would come for me here; I knew that I wouldn't be able to heed Effe, and she would find me."

Alia's mind emptied, not grasping how Dorian could have tried to spare her even when she'd been openly hostile to him. She had been a prisoner dragged before the King's Council, and he, the newly named Master Mage. Dorian had managed Lena's outburst and sorted her aura. And then later that day, when he had come to train Lena, she had threatened to kill him. It was a wonder that he hadn't handed Lena over to Effe in that moment.

"I flickered to the coldest peak in Parth—putting the entire continent between you and I." Dorian's hands shook. "And still, I could feel you. Our brief meeting was all that it took to become attuned to you. Your magic, your anguish, it beckoned to me."

It had taken her much longer to form that connection, to recognize that Dorian could truly understand. He'd known right away. He'd known everything.

"When the Oucura attacked, it felt like an entire mountain pressed down on my chest. I was compelled to return to your side. All the while you despised me, I was wondering what it would feel like to hold you. To be the one to inspire the tumult of sentiment that propels you. And then in Alasar ..."

Alia soothed Dorian's curls, pushing them back so she could see every expression.

"The Tiarcon trapped me as an eagle, just as Vincent did. And being trapped that way, rather than controlling the shift, my awareness falls away. I think that is why I can't remember the time I spent under Vincent's power; I was something else then. It was the same in Alasar."

Her fingers tightened involuntarily, itching for the power to end

Bergan and Vincent.

"But you." Dorian met her gaze. "Even trapped in my other form, I could still feel you. I knew you needed me."

Her throat went dry, remembering the choking pressure of Bergan's hand, the relief brought on by Dorian's sacrifice.

"It is unsettling," Dorian murmured. "To want you, to need you this much."

It *was* unsettling. To think of how many times he'd been at risk because of her, how he greeted every awful thing she did with understanding. Perhaps it was just the haze that came with infatuation, the thrill. That would fade. And it would break her when it did.

So, she responded the only way she knew how. "I'm going to kill Vincent. Despite what Cormac wants, I'm going to kill him."

Dorian shuddered. "I can handle Vincent."

"Dorian—" She sighed deeply, knowing she couldn't hold back any longer. "If Ruben were to appear in front of me at this very moment, I don't think I could fight him."

"It is not the same. I'll have a chance this time, I'm ready to confront him."

"And if it all happens as you hope, if you get your hands on Vincent, if you get your answers, what then?" Alia challenged.

"Then I'll kill him. Make your promises to the King. It'll be my hand that strikes him down, and you'll have fulfilled your charge," Dorian said without hesitation, fingers trailing down Alia's back. "Don't worry over it. It is my concern."

"And what if that makes it mine?" The words were out before Alia could stop them, emotions escaping the walls she'd built. The vulnerability was scorching, idiocy keeping pace with the beating of her heart. But it didn't stop her. "I mean it, I won't let him have you."

Because Dorian was hers now. Whether they'd made promises or not, this feeling in her chest was certain. She'd break every cage in this realm if Vincent ever tried to put Dorian back in one. The Undoing simmered in agreement, pledging its power to the cause.

"You weren't listening." His hand threaded through her hair, bringing her forehead to rest against his. Alia breathed him in, basking in the moment of darkness before his sight illuminated her world. "No matter where I am, what I am, I'll still feel you. You'll have me."

The Mandals approached the last day of the continental summit as if nothing at all was amiss. Brida's absence was explained away by the time needed to rest in the infirmary with promises that she would rejoin her delegation at the closing banquet. The same banquet that the Mandals were certain would be the site of Vincent's attack.

The same banquet Alia now sat in the center of. Rows of tables filled the hall, seats full of Mandal's nobility and the visiting delegations. The royals sat at the front, projecting levity and calm. Flora joined her at the table, barely eating, as some nobles began to stand and circulate.

"Have you recovered? You said before that you were feeling ill." Flora was really asking if they had prepared, if measures had been taken.

"I am quite well." She felt more confident when Baldric approached. Though there was no sword at his hip, Alia knew that he was covered in blades.

Baldric looked at Alia from head to foot, taking in her elaborate gown. She'd needed more extensive armor for this night, a tightly-woven plum bodice, embroidered with golden waves, leaving more of her chest exposed than she normally liked. The sleeves billowed at her elbows, the slim silhouette swelling to full skirts at her hip. "Practical."

Flora was watching Baldric intently, likely trying to discern if Alia had told him anything. "Why be practical when you could be beautiful?"

"Always so helpful, Flora." Baldric scanned the room.

Cormac was in the center of the royal table, positively jubilant about the agreement the three parties had come to. A fine actor.

"How will they seal the agreement?" Alia asked.

"They'll do a signing and an oath there." Baldric nodded toward the head table. "Any time now."

"You're sure they're away?"

"I escorted them to the door myself," Baldric assured her.

Lena had refused to be in Alia's presence, but Ossian had readily embraced enforcing Alia's order to take Lena to Finn.

"And—" Alia lost her words when Queen Elowen returned to the hall. Her sister, every inch the regal queen she trained to be, walked in with her head held high and wearing a gleaming grin.

"She was supposed to be halfway to the Meador lands by now."

"She wouldn't leave her people." Baldric drew close and placed his cheek against hers. "The boys are away with their grandmother."

"I'm going to kill her." Of all times for Elowen to reveal her stubborn streak.

"Hold yourself together, Ali."

Cormac raised his hands, silencing the musicians and drawing the attention of those assembled. He clasped Elowen's hand. "It has truly been an honor to host our esteemed friends from Parth and Royce. And it is my privilege to announce that we've come to an agreement built upon shared defense, mutual prosperity, and above all—commitment to the persistence of Entien." He looked at Prince Everett as he spoke, baiting the disingenuous royal.

Harlan had moved from Cormac's side to the back of the hall. A few of his men clustered nearby, never taking their eyes off their captain as he maneuvered. Alia spotted Dorian on the opposite side, standing beside a Roycan guard.

"So let us raise our glasses before we sign," Cormac continued with a gleaming smile. "To our allies."

The Roycan mimicked Cormac's toast, raising their glasses in turn. But most of them didn't live long enough to touch the cups to their lips. A shiver of magic fell over the hall, mages stationed at every corner, flashes of flame, glimmers of water, and wisps of wind targeting whatever defense the Roycans might have endeavored. Within seconds, only Prince Everett remained breathing, the rest of his delegation burnt or vainly clawing at their throats for breath.

Flames twisted in Cormac's eyes, drinking in the scene as Mandal soldiers poured into the hall. Alia could feel magic spouting overhead, barriers and protections encasing the hall where most of the palace inhabitants had gathered.

Baldric fastened his hand around her arm rather than pick up a weapon. He pulled her towards the balcony, away from where Cormac was announcing an explanation to the horrified Parthian King.

Alia whirled, trying to get away from Baldric. "Cormac acted too soon; he's not going to come."

"He will." Baldric grunted as he fought to hold her. "The Roycans were his vanguard, designed to be slaughtered. His designs don't hinge on them."

And then she felt it.

The discord was so consuming that it could only emanate from one man.

Vincent.

Alia's whole body tightened, and Baldric braced her back. "He's here."

"Then we have to go."

Baldric took a small pouch out of his pocket, casting its powdery contents into the air. A cloud washed over Alia and Baldric, tingling her skin. Baldric's arm was around her waist, pulling her forward and out of the hall.

"There is a whole explanation that I don't remember, but as long as you don't use your magic, no one can see us. If you don't use your magic, Vincent won't be able to find you."

"Find me?"

"Did you really think we'd send you to him?"

"I need to kill Vincent."

Baldric grunted as he hauled her up a flight of stairs. They weren't the only ones running in the corridor now. Screams erupted around the palace. She stopped fighting Baldric and instead followed his lead so that she could reason with him when they finally slowed.

Baldric took her several flights higher, and she knew where they were headed. They climbed their way to the garden. Baldric led her behind a hedge, revealing a small space that no one passing would be able to see into.

"What now?"

"Lena planned it all out. We wait for Harlan to come fetch us." Baldric grasped a dagger out of precaution.

"Our home is under attack, and we're just going to sit in the garden?"

"You may not be as used to this role as I am. But tonight, you are a liability. The best thing you can do is to stay out of enemy hands while Dorian, Harlan, and Cormac defend the palace. Your magic, while formidable, can be neutralized. And Vincent is sure to exploit that." Baldric swung his sword at an invisible opponent.

"How can you stand hiding here while your fellow soldiers are out there fighting?" Alia tried to appeal to his sense of honor.

"Part of being a good soldier is playing the role you're given, rather than the one you see for yourself."

"Says the quotidien who accompanied me to Alasar."

Baldric's lips twitched. "That was just a job that no one else wanted."

"I need to protect them."

"That is exactly what you're doing. Here with me."

Alia balled her hands into fists.

Alia couldn't stop imagining what was going on inside the palace, what horrors Lena and her friends may be facing. "What about Elowen?"

"Harlan will look after her," Baldric said evenly. "He always does."

Alia folded her arms. "And Dorian? Did he know of this?"

"If the Master Mage can't look after himself, then we're all lost. And no, we didn't tell him because he couldn't be trusted not to tell you."

Perhaps Baldric was trying to distract her from the sounds of battle all around them, but he was still being a prick. Alia fell silent, imagining the deaths of everyone she loved.

They could hear shouts and clashes.

Alia sat, pulling her knees into her chest and wrapping her arms around her shins. Baldric paced.

And they waited.

23

They waited until the screams quieted and their limbs locked up. Waited until Alia's mind was so filled with images of carnage, she could barely stand to let herself think.

And still they waited.

"What did Harlan say again?" Alia asked for the hundredth time.

"He said he would come to us once it was safe."

Alia could sense his anxiety; he also thought it had been too long.

"We could venture out. We need to make sure the Spear is protected."

When Baldric didn't deliver a flat denial, Alia perked up. "Perhaps just a quick look at the hall," he said.

"Less than a minute," Alia promised, getting to her feet.

"Stay behind me and follow my every command."

"Fine." Alia would have agreed to just about anything at this point.

The trip down to the palace was fraught with the signs of battle. Dead Mandal guards and soldiers littered the stairway and corridors, as well as the bodies of servants and noblemen alike. Baldric shook with anger at the sight of his fallen comrades, picking up a sword from one of the fallen. Alia steered him with her hand on his shoulder.

"This was not supposed to happen," he whispered.

They continued onward, shrouded in magic and shadows, and dread grew in Alia the further they travelled. The bodies multiplied the closer they got to the hall, piled in a tangle of limbs. Alia searched for familiar faces among them, looking for evidence to contradict the feeling in her chest. Her fingers itched to seek out signs of life to heal, but to heal would be to bring the fight upon them.

The hall, which had been a site of celebration a short while before, was now both prison and tomb. Soldiers clothed in Veillanti yellow guarded the entrance, making Baldric bristle as he walked by undetected.

Seeing Elowen in chains with a blade to her throat was a sight Alia had not been prepared for. Their proud queen was on her knees, her king was nowhere in sight. King Reglund was chained beside her, badly injured. The lords and ladies of Mandal's great noble houses were similarly bound behind them.

Elowen was in a state of disarray that Mariana would have never allowed. Vincent was circling her, and while her lips trembled, her shoulders were firm.

"I'll ask one more time. Where are the heirs?"

"I haven't the faintest idea," Elowen responded metallically, staring straight ahead and beyond Vincent.

"I need the blood of Mandal's king, the current or the next." He turned back to Elowen, "If you won't tell me where they are then you have outlived your use to me."

Alia panted, wondering what had become of Cormac. She scanned the hall again for her king. Harlan was bound and on his knees, sending Alia's hopes plummeting.

Elowen lifted her elegant head, holding herself proudly, before she shut her eyes. Alia broke to see her sister accepting her fate. Alia couldn't let it happen. Before she could look to Baldric for permission, a great yell came from the prisoners, a madman unleashed. Harlan burst through his chains, a fearsome opponent to behold as he cleaved through two guards to make his way to Elowen.

While Harlan distracted the Veillanti, Alia brought Baldric's hand into hers. She motioned to the chains and the door. Baldric granted her permission, knowing that in doing so, they would be exposed, and he would break his promise to Lena.

Vincent had apparently grown tired of Harlan's uprising. He reached out with one hand and Harlan's entire body became immobile. Harlan was lifted off his feet, and Elowen rose to hers. "Stand down, Captain," Elowen said gently, so full of emotion that Alia couldn't look away.

"My queen—" Harlan began.

But with a sharp jerk, Harlan's head twisted to its side.

Too far.

She heard the crack as his neck broke.

There was no healing that could be done for him.

Harlan.

Alia let out a shriek to match her sister's, and the Undoing burst forth from her, seeking out shackles wherever they could be found. With all the ferocity she could manage, the Undoing shattered the chains retraining the Mandals and Parthians, freeing the prisoners in the hall. She then turned her attention to the soldiers, striking them down with little thought to the fact that they were mortals and not creatures from another realm. The distinction no longer mattered to her.

Baldric was fulfilling his end of the bargain, ushering their people out of the hall as Alia turned to Vincent. The Veillanti mage was smiling.

Alia knew she had to hold his attention to allow the rest to escape. She reached out with the Undoing, the black darkness spilling from her and surrounding him.

But before she brought about his death, a spell from Vincent's lips struck her. It was a similar feeling to the spell that Dorian had once done, making her darkness swirl around her instead of outward. She lost connection to Vincent, lost the ability to feel anything besides her own pain. The darkness was pulled back into her, where it always festered.

Cut off from everything around her, she could at least see that part of her effort had worked from the translucent barrier. Most of the prisoners cleared the room, the few surviving Veillanti grappling to bring them back. She couldn't see Baldric any longer.

But Elowen hadn't run with the others. She knelt beside Harlan's body, weeping. Alia's friend had been a force in life, full of laughter and strength. He looked smaller now. Only a shell was left behind.

A shell.

Alia fell to her knees, her forehead resting against the unseen barrier. Tears threatened to take over, knowing she'd never talk to her friend again. Seeing Elowen fall apart reminded Alia that she needed to press on.

Alia regained her feet, feeling her calm come back to her.

Vincent eyed her with cool interest. His dark eyes flashed, the haunted red lines casting a menacing sight. "You wield a power that you do not deserve. I will relieve you of it."

"Why not now?" Alia wanted Vincent's attention on her. Not on Elowen or on trying to recapture her countryfolk.

"Are you so anxious to be free of it? I would have expected Dorian to come for you by now." There was mild irritation in his voice.

"You can't take his magic, can you? He's always been able to resist you."

An outbreak of shouts reverberated through the room, and Vincent's attention shifted towards the entrance of the hall. Vincent shouted orders at soldiers with yellow insignias and several more mages in robes. "Now, since someone let the princes slip away, I have to find myself a king."

She allowed herself respite at the knowledge that Cormac hadn't perished before shifting her attention over to Elowen, who was still at Harlan's side. Alia toyed with Finn's bracelet, knowing she would have to use it if she wanted to make any sort of stand.

Where were Dorian and Cormac? Dorian could sense her, so he must know where she was. Alia wondered if her magic still reached out to him while she was trapped. But perhaps it didn't. Perhaps he thought she was already dead.

She wondered if he had found the strength to shift into his most powerful form, or if fear held him in his mortal body. Her heart ached for him; she'd promised protection only to be pulled away.

She felt along the sides of the prison that Vincent fashioned for her only to be met with hard walls. She reached out with her Undoing, seeking to exploit a weak spot or shatter it altogether, but her magic just crept up the sides, unable to penetrate and unable to grasp onto anything. Next, she tried healing, to no avail. She tried to erect barriers within the cage to push the walls out. Nothing. She tried to think of something Dorian had taught her over the past few months and nothing worked.

Alia slammed her fist into the barrier once again, only managing to make her hand throb. She was using too much energy and was beginning to feel weak. Locked away, she couldn't even pull from Finn's bracelet.

"You need to get out, Ali." Elowen didn't take her eyes off Harlan. "You need to make them suffer." Her sister's royal countenance was twisted into a menacing mask.

A handful of Mandal soldiers burst into the hall. "Elowen! Alia!" Edgar Meador was among the newcomers. It seemed that he had decided to be loyal to his kingdom after all.

"Father!" Elowen wailed.

"Get her out of here," Alia ordered.

Edgar assessed the situation, his lips pressing into a thin line when he saw Harlan's broken body on the floor. His forces clashed with the Veillanti soldiers. He instructed his men to disengage and take Elowen to safety, ordering them from the hall. Soon, only the two Meadors remained in the room strewn with blood and iron. Edgar ran his hands along the sides of her invisible prison, muttering to himself as the clash of battle rang out behind him.

"You should get out of here. Elowen needs you."

"And so, it appears, do you," Edgar said with a frown.

"The mage will be back for me."

Edgar snorted. "They thought he could take our palace easily. There is no way they can hold it; we are massing at each corner."

"Perhaps they thought they would have a Mandal ally."

Edgar cleared his throat. "I would never betray my kingdom." He placed his hand on the barrier.

"It is far too late to be noble. Go. Get Elowen. Follow Mariana and the princes. Live, Father." There was nothing he could do for her, so he might as well save one of his daughters.

For a moment, Edgar looked like he might heed her. "I never thought I would hear you call me father again." His shoulders relaxed and he braced himself against the barrier and settled in. "Many times over the years I've wished for things to be different." Edgar reached for her but was blocked by Vincent's spell. "Your mother told me about Ruben."

Alia could see the simmering rage in Edgar's eyes, eyes that were so much like her own. His bottom lip shook as his expression rebelled against the tightly controlled lord, belying torment. "I asked him to monitor you for signs of the Undoing, not trigger it."

Her father was literally reaching for her, wanting to hold her. It was something Alia hadn't let herself think on, the dearth of comfort she never received, the protection never extended to her. She had seen Finn embrace Lena, observed that closeness with so much reverence, but she could not recall what it felt like to be in her father's arms. That had been taken from them by Ruben, by Mariana, and from the coldness that characterized the Meador line.

"It doesn't matter now," Alia dismissed, wanting more than ever to forget.

"I never knew what you wanted from me."

Vincent flickered before her and looked at Edgar like he was an insect. A twitch of his fingers had Edgar flying into the far wall. Alia watched him crumple to the ground before focusing her attention back on the menacing mage.

It was then that Alia realized that Vincent hadn't returned alone. Cormac lay at his feet, eyes closed and body splayed out on the ground. Alia couldn't see, couldn't feel if he was still alive. She screamed his name, but it did nothing to rouse him.

"Fetch the Mandal bitch," Vincent instructed the Veillanti soldiers.

Vincent had said he needed the blood of the king, and now it was pooled at his feet. Alia's mind began to make the connections—Flora told Vincent about the Spear of Orlast, and how only the king of Mandal could open the chamber. He had the king; all he needed now was to be told the way.

Flora was brought into the hall, dragged by her crimson tresses. At the sight of Alia and Cormac, her struggling intensified, and her screams became shrill. Alia sensed Flora's desperation, a woman caught firmly in the grasp of the cruel mage, torn between protecting her family and the country she loves.

Vincent spread his arms wide in welcome. "There you are, Flora. I told you I could secure your king."

"I told you he needed to be alive!" Flora shrieked.

Vincent gave Cormac a swift kick to the abdomen, eliciting a groan from the limp monarch. "And alive he is."

Vincent's next move would be to make Flora show him the way to the Spear of Orlast deep under the palace. He would take Cormac with him to use the king's blood to open the chamber.

And then Vincent would destroy the Spear, bringing Entien's protection from Alasar to an end. There would be no fight against Bergan, it would be a slaughter.

Alia resumed her pounding on her prison, again trying to capture Vincent's attention and slow him down from his destructive purpose long enough for someone to come to their aid. "He won't spare you!" Alia shouted at Vincent. "Once you've served your purpose to Bergan, he'll cast you aside just like any other lurcher."

Shadows gathered around Vincent as his annoyance flared. "Which is why I'll have you."

"The Undoing is useless against Bergan." Alia felt the mist spool around her.

"Your ignorance is your downfall."

"Dorian will never be yours." Alia lifted her chin and challenged the mage. "He has bested you before and he will do so again."

"Everything Dorian knows, he learned from me." Vincent's lips curved into a smile.

Vincent's next spell overtook her with minimal effort.

The world around her went dark, shifting her. She was no longer in the hall. She had been transported to the Tower. She tried to hear the sounds of the battle but the room was silent.

Panic gripped her.

"Lay down here, Alia." A voice came from behind her. Alia's skin erupted in bumps as she froze, made completely immobile in terror.

She knew that voice.

She hated it.

Knowing the scene in front of her was an invention from her own mind did little to quell her fear. Ruben was conjured from her memories— thinning brown hair, a weathered but disarming face, and an unintimidating stature. His robes, while plain, were spun from the finest thread, signifying his noble station. His voice was soft and even, that of a trusted teacher. Twelve-year-old Alia listened intently when he spoke.

"The easiest way to learn how to heal is to heal yourself," Ruben began to explain.

It was one of the first times, one of the original deceptions he had used to put his hands on her, to hurt her, and call it instruction. Every inch of her body was in agony, but she couldn't move. She felt no connection to her limbs or her magic; she couldn't even bring her arms around herself in protection. Vincent had sent her here to relive this, unable to alter the course of the memory.

But the grown Alia, somewhere far from this moment all those years ago, was screaming.

"This is how you learn," her torturer explained. "Now to heal yourself, close your eyes and feel inside your bones, your blood, your heart. Feel every bit of pain, the disruption. Let me in, I'll help with the pain."

This was where she had been made, where an undeniable darkness had taken root and grown inside her. In this office, in these hours, Ruben had created her, twisted her.

She used to be more light than dark. But now there was no way to distinguish what had belonged to her from what he had put there.

Dorian had spoken of suffering this spell at Vincent's hands and while he had been held captive at Bergan's holdfast. Dorian had endured this for days there and for months in Veillant.

She'd rather die than stay here in these moments. She'd rather die than have to live this again. Alia tried to feel her magic, tried to summon a wisp of Undoing to kill Ruben herself. But there was no magic, and there wasn't even a Ruben to kill. Finn had seen to that.

Stop. Please stop.

"Well done." Ruben praised her healing. "Now again."

And again. And again. Her mind hadn't been able to comprehend the extent of the abuse, but even she had known it was wrong.

Help me.

But no one helped her then. She could almost feel the darkness blooming within her. The shame, the pain. The rage.

Stop.

"Breathe." A voice came to her. Not Ruben's voice, but a woman's, deep and smooth. Alia turned to see her, towering and foreboding, leaning against the bookcase. "You're going to drown yourself." The woman stepped forward and tapped on young Alia's forehead, popping Alia's consciousness free. The scene still played, but Alia was outside of her embodied memory rather than trapped within.

Immediately, Alia drew her arms around herself. She was in control of her body, could shield it. Alia took in the caramel-colored hair, the woman's broad features carved with perfection. "Deanna."

It was the woman from Bergan's holdfast, the one who had taunted him. She had distracted Bergan from killing Baldric and allowed Alia to get her footing to challenge the Tiarcon. She had been in Finn's estate when Alia was first reunited with him, the emissary from the Tiarcon of the Forest. The emissary who had wanted to drag her back to the Forest to be stripped of her magic and punished for her theft. The woman from her visions, her bloody fate.

"We were never properly introduced. But yes, I am Deanna, and you are Alia." She turned to the recreation of Alia and Ruben, scrunching her nose.

Alia was unnerved by Deanna's presence, and yet grateful. "Can you make it stop?"

"Are you asking me to end this or end you?" Deanna stepped forward, her eyes twinkling. "The spell really lacks imagination. In Alasar, we like to design our own nightmares."

Alia was desperate to get away from the sound of Ruben's voice, from the pain, but Deanna was one of Rowthra's subjects. If she were here, somehow in Entien despite the veil, it meant that the Tiarcon was coming for her. There would be a more terrible scene waiting for her at the hands of the Tiarcon of the Forest.

"Or I could just put you back." Deanna leaned over the recreation of Alia's twelve-year-old self, ready to tap her forehead again.

"Wait!"

Deanna straightened and gave a self-satisfied grin. Deanna snapped her fingers, and they were alone in the quiet. Alia wrapped her arms around herself again. She took deep, hacking breaths as tears escaped from her eyes.

"If only Bergan had known how easy it was to break you."

Alia tried to compose herself, still hearing Ruben's words in her head, the inculcation taking root. "What do you want?"

"You've found yourself in the middle of a war." Deanna dodged her question. With a wave of her hand, she displayed the scene in the hall. Alia was looking down on her own body, nearly completely obscured by the deep purple mist of the Undoing filling the box Vincent had crafted for her. Deanna hadn't been lying about nearly suffocating herself. Her body was motionless and limp, with the appearance of death.

The hall was full again; the Mandal forces resurged, engaging the remaining Veillanti soldiers. A small contingent of Parthians, Octavius at the helm, fought beside the Mandals.

And Lena.

Her daughter was down in the battle, a garnet beacon decimating any mage that dared to stand against her.

Alia screamed, horrified that her daughter was not in Alasar, where she was sent, but here in the bloody center. Dorian was beside her, trying to sort his way to Vincent through Veillanti mages.

But Vincent was focused on another. A body was slumped against the invisible barrier containing Alia's body. Edgar Meador, dazed and bloodied, lay at Vincent's mercy. From his appearance, he had put himself between Vincent and Alia, protecting her with the only weapon he had left. His body.

With one hand raised, Vincent stripped off Edgar's armor, reducing the Mandal lord to his tunic. Magic tore at the fabric, exposing Edgar's chest.

The gold amulet glinted in Vincent's hand, the same one that he attempted to press into Alia's flesh. The amulet was designed to transfer magic and was etched with Vincent's spells and emboldened by murdered mages.

But Edgar was quotidien; there was nothing Vincent could gain from him. Still, the Veillanti mage pressed onward, the amulet burrowing into the skin just below her father's collarbone, where Alasarans boasted their sworn marks.

Do you know what it sounds like when someone is having their magic severed from their body? How quickly the light fades from their eyes once it's gone?

Edgar's screams of agony stole Alia's breath. His body arched with pain. And between the amulet and the matching one melded to Vincent's breast, mist moved through the air. An oddly familiar mist, the kind that haunted Alia for too many years.

The Undoing.

"How is that possible? He doesn't have any magic." Alia spoke the words aloud, only intending them for herself.

"Not anymore," Deanna mused with detached interest.

The air cleared, and Vincent stumbled away. Her father was dead, empty and discarded. The loss washed over her, merging with raging confusion. Another Meador lie, another violent end.

Vincent reeled, his pale countenance sapped of its meager warmth. His skin crawled, lumps and surges beneath his skin, the red around his eyes bleeding across his skull.

"Ah," Deanna said. "What do you think he'll become?"

"What do you mean?" But Alia knew. It was the threat that had hung over them since Ossian raised the possibility. Vincent's mortal form could only take so much magic, could only withstand so much strain before it was forced to change, to survive.

Locumten.

While they watched, Vincent threw himself down on the floor, sweating out the Undoing.

"He's fighting the transformation. Trying to salvage a part of himself."

"Is that possible?"

Deanna shrugged with a smile.

Alia tried to access her magic but felt nothing. "You're still down there," Deanna explained, as if she could read Alia's mind. "Just your consciousness is here with me."

"What do you want? I need to go back."

Deanna let out a halting laugh. "You want to go down into that mess?"

"Yes."

Deanna thought for a few seconds. "I suppose that bodes well. I'll make you a deal."

Alia squared her shoulders. "A deal?"

"I can send you down there, break you out of the cage even."

"And?"

"And then after, you will do something for me."

"What?"

The Alasaran shrugged. "Whatever I decide."

Alia winced as Vincent recovered enough to singe Lena with shadows. "Just tell me what you want from me."

"You're the one who wants something," Deanna snapped, knowing that she had Alia in the corner. "Or I could just put you back ..."

"You're going to take me to the Tiarcon of the Forest. She'll take away the Undoing, fine. She'll kill me, fine. Just don't hurt the rest of them."

Deanna narrowed her eyes. "I will set you free to fight your battle. And after, you'll do something for me. Or you can go back to where I found you," she repeated as if Alia had lost her wits.

Alia yelped as Baldric's chest caught the edge of a Veillanti blade. Time was short for her to save them. Cormac was stirring, and Vincent's limbs were elongating, his head almost entirely red.

Whatever Deanna had in mind for her, she would have to endure ... later. After.

Deanna held out her hand, and Alia seized it. A green vine shot from where their hands met, wrapping around Alia's forearm with a fiery burn. In seconds, the vine had sunk into Alia's skin, leaving a whip-like mark—a memory of the accord she had entered into.

Deanna pulled her arm in and whispered, "I'll be close."

Returning to her body was an overwhelming sensation. Deanna had been true to her word—Vincent's prison had been destroyed. The deep plum mist that had surrounded her was starting to drift out into the room.

The darkness had been mounting as she was forced to relive her torment. It merged with a swirl of rage at Flora's and Cormac's wounds, Harlan and Edgar's bodies still in sight, and from the audacity to attack the place she once more thought of as her home.

She cast the Undoing over Vincent as the mortal mage struggled to control his transformation.

"How did you—?!" Vincent shouted, attempting to shield himself from the mist enveloping him.

He managed to cast off Alia's attack, stumbling over a Roycan corpse. Alia seized on the chance to grasp Baldric's shoulder and heal the gash across his chest. Baldric coughed blood and grimaced.

"He's transforming," Alia panted. "Where's Ossian?" If Lena were here, the commander could still be as well.

Baldric wiped the blood from his chin, scanning the hall. "I'll find him."

Alia turned her full focus to Vincent, lashing him with a new round of the Undoing. Lena attacked with an onslaught of storm winds, pinning his arms to his sides and covering his mouth.

Dorian's magic joined theirs. "He's yours!" Alia shouted to the Master Mage.

A tremor stole Dorian's resolve; Alia knew the feelings he was grappling with—she had long imagined having Ruben at her mercy. Vincent struggled against Alia and Lena, but they held fast. As he struggled, unbridled dread filled Alia, like she was falling through air, whipping around with nothing to grab onto.

Chaos.

There was no end to Vincent's defenses as he wielded his magic, gifted and taken. The Undoing scattered as it was chased by shadows, mixing until she was unable to discern her magic from Vincent's. Alia's grip on the Undoing faltered, dispersing it through the hall to other targets. The effort of dragging the mist back had her on her knees, and Vincent was once again freed as Lena was forced back into the wall, her garnet tethers blinking out.

Dorian's hands concocted a dark cloud, which crackled as it floated to Vincent and struck him with bolts of lightning. And then, Dorian took his other form, a golden eagle. Alia almost lost her concentration at the sight of him. Dorian spread his shimmering wings, beating the air in the hall so powerfully that those closest to him fell.

"Now!" Lena shouted, struggling to regain her hold on Vincent, who was thrashing about as his skin sizzled. But the sight of Dorian as an eagle, his prized possession, had reinvigorated the mage. Vincent's eyes followed Dorian as a torrent of golden light came from the eagle's mouth with a mighty cry. It struck Vincent, forcing him to the ground. Vincent screamed, but he still drew breath.

"He's holding back," Lena said.

She was right, but still Alia waited, becoming a spectator to the battle raging between Dorian and Vincent.

Sun against shadow, calm against chaos.

Doubt edged in, overpowering Alia's faith in Dorian. He had told her that he was anxious to face Vincent, to be the one to kill him, but now he hesitated.

Vincent was dangerous. To her, to Lena. He was deadly as a mortal and could become even more powerful as a locumten.

I should have torn it all down for them.

She couldn't leave it to Dorian to get rid of him and end the threat to their lives. He had been through too much. Vincent knew about the Spear; there was no telling if he had also given Bergan the information. He could be close to transforming into a locumten, and then he would be even more destructive. Cormac's dream of a captive mage was folly.

With Vincent distracted by Dorian, the Undoing reached him easily. It coursed through his body, washing over defenses into a dark heart. Her power wrapped around his heart, encasing it in darkness, poised to crush him. At the last moment, Vincent focused on her, shadows searing through her like sheets of hot steel. Alia fell, the Undoing returning to protect her, shielding her as she healed.

Alia regained her footing, the shreds in her dress and bloodstains the only sign of Vincent's vicious spell. The Undoing swirled around her; it was part of her, tied to her. It was her strength, tinged with darkness.

Her eyes closed, the ghosts of the memory coming back.

Alia listened, not trapped, but searching for something. Even within the battered twelve-year-old girl, there had been a spark. The Undoing awakening, growing, holding her together. The Undoing had always been there; it wasn't Ruben who had created it or placed it there.

The Undoing was *her* darkness, her finest weapon.

She had needed the dark to survive, to fortify the spaces where light had been stamped out. The two sides moved together now, wielding a force of their own.

And Vincent was a pestilence. Just like Ruben. He stole and murdered, desperate to amass more power. He knew no bounds, no consequences.

Balance was demanded, and she would deliver it.

The torches on the wall shuddered as Alia's hands began to glow once more, her magic racing to her fingertips, bursting forth into the hall like a swarm, filling the air, blotting out all light, and completely within her control.

"Undoing Mage," Octavius called to her, his hands outstretched at Vincent.

His eyes bid her to lead the offensive as he activated unseen magic. Vincent's form twitched, straining under the onslaught of four mages. His cold eyes glazed over as his defenses faltered and he began to shout. Whatever Octavius was making him see, whatever he was doing to his mind, it was excruciating.

The Parthian mage nodded to her then, blood running from his nose and ears, arms shaking. Another mortal with high magic.

"Dorian. I can give them back to you. The years, your memories," Vincent broke free from Octavius long enough to taunt.

Alia risked a pause to look at Dorian, who had shifted back into a man, staring down at Vincent. His intensity failed him, eyes wavering, losing their sharp point.

"Don't you want to remember?" Vincent's face twisted into a grin as he saw Dorian's shoulders shake.

"I want to remember," Dorian called out across the hall. "Alia, please. I need to know."

Alia looked at her daughter, who knew well what she was about to do. Lena gave her a slow nod. Alia's hands dissolved, consumed by mist. The Undoing gathered and swooped down, curving into Vincent's screaming mouth, clawing at his bloodshot eyes. The mismatch of magic within him began to pull apart, the pieces that never belonged to him deserting him in his moment of need. The Undoing crooned back to her, seeking permission to serve out its purpose.

Alia turned her gaze to Dorian as he was pleading with her, sending waves of his own power to try and dissuade her. She could feel his anguish, the desperation to feel whole again, to know himself, to have ownership of his life.

But some things were better forgotten.

Alia closed her fist of swirling mist.

Vincent twisted and collapsed. Even he needed a heart to live. His aura pulsed out, one more round of crippling chaos, leveling all those fighting in the hall.

And as the last effects of Vincent's cobbled magic waned, Alia felt a satisfying calm settle in. The magic, taken from the mortals, would travel to the veil, strengthening it. A balance restored with the destruction of the chaotic aura, a stasis between warring magics.

In the wake of Vincent's destruction, Alia could feel the two realms grating against each other, two realms where there once had been one, five Tiarcons where there once had been eight. Begging for balance to be restored. There would be no peace until then.

Gathering from its prey, the Undoing took to the air, ravenous and searching. Alia called to it, to the part of her that wanted vengeance, and braced herself for the agony of her worst moments. Ruben's abuse. Her mother's rejection. Finn's death and betrayal. Lena's imprisonment. Harlan. With each image, with each emotion, the Undoing bid her to remember what had happened and how it felt, but that she survived and should not misuse this power to perpetrate more of what she suffered.

The view of the hall faded altogether, once more summoning the Tower, once more summoning Ruben. This memory was dredged up by the Undoing, rather than an exterior attack. The steps that she took to the Tower were not of her choosing. Ruben's claws were so deep inside of her that he could control her from afar, seeping into her mind at his choosing.

He was sitting quietly when she arrived, scribbling in his record book. The mage was calm as ever, a smile greeting her, the true joy at the completeness of his control. "Lie down, Alia," he bid as if she had any choice. She moved to the table, a platform really. Her eyes caught on the window, the tranquil sea waiting for her outside. She focused on the sound of the waves, the sparkling of the sun on the surface, and the fresh brine that she could smell even up here. She was within the sea, not immobile in the Tower.

"We have to address the lies you've been spreading. I'm not angry, I just don't know why you've invented such fantasies."

Alia trembled internally, knowing the glimmer of lucidity was going to be stamped out.

"But despite your childish behavior, I'm very proud of you. Paired to the Prince, to bear Mandal's next ruler. Our hopes finally realized. You will bear a royal child of magical prowess, our child, and my nephew will accept them as his heir." It was Ruben's dream, his singular goal to seed the next generation of Mandal mages with high magic. His high magic. An unparalleled army of mages, mothers handpicked from his most talented students.

As soon as her marriage took place, he'd renew his attacks, force her into carrying his child, using her body as a vessel for his ambition.

"You can't tell others about us, Alia; their lesser minds cannot see the purpose of what we do here. How precious we are to Mandal. I am helping you, making you strong enough to manage the darkness that plagues your bloodline."

The inculcation took root, penetrating her mind and weaving itself into her thoughts as if it were her own.

Alia gained awareness within the memory. This was the final night, Ruben's last attack and her first.

She tried to squirm against the inculcation, fight his control over her body as his words bit at her, fangs sinking in and holding fast. Alia's insides writhed in agony, trying to grasp on to anything that might pull her free of Ruben's influence. She felt her anger build with each breath, each word out of his mouth, each time she tried to shield herself, only to be imprisoned in this spot. The pit of her stomach roiled.

"If you give in, it'll devour you and everything you love. You can't outrun the darkness you carry inside of you."

And she flinched.

It was too slight a movement for Ruben to note, but Alia felt the minute tensing in her arm and the twist of her elbow. Ruben kept going; he hadn't released her. She had broken through the inculcation. Sensation returned to her face, tempting her to speak and prove that she could. Her fury continued to build, the desire to pounce on the Master Mage, to make him as powerless as he had always made her.

But before Alia could demonstrate control, her head pounded, as if a hundred voices were shouting at once.

'No one else would have you if they knew.'

'Without me, you can't contain that darkness inside of you.'

'You belong to me.'

They had a hold on her—the voice that she heard in her head, her beliefs, her memories. She could sense the parts of her mind, those that were hers and those that were his. A darkness invaded her mental landscape, curling over the scars that the inculcation had left behind.

That had been the first target of the Undoing, the effects of inculcation fading away, her mind awakening at the same time as her magic.

The mist began to pour from her hands and encircle Ruben, his screams of indignation shifting to screams of terror.

Alia drank in the feeling as the images faded, sending her back to Mandal's hall, the Undoing coiled within her.

"Mother!"

Alia turned towards Lena's call, trying to acclimate back to the hall. Her daughter was being reinforced by Ossian, the commander bloodied but still on his feet. Baldric was on the ground, cradling Cormac in his arms. "He refused to hide," Baldric explained the many wounds on the king's body. The remaining Veillanti forces were captured by the Mandal warriors, their leaders now fallen. "Stubborn, asinine, bastard of a king."

Cormac was weak, but she could still feel the life within him. Casting a glance over her shoulder, she saw that Lena moved with her and Dorian was standing over Vincent's body.

Alia knelt at Cormac's side, placing her hands on his cheek and chest. She pulled from her bracelet to find the energy to heal him, feeling all the cracks in his skin and bones and knitting them together. As she worked, Cormac's eyes fluttered open. His hands closed around her wrists and then travelled to her shoulders, pulling her in and crushing her against him. He began repeating her name over and over again into her ear.

Alia managed to disentangle herself from the king, pushing back to her knees. Baldric looked to his side and Cormac and Alia followed his gaze to where Harlan still lay.

Cormac crawled over to his friend's body, and Baldric helped him along. Alia and Lena kept a few steps away, hands clasped. Cormac reached over and closed Harlan's eyes. Baldric retrieved his sword and folded his arms to his chest. "My friend," Cormac said, placing his hand on Harlan's. Alia clung tightly to Lena before turning away to face the body of Edgar.

Lena let out a gasp when she saw him, rushing to her grandfather's side to check for signs of life. She used her magic to straighten his body, giving him the look of peaceful sleep. Alia knew she wouldn't be able to sort through her feelings about her father, how he had died, how he had lived. The magic he'd kept from her, leaving her to face hers alone.

Mandals were partaking in similar activity all around the hall as they claimed their fallen.

"I sent you across the veil." Alia faced her daughter.

"I went. Ossian fulfilled his duty. And then I turned back," Lena answered.

"I didn't—"

"I know." Lena threw her arms around Alia. "We thought you were dead, Dorian and I. We heard you screaming and then everything was quiet. You were lying there, you looked—"

Alia shushed her, thinking of her deal with Deanna and the vine mark visible on her forearm through her torn dress. "I'm here. I'm still here."

For now.

Alia looked up from Lena's shoulder to see Flora. Her friend returned to the hall, relatively unmarred, a rose among the debris. Her eyes were wide, taking in the carnage. Her chest heaved, likely blaming herself for all of it. "Flora needs us."

Alia caught Flora before she fell faint, overwhelmed by what she saw. By Harlan, by all the cold faces. "It's over, Flora."

"I did this."

"Vincent did this. Go to them, Flora. Go to your family."

Lena offered to flicker, which Flora accepted readily. Lena had to get her out of the city regardless, as too many had witnessed Flora's role in the treason.

That left Alia to face Dorian. He had not moved from Vincent's side. She approached slowly, not wanting to startle him.

"Dorian—"

He snapped out of his trance and took a step towards her, his eyes blazing. She retreated.

"Why?" Dorian spat the word.

Alia summoned her last remaining bit of strength. "I couldn't let him live. He was about to become immortal."

Betrayal darkened his eyes. "You didn't think I could kill him."

"I didn't know if you would."

It might as well have been Dorian's heart encased and pulled into sections, the Undoing bisecting vein from pump. The Undoing savaged the bonds between them, the space going cold. She was the Undoing. She had done this.

"I thought you understood."

His words struck a blow to Alia. Even with what he had survived, Dorian had never let all he suffered taint him, had actively shunned it. And now he was overtaken by darkness, the way out blocked by her.

Alia bowed her head and stepped away. She had no defense, only the truth thrumming through her that she would do it again. Understanding Dorian's anger, what she had taken from him, only made it worse.

Being hated was something she knew how to weather.

24

Small boats dotted the blazing horizon. Each was fashioned for only one passenger, its first and only. Alia couldn't count all the ships carrying the dead onward for one last journey with Harlan and her father among them.

The royal family led the Mandal procession to the shore, joining with the Parthians who had stayed behind. Bowmen readied burning arrows from atop the cliff. The princes notched arrows, one for Edgar and one for Harlan. Elowen stood beside her husband, openly sobbing, flanked by her mother and her sister. In one night, the Queen had lost the man she loved and her father, her grief robbing grace. Mariana held her head high and her shoulders square, giving her husband a strong send-off.

Lena leaned into Alia and wrapped an arm around her back, a brace in case she needed it. Alia gave her daughter a grateful nod and turned her attention back to the sea as the arrows flew. The flames caught, taking Alia back to the massive pyre lit in the meadow earlier that day. Vincent, Brida, and the rest of the enemy dead were not granted a final journey to the Sunset Realm. Only Prince Everett remained alive, sustained in Sheath's dungeons.

Alia had gone to watch them burn, to seek some sort of resolution. Dorian had been there as well, watching the final demise of his old enemy, his old friend. The silence between them stretched on.

As the sun relented and the fires started to go out, the onlookers on the shore dispersed. Elowen had to leave as she disintegrated into wails. Mariana went with her, tucking her daughter against her hip.

"What should I be feeling?" Lena asked, searching Alia's face for guidance. "We won the battle, but …"

It didn't quite feel like a victory. Alia looked over the dead, saw the scars that the ordeal had torn open, and knew that more was to come. War with Veillant was inevitable now, and Royce would have to be dealt with. Alia struggled even more, knowing that soon Deanna would come for her. She would be separated from Lena, and she would have to sort through it all on her own.

"I'm proud of you," Alia said instead of offering a hollow answer. "You stepped in to defend a kingdom that you owe nothing to. Without you, there would have been many more boats."

Lena bit her lip, looking to the ground. "But what if Effe was right, what if I'm destined to destroy all of this?"

Alia caught Lena's shoulder, turning to face her. "They have no hold on you." Alia forced emphasis into every syllable. She had already recanted the word she spoke to Lena to get her to leave, but she felt the need to do so again. "I am not afraid of which choices you will make."

"As if you'd let me make a choice without stepping in." Lena tucked her head into Alia's shoulder. "Are you sure you're well?"

Don't you want her to see you well, despite it all?

"Yes." Alia faked calm. "It's a relief." To know it would all soon come to an end.

Lena's frown persisted, even as she backed away to join the contingent of mages who were gathered to send off their fallen. Madeline embraced Lena, pulling her into their circle. Lena had a place in Mandal, a group that she could lean on when Alia was gone. She dropped her gaze when she saw Dorian among the mages, staring back at her, face marked in anguish.

"Thus begins my reign," Cormac said. The two of them were the only ones left on the stretch of shore.

Alia pursed her lips, not surprised that Cormac would look at the deaths of hundreds and see only himself. "With a victory."

"Odessa still lives." Cormac looked back at the horizon. "And Vincent doesn't."

"I had to kill him or lose the Spear."

Cormac grudgingly accepted her excuses, especially given that he was unconscious through most of the battle. "Harlan was the only one of you who never left me. My most loyal friend."

Alia's mind instantly went to Harlan and Elowen, her expression making Cormac chuckle. "He told me. I'd always known. I would have let them be, were it not for my sons, if not for the fact that no one can get out of a royal marriage. Not even the king."

Alia tried not to show her surprise.

"Elowen was owed something true. She tried with me; she really did. But something in me could never let me love her, would never let me trust her." Cormac looked at Alia, and she readied herself for an attack that never came.

"Harlan died defending his queen and his country," Alia finally offered. "He would have been proud of his end."

"Oddly conciliatory tonight."

Alia had no real response for him. In truth, she felt nothing. No grief, no anger, nothing except emptiness. "What of Flora?"

"Still eluding our soldiers. But she will be found and brought to account for her treachery."

"She didn't have a choice."

"She did." Cormac's features hardened. "How many have given their lives and their family's lives to the kingdom?"

"That's not fair."

"Do not lecture me about fairness," Cormac snapped. He reached out to grasp the collar of her dress between his thumb and forefinger, fixating on the fabric near her collarbone.

"I know what waits in Alasar. There can only be one enemy."

"There is never only one." Cormac continued to rub his fingers together. "I wanted Vincent alive."

They stood face to face for another few moments.

Alia's face tightened. "If you really want to do right by Harlan, you'll care for Elowen now. You'll try again, for him. And you'd stop smoking that poison and be there for your kingdom. You aren't a good king, but you could be. The realm needs you to protect the Spear."

Cormac's eyes narrowed. "You have no standing to judge me, nor do you know my reasons. I have a war to fight, and I intend to employ every asset I have. Imagine the Veillanti's rage when they see Dorian with the vanguard."

A shrill whine invaded Alia's thoughts, rage blocking out everything else. "Don't threaten him."

"Then for once, Ali, obey an order." His jaw tightened. "You either stay in your place or I'll put someone else there. Dorian, Lena. Any of you suits me."

The king headed for his guarded carriage before Alia could retaliate.

Sheath was stuck between a victorious chant and a mournful cry. Cormac had just made it clear that this was just the start of his conquest, and he was determined to drag her into it. Deanna was coming. And when she came, Alia was under no delusion—she would suffer. She couldn't look at Lena without thinking that soon she would be leaving her, whether pulled by the vine around her arm or by her death. There was nothing except sinking acceptance that her fate had already been written.

She stopped when she caught sight of a familiar pair in an alleyway, Ossian and Baldric. As Alia watched, Ossian threaded his fingers through Baldric's hair, lifting Baldric's face to his and pulling him in for a kiss. Baldric responded with equal ferocity, bringing the Alasaran ever closer. Alia almost smiled, watching her friend hopelessly entranced by another, an Alasaran of all people. She turned to give them privacy.

"Lady Alia," Ossian called her back. When she retraced her steps, Ossian bowed before her. "I am bound to return to the Tiarcon now that the mortal mage has been dealt with."

Alia failed to muster a smile for the departing Alasaran. "Enjoy getting your wings back." The accord burned, knowing that she wanted to speak of it to Ossian, beg for Finn's protection. Perhaps she should go back with Ossian, go to the next realm before Deanna had the chance to fetch her.

But she was forced into silence.

Ossian gave Baldric one last embrace and turned for the palace.

Baldric linked arms with her and pulled her off the city street towards the Wall. "Let's get this over with."

"For Harlan." Alia let Baldric guide her along

They approached the Wall, ladders already placed along the cliff face. There were too many new names to be added.

"Right here." Baldric shifted a ladder, producing a chisel in his hands. "He'd want to be with his parents. And George."

Baldric knew exactly where the names were. He began hammering away, leaving Alia blinking up at him. Each strike of the hammer on the chisel shook Baldric's shoulders, the clouds of splintered stone swallowed in the spray from the sea.

Baldric descended faster than Alia expected and thrust the chisel into her hands.

"I can't," Alia protested.

"For Harlan," Baldric threw her words back at her.

Alia trembled, steeling herself as she climbed rung by rung, her shoes catching. Each time she tried to picture Harlan's face, the ache was almost too great to bear. She wanted to bury the thought of him, every smile, every embrace. Bury it until it couldn't hurt her anymore.

Alia reached the place where Baldric had begun his work, leaving her to etch Harlan's family name. Her shoulder ached, lacking the strength to quickly complete the task. With each strike, she cursed the realm, the powers that shaped fate, that decided to take the best of them away so soon.

When she finished, she paused to run her fingers along the indentation that Baldric had completed.

Harlan.

"I loved you the best I could," Alia whispered the vow that Harlan had made to her while looking at that very spot. She closed her eyes and willed the wind to take her words away to the next realm, to reach Harlan.

Harlan Gust.

A piece of him to live on in Entien, to be remembered and celebrated, even as his being traveled to the Sunset Realm.

Baldric stretched his neck. "He'd want us to have a drink."

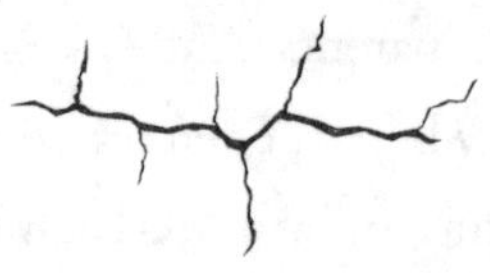

The pub clashed with noise and filth, exactly the kind of environment that Alia needed to drown out her mind. Baldric fetched them a few tankards of ale and ushered her into a corner table.

"I'm sorry that I left you."

Alia swallowed. "Left me?"

"Vincent got his hands on you when I left you alone."

"Hush, Baldric. You organized the remaining forces. Made sure there was something left when I got out."

"Still." Baldric frowned. "Something happened to you in there, I can see it. And I've never heard screaming like that."

"Best not to dwell on it."

"You can talk to me. Our list of friends is dwindling."

Harlan, dead. Flora, a fugitive. Alia downed the rest of her tankard. "When is Ossian supposed to be back?"

"How would I know that?" It was Baldric's turn to take a long drink.

"I never thought the Baldric who could barely stand in the presence of magic would fall in love with a shapeshifting Alasaran."

Baldric ran his hands through his hair, dimples showing. "It is probably a novelty to him, spending time with the pathetic mortal."

"He doesn't seem like someone who pursues novelties."

"You don't know him."

"What do you actually know about Alasarans?" Alia leaned forward, thinking of Deanna.

Baldric shrugged. "I only ever asked Ossian about himself. His family, his service. They aren't so different from us. Why?"

"I need to be prepared for what comes next."

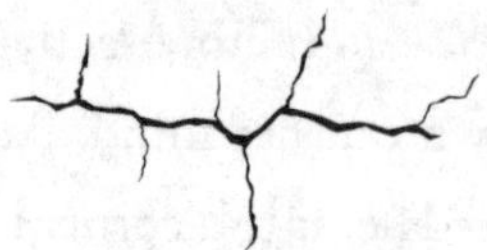

By the time Baldric and Alia stumbled back to the palace, both were uproariously drunk. Baldric took pains to deliver Alia to her room. When they rounded the corner, Dorian materialized before her door.

"Don't look so cross, Mage. She was just out with me, not her husband." Baldric was reduced to high-pitched laughter.

Dorian's feet shifted, but his expression remained stern and fixed on Alia.

"What is your—"

"Go on, Baldric." Alia braced herself on the wall with one hand to try to stop the hall from spinning.

Baldric looked from Alia to Dorian, not at all listening to her. "What did I miss?"

"Baldric, please."

"Stop looking at her like that." Baldric stepped up until he was inches from Dorian's face, trying to bring himself to match his height. "What right do you have to ever look at her like that?"

Dorian's brow furrowed, his hands coming up to push back on Baldric's shoulders.

"He's in a fighting mood," Alia explained to Dorian, pulling at Baldric's hand and placing her palm to his cheek. "Go off to your rooms before I ask Dorian to magic you there."

Baldric balked and gave Dorian a suspicious glare before hurrying off in the opposite direction.

Alia faced Dorian, finding it hard to keep her balance.

"I was hoping we could talk," Dorian said, his anger permeating his aura.

"I'm in no condition."

"Alia."

Alia groaned. "Give me a moment." She extended her fingers, drawing out the bits of alcohol in her blood.

"Here," Dorian offered his arm once she removed enough.

He flickered to his quarters. The room had housed a sun only days ago, Dorian's fledgling attempt to sustain Mandal despite the constant dark. It had been cleared out, ripped away, and replaced. Snuffed out.

The loss echoed through her. "Tea?" Alia managed as Dorian dragged a pair of wooden chairs forward.

With a wave of his hand, a full tea tray appeared at Alia's feet. Dorian watched her as she prepared her cup, crossing and uncrossing his ankles as he sat beside her.

"Harlan, your father ..."

"Just get on with it."

"I want you to explain."

"Dorian." *Please.*

"I have dreamt about what it would feel like to be rid of Vincent. To not have to worry that he was going to—I thought I would finally feel free. But now I just feel ... nothing."

She understood that feeling all too well. She thought of the feathers carved into Dorian's skin, all the pieces of him scattered across the realm.

"Have I not shown you the lengths I would go to for you, what I would do for you? And you couldn't give me this," he said.

Alia wished that she were drunk again. Hurting Dorian was not something she had wanted to do, but she knew she couldn't run from it.

"I am sorry," Alia said, the words sticking in her throat from saying them so seldom with actual meaning. "And you're right."

Dorian's shoulders sank with disappointment.

"He was taunting you with memories that he probably didn't even have, that you wouldn't have even wanted."

"That wasn't your choice to make."

Alia straightened her back; she couldn't argue with him.

Dorian took a deep breath. "You think so little of me."

"You know that that isn't true." Alia's voice broke for the first time. She wanted a novel explanation to form in her mind, one that could absolve her and bring him the comfort he needed. But all that resounded were empty apologies and misplaced confessions. As if telling him how she felt now could undo the betrayal.

"But not enough."

"I am sorry." Alia bowed her head.

"That's not enough."

Alia wished that the darkness inside of her would swallow her already. Dorian was so good, too good, and he couldn't balance her out. It would cost him too much. "I'm not."

Dorian turned his back on her, an invitation to leave. She was shocked she could still feel worse.

"Cormac threatened you. To send you in the first wave to Veillant," Alia divulged.

A slight tremble went through his shoulders as he shrugged.

"You should leave Mandal." Alia pressed on.

"Is that what you want?"

"It doesn't matter what I want anymore."

Alia set her teacup down and stood, hurrying towards the door. But before she could get there, Dorian flickered in front of her. He looked down at her, cupping her cheek in his hand. He kissed her, feverishly, as if it was against his better judgment. Her hand reached to rest on his chest, hoping that the contact could fix what she had broken, could make what he said untrue. She embraced the lights dancing before her, Dorian's light.

But as Alia reached to tug him closer, Dorian grabbed onto her forearm and pulled away from her lips. "What is this?" he examined the vine marking.

Alia snatched her arm back and tried to duck around him for the door.

"Alia!"

His shout made her stop short. "Just let me go," Alia pleaded. "There is nothing you can do."

His face dawned with recognition. "You entered into an accord."

"I made a choice."

"What did you promise them?"

"You know I can't speak of it." Her arm already throbbed.

"Who?" he demanded anyway.

"Dorian, I'm not an imbecile. I know what this means. I made a choice. I couldn't watch anyone else die."

Dorian's pallor deepened. "This can't be undone."

"I know that."

Dorian tried anyway, gripping her forearm and muttering a spell. The mark burned hot but didn't fade away.

Alia cursed.

As if alerted by Dorian's attempt, Deanna appeared. "That tickled," she said. "I had almost forgotten about you, mortal."

"Something is here." Dorian's neck twisted as he tried to discern the attack.

Alia focused on Deanna; her death came to claim her.

"Time to make good on your promise," Deanna announced. "I let you send off your dead."

"Fine," Alia resigned herself. "What do you need me to do?"

"Alia, who are you talking to? Can you see her?" Dorian tried to shield Alia.

"You have to come with me first, then I'll explain everything," Deanna said with a predatory smile.

"Go with you … to Alasar?"

"Of course."

"Dorian." Alia tried to keep him still. "You have to tell Lena I'm gone. Tell her that I love her." It was a hollow send-off. She was leaving Lena in the hands of a war-bent king, Flora's fate in the balance. And Dorian in certain peril.

"You can't have her!" Dorian shouted at the ceiling. Dorian pulled Alia behind him and spun, once more willing to risk all that he had in order to save her.

But she couldn't be saved.

The Alasaran chuckled as Dorian tossed spells in every direction. With a flick of Deanna's fingers, she opened her hand to Alia, and like a tether, she responded, moving into Deanna's hands.

Alia turned in time to see Dorian's spells clear, his chest heaving as he cut a feather into his arm, sacrificing another piece of himself to try to free her.

She met his eyes as they shone with tears. "You can let me go. You all must let me go."

Dorian's blood dripped to the floor.

And Deanna took Alia to the other realm.

ACKNOWLEDGEMENTS

This story began as a personal outlet, focusing on nonlinear healing, complicated daughters, mothers who fell short but kept trying, and people who internalize things that were never their fault. And while sharing this book with the hope that it contains meaning to someone else has made this whole process worthwhile, it also made it equally terrifying.

I am grateful to every person who helped turn that outlet into this book, and those who provided encouragement along the way.

To my husband, whose only condition when I said I wanted to seek publication was that I couldn't give up, thank you for being the first and loudest person in my corner. To my daughter, wanting to make you proud is the strongest inspiration I've ever felt.

To Dr. Lauren Reed, for making sure aspects of trauma and abuse were treated with proper care, respect, and realism. And who, beyond being a brilliant reader, is an unmatched older sister who has taught me most things worth knowing. To my mother, who has read everything I've ever written for decades, and my grandmother, who passed on her dream of being a writer to me with unfailing support, your encouragement means everything.

Thank you to my early readers: Courtney, Molly, Kathleen, Lindsey, Sarah, and all the friends who continue to carry me through the dips and celebrate each milestone.

To the talented Anna Jean Hughes, the first editor on this project, thank you for giving me so much insight and confidence to keep pushing through.

To Alex, Tina, and the whole team at Rising Action Publishing ... there is no way to properly thank the people who believed in this book enough to invest their expertise and resources. I know definitively that this book could not have found a better home with a more thoughtful and passionate team.

ABOUT THE AUTHOR

Author Photo by Lia Giannotti

JL Lienhardt is a lifelong writer and reader of fantasy novels, favoring those that explore contemporary issues through engaging magical worlds. JL lives in Michigan with her family.